MW00587737

ALSO BY SUSAN MINOT

Why I Don't Write and Other Stories

Thirty Girls

Poems 4 A.M.

Rapture

Evening

Folly

Lust & Other Stories

Monkeys

Don't Be a Stranger

Don't Be a Stranger

SUSAN MINOT

Alfred A. Knopf
NEW YORK
2024

THIS IS A BORZOI BOOK

PUBLISHED BY ALFRED A. KNOPF

Published in the United States by Alfred A. Knopf,
a division of Penguin Random House LLC, New York,
and distributed in Canada by
Penguin Random House Canada Limited, Toronto.

www.aaknopf.com

Knopf, Borzoi Books, and the colophon are
registered trademarks of Penguin Random House LLC.

Library of Congress Cataloging-in-Publication Data
Names: Minot, Susan, author.
Title: Don't be a stranger / Susan Minot.
Other titles: Do not be a stranger
Description: First Edition. | New York: Alfred A. Knopf, 2024.
Identifiers: LCCN 2023050438 (print) | LCCN 2023050439 (ebook) |
ISBN 9780593802441 (hardcover) | ISBN 9780593802458 (ebook)
Subjects: LCGFT: Romance fiction. | Novels.
Classification: LCC PS3563.I4755 D66 2024 (print) | LCC PS3563.I4755 (ebook) |
DDC 813/.54—dc23/eng/20231026
LC record available at https://lccn.loc.gov/2023050438
LC ebook record available at https://lccn.loc.gov/2023050439

Jacket image by fstop123/Getty Images
Jacket design by Janet Hansen

Manufactured in the United States of America
First Edition

Contents

PART I

PART II

PART III

PART I

A new person is to me a great event,
and hinders me from sleep.

—RALPH WALDO EMERSON

1

The Comet

She stayed as long as she could in the bath. There her mind could be mercifully blank. Soon in the stillness of the hot water some rumination would begin, but the bath was the place she did not try to steer her thoughts. She let her mind roam. Before her were white tiles, but in her mind's eye was a montage of images, her young son's face, his slender neck and unruly hair, people's faces, the picture of dust in Iraqi air on the *Times* front page. She thought of sex, sex she'd had in that bathtub, sex she'd like to have, of bills, of writing, the writing not done, the bills not paid, the movie she'd seen the night before, the funny quip in the mental ward. She thought of the flat sidewalk outside the apartment, the sandstone steps down, an interesting coat she'd seen on a woman. She might think of the dead, her mother, her father, her friend in the hospital room, the lover lost in a crevasse. She didn't think of who she was, that was a clear pane. Anyway by her age one should know who one was. Ivy Cooper was fifty-two.

. . .

When the doorbell rang, a shrill old-fashioned bell clanging high up in the hall, she was still in the tub. Not quickly, but not slowly, she undialed the drain and stepped out. She wrapped herself in a towel and walked with damp feet down the old wooden floor.

The apartment door was never locked, but he wouldn't know that. She opened the door to a man with a shadowed face in his midthirties wearing black-rimmed glasses. He was standing oddly close to the threshold.

I'm early, he said.

He was smaller than she had expected, but still taller than she. He was broad in the shoulder, wearing a thick cardigan the color of caramel over a plaid flannel shirt. His hair was a shiny mass of tangles, with a part down the middle, and bound in a ball at the back of his neck. The face was handsome—full mouth, bruised eyes—and it gave her a jolt. But the jolt was more than that, there was something familiar about him. Yet he was a stranger.

Hello, she said, holding her towel in a fist.

They did not introduce themselves, but kissed each other's cheeks.

Come in. She stepped back and he came forward and she shut the door. She directed him toward the living room past the coats lumped on hooks narrowing the already narrow hall. The living room was wide with a high ceiling, tall bookcases with more books piled on top to the ceiling. At one end were three tall windows facing the street with the black ladder of a fire escape across it, a fireplace and mantel against the far wall and at the other end wide pocket doors opened to an airy kitchen with open shelves holding plates and bowls and glasses above a sink and a countertop of terra-cotta tiles. The stove was an ancient enamel Royal Rose. One diagonal window faced the neighboring building, a plastered wall which looked European, with an armchair nearby. The long kitchen table was covered with overlapping tablecloths, some Indian, some embroidered linen.

Ivy told her guest to have a seat. She'd be right back, their friend Maira should be there any minute.

The man sat obediently in the center of the white couch against the wall opposite the fireplace in front of a rough wooden coffee table.

Sorry there's no music on, she said, backing out of the room. Just let me get changed. Out of sight she called more loudly, Be right out.

There was no response and the silence kicked up her nerves. Or was it his beautiful inscrutable face?

What to wear. She opened a crammed closet—some of the clothes she'd had for decades—not liking how one had to care what to put on, but caring nevertheless. Caring hoped for satisfaction and she'd found it was best not to expect—well, if you could help it—anything.

She usually had music playing in the apartment, but tonight hadn't made a selection, in case the stranger wouldn't like it. He was a musician. As a writer, Ivy knew she was extra judgmental about writing and figured a musician would be the same. She wanted the stranger to think well of her. And already she'd held herself back, before they'd even met, wanting to please. Though, truth be told, she wasn't always sure whom she was hiding. At her mortifying age, you'd think she would have figured this out by now. She hid that, too.

Maybe a skirt, she thought. It was the end of September, still warm in New York. And the soft grey shirt with the low neck.

Maira had wanted to introduce her to Ansel Fleming for some time. It was not a setup, Maira said, though frankly Ivy wouldn't have minded a setup. Just someone to have coffee with, said Maira. Though Ivy didn't need a new friend, already neglecting many of her friends, since the eclipse made by motherhood. Maira was an expansive person, always wanting to introduce you to someone. Her circle of friends was forever overflowing like a flooded river with Maira on its banks, her wrists in bangles and fingers weighted with rings. She was a designer.

Looking in the mirror Ivy rubbed lotion into her skin. *Prepare a face to meet the faces that you meet.* The bell rang again, shrill in the hall.

Will you get it? called the deep voice in the living room.

But Maira knew the door was open and was already inside. Hi, came her cooing, inviting voice, and Ivy heard the sounds of greeting. She heard, Where's Ivy? but not the low-barreled murmur answering.

I'm coming, Ivy called. She put an elastic around her hair and pulled the tail over a shoulder. Now that Maira was here, she didn't have to rush. But she felt a rush inside. She took the elastic out and redid it, lifting it instead into a twist.

She could hear Maira's smooth voice. She was a good friend and Ivy had met many people through Maira. Maira had many friends and might make a new one tomorrow, at the table next to her in a restaurant, noticing something about them, shining her sparkle.

Ivy zipped on boots, leaving her knees exposed. She felt an inviting fogbank waiting in her living room and savored it before entering.

Maira stood and kissed her hello. She was tall and thin, in a black dress with leather panels and orange platform shoes which made her even taller. Her light green eyes with long eyelashes looked intently at whomever she was speaking to, gathering information. Where was Nicky tonight? Out at a friend's sleeping over. So grown up now, Maira cooed.

Ansel Fleming sat at the end of the couch, hands dangling from the knees of his jeans. As Ivy and Maira got drinks in the kitchen, Ivy felt drawn to the quiet space where Ansel Fleming was, apart from the conversation. A beer for Ansel, wine for her and Maira. Maira had arranged for them to meet here before driving to their dinner in Brooklyn. Maira's evenings were often divided into a series of dates—the drink before, the dinner, the drink after, the drink after that. These days, when Ivy went out, she had to try to be home as early as possible to keep down the astronomical cost of the sitter.

Ansel poured beer slowly into a glass. Maira asked him about his recent shows. He'd just been in Austin, right? Had he seen their friend Topper? Yes, another baby on the way, Ansel said. So I heard, Maira said. Brave at his age. Maybe, Ansel murmured. And Carla? Had Ansel spoken to her lately? Maira had, she talked to Carla every other day. It was amazing to Ivy how many people Maira spoke to every other day. Her husband, Tony, for a long time ran the business side of her design company but he rarely came out with her, though that never seemed to bother either of them. They had two children, her daughter from a previous marriage who was in film school and a son between them both about to graduate from high school and far from ignoring them, Maira knew everything they were doing, too.

Ansel removed something from his pocket and set on the table a stack of plastic CD cases.

What's this? said Maira, on cue.

A couple of new songs, he said. And old ones, bringing them to my man Christopher. Christopher was the six-year-old son of the hosts awaiting them in Brooklyn.

Well, we have to hear the new one, Maira said.

Ivy, he said, do you have a CD player? He spoke as if he'd arrived from another planet.

Mutant Ninja Turtle okay? she said. He didn't laugh. Ivy reached under a nearby lump covered by an Indian bedspread and from Nicky's toys extracted a rounded green CD player with a red handle and two yellow flowers.

Ansel Fleming clicked open the holder and with a careful thumb and finger set in the CD.

Maira straightened her back, preparing to listen. She lifted her eyebrows to Ivy—an extra treat.

The music started as a low beat thumping the chest, then lifted into a trickling and jaunty tune. Ansel's chin pulled in and ticked side to side. His shoulders tinily moved. Maira's head bobbed, her features serene. Ivy remained still, elbows planted on the low table, waiting to respond. The lyrics came and she concentrated to make out each word. The singer was flying into a city at dawn and wondering where a you was and when he would he see the you again. The vibe was frisky and laid-back, as if the singer was confident he would. Ansel's face listening showed no self-consciousness, seemed simply mildly pleased. She saw something in him unusual, as if not touched by the usual things.

The song dwindled to its end.

That's it for now, he said and snapped the CD out.

Love it, Maira said. I want more.

Are you handing out CDs? Ivy said.

No, he said. These are taken.

Ivy wasn't sure what one said to a musician after hearing his song. She wondered who the you was. But she wouldn't ask. A musician was utterly mysterious.

Before they left, Ivy went back to her room and changed her skirt for dark jeans. She felt the strangeness of not having Nicky a few feet away from her. The concern she had for him when nearby altered when he was absent, into a slight increase in worry, as one would have in a spaceship, noticing the door ajar to the universe beyond.

Ansel said he knew the way and would drive. Ivy sat beside him in the passenger seat of her old Volkswagen with the slightly loud muffler. She had an odd feeling beside him, both nervy and sedated, and found herself more interested than she'd expected to know what he was like.

A musician? Ivy had said when Maira suggested introducing them. They both understood she meant probably a lot of women. But Maira had said no, he wasn't like that. He left his gigs and would go home alone. I never see him with anyone, she said. They stopped at a light on Broadway and figures through the windshield crossed in front of them, silhouettes with the variety of city lights behind.

Look. Ansel pointed to an old man and woman holding hands as they passed in the headlights. That's sweet, he said. Keeping it alive.

Ivy winced. Immediately she wondered if the sentimentality

was sincere or was he trying to impress her with sensitivity? It relieved her to dismiss him a little. He wasn't as compelling. And if he wasn't as compelling, he wouldn't matter.

How do you know where we're going? Maira said admiringly from the back seat. The car slid down the bridge onto Atlantic Avenue then turned into the leafier patchwork of Brooklyn neighborhoods.

I did live here for ten years, Ansel said.

Of course you did, Maira said. I guess I always picture you in Chicago.

Ivy knew he'd grown up in Chicago. Maira always filled you in on who you were meeting. She had heard his history. So she knew the larger outlines of his story: he'd spent seven years in jail and had gotten out almost two years ago.

They crept up a sloped street with the park at the end in ruffled darkness and found a parking place. The town houses, though each individual, were connected in one united front on both sides of the street. They rang the bell at a door with an eyelid window above. The door opened to a woman in a long flowered dress with pleasure in her eyes.

Tina was an old friend. Ivy had been in her wedding, knew her family. Tina had met Ansel Fleming through Maira that summer—he'd performed at a benefit on the island where they summered. They had spoken about him maybe giving Tina's son guitar lessons. Tina led them into the living room, holding her neck high, as if above waves, as if being a hostess was being a buoy. Her husband, Nate, in a crisp purple shirt, tipped his forehead down from his height and mirthfully offered them drinks from a table covered with bottles. People sitting on white sofas holding drinks were loosely introduced. Some Ivy knew, some she'd met, some not at all. Everyone smiled, some turned, some stood up, some kissed. Beyond the living room was a large bright kitchen with a table set and beyond it a dark open door with a few figures outside smoking on a slate backyard under golfball lights. Ivy went upstairs to say hello to the children Christopher and Mabel who sat hypnotized in front of a TV with their sitter, an older woman whose name Ivy didn't know, cozily beside them. Ivy thought of her Nicky, sleeping on the foldout mattress in his friend Oscar's room.

When Christopher was told by his mother that Ansel Fleming was there he sprung up to find him.

At dinner Ivy was surprised at how pleased it made her when Tina pointed to the seat she should take, then pointed Ansel Fleming to the seat beside. Till now, Ansel had been absent, occupied with Christopher, and Ivy had been aware that where Ansel Fleming was seemed to be more substantial, and held more dense molecules than were in the rest of the room. He had qualities independent from everyone else there.

Ansel placed two BlackBerry phones on the pink tablecloth to the side of his plate away from her.

Expecting a call? she said.

He looked at her without answering.

People at the counter were putting food on their plates and sitting down, chatting, laughing. Near her in Ansel Fleming were the echoing sounds of trees shaking against each other.

The pink table was set with mint-green plates trimmed with gold beading, probably Tina and Nate's wedding china. The pooled voices swirled over the lit candles. Handsome husbands in glasses, smart wives in satin shirts with a slash of crimson lipstick and tumbling hair.

Ivy ate—chunks of chicken in yellow curry sauce, white rice, green salad with unpeeled cucumber slices—but her attention had collected in her arms and her chest and was tuned in to the stranger beside her. People were discussing where to get the best coffee. She thought of the conversation from Ansel Fleming's point of view, and cringed at its cliché. Now they were talking about the difficulty of getting their children into schools. She searched for a question she could ask him that she didn't already know the answer to from Maira. He'd been raised by his grandmother, had gotten a scholarship at a prep school. He'd had early fame, with the Rebels, and dropped out of college. Online she'd learned about his decision to go solo as a musician, then of the arrest, of the public campaign for his release. Ivy remembered having vaguely heard of the campaign at the time, some eight years before. Maira had been involved, but Ivy was living in another life then, on a farm.

What do you do with your days? she said finally.

Well, said his deep voice. He worked, on his music. He traveled, he performed. He visited schools.

I like to talk to the young people, he said. They know what's going on. He said he was there to tell them there was nothing cool about being in jail. A lot of them thought that it was a badge of honor, but he wanted to convince them otherwise.

In one ear, Ivy could hear Tina telling a funny story about being on vacation with her family in the Virgin Islands. It involved an iguana.

I know you're a writer, he said. Maira gave me your book when I was away.

Ivy was surprised. Maira hadn't told her. She was struck by the phrase *when I was away*. She said that had been nice of her.

Ansel said nothing further about the book and she liked him for it, even if it did make her wonder.

How do you like that? he said.

What? For a moment she thought he meant the curried chicken.

Writing, he said.

She wanted to answer him sincerely, not her usual reaction when asked about writing. But a dinner party was not especially conducive to sincerity. She felt at a loss. It had been early in her life when she'd found simply that putting words on a page was pleasurable. Writing filled up spaces she hadn't known were empty. As a teenager it was a compulsion. When writing, she could feel herself, at the same time that she disappeared from herself. When she emerged from the page to face the walls of her room it was as if she'd been spit out of a warm place back into a hard-edged world.

She told Ansel Fleming that she'd found out early on she liked to write and since she spent so much time doing it figured after a while that she should see if she could make a living at it. But she still didn't really think of herself as a writer, writing was just the thing she did. She had spent a lot of time alone, but it was different now. When she became a mother things changed, including writing. She wrote a lot less.

It's great to be a mother, Ansel said.

Yes, she said uncertainly. Though I'm not sure how good I am at that.

I bet you're a great mother.

How would he have any idea? But she liked him saying it.

Well . . . , she said.

Ansel Fleming felt like a glass hill she was sliding on, trying with an ice axe to find a place to stab and stick. Which she was finding she very much wanted to do. But the pressure was making her mute and she glanced down the table to the loud voice talking.

One of the men she didn't know was saying, You live your life that way and then you grow up and think, Get me the fuck out of here.

Ansel didn't seem to be listening to any of them. Ivy felt he was apart from these people. She had the feeling he was more real, even than herself. Especially herself.

What's this? Ansel said, pointing to the back of her head.

What?

The color.

She touched her neck where her hair was swept up in a twist. The top hair was bleached very light, on the back of her head the roots were dark. Two tone, she said, explaining nothing.

He nodded gravely. Ivy felt an upwelling urge to laugh. She wasn't even sure at what—his earnestness, his beautiful face?

Ivy heard a woman say, I've given up trying to quit. I've quit quitting.

Can I get your number or email from Maira? Ansel said abruptly.

Ivy's chest zinged. Well, she said in a teasing tone, or you could get it directly from me now.

He laid a palm on one of his phones. Yes, he said with a nod. Okay.

He tapped purposefully onto the keyboard as she dictated. With his head bent forward, she could study *his* head with its tangle of shiny hair like licorice.

She wondered how long his hair was. She wondered what kind of sex he liked. And what it would be like to have it with him.

Nate in his purple shirt was moving around the table, pouring from a wine bottle, reaching over peoples' shoulders. He tilted the bottle at Ivy's glass. More?

She nodded and he poured.

Who's driving home? Ansel said.

Oh, she said and sat back. I can.

He turned his face to her, eyebrows raised over the low-lidded almond eyes, chin drawn in, unconvinced. Her vision *was* slightly swimming from the wine and she flushed, upbraided that he could tell. Again she felt his judgment. Ivy regarded herself as relatively responsible. She maybe wasn't overly cautious, but not reckless.

She pushed away the base of her wine stem over the pink cloth and reached for a glass of water. I'll switch, she said.

He laughed now, a quick low grunt. He set his beer bottle to the side, a chess move. *Checkmate.* I'll drive home, he said.

Goodbyes were said in the white-couched living room still bright with lamps. Maira, Ivy and Ansel stepped out the front door into soft darkness with September leaves still thick and black around the streetlamps. On the flagstone walkway, Ivy felt a hand at her lower back guiding her. As if she needed someone's guidance! But she liked it, the cheekiness of his confidence and the wave of pleasure she got from his attention. Earlier in the evening she'd heard him tell Maira he hadn't been to someone's house in a long time, and yet it didn't show. The imprint on her lower back seemed an eerie branding.

. . .

He drove through the light-dotted night. At the bridge, a swath of red sparkles swarmed up the rise. Maira, still eagerly gathering information, was perched forward between the front seats. What song was Ansel working on right now? she said. Her earrings jangled comfortingly near Ivy. What was that song? she said. *All I have . . . ?*

Ansel cleared his throat. Shall I sing it?

Absolutely, Maira said and sat back to listen.

Ivy watched his hands on the steering wheel as Ansel sang. His rough voice was unabashed and clear in the car.

". . . I give you this . . . when nothing else holds . . ." His voice had a raw rasp. In the rearview mirror Maira was bobbing her head, enjoying it. Ivy contracted slightly, feeling self-consciousness for him. The singing felt a thing maybe too close or too fast. His hands were sturdy and well shaped and their place on the steering wheel reassured her.

Bars of shadow flickered over the car as they crossed the thrumming bridge. Below, the river was black and shimmering. The buildings cut into the air in stacked blocks radiant with tiny lights. Seeing them, one had to reflect to register the people dwelling inside, or the engineering it took to build such monstrous things.

Should I take you home? Ansel said, tilting his head toward Ivy. It had been a long time since a man had sat beside her in a car and offered to drive her home. If he did, would she ask him to come up? Would he have wanted to? It was rare that she didn't have Nicky in the apartment and she felt the freedom of the fact tonight. She actually could do it. But she wouldn't. It was nice to imagine it even in a flash.

I don't think I'm the first stop, she said.

They worked out who lived where—Maira was farther uptown, Ansel was farthest down.

So we'll drop Ansel first, Ivy said.

Are you sure? he said.

Yes, she said, though she was not, and she liked that he asked. They drove across on Canal with the now darkened storefronts which spilled purses onto the sidewalks in the day. After passing the curving roads that snaked down into the Holland Tunnel, Ansel turned uptown. He pulled the car over to the curb.

Is this where you live? Maira said, not hiding her surprise at the high modern building with black glass windows.

This is me, he said.

Ivy opened her passenger door to get out so she could drive.

Watch out! Ansel shouted.

She quickly pulled the door in. What? She looked down the avenue to car headlights in the distance.

Careful of traffic, he said. He came around to her side of the car, looked both ways, then opened her door. He escorted her to the curb.

Well, you're looking out for me, she said joking.

I want you to be safe, he said with no irony.

Maira got out too and hugged Ansel goodbye. He waved to Ivy. I'll give you a shout, he said and walked inside through his glass doors.

Each day they were up by six-thirty. Sometimes in the night Nicky would have crawled into her bed and be a unit of heat beside her, arms flung out, mouth parted, his foot tucked under her knee, or into her elbow.

They would get Nicky dressed first. Then he would sit in front of his cereal or English muffin or dry granola at the kitchen table while she dressed around the corner, talking to him.

How come Dad is a poop head? Nicky would say.

Is he?

Yes.

Well, people are who they are, I guess.

Can I get some more Legos today—?

We'll see.

Does *we'll see* mean yes?

It means I haven't decided yes or no, Ivy said.

I think it's yes, or you would have just said no. Right, Mama?

I guess.
Why do you always guess everything?
Because I'm not always sure.
You should be sure, Nicky said. You're a mother.

Then they walked to school, Nicky taking three steps for every one of hers. School was an eight-minute walk. She'd seen other parents with children boarding the bus, but Ivy thought how if they were still living in Tanzania, they'd be walking everywhere, so they walked each morning, first down the red sandstone steps of their brick building with 1885 stamped above the doorway, past the stoops and iron grating and town houses to the corner. They crossed Sixth Avenue amid speckles of rain. She would hold the umbrella over them. He would hold her hand. The trust with which he accepted that she was the person whose hand he ought to hold never ceased to amaze her. The bus whizzed by them, pulling air. On Christopher Street they walked by the store windows, boutiques with well-cut dresses on mannequins, earrings hung on a pyramid display, carefully placed expensive boots. The small shops never had a customer inside. They were spaces for people with money and refined choices. Across Seventh Avenue came smaller stores—the head shops with the glass pipes and Native American feather-dripping dream catchers, small S & M establishments whose male mannequins in captain's hats had muscled torsos in corseted leather or gold jockstraps. Nicky hadn't seemed to notice any of it till one morning he stopped and pointed to a small figurine of Superman carrying a lifeguard. Look, Mama, he's saving the man.

At the brick school building they would enter one of the three blue doors and go up two flights to his classroom where Ivy would leave Nicky in the care of others.

Returning home she took a different street, past young people walking briskly to work, returning from exercising. She stopped at her coffee place with the red circle on the glass and waited in a small wooden room in a short line. Now and then the line was long, crowding the stools by the mirror and the worn beam counter salvaged from a barn. She eavesdropped on conversations, the mother instructing her child in a stroller, girlfriends discussing the night they'd each had. This was her daily contact with adults. The coffee place fit four small tables, and an uncushioned window seat. Nearly every morning the same three men and one woman were there, reading their papers, talking to each other. They took up two tables and talked across the room to each other, about the political headlines, often about what she couldn't tell.

One morning she overheard two women sitting facing each other, hands around paper coffee cups.

One said, She didn't want to believe he was a murderer.

The other: She doesn't think he did it?

Well, she does now. He's serving life.

On the wall were black-and-white photographs of coffee fields and canvas bags which looked as if they'd scaled Everest. A vintage pastry display held coiled croissants, dark muffins with nuts, scones with red currants and green donuts the color of moss. Ivy glanced out the windows to the people passing. A flock of strollers was pulling into the day care next door. A woman's hair billowed like a spinnaker. Ivy often found herself looking out windows, as if answers might be passing by and she didn't want to miss them.

Out the creaking door, she carried her lidded cup of latte past the children being herded into the day care, past the fire station. She could still see the wave of flowers spilling across the sidewalk years ago in front of the station where none of the firemen responding to the call on September 11 had come back. It was a memory like no other one, historic, wide and shared with nearly everyone.

She had the day to work. She had held off applying for a teaching job till the following fall. She wanted to work, but dared not teach without more solid coverage for Nicky. When he was a little older, she'd be able to juggle that more easily. If she had to work and was not available to him, who would take over? No one. So for now she would make do with the articles, ones she pitched or was asked to do, while continuing to work on her next book.

She spent the day alone. While Nicky was in school, her concern for him was suspended slightly; that is, she didn't have to be one hundred percent alert. Theoretically this was the moment allowing her the time to write. But it was not always easy to focus; it was not easy always to believe it worthwhile. When engaged in her work, she was absorbed and everything else around her disappeared. When she was not engaged, a quiet resentment rose up like floodwater in a basement, that her life was not more productive, not more worthwhile, not more intense. The feeling was mortifying and she swatted it down internally. Once when she'd started to describe the dissatisfaction to a sympathetic friend she immediately stopped herself. Out loud, she heard how spoiled it sounded. Look how lucky she was for God's sake.

She sat down at the end of the kitchen table farthest from the sink and the stove, as if to distance herself from the domestic. She once had a separate room to work in—the narrow quiet back room—but that was Nicky's bedroom now. She also once had the feeling she could write all day, words spilling in a waterfall, both foamy and clear, pouring into a green pool, out of her pen onto the paper. The only thing then which kept her from writing constantly was the nervous recognition that she'd miss the things other people were doing and become even more separated from life than she already felt herself to be. To stay so much in the world of writing she would not learn about the world, and she had a lot to learn. How could she write without learning how to live. The netherworld of writing offered a suspension in reverie, but she was just as interested in engaging, watching people in action, seeing new places, studying whatever was in front of her. She'd learned that if she didn't make the effort to engage with that world, she'd lose her connection to it, lose her ability to be with the people in it and to love them, and possibly vanish in a mist.

The day after the dinner with Ansel Fleming she found her attention being drawn away from the table in front of her and back out into the world. She typed his name into the search space.

She had not gone onto this new-to-her site Twitter. Her one visit to Facebook had been instigated by an encouraging friend who offered to set up an account for her. She watched over his shoulder, when within seconds of registering, a message came, a hello from a man she'd met once at a wedding—a person she barely knew!—causing strong heart palpitations. It was as if she had bored a hole out into the world, a tunnel which might pour poison back through it. Panicked and ambushed, she'd immediately canceled the account.

She understood about YouTube, because that was like a miniature movie theatre, and movies did not frighten her, movies she loved.

In these eerie places she was able to find out more about this Ansel Fleming. The weirdness of it was exciting and maybe a little discouraging. It was a cheat, to engage with a person's information without them having to be there. But there he was, at the end of her fingertips, singing on YouTube. She could watch and listen to him speak more than he had during the evening she'd spent with him. She could listen to him talk about prison, about the kindness of people he worked with. He used the whole name of the boarding school where he'd gone, Adams Emerson Academy, which Ivy had always heard referred to as simply Adams.

There was a clip from nearly two years ago, just after he'd been released, of him performing outside. His hair was pulled back in its usual tangle but she could see it was much shorter. A dark T-shirt was snug around his upper arms holding a guitar; he was sitting on a chair on a platform at the edge of a park. A loose crowd stood in front, wind blew across the microphone, Ansel looked uncertain. He played a lovely song, tentative. Each time she heard his songs she liked them more. She noticed his mouth slanted slightly to the side as he sang. Could she trust that mouth? There was something in it both arrogant and sincere, something stubborn and vulnerable. She couldn't read him, but he didn't seem to be a lying sort of person—much of what he'd said to her so far had been almost startlingly sincere. In a black-and-white clip he sang at a club, the frame close on him with a black background and a guitar tucked under a round shoulder. This time his singing seemed to be focused inward, not out, giving it an extra power. After short clattering applause, he made a self-deprecating comment and laughed with a glowing expression.

That Monday Ivy arrived early for Nicky's 2:50 P.M. school pickup. Unusual. Usually she arrived on time, or a minute late, to avoid standing around with the parents in the garagelike room where the third graders were released. You were not to go upstairs to the classroom for pickup. The dark green painted room doubled as a gym, so the brick pillars were wrapped in wrestlers' padding. To Ivy's distress, this public school did not have any sports programs, another frustration that Nicky could not run endlessly around as children needed to do. The people waiting for the children were either family members or minders. Young babysitters sat propped against the wall, while older more maternal minders, nearly always with brown or tan skin, chatted with each other, or stood apart. The minders did not have the same look of expectation you saw on the family members' faces. Mostly family members were mothers, but there were a few fathers, this neighborhood having a bohemian and international streak. Some waiting were young grandmothers, some were older grandmothers. Soon the children would burst out of the stairwell door, having come slowly down—one step at a time—from the third floor, a stream of small people dragging coats and backpacks spreading out into the room like an alarmed school of fish. In the first year here after the split, Nicky had met his mother's arrival with a low brow and angry stony eyes. Ivy had tried to ignore it and be chipper. But Nicky was fuming. Where was his father? Far away. Sometimes she would address his mood. Is something bothering you, my angel? Immediate response: Yes, you.

Often after pickup they would go to the park. Often his classmates were there too, swinging on the monkey bars. Nicky would wear himself out, but not, Ivy noted, from running on green grass under green trees, but by jumping around on rubber and concrete. The walk home afterward, if he'd gotten too tired, could be harrowing. Nicky would throw himself down in a fit of rage and refuse to move, legs stiff and resolute as a sit-down striker. It was these moments when Ivy would feel as if her head was being microwaved, so keenly was she aware of both their misery, and she had to scour herself for scraps of patience. She wanted to sit on the ground and cry, too. Then a strange paralysis took over and she'd be overcome with waves of homesickness. People passed by ignoring them till a woman—it was always a woman—would smile knowingly, amused at the boy scissor kicking his heels on the gum-blotched sidewalk. Ivy wanted to scream it was not funny. The fact she was unable to be amused or at least see the stupidity of letting it undo her only added to the frustration and fury. She was incompetent and weak and at the end of her rope; she was letting down her son; she was in hell.

The doors opened and the children burst out. Seeing her child after nearly six hours away from him still gave her an emotional charge. Today Nicky came running to her, his mouth open in a smile. He practically threw her his backpack, confident she'd take it. We're going to the park, he said, and ran past her. Oscar and I have a contest with Izzy! Her nerves relaxed; he was happy and engaged. The relief, the blessed relief.

She got an email.

Dear Ms. Cooper,

I was passing through your neighborhood yesterday and looked around for diminutive blondes but didn't see you. I hope you are well. You have hosted me at your place so maybe you would allow me to do the same.

AF

Dear Mr. Fleming,

That would be very nice. I am free next week after Monday so let me know what night would be good. We could go out and get a bite or maybe see a movie? I look forward to hearing from you.

Ivy

In the darkening room, not turning on the light as night fell and the room settled grey with the lure of a languid mood, she felt her body and its healthy appetite.

But in the following days she heard nothing more. Well, she thought, it had been interesting, he was an interesting person. She had been open, but she didn't linger over the thought.

After a week he emailed. *What about Thursday at my place? I'll give you some music.*

She was embarrassed by how pleased this made her, and was glad no one saw. She waited to email back despite wanting to immediately and therefore didn't wait long. Why was one supposed to wait? Not to appear eager? She had always wondered at this logic everyone seemed to support. Others must understand it better than she. Though she understood the instinct not to show too much of oneself.

That would be great. What time? Must book sitter.

6 good?

See you then.

On that Thursday morning, Ivy got an email from her sitter Caitlin saying she was sick and couldn't make it. Caitlin was Nicky's main sitter, and Ivy had secured a relative commitment, promising Caitlin at least three nights a week and acknowledging her graduate school schedule. Ivy turned to the long list of alternatives. Most of her sitters were college girls, but many were recent graduates, overqualified young women with office jobs at magazines, or studying for the bar, freelance stylists or aspiring filmmakers. One was a middle-aged woman from Ukraine. Ivy called, texted, emailed. On the fifth try she got Alana. But Alana didn't get off work at *Vanity Fair* till six, so she could make it by six-forty, was that okay?

Ivy emailed Ansel: *Can we make it 7? Sitter adjustment.* She felt the curtness of her message slicing herself down, curating herself so he wouldn't need to hear the details of her life. Even if she felt she had much to tell.

And frankly, she almost wanted to write: *Do we need to exchange life stories?* The thought of telling hers was exhausting. Relating even the facts of her marriage, then divorce, was a deflating prospect.

It had been over a year since she and Everett had split and she had not had any important person in the interim. Everett's body was the one still closest to her, the one she had imprinted on. She was eager for that to change. Everett for his part had managed to get a new girlfriend, quite swiftly in fact, and Ivy knew that her finding another body would be an important step away from Everett. Maybe this was her chance.

Maybe she could also enter another world, Ansel Fleming's world. That he was thoroughly unconnected to her life was terribly appealing. She thought of his time in jail and of how far that was from her life, and instead of being alienating it had extra weight. She knew this seemed reductive, but the experience gave him an added dimension. Then she thought of how at the dinner he had chuckled at something she hadn't thought funny, and then of how he'd not laughed when she cracked a cynical joke. So, maybe they weren't on the same wavelength. If you don't laugh at the same things . . . She thought of his hand on her back. That was something else. Well, she'd find out. She sensed some alignment with him, something magnetic. Perhaps it was simply physical attraction that had made her nervy, having to look away from him. She thought now of being in her towel and opening the door and the surprise of his face with the whites of his eyes behind the glasses and his straight teeth and full easy mouth, the slightly lowered eyelids, lids which said, Don't fuck with me. She thought of his hands on the steering wheel.

Her LG phone rang. No one called anymore, now that you could text. She was outside Nicky's school at the three blue doors. She stepped aside not to block the arriving parents. The name on the screen: Ansel Fleming. She answered, heart thumping.

Hello, Cooper, he said. I got your message. Seven is fine. But I wanted to tell you I have to get up very early tomorrow for a video shoot in the morning.

Oh, I'm sorry I had to change, she said. She looked at the trees across the street where a private school was hidden behind a brick wall. I promise I won't tire you out. Her hand covered her eyes. What had she just said?

He laughed. Okay, see you then.

Because often while waiting she thinks of what is lacking, of where she is letting down her son, she thinks of the small concrete roof area on the fourth floor where the children have recess. The urban way. Like a prison, she thinks. Near her were parents chatting, their weary faces seeming to reflect their job as being one of a continual slog of care. It was an obligation, rarely abandoned by a mother. Ivy noticed that those parents who appeared snappier and less rundown were likely those with an outside job.

Nicky's teacher Angela emerges first, a figure of firmness and understanding with loose springy hair. Under her spell, the children look intently to interpret their teacher's expressions. She holds the door with composure as chaotic figures come pinwheeling through, hair sparkling with barrettes, shoelaces untied. Boys pretend to zombie-walk. A girl in red wraps her arms around the shiny black leggings of her babysitter. A boy with pointed ears joins a woman with the same feline face. Nicky is walking beside his friend Jackson, a redhead with dark lips. They look as if they are in legal conference. Love rises in Ivy seeing her son, a feeling of joy and worry interwoven. Every now and then she will notice he has changed. He is a new version of himself with his same personality, but different ways of expressing it. He is older. And Ivy will have to adjust to something new.

Jackson and Nicky inform her they want the monkey bars.

Jackson finds his sitter, a woman named Fabiola, tall and glamorous in a blue turban, and they all walk toward the exit door together. Outside, Nicky separates from his mother to walk beside Jackson, matter-of-factly passing the ice-cream truck parked five steps from the exit. Ivy has limited the purchase of a SpongeBob popsicle or a vanilla soft swirl to only once a week, usually Friday, to avoid the daily negotiation. Ivy and Fabiola follow them. Ivy had learned that Fabiola has two children back in Haiti and that she is going to school here. Ivy asks her the names of her children, thinking she probably has already asked her and she really ought to write them down so she can remember. Fabiola looks no older than thirty.

The day is shadowless. On Leroy Street they all turn toward the park, under a row of canary-yellow trees glowing along the chain-link fence.

Somebody threw up, Nicky says. Underfoot the squished orange gingko fruit smells of vomit.

The park gate creaks open. A mother changing her baby on a green bench looks vigilantly up to make sure the latch is lowered after they enter. A sign says you may not enter unless in the company of a child, a twist on usual signs forbidding children. Fabiola smiles goodbye to Ivy and walks over to two women she knows sitting in front of strollers. A small dry fountain sits in a dented concrete base and inside the fenced-in area are two different jungle gyms, each with slides, one with a small house and roof, one with monkey bars. It is to this second one that Nicky always goes. They've never even explored the other one.

Ivy spies a dad she knows, reading the paper. Luckily he does not see her. She does not want to talk, she wants to sit alone. She thinks of how she has no idea what to expect later tonight, but feels it like a secret. Various vague scenarios curl like vines dimly in her mind. Later, on the swings, Nicky calls her. He wants to be pushed.

Higher, he says, higher. The goal seems to be the thump when the chain sags.

What did you guys do today?

Nothing.

Really? Nothing.

Nope.

She tells him that she's going out tonight, that Alana will be coming.

I know, you told me, he says.

That okay?

He shrugs, seeming genuinely unconcerned. Ivy can't tell if he doesn't care, or if he's hiding that he does.

Going out was something she made herself do, reasoning that if she didn't see people *some* nights, she'd have no adult interaction and that couldn't be good for her state of mind, could it? Sometimes this seemed reasonable. But she always felt discomfort, unsure how much was guilt, how much her own reluctance to leave him. Hard always to parse out the elements of discomfort.

She fed Nicky a dinner of chicken fingers with ketchup and steamed broccoli and gave him a bath. Knowing she was leaving this evening made her duties sweeter and she felt the difference between giving genuine care and performing it robotically. The doorbell rang and Ivy let in Alana, looking chic in a fitted black dress with three-quarter sleeves, a shiny curtain of hair over one eye. She slid off her flat black shoes from dark stockings. Ivy noted she looked far more fetching than herself in jeans and a thin boat-necked striped shirt. She'd purposefully not dressed herself with any fanciness. If Ansel Fleming liked her, then it shouldn't be because she wrapped herself in a pretty package, she thought, but the truth of it was she didn't have the energy or perhaps the confidence to make a more dramatic presentation. Ivy noticed clothes, and admired the effort and even delight which people took in presenting themselves, but she felt the attention strangely embarrassing, even as she wished she took more care and had more boldness. It was hard to muster it. Almost to spite herself she chose the clothes in her closet which were the least striking, relying on the principle that clothes did not define the person, even if she thought so when she looked at other people. It was perverse, she knew, but there it was. She admired those with the talent to choose the right and interesting thing to wear. It was a skill. And the times when Ivy was dressed in something which felt both fabulous and not ridiculous were so rare she had to consider them a fluke, something meant for her only when the stars had magically aligned. Still it was so pleasurable that she wondered why she did not manage it more often. The truth was she was happiest with no clothes on at all.

Nicky in his elephant pajamas, hair wet, was sitting on a floor cushion, coloring on the low table made from worn dhow wood. She and Everett had bought the table in Zanzibar and had shipped it back in a container along with some of the contents of their house in Tanzania when they'd moved back to the States.

Alana glided onto the couch behind Nicky, and leaned over his shoulder with interest, her prayer hands tucked between her knees. They murmured familiarly with each other.

Is that a horse? Alana said.

No, a spaceship, said Nicky. There was a pause. But I'm going to put a horse in it.

Ivy hoped that Alana stayed as interested in her son when she was gone; there was no way of knowing. But Alana seemed sincere and dependable, besides being wildly overqualified, and Ivy was grateful.

Good night, my pumpkin, Ivy said and kissed the top of his head. He hitched away his flannel shoulder, irritated. He didn't like goodbyes. Who does?

After saying good night three more times while she looked for her wallet, then her phone, then went back to the bathroom to check her lip liner, she put a scarf in her bag, and went out the apartment door.

She walked to his. It was a mild evening, no longer summer, but still warm. What would they talk about? Now, after her online investigations, she had even less to ask him about, that is, things she genuinely did not know. Maybe a musician didn't like to talk. Who would want to talk when there was singing instead? Ivy hadn't the first notion of how one went about making the magic of music. She was curious about its wizardry. Maybe he could describe it. At the crosswalk she dashed across just as the light turned green. She arrived at the checkered black glass façade. The building ran half the length of the block and was about twenty stories high, not the usual prewar apartment building where many people she knew lived, not the old walk-up or the basement in a town house. She pulled open a glass door by its Plexiglas tube handle and entered a stark lobby with an austere grey concierge island and behind it a young man with hair shaved on each side. She told him she was here to see Ansel Fleming. Leaning back in a springy chair, he seemed to look at her in a certain way. Who were the others announced to see Ansel Fleming?

Three G, he said.

She saw no elevator or stairwell, just the matte walls of the lobby sealing them in. Where do I—?

Around the corner, said the man.

Going up in the gray steel box elevator she felt too much herself.

The door slid open silently to a deserted carpeted hall. She had the odd feeling that no one lived here and it was a front for something else, not as it appeared. Partway down she saw an open door and a shoulder jutting out. She walked toward it and Ansel's head tilted out with a solemn expression. Hello, she said. He kissed her cheek and moved aside for her to enter. He wore a dark T-shirt and jeans and was in his socks. She was conscious of how he was the three-dimensional version of what she'd recently been looking at on her small screen.

Should I take my shoes off? she said. Along the hall was a neat line of shoes: cowboy boots, sneakers, tie shoes, work boots.

Not if you don't want to, he said.

I think I'll keep them on, she said.

At first glance everything in the modern apartment seemed to be either black or white. There was a kitchenette with a black counter and cabinets, a chrome fridge and, beyond it, a sitting area with a glass coffee table, white shag rug, black leather couch and the large windows she'd seen from the street. There were black bookshelves against the white wall and a large black TV screen. A long table held a large computer console and keyboard, with a few papers, and a standing microphone jutting up beside two leaning guitars. A black-and-white piano keyboard hovered nearby on a stand. On the wall were framed blown-up black-and-white portraits of Janis Joplin and Jimi Hendrix with blank white backgrounds. On the far side of the room were some small framed snapshots, atop the heater, the only sign of a personal touch.

Ivy reached into her pocket and took out two eggs. I brought you something, she said. These are from our chickens in Virginia.

Ansel took them, unsurprised. I love eggs, he said. I'll cook them. He went to the fridge and set them in the empty plastic egg container. Would she like a drink? His hand was around a bottle of beer. He also had white wine. Yes, she'd love some wine. He took a glass out of an upper cabinet, poured from a bottle and handed her the glass.

Would you mind if I put some ice in? she said.

His chin drew into his neck. He did mind. He bent down to the freezer drawer and extracted a tray with some effort.

Was that wrong to ask? she said.

If it had been a very good bottle I might have been offended, he said, and dropped two ice cubes into her glass.

Oh, sorry, she said, not sure if he were joking. Thank you.

No problem, he said flatly.

She felt on tenterhooks, felt she appeared ridiculous. The worry made her realize she very much hoped he'd like her. She took off her jacket, pretending she felt welcome. She asked him how long he'd been living here and was surprised it was more than a year and a half.

Right after I got out, he said matter-of-factly. I'm still filling the bookshelves. A friend took me to Ikea.

It's nice, she said.

The apartment belongs to a friend, he said. I rent it from her.

Again, despite wanting to ask more, Ivy commented on what was in front of her. She didn't want to look as if she was gathering information.

What's this? she said. On the counter a paper towel was spread with a selection of penny candy—jelly beans, candy corn, chocolate kisses—laid out as if for a sale.

A friend sent me that, he said. So thoughtful of her.

For Halloween?

I suppose so, he said. I wish wish wish I could be thoughtful like that.

You're not? she said.

Not like that, he said.

She stood at the kitchen counter, holding her wineglass. A small pile of CDs was also on the corner. He saw her looking at them. Those are for you, he said. She looked: three of his albums, his face on each cover. One was the CD he'd played for her and Maira.

That is so nice of you, thank you, she said. She had the pleasurable feeling that she'd be able to keep something of him now. I can't wait to listen, she said, and learn them.

He put the wine bottle back in the fridge and as he walked behind her he ran his hand along her belt hoops. I'm flirting, he murmured.

She wasn't exactly shocked, but felt an alarm like a wave go through her. Did he really just say that? Narrate his move. She remained still, unable to speak. It threw her, but in a pleasant way. She'd been in the apartment for barely ten minutes, she thought, and it was as if he'd seen the sign over her head: I'M LOOKING FOR A NEW PERSON TO IMPRINT ON. Maybe they were on the same wavelength after all. But why couldn't she address more directly what was going on? Why couldn't people? It made her feel disconnected, but also engaged in some mysterious progress. And yet untethered. Then it occurred to her that coming to his apartment might mean, in his book, that she was presenting herself as available. She hadn't thought it completely through but guessed it could mean that.

He sat down at the table with the computer console, his back to her. Want to hear my new song? he said. She said she did and carried her glass over to the couch and sat. She didn't particularly feel like drinking, she was already heady.

He clicked some keys. Music filled the room from crisp speakers. The song was slow, which for some reason relieved her. Out came his raspy voice. The music swelled into the corners. She tried to let the song wash over her, but felt his presence there, the creator. How was one to sit listening with the musician nearby? She glanced at him. His head nodded with the beat, his hair piled in the tangled swirl at his neck. She tried to follow all the words, the way she understood things. *Somewhere in the space of me and you . . . , it was my fight, make no mistake* all hitting at a heartbeat's pace. Thank goodness she liked it. On the glass table were two piles of photography books. Black and white! She noticed a five-foot-high DVD case packed with DVDs. She wondered if they were his. The song ended.

She told him how much she liked it. Really liked it.

He swiveled on his chair and faced her, hands on his thighs. Thank you, he said.

She said she found it hard to take in a song after hearing it only once, and did anyone else think that? He said he supposed they did. She asked if this was the song he'd be filming a video of the next morning. He said it was.

The phone face up on his desk buzzed. He glanced at it without interest, but picked it up and slipped a white earplug into his ear. Excuse me, he said, looking unnervingly straight at her. It's the producer. I'll only be a moment.

He stood and walked gracefully toward the doorway cut out of the white wall, saying, Hey. Yes. Yes, I told them seven A.M. They know. They'll have them there. No, they can pick it up after . . .

He disappeared through the door.

Ivy stood and crossed the thick shag rug to look out the windows. Venetian blinds were pulled up in a pleated line at the top. Across the street was a wide sandy-colored building with cornices and a few windows lit, showing offices. She looked at the snapshots in their frames: Ansel holding a plaque next to a man with curly white hair and a silver tie. Ansel smiling radiantly with a small boy on his lap. Ansel between two taller blonde women in dark clothes. Ansel in a red-and-white baseball jacket with his arm around a small woman with a short wavy '50s hairdo and pearls.

Sorry, he said behind her.

Is this your mum? she said.

No, he said. My gran. She's the one who raised me. We've been through a lot together.

Jail, thought Ivy.

There's no one better than my gran, he said.

And your mum? She turned around.

She wasn't around much, he said and took a swig from the beer bottle. Last time I saw her I was eight.

That must have been hard, Ivy said.

It is what it is, he said. I didn't know anything different.

I lost my mother, too, Ivy said. When I was eleven. She and my dad both died.

Ansel did not say anything. Then after a moment, I'm sorry.

On hearing this people usually said, How did they die or When did that happen and so who raised you, but Ansel asked no more questions. Maybe he knew her story from Maira already as well.

They both moved to the sofa and sat, Ansel at one end at a distance from her. He was not flirting now. Had she discouraged him? She did not know how to do this. He took a long swig of beer. Ivy sipped the wine, feeling polite. She asked him if he had any siblings. Yes, two sisters. They were both older. And your dad?

Never knew my dad, he said. Not sure my mother did either.

Oh, she said.

So here they were, she thought, trading histories. But he wasn't saying much.

But he must have looked like me, Ansel said, because I don't look much like my mother.

Oh, Ivy said again, not wanting to pry but with many questions.

My sisters look more like her, but they had different fathers, too.

Ivy nodded, not sure how to react.

He talked then about his grandmother and how devoted she had been and how he would never be able to repay her. He turned his wrist and showed Ivy the tattoo of *Halia* written in script, his grandmother's name. Is that—? Hawaiian, he said. Seeing a notebook behind him on the table, Ivy asked him if he wrote his songs there. Yes, he wrote by hand in a book. She told him how music was so mysterious to her and she was in awe of it. He said it wasn't that amazing, it just came out. He could write a song anytime.

Exactly, she said. That is amazing. He shrugged, pursed his lips. That was nothing.

He stood and walked back to the table, moving like in deep water. Want to hear another one I'm working on?

Definitely, she said.

He studied the screen and fingered the keyboard. She realized he wasn't wearing his glasses today and how it opened his face. After the music started, he stood up and came back to the couch and sat close to Ivy. There was an electronic fizz, then a guitar slid in with heavy plucking. There were other sounds she couldn't name, watery sounds? Whispers?

Wait for the beat break, he said.

The music spilled out and his voice joined it. Ivy tried to make out the lyrics swimming across the air. He was *no longer waiting*. There were *choices we have to make*. There was a *you*. The beat carried the words austere as a barge. There was the tinkling of icicles.

She thought of how music entered a person without your needing to think about it. Reading wasn't like that. You needed to give it all your attention.

Then she felt his hand on her lower back. It rubbed her shirt lightly, encouragingly, friendly. It went side to side with the music. It went up her spine, paused, then went down. She felt her outline shimmering. She glanced at his profile looking straight ahead, head bobbing, his hand on her back as if separate from him. She reached around and put her hand over his.

He turned his head and faced her. Too soon? he said.

No, she said. It's nice. I'm holding it back.

His other hand squeezed her arm.

The song finished.

I'll put on something else, he said, pushing up from a knee. She asked if she could use the bathroom. His chin pointed to the half-open door.

. . .

The bedside light was on in the next room. Dark comforter, neat white pillows. More black bookshelves with empty spaces against the white wall. More black-and-white photographs. Did they all belong to the friend? Or were they his? One large abstract painting showed dark tire tracks crisscrossing snow. This room had the same three windows facing the street, in front of these, three guitars in stand-up holders, one a white shiny electric. The small bathroom had a sink which just fit between a tub on one side and a glass-enclosed shower on the other. Ivy looked into the mirror at the stranger she was. Her reflection was nearly always a surprise, the features wanting a slight adjustment, the hairline not quite right. She closed her eyes to make contact with the self inside, feeling unmoored and happy. Where was she? Who was he? She opened her eyes and as if answering saw Ansel had the exact same body lotion she used. She then saw the same coconut shampoo. She noticed his toothbrush was one of those two-toned cheap ones, exactly like the one she had now. On a lower shelf was an unopened box of soap: her brand, though his was almond to her verbena. It was like *The Twilight Zone*. She knew it was only a coincidence, and yet.

Returning past the tucked-in bed, she tried to calm a sort of splashing frenzy in her mind—feeling too out of practice for this, she thought, too moved.

The muteness which happened around someone to whom you were attracted overcame her, shutting down something natural. She entered the room blank and calm. Returning to Ansel, she felt him a slight degree more familiar. His songs felt like a breastplate over her chest. He'd put on a symphony now, slow and swelling. He was sitting at the end of the soft couch, with his arm along the backrest. At the end of the arm his hand moved, gesturing to Ivy. Come here. All the way over here. Again she felt the relief of no words. He did not watch her as she floated over. He was letting her come on her own. She sat down close to him and put her shoulder in the curve his arm made and tilted her face up to his. His face was as smooth as a rock face, or a hillside, his eyes with a darker smudge around them, as if always in the shade. He turned barely and she stared close-up at his mouth, neutral, unmoving. She felt his not hurrying as showing his confidence and this made a strong impression. She was having difficulty breathing. She brought her lips to his. The first time you kissed a person there was a kind of shock, an unlocking which never happened that way again. This moment of contact could be almost psychedelic, behind her eyes were striped with light, the back of her forehead black color splashed on black. She wasn't breathing. It was wonderful.

After a few moments she pulled back for air. The tightness in her chest had relaxed.

One's face got this close to not a lot of people. Unless you kissed a lot of people. The awareness of this always flashed on her, whether thought came with it or not, that the person she was kissing had now entered into that category of people in her life, ones she got this close to, and how he would always now be one of those people. They continued to kiss.

After a while he smoothly and abruptly pulled her up to standing, turned her around and steered her by the shoulders through the door into the bedroom. Still holding her, he timbered like a tree with her onto the comforter. She still had the giddy feeling of wanting to laugh, but this had gotten serious, her body electric and vibrating, being swept off into rapids. She was aware of not knowing his body, though tight against her, or knowing him for that matter. She thought how Maira had mentioned he was monklike. She never saw him with anyone. Well, Ivy thought. Well, well. So did that mean this—? Stop thinking, said a happier voice. Stop thinking, for Christ's sake. And down the rapids she went. But she kept the awareness of what she knew about him and what she didn't, how he'd been in jail and not believing in the idea of prison and of all the years he'd not been free—seven!—and all she'd done in those seven years. And how she couldn't begin to ask him about that, it was too enormous. What would one even say anyway? *What was it like?* Was it respectful not to ask? Or were people too careful and maybe he wanted it to be acknowledged? Who knew! Blurred frothy thoughts tumbled in the sensations. She was breathless and happy and off-kilter, in this room where she'd never been with the one light on, her arms around a stranger who was now unsnapping her jeans. Through his T-shirt she felt the dip of the muscle between his shoulders, his body solid and dense. He took her hand and placed it on the bulge at his crotch. Lord God, she thought, where am I? Fuck, she thought, who cares?

I haven't— she began. His face was pressed to her neck.

What, he murmured.

I haven't actually kissed anyone, she started and paused, but my husband . . . in the last ten years. This was the first mention of Everett, of the ex-husband.

Ansel may or may not have heard. His gaze was roaming over her body, his hand slid under the waist of her jeans.

She really almost did laugh out loud, it was so surprising. Oh, she said and pushed herself up on an elbow.

He stopped. What?

Nothing, she said. I mean, it's okay. I'm just. I don't know. It's nice. I'm just really—She shook her head, what was she saying? He smiled and helped her pull her shirt over her head.

For a moment she was up on the ceiling in the corner looking down at herself.

He pulled her onto his chest in her black tank top. She lay a forearm down. You know, she said. I'm rather older than you.

He stroked her bare arm, focusing on it. And your point is?

I guess, she murmured. I just thought . . . full disclosure?

But he wasn't listening. His hands moved down her back and slipped commandingly under her jeans waistband onto her bare ass. She crushed his mouth. He kneeled up and reached for her boot and tugged. It didn't come. He looked at it, located the zipper and unzipped. She was on her back, watching this stranger loom over her. What the hell. She bent up, unzipped her other boot and heard the sex sound of it hitting the floor. So this was happening, she thought. No, she told herself, smudge the brain to stop thinking. Just feel. She peeled off her thin socks one after the other. The bare skin of her soles felt the bedspread, felt the weave of his jeans.

He lifted his T-shirt over his head and some of his hair came undone, falling in thick strands past his shoulders. When the skin of his chest lowered down and met the skin of her chest, the reflection came, not for the first time, Why does anyone do anything but this?

The newness lasted only a moment before she started already to be familiar with the shape of his upper arm, the width of his hips, his sturdy neck.

She kept batting away the thoughts which didn't belong—where would this lead? what was she doing?—and instead focused on the sensations zooming through her. Ah, her body hummed, ah, so this is how he moves. This is how he does not smile.

Later, they lay in the bed's yellow lamplight with the rest of the room in grey shadows.

Ansel got up in an unhurried way, and she watched his dark back and paler butt move unceremoniously to the bathroom. She heard the sound of the shower through the open door. She liked his lack of modesty, and did not want to care about his not speaking, because she also liked he wasn't behaving in an expected way. After a few minutes she sat up too in her new wonderfully pummeled body and stood on hollow legs.

She came into the bathroom where Ansel was behind the shower glass, under the water, moving white suds over his dark chest. His hair was tied up, away from the spout.

Can I come in? she said.

Sure, he said neutrally, not unwelcome, but not overly inviting.

She stepped in, feeling scrawny and pale beside him. Her face felt raw, probably pink, and her hair was in a puffed tangle. He stepped aside to let her have the hot streaming water. After rubbing her arms and wetting all her body, she stepped aside for him.

You keep going, she said. He stepped back into the shower,

and she could see more clearly the large tattoo she'd noticed in bed, the foam-edged waves of that famous Japanese painting. At the bottom of his neck was an eye radiating rays.

Why the eye? she said.

Special meaning for me.

I have a key chain almost exactly like that, she said.

He didn't comment.

And the wave? she said.

I always thought it was a beautiful picture. He stepped out of the shower and set a towel for her on the toilet seat.

When Ivy came out after drying off he was finishing putting on sweatpants and a white T-shirt. He went into the other room. She collected her crumpled clothes from the floor and dressed with fingers that seemed to tremble but with a kind of energy adjustment, not nervousness. She sat on the bed to put on her boots. Through the door she saw his white shirt bending in the gloom of the unlit kitchen. He straightened and faced her. I admire what you do, he said from far away with a kind of formality.

Thank you, she said. Her voice felt deeper.

She found her jacket on an armchair and her bag on the counter beside the CDs, still there. His getting dressed and leaving the room meant there would be no lingering, it was time for her to go. Thanks for these, she said and put the plastic squares in her bag. Can't wait to listen.

You're welcome, he said, heading to the front door. He turned before opening it. If you are alone so much, he said offhandedly. You should use me.

He stood in bare feet with his beautiful face and arms. She was taken aback, mainly because the offer was an unexpressed version of what she would have hoped for if she had thought it through. Which she hadn't yet. He was describing it before she could.

I may, she mumbled, feeling it wasn't all she might have said. She had many feelings, but did she need to get into them? She liked how Ansel Fleming seemed to edit out the extraneous. What really did she need to express anyway? That she was happy? That she felt relieved? Baffled? In fact, the buoyant feeling she had didn't want to express itself. He opened the door.

Have a great shoot tomorrow, she said.

You're taking a cab, he said.

No, I'll walk home.

Take a cab. He looked across the room to the dark windows as if there was danger out there. She hadn't looked at the time, but it couldn't be later than 10:00 P.M. She laughed.

I like walking, she said. Anyway, tonight I'll just float home.

He stood, waiting for her to go. She kissed his cheek, despite the urge to hug him again close, but he was no longer offering himself.

Night, she said, beaming. Thanks.

Good night.

Thanks, she thought, purring down in the elevator. Now that was an understatement.

She crossed the lobby, passing the high counter with the concierge's eyes just above it. She felt he was seeing through her clothes to her skeleton where sex radiated off her. She kept her expression bland lest anything blissful show.

Outside, the air was light grey and on the sidewalk bits of mica glittered like fairy dust. The hum of the city sounded like surf rumbling. She turned up the avenue on soft invisible feet, changed, no longer the same self that had walked down it earlier.

Her chest felt lifted with helium and her throat so thick with joy she could have coughed it out in sparkles or stones. This was the feeling one waited for. She was returned to some joy and had needed another body to get there.

There was little traffic on Hudson. She saw herself from above, a figure walking up the expansive street, enchanted. Taxis thumped the potholes. Potholes were enchanting. She passed the park where she took Nicky, lit up yellow with the floodlights over the buttery gingko trees. Building corners were sharp and decisive, shooting heavenward. Up in a lit window she saw a white ceiling and a green wedge funneling from a green lampshade and the shadow of a person moving. The sky was dove grey. It was hard to remember how one didn't always see the miracle. She glanced inside herself for that place where despair usually sat, but couldn't find it. Her feet kept walking, unattached to her legs.

The young figure on the couch sat leaning over her blue hands. Oh hi, she said, looking up from her computer. Did you have a nice night?

It wasn't something Alana usually asked and Ivy blushed. Did it show?

She went to the secretary desk where she kept the envelope with cash. The envelope was there, but empty. How quickly it happened. She could barely remember taking out a final bill. Her feeling about finances was that if she looked too hard at them they'd turn you to stone. But tonight the empty envelope didn't worry her. Worry couldn't touch her. What was the point of worry anyway? Her ex-husband, Everett, defended the worrying he did as being preventative. If he worried about something, it was much less likely to happen.

She found some bills in her wallet and paid Alana her sixty-five dollars. They chatted as Alana put on her coat. Alana's job at the magazine was okay for now, but she was probably going to apply to graduate school. She hadn't decided if it was going to be in writing or in law.

After Alana left, Ivy walked down the hall to Nicky's room, the narrow room once her office, where her desk—a wide slab of plywood set on file cabinets—had been replaced by a chunky loft bed, raised up to make space underneath where he could play and which the door hit when open all the way. At the one long window was a bureau across from a shelf holding small bins filled with either toys or clothes. Ivy stepped onto a footstool to reach the upper bunk where Nicky lay sleeping and kissed his quiet face in the bliss of sleep.

In the bathroom mirror she looked at her own face. Her eyes looked puffed and her mouth beaten. It made her smile that it showed, and made her look like a stranger. The look reminded her of something. She'd seen it before. Then she remembered, the otherworldly pummeled look she'd seen on her cousin Margaret's face hours after giving birth.

She listened to the CDs. With each song she pictured Ansel Fleming in a different scenario. There were subway platforms and front rooms, cafes and bedrooms. She listened intermittently, not to overload herself. The spell of him was lingering on its own, without the songs. The earlier albums were lively and edgier, full of curses and anger and righteous complaint, the later songs more pensive, gentle, even hopeful.

She wanted to text immediately but, having learned at different points in her life that her instincts were not always in line with the common wisdom, did not. She did not hear from him. After two days she wrote him thanking him for the music. She told him he was transporting. He responded, Thank you for your kindnesses. So that's how he described it, *kindnesses*.

The weekend went by. With each day Ansel Fleming felt both more strange and more vivid. She still had the floating feeling she'd had leaving his building. It was as if she'd pushed off on an icy pond and her skates were gliding much farther than her push had promised.

. . .

After five days she wrote, *How long do your spells last?*

The dots flickered. He had an answer. *9–13 days.*

Good to know, she wrote back, smiling.

The next day he wrote, *9 days is a gross exaggeration.*

But after nine days the soft feeling was still with her. It was too lovely to describe to anyone. Besides, what if it was nothing. She savored it as a secret. Yes, it was making work less compelling, but so what, this didn't happen all the time. It hadn't happened to her in a decade, since Everett. Maybe it would never happen again. She'd allow it, the new dimension of it.

Instinct kept her from texting more. She wanted him to come after her. In fact, she quite needed it.

At last an email came early in the afternoon.

I was running by your house early this morning and thought of you. I looked for diminutive blondes but didn't see you. Hope you're making magic over there.

She responded immediately, electrified, caring nothing for the common wisdom. *You should have come up and gotten into bed with me. Though it might have surprised Nicky.*

His response: *I have a window this afternoon before 3. Want to sneak away?*

She was putting a cake in the oven for Nicky's birthday. She couldn't sneak away. Did he want to come to her?

The doorbell rang twenty minutes later. Going to answer it she felt the echo of their first meeting, except now she knew who would be there. But he was still a surprise. He wore a crisp white shirt with two pockets on the chest, no glasses, those sad vivid eyes. His face was bigger, ablaze.

She backed down the hall as he sort of stalked after her. How are you? she laughed.

Hungry, he said, placing his hand below her neck and focusing past her. I didn't have lunch.

Oh, can I make you something, some eggs?

His hand pressing her chest steered her backward to the bedroom.

After, he said.

The usual afternoon was now a flying carpet. He pushed her onto the bed and she watched, propped on her elbows, as he stood in the doorway unbuckling his belt and stepping out of his pants. She wondered if he found this as surprising and thrilling as she. Oh who cared. It just was.

He moved over her, quickly lifting off her shirt, then pulling down her red pants, tugging them when they stuck at the ankles. His expression was solemn and she felt again like laughing. Was this how other girls were, waiting for him, docile? Was this how he handled them, too? She even felt like she was another girl, open and quick and easy, a girl she might not find familiar but was happy to be.

The bed was a raft and his pressing body tilted her on it. The window was open letting in a warm air with the city hum in it. It kept hitting her, the surprise of him like waves slapping. The slick wet of their skin, the dark slash of his hair.

Then the raft was still. His body with its wet curves.

Did he want to shower?

No, he said, and wiped his chest and ribs with a towel she'd given him. Sweat shower.

In the kitchen she beat the eggs. He sat at the table in his bright white shirt. For about twenty minutes each day sunlight found its way over the flat rooftops of the backyard space behind her building into her angled kitchen window and splashed brightness over the old wooden floor and the draped armchair and the carved mantelpiece. Ivy would sit in the sunshine and work, writing, reading manuscripts.

I walked up here to you, he said. He told her he wasn't used to walking around in the daytime, it made him nervous. Night was okay. He didn't have the same anxiety at night. He'd been like that, he said, before he went in the joint. The joint, she thought.

At the open kitchen window were terra-cotta pots where Ivy had planted parsley, mint, basil and rosemary. She picked some sprigs as the eggs turned yellow in the pan. Ansel asked her about her writing routine and she shrugged and laughed. It was no longer organized. She crumbled feta cheese over the eggs and said her habits were pretty scattered, though they hadn't always been. He nodded at her with a serious expression. It's important to keep at it, he said. Again she felt shown up by his intensity. She used to have that. She used to care that way about her work, but now . . . now life had more pressing concerns. Art and making offerings to the world had been taken over by life. She had a child. And her marriage had cracked apart. Ansel was still free and she envied he could still live in that intensity. Also, he had youth. She didn't exactly envy that, but she saw its uneven delights. Either way, youth always had an advantage.

Every day is one more day than I thought I'd have, Ansel said.

She felt thoroughly frivolous beside this person.

She diced some tomatoes, added olive oil and basil and put it on their plates with the eggs. Sitting down, she told him again how much she liked his music, which she hadn't said in person, and particularly that she liked the second album, called simply *Ansel Fleming*.

That was the one I finished right before I went in, he said. I didn't get a chance to promote it, he laughed. Needless to say.

Each song is so different, she said. Each one really—she paused, not knowing how to talk about music—has its own . . . form. And is strong.

Thank you, he said.

They ate. The cake she'd taken out of the oven before he

arrived was cooling down at the other end of the table. Ivy felt the colors around her jewel-like.

She asked him about his grandmother. He told her how hard she'd worked all her life, at the same job, at a hospital supply company, supporting her three grandchildren, all on her own. She rarely spoke of Ansel's mother. Her attitude was there are some things you can help and some things you can't. She'd been the one who'd organized it so Ansel could go to a good school, with a scholarship, somewhere else from where they were. His sisters had left home young, so Ansel was with her the longest. He said again how much he loved his grandmother and how she was the best thing in his life. She had grown up in Hawaii and met Ansel's grandfather when he was stationed there and married him and returned with him first to Arizona where he was from. Ansel said he was part Navajo. Then they moved to Detroit where his grandmother got a job and supported them. After they were married two years, her husband went out one morning and never came back. I don't think she ever got over that, Ansel said. He said it as if it was just occurring to him. Had he not said it before?

He also said, I worry about her. He didn't say why.

Their plates were empty. Did he like pears?

I love fruit, he said.

She had a pear in the fridge, it was ripe.

Could I have a knife, please? he said. He peeled the pear with calm deliberation, then sliced it.

You're easy to talk to, he said.

Her heart expanded. She wanted to swat it back down. Come on, now. No expectations. But his saying something beyond the physical interface fed the story which had been forming in her mind from the beginning that she'd met a person who would be important to her. Maybe she'd know him for a long time, maybe he would change things. Something.

He had to be going, he said. He had an interview, at a radio station in Midtown. He would take the subway to that, he laughed, and his face expressed both trepidation and determination.

She said she had to go soon, too. To pickup. She threw out

the line to see if he would note a detail of her life. He didn't say anything.

At the door he said, Stay out of trouble.

She thought of prison, but didn't make a crack, feeling it beneath them. Before the door closed, he said, I'll be keeping an eye on you. She said nothing, aware of letting it mean too much.

She went back into her apartment. It was no longer too crowded or oppressive. It was fine. It was better than fine, it was precious. Okay, so she was a cliché of postcoital bliss. She'd take it.

The cake needed to be frosted. Fifteen minutes before she had to leave for pickup.

The impression he left felt nearly three-dimensional, an aftereffect of sex. Pieces of him hovered over the bed as Ivy smoothed the sheets, his hands at her crotch, his dick in her, his face an inch from hers. She punched the pillows and propped them against the wall, but saw more vividly the earlier bed with them still on it.

A chunk had been sliced from her usual world and was replaced with a glowing wedge.

She peeled the red top off the icing container and added a few drops of green dye. But what did *he* think of this, what did he have in mind? She had no idea. Though she could be pretty sure he was not looking for a single mother with a son—and an older mother at that. She laughed inwardly. For God's sake she'd seen this person, what, three times, and two of those times they'd had sex. Why did a person need to think about what it was or wasn't or would be? Couldn't she just let it wash over her for once? Yes, she could. This time, she would. She spread green frosting over the cake, squeezed from a pastry cone a white fluted border and wrote Nicky's name in translucent blue loops. Each lover had a certain geometry, and there were echoes of each other at first, but Ansel Fleming was different. His direct beeline to sex, without the usual preamble of getting to know the person—that was new. And hadn't it been just what she'd been wishing for? That she'd happened upon a man with the same idea quite amazed her.

Thoughts tumbled around in her, light and soft, so different from the heavy ruminations of divorce she'd been dragging around. She had pictured Nicky, displaced atop a wagon piled with upended chairs and baskets, rolling off in a swaying caravan down a muddy road, away from his father. Having allowed for that to happen, she deserved nothing good. She covered the cake with a cardboard box and hid it out of sight on top of the fridge.

Ansel Fleming. She was baffled he'd even looked at her. It was all so surprising. She had no clear reading on this. There was no steering it. It would have to steer itself. The less she followed the usual ways the better. Where had those usual ways gotten her anyway?

On the sidewalk she walked quickly to school in the warm air, passing figures in the dappled shade, thinking, No one has the least idea of the radiance in me.

2

Radiance

Let everything happen to you: beauty and terror.
Just keep going. No feeling is final.

—RAINER MARIA RILKE

In the following quiet days she listened to music in her new rooms gliding this way and that, letting sound flow through her.

On the walk to school, Nicky's small hand wrapped around her fingers and Ivy felt love and gratitude for this little person walking upright on tiny feet, breathing, his eye roving like a bird's. Certainly all the people they passed were equally valuable, but she felt it for this boy humming to himself on the way to school.

And now with Ansel Fleming she had added another tenderness, somewhat ragged and a little depraved, as if on the flip side of her heart. Something more selfish perhaps, something to hide.

The spell was now too expanded not to tell someone. She called Maira, left a mysterious message, and Maira called her back. Maira was delighted and, Ivy noted, surprised. I didn't picture that happening, she said with a laugh. But she thought it was great. Nothing she liked better than for people she thought were great to find each other.

. . .

That weekend Everett was scheduled to come to the city from Virginia to celebrate Nicky's birthday. It was four days after the actual day when she'd had neighborhood friends with their children to eat the green-and-blue cake, but Everett would not have missed marking it, and the weekend meant he could spend time with Nicky. Ivy used to think of celebrations like birthdays and Christmas as obligatory, and did not like being told what to do or how to behave, but after Nicky's birth a sort of phantom person rose up in her, one caring about holidays. It was on his behalf; holidays had been made for children. The phantom person—she supposed it could be called being a mother—altered other attitudes. A schoolroom was now more important than it had been. Cleanliness and some measure of domestic order, which had never been priorities, were now elevated, since they expressed care. Eating meals at usual times, something Ivy had long dispensed with when first living on her own, was also crucial. She had been surprised at how quickly these conventions, as she saw them, rose in value.

During his visits to New York in the first year of their not living together, Everett would stay with them in the small apartment, sleeping on the wide couch in the high-ceilinged living room, suffering the street noise and never failing to point out that New Yorkers must be insane—to be able to sleep with all that racket, not to mention pay that much for food, to wait in that long a line etc. This time he was staying with Ivy and Nicky one night, then taking Nicky with him to Brooklyn to join his new girlfriend, Rebecca, at her sister's. Ivy had met Rebecca in Virginia, where he lived in Dover. Rebecca came to Dover on the weekends from D.C. where she worked, and Ivy had seen her at holiday parties, but had never actually spoken to her. But she knew who Rebecca was. At the end of the previous summer Nicky had spent some time with Rebecca at the farm and, when asked what she was like, said Rebecca was nice and okay and fine. Nicky was straightforward about his take on people so Ivy saw this as positive.

Everett arrived by train with his knapsack, appalled at the crunch of the Friday rush-hour crowds on the subway. There he was again, not seeming to age, the same appealing face, wide forehead, strong bones, the face she knew so well, no longer hers. He'd gotten a haircut and it made him look fresh and younger.

Everett flopped on the sofa and Nicky immediately scrambled onto his lap, both looking relieved to be with one another. Ivy ordered takeout Mexican food and they all went to the restaurant to pick it up, walking back through an early darkening Washington Square past tourists staring up at the lit arch. Nicky walked in between them, holding both their hands, like an intact family.

What's your favorite color? Nicky said.

Green, Everett said immediately.

Mum?

I think blue, Ivy said. Today at least. It changes.

Yours, Skeezits? Everett asked and Ivy noted his kind tone. Everett did not always try to please and she was grateful he was making an effort.

Nicky paused, suspended in the attention from both parents. He looked at the glittering lights in the windows of the town houses surrounding the park, then up at the clouds streaked with moonlight. See-through, he decided.

Good choice, Everett said.

Shadowy figures slid by, detaching themselves from the trees. A hooded man passed near them muttering, looking directly at Ivy with dart-like eyes. Everyone ignored him.

What did he want, Mama?

He was asking if we wanted to buy drugs, she said.

Really? Everett said. Do you have to tell him everything?

But we don't want to, Nicky said. That's why you didn't answer him.

We definitely do not, she said. Who knows where they came from.

Everett said, It's illegal and you are never to think about drugs.

Nicky said, I don't think I'll want to try them anyway.

You people, Everett said. New York.

. . .

They were not like one another and Ivy had liked the difference. He cared little for social life and was self-sufficient and dutiful. She liked being near those appealing qualities. Everett, on his side, liked the things about Ivy which were similar to him—wanting to be in nature, wanting to help in the world and understanding what he liked.

Their differences were less apparent when they first met, both of them being far from home. Meeting in a foreign place, people might seem more familiar than if they'd met at home. It had been at a wedding in Kenya. At the bar beside women with feathers in their hair and men wearing wrapped kikois and jackets, Ivy was introduced to Everett Scott, an American friend of the groom, wearing a light blue shirt and khaki jacket. He had short thick hair, a strong jaw with a pointed chin and a clear gaze. A heat ray moved through her body. Neither of them knew many people at the wedding so they served themselves at the buffet and sat together in the dark green garden under the looping lights at dinner and she learned that he was working in Tanzania in agricultural planning. They discovered people back home they knew in common, no one close. Later when she danced with him, this new man surprised her by being unbridled, adeptly swinging her around and making jaunty almost comical moves, swept up by the music, not like his reserved manner. But he kissed her goodbye on the cheek.

He was perplexing to her, his good looks, his dryness, his matter-of-factness. When they met again some weeks later when Ivy visited Arusha for work, she learned he'd not been unmoved by her after all.

His lovemaking was earnest and boyish with a passion that seemed to surprise Everett as well. Ivy saw him as a forthright good man and was almost proud of herself if not surprised by the attraction. In his job Everett often ended up dealing with extreme matters—sudden flooding, drought, displaced persons—but Ivy never heard him boast about his management, nor complain. Her relief at finding a man who did not drink too much, or sleep with other women, and seemed to understand commitment had her spellbound. She fell in love with him quickly, not unusual for Ivy. Soon she had moved into Everett's house, a stone building in a leafy garden. It felt like home. But home for Ivy had always been someone else's.

Cramming himself against the wall on Nicky's raised bed, Everett lay beside his son and read him an old favorite book (crows, rooftops, loyalty) while Ivy washed the dishes. They were all in bed by nine. Ivy still was not used to the oddness of being in her bed with Everett sleeping on the sofa in the next room. Nine years of habit told her body it should be otherwise. A part of her even thought, Why can't we still just sleep together? Because, was the answer. It was the logic you gave a child when no explanation was necessary. *Just because.*

The next day was Saturday and they went up in an elevator to go ice-skating.

The rink was three stories above the Hudson River. Enormous glass panes looked across the water to the factory stacks and skyscrapers in New Jersey. The white rink was surrounded by white boards so on a sunless day you felt blended in with the sky.

There were a good number of people skating today. Everett and Nicky glided beside each other, their cheeks reflecting the cold white ice. Nicky's hat was shaped like the head of a hound dog with long earflaps; Everett wore no hat, rarely feeling the cold. Nicky was chopping his hockey skates, leaning forward. Everett rented hockey skates for all of them including Ivy, who skated on both, because figure skates were for sissies.

After skating they would meet Rebecca when her late-afternoon train arrived and Ivy would pass along Nicky to his father and his new girlfriend. The oddness and pain of this were mitigated slightly by the prospect of having a night of her own, when she wasn't having to pay a sitter. She'd planned to meet Irene for a drink. She had purposefully not texted Ansel Fleming yet to see if he was free. She figured the more last minute it was, the less it would show she cared. Her behavior would convince her emotion. And yet her emotion was lifted regardless in anticipation of a free night.

She had stopped skating for a moment to lean back on the sideboards, and watch the people sweeping by. A stream of humanity gliding or wobbling, dark outlines against white. Then her people appeared, more radiant than the strangers around them. Nicky's eyes were focused, gleaming with a determination to impress his dad. Their son's face was brighter, no question, when his father was there. Another nick to her heart.

Nicely done, she called and Nicky smiled, grateful.

Everett moved gliding on air, his shoulders filling in his blue canvas Carhartt jacket, his thick hair cropped close to his head. She had never not liked the way he looked, his defined jaw, his direct gaze. She had liked it right away, and liked his dense but graceful body. She'd liked his physical ease, the way he threw himself under a truck to look, then slid out, barely smudged. He always weaved by, instead of banging into things, and had a way of bending his forearms, muscled from work, meditatively behind his head, of crossing his ankles like a dancer stretched out in a chair. But he was aware of none of it. And she had liked how it matched up with his character, the certainty of his self, having a deliberateness with which he applied himself to matters he cared about. She had liked how he never felt the need to justify his behavior, as many people do, but was himself unapologetically, a solid person not distracted by sparkly things. He had a drive, but it was without the calculation of ambition. He seemed to want to do good and to work hard, not for himself, for the community around him. He was still that way, Everett.

Why aren't you skating, Mum? Nicky said.

I was. Just resting.

The boys—they used to be her boys—skated past.

Ivy had removed Nicky from their home in Virginia, so

Everett had become a father who lived far from his son. This drastic change made for a continual simmering fury on Everett's part, and a continual cowering state for Ivy. It was Ivy's doing, and it was Ivy's fault. The option of staying in the small town would mean she saw only the people she'd known through Everett and when she pictured herself renting a cottage down the road . . . well, it looked not only lonely and unworkable, but she genuinely believed it would serve Nicky better if his mother had a robust life in New York. She could offer him expansion. She would build on the life there she'd once had and be with her friends. Her closest family member, cousin Margaret, was nearby in New Jersey, and Ivy needed family support, something beyond Everett. But the fact that she'd taken Nicky to a place far from his father was a thing she never thought of without guilt. She had not seen any alternative as feasible, but that did not alleviate her guilt.

Ivy felt her phone in her pocket. She would not say anything about it being last minute. Why describe it? Just be straightforward. She took her phone out and typed, *Want to watch a movie tonight? Am free. I have a screener.* The message whizzed off.

The next time they came around, Nicky banged into the boards beside her and Everett glided up behind.

Can't keep up with him, Everett said.

A trio of teenage girls in shiny leggings and pom-pomed hats careened by, shrieking, clutching at each other's elbows.

People here are nuts, Everett observed.

Ivy barely felt his remark; she was cushioned and content. Behind her eyes she could look at the image of Ansel Fleming.

Want to try backward? she said to Nicky.

I can do that, he said immediately and wiggled his heels side to side, staying in one place.

That's the idea, she said.

Don't listen to your mother, Everett said. Try pushing backward a little, and use your calves. Everett demonstrated, swaying side to side, backing away from them. Having been an ice hockey player in high school Everett was a natural graceful skater. He stopped with a spray of ice shavings and came skating back. Nicky frowned, he'd never be able to do it like that.

Usually Ivy would have intervened and tried to soften Everett's curtness. But today she didn't feel the need.

Nicky was her main thing, her continual thought. But having something else to think about, a place to spread her attention, could only be good for Nicky. In fact, it seemed to her that in the last two weeks, since she'd met Ansel Fleming, Nicky's attitude had been decidedly more calm and curious, rather than angry or irritated toward her. Or maybe it was her attitude which had changed . . .

She would not check the phone. She would wait. But having a phone to check . . . and someone at the other end . . . that was new. It fueled the reserves.

You have him? she said to Everett. I'm going to do some laps. And she pushed off.

She whizzed past the moving people, taking long strides. Sweeping around the corner at a tilt, she had the arrogant feeling that no one felt as good as she. She thought of the moment in the afternoon asking him if she could make him something to eat and the thrill of his *After.* The body had often been the place for her of the real proof, and this confirmed it. There was a bruise she'd noticed that morning on the back of her thigh. Evidence.

Don't check the phone. The longer the wait, the more chance there was for a response. A loud alarm filled the high arena, a screeching *beep beep beep,* and the skaters all herded obediently toward the entrance gap to clear the rink. The white boards pulled back at the far end and the majestic Zamboni appeared and entered like a tank. It swept close to the corners, moving like a woman in a hoop skirt, leaving a thin glaze of water over the surface behind. People watched for a while, hypnotized by the shine and the transformation.

Ivy walked in her skate blades on a rubber floor made of huge black puzzle pieces fitted together. Nicky was standing tentatively in front of a snack dispenser. He requested pretzels, knowing candy would be denied.

Maybe we should get actual lunch, Ivy said and unwound her scarf in the windless room.

Behind the cafeteria railing which supported their tray, they viewed pizza with thick cushions of white cheese, sugared donuts, hot dogs, white rolls, bagels, white bread. Into red cups machines poured sugar water. Ivy ordered a cup of tea, Nicky a toasted bagel, Everett a slice of pizza topped with broccoli. They walked in their blades to an unoccupied round orange table to which rounded plastic orange chairs were attached. Music throbbed from speakers, louder now without the hiss of skates on ice, and layered with chatter and children shrieking. But none of it was irritating, not the badness of the songs nor Nicky's hot chocolate spilling on her jeans. Ivy had a liquid place in her mind where she floated.

Can't you afford gloves with fingers? Everett said.

They're meant to be— she began, then saw Everett wasn't really asking.

Sit here, love, she said to Nicky, and took off his hat.

I want to sit there, he said, pointing to the seat on Everett's other side. She slid over his plate with the bagel on it.

You shouldn't give him everything he wants, Everett said.

If they were still married, Ivy would have been compelled to challenge this sort of statement. Despite the righteous intention, the impulse only served to keep them on a well-worn path of bickering. It took the devastation of their breakup for her to learn to stop offering a defense. She wondered now of the difference it would have made to their marriage if she'd seen the wisdom of this while they were still together. But who was she kidding, she wouldn't have been able to do it then. If you are married, it matters that you are in agreement. And when not in agreement, it ought to be acknowledged.

Everett took a wide bite into his pizza. After swallowing he said to Nicky, Aren't you having any food?

He's having a bagel, Ivy said, unable to stop herself. A bagel's fine. She felt Nicky's gaze on her, noticing the old engagement.

You're going to spoil him, Everett said.

Ivy glanced to the table beside them. A husband and wife and their two girls were all eating, each person with a calm unexpectant face.

. . .

After eating they returned to the ice which after the cleaning was like polished white marble. Ivy thought of how everyone's feet were hovering an inch off the ground.

She could wait no longer and while gliding along, Ivy checked her phone. There was a text. *Sorry,* it said. *Working. Be well.* The small cloud of joy in her shattered and tinkled into icicles at her feet. She kept her chin up, skating on, but found that this was the first unsettling moment she'd had in a week.

They waited outside Penn Station on the less populated Eighth Avenue side.

A woman in a dark blue parka with a fur hood came out of the swinging doors, pulling a wheeled suitcase, walking toward them. They all greeted each other. Rebecca's thin glassy hair pooled like syrup on her fur hood. Straight nose, pale mouth and an accepting expression conveyed someone not bothered by trivial things. The tidiness of her suitcase and small pocketbook showed she was squared away, someone who followed through, who would do her taxes on time. Ivy knew she worked on the managerial side of running NGOs. She said hello to Nicky and winked at him, showing they had an understanding.

Meeting Rebecca now as the woman sleeping with the man she'd slept with for so many years, Ivy could not help assessing her erotic attributes. The simplicity of her sneakers, regular jeans, had an understated allure. Ivy glanced at her hands—one's hands said a lot about a person—but they were covered in dark green gloves.

Welcome to the mayhem, Everett said glancing at the people walking by. How was D.C.? Ivy knew this was Everett being positive and polite. He was one of those people who found it easier to be kind to strangers and who let himself become progressively more irritable and unbending the closer he drew to a person. So he was still in the polite phase with Rebecca, she thought.

Just the usual frustrating meetings, Rebecca said calmly. Two peas in a pod, thought Ivy. They exchanged more hellos.

Everett gallantly took command of her suitcase handle.

Are you still living in D.C.? Ivy said, knowing the answer.

During the week, Rebecca said. But I'm helping my parents move to Florida so I've been going back and forth there, too.

Oh, said Ivy. That's nice of you.

Well, not really. Apparently it's my job, Rebecca said.

Everett gave his ex-wife a look. *Go.*

Ivy bent to Nicky. Okay, my little one. She took his shoulders to hug him, but Nicky had crossed the divide and stood close to his father, blithely ignoring her. Then his dark eyes bore down on her, as if to say, Why are you still here? But Ivy had been lingering, her instinct suggesting that tolerating the four of them together would help stamp its normalcy for Nicky. And perhaps for herself.

Everett's instinct, as so often, was not the same as hers. Don't you have to be somewhere? he said.

Ivy laughed. His directness had been something she'd always liked, even when it skewered her. Not really, she said. But I'll be going.

Nothing planned for your night off? he said.

Meeting Irene, she said. But that wasn't for another hour. And Irene had time only for a drink.

Ivy told Rebecca it had been nice to see her again and again said goodbye to Nicky, checking herself not to bend down once more and hug him. He was ramrod stiff beside his dad.

Bye, she said. Bye, and walked quickly to the corner, crossing before the light changed. Deciding not to protect herself from a scene which might hurt, she looked back. Everett was on the avenue hailing a taxi—special treatment tonight—and Ivy watched the three silhouetted figures, the small hound dog head between the man and woman, a yellow cab stopping. She saw them objectively. The man placed the suitcase into the popped trunk, and the woman went first into the back seat, followed by the little boy, then the man. They were an intact family unit, the geometry fitting with the three of them. She wasn't sure that she and Everett and Nicky had ever looked quite like that.

. . .

In the middle of the night she sometimes heard noises coming from Nicky's room. She got out of bed and moved down the hallway into the shadowy room, never as dark as in the country, always lit with a city glow. She stepped onto the low stool to reach up to the figure sleeping on the bunk. Sometimes he was quiet by the time she got there. One night she found him whimpering, but still asleep. She lay her hand on his chest.

It's okay, she whispered.

His eyes opened, dark spots in the grey light. But he wasn't seeing her.

You're going too fast, he muttered. It's going too fast. It's pounding.

Mumma's right here.

Stop going so fast, Mama, he cried out suddenly, breathlessly. His eyes still did not register her, but he had sensed her there. You're hurting me! Stop pounding! Right here! He banged his chest. You're hurting my heart.

She laid both hands on his shoulders. It's okay.

Why are you letting it go so fast? His head thrashed back and forth. You're hurting my heart, making it go too fast.

I'm right here, she murmured.

Leave me alone! Put me in my bed!

You're in your bed, sweet. You're right here.

You're not making it stop! Take your hand off my head. It's too hard. Too fast.

She lined her arms alongside him as if protecting him from shrapnel.

His breath came jerkily, painfully.

It's okay, my angel, she murmured. It's okay.

Finally his breathing began to slow. He burst into tears. His eyes looked around, saw her. Why does it go so fast? he wailed, tears leaking down his temples. Why, Mama?

I don't know, my love.

After wearing himself out with crying, he fell back asleep.

Back in her bed, face to the ceiling, tears leaked down her temples. After Everett's visits, Ivy learned to expect days with these extra moments of turmoil for Nicky. One evening as she was cooking she'd heard high inviting sounds coming from the corner of the living room and saw Nicky with the figurine of a Dalmatian in one hand swirling around a policeman in the other. Are they dancing? Ivy called. No, he said, they're getting divorced.

The thin shadow of a loose cable wire trembled on the wall by her bedroom window. Having a child in distress delivered yet another new version of worry and of pain. How could one bear it?

One felt one could not, then in the morning one woke and one had.

Sunday evening. They were out of soy milk and Nicky liked a warm glass after dinner. She rarely left him alone in the apartment, but if she dashed to the corner bodega it would be easier than having to coax him away from his evening movie. When she stepped out of her building, her heart pounding irrationally to be leaving him, the peace of the evening dusk hit as a smack: to be out of the apartment, among the gentle movement of people strolling by, had a memory of an earlier life. A ponytailed woman in blue hospital scrubs jaywalked across the empty street holding a paper coffee cup. The opposite of me, Ivy thought—a purposeful worker, a doctor or nurse, who'd worked long hours, uncomplaining, making a daily difference in each person's life. Feeling purposeful as a mother came and went. You had to check if it was there, like taking the pulse of a person in a coma.

She thought of the mothers who wrote of maternal wonders and satisfactions. When Ivy sliced chicken or folded small shirts into kerchief-sized squares, she knew this was caring, though these felt more like things which simply ought to be done. Like washing the floor, or renewing the lease. Loving your child existed in its own altogether-different place.

On the stoop of a town house sat a child of two or three banging her heels against the steps. Parked in front of her was a massive black car, unloading a family returning from a weekend away. A handsome father held a baby in one arm as he opened the side door to let out a small boy who ran to his sister and shoved her over so he could sit. In the passenger seat, in a yellow door light, sat a woman, the mother, staring forward with the black wire of an earbud grazing her cheek, speaking soundlessly into a mic. Her posture was regal, her concentration steely. Ivy recognized her as a film director she often saw in the neighborhood. The woman was usually alone, often talking this way into a wire as she walked pensively with long flapping pants, unencumbered by a handbag. Ivy had met the film director a few times, at parties over the years, but the film director never remembered Ivy. An older, dark-skinned woman came out of the building and picked up some of the bags the father had set on the sidewalk and carried them up the steps past the children. Ivy marveled at how the film director maintained a calm focus, in the front seat, taking care of business, oblivious of all around her.

Before dinner they sat on the rug with Nicky's *people,* small figures made of wood or plastic, most of whom were technically animals.

Mum, you're not really playing. You're cleaning.

Sorry, Ivy said. She was separating the Sunday newspaper sections she'd not yet read. Just one sec.

Whenever you're cleaning, you're letting your people down, Nicky said. He sat cross-legged on the thick rug facing a carefully arranged semicircle of the figures.

She turned back to him, feeling only partially in her body. Sorry, sorry. You're right. Okay, where were we?

Nicky moved the figures, making them bounce, making them glide. The unicorn flew. Two figures fought with each other. Nicky said, They're fighting in Paris. Ivy's head hummed on two frequencies. One frequency was loving her son. The other radioed tediousness. It was hard to tell which was more difficult to tolerate: the tedium, or the sacrilegious acknowledgment of the tedium.

Breathing heavily with importance, Nicky stood up. I have to go to the bathroom, he said. You keep being everybody.

. . .

The thought of when she would see Ansel Fleming remained unfrantic in her mind. But after a while it began to flutter, like a missing person poster tacked to a tree forgotten. She did not need to make a move, but she felt the flutter of waiting for him to.

That week she went to a morning yoga class. After stretching and twisting and being upside down, her mind also felt more flexible. So, all her resolve to wait for him simply fell. Without preamble even in her own mind, she texted. *What are you up to this morning?*

The reply came immediately. *Had my coffee, getting to work. You?*

Just did yoga, heading home.

And his reply, like a prize.

Fancy coming to visit?

Her nerves shook like strings. *Right now?*

She unlocked the rusty blue Schwinn. It was heavier to move now since she'd put on a back seat where Nicky could ride. It felt light as a feather flying down Seventh Ave. Twelve minutes later she was humming up the elevator to the third floor.

He opened the door.

It's the daytime, she said. I shouldn't be here.

But you are, he said.

He led her in and returned to his seat in front of his giant computer screen. Want to hear a new song? He patted his knee for her to sit on it.

Soon they were in bed. The muscles on his body were smooth and thick and substantial. She marveled at his skin, kissed his neck. Your hair is so long, she said, wanting to say something about him out loud. So much beauty, she thought. But she didn't say that out loud. She thought how she knew so little what was inside him. That would come, she told herself, that would come.

. . .

Every day, every six hours, he told her, there was roll call. Ten o'clock at night, you stood next to your bunk, your name was called and you'd answer yes, present. Four A.M., same thing. Some guards might give you a break and see you were there sleeping and not make you wake up.

She had finally asked him to tell her about it, daring because she was naked beside him.

Jesus, Ivy said. She thought, Seven years. She didn't know how even to measure it.

He'd been in two different prisons. The first was too far away for his grandmother or any friends to visit. At the beginning, he wasn't thinking about anything but appealing his sentence. That took over. He stopped thinking about music. Music had been the thing that got him in here. He'd wanted to raise money to make an album and wanted to do it on his own. His experience with a label hadn't worked out and he wasn't the first person to try this other way to make quick money. He'd seen other musicians do it. So, when he came across a person offering him a short-term business proposition, he'd taken it.

Needless to say it was a mistake, he said flatly. His face looked untouched, as if this were someone else's story. The shock of being caught had been bad, he said, but worse was the betrayal by his friend who it turned out had set him up. This friend testified against him. That had been almost worse than the sentence. So now, he said matter-of-factly, he wasn't going to trust anyone again ever. He'd had seven years to think about that every day. He would make sure that never happened again.

He also had a lot of time to think about his own part in it.

The prison where he ended up serving most of the time was not high security. There wasn't even a fence around it. Outside the building was just a field which you could without too much difficulty walk across if you wanted to leave. But if you were caught, which you probably would be, your time would be doubled and that wasn't worth it.

Ivy's cheek lay against his shoulder as he talked. She murmured questions and he kept talking.

All his focus was on the appeal. Trafficking drugs is a nonviolent crime and he was a first offender. Both helpful things. But the drug laws were as strict as they had ever been—and since he'd crossed state lines they were even more punitive. He was twenty-six and had been sentenced to fourteen years. More than half his life again. He spoke on the phone a lot to his lawyer, calling collect on the pay phone, and tried to stay in touch with people on the outside as much as he could. Some organized support for him. He appealed to celebrities he'd met during his early successful years. Some contacted politicians, legislators. He decided to get a law degree himself. The United States did not offer law education to its prisoners, but the London School of Economics did, so he enrolled.

He ordered the books and took the law courses. One of the rules they had in the joint—there were a lot of rules, always changing—was that you couldn't have more than three books in your possession at a time. Great rule, he said. Keep the inmates from reading too much.

So he had to study three books at a time, then replace them with three more.

She asked him about other rules.

The rules were always changing, he said. They particularly liked to keep taking things away from you. Suddenly no more football shirts, no more orange juice. Just in case you started to feel that your life was your own, they'd make another rule.

I can't imagine, she said.

He glanced down at her. She felt it a stupid thing to say, not because of his look, just because what could one say.

But you did get back to music, she said.

He nodded curtly. His attitude wasn't thoroughly reluctant, but she could see he did not relish telling the story. His attitude seemed to be, This is the story I tell. It may not be the one I want to tell, but it's the one I have.

It was after he'd been inside—*been inside*—for a couple of years. A guy who knew he'd been a musician had a spare guitar and gave it to Ansel. Maybe he could use it. Ansel laughed at him. I can't play that. He'd made music only electronically. But for some reason he took the guitar. Maybe he could learn. He started to play around with it and to teach himself. Then after a few months they changed that rule: you were not allowed to have instruments anymore. They took the guitar away. Now he wanted it. Figuring out how to play had passed the time, and he remembered that he loved music. Then he found out that if you taught music to other inmates, you'd be allowed to keep an instrument. So he thought, I'll teach. He got the guitar back. The only problem was that he barely knew how to play. So he kept teaching himself. He'd learn new chords each week, just in time to explain them to other people. That's how he got back into music. That's how he learned to play the guitar.

She lay against his woolly chest. She thought about having everything taken away, about how she could not relieve him of any of his suffering, could not take it into herself, the way she'd taken him into her body. His reality seemed to weigh so much more than her own.

She asked him how often he thought about it, about being there.

Every day, he said. He'd been out nearly two years, and he thought about the people there probably every hour. It made the day better when he thought about it, because he was relieved that he wasn't there anymore, but he also wasn't going to forget about the people back there still locked up. He always kept them in mind.

It was always loud in there, he said suddenly. The only time you had any quiet was taking a shower. So he would take long showers which he was allowed to do because it took a long time to wash his hair which reached down his back. He had decided not to cut his hair as long as he was in.

She saw a hard look come into his eyes as he seemed to see it again. It was so loud, he said, shaking his head. The TV was always on high volume and everyone was talking. He used to try to get away from it as much as he could and read on his bed or play his guitar, but everyone was in the same room. Now when he visits his sister and she'll have *Judge Judy* on or some shit he'll say,

I can't listen to that shit and she'll turn it off for me. He laughed at this.

He got up, put on sweatpants and went into the kitchen. A man's back, she thought. Was that the strongest side of him?

Want some fruit? he called.

She fished around for her underwear.

He returned with a white plate and on it a pear—like she'd given him!—which he had skinned and sliced. She sat against the pillows, in the place he usually was. He sat facing her and handed her a slice which she ate, then he gave himself a slice. She thought, Here I am in my plain black bra and underwear in another postcoital cliché, sharing fruit with a man, as if it is something I always do.

It did not feel altogether odd, but partly.

He was talking about the music gigs he had in the next month and as if on cue his phone rang in the other room and he walked back to get it, plugged in earbuds and strolled around, talking to someone—his manager? lawyer?—about signing rights over, about venues, about contracts. His voice deepened, taking pride in taking care of business. He leaned down and took a last slice of pear. Watching him, she thought how likely it was that there had been other girls also sitting in their black or red or white underwear while he talked on the phone, so relaxed he was, so unsurprised to have her there.

She picked up the empty plate and carried it to the sink. Ivy found her clothes on the floor and her hair tie, lying half under the bed like a relic from her other life.

She came back into the living room and felt again the difference in one's body after sex, of how it had been another version of herself two hours before. But there had been more than that, she was also altered by all he had told her. She had added more to herself as well.

She put on her boots. He was in the kitchen, closing the fridge door.

When he turned around he started a little, like a colt, surprised to find her near. Her arms were lifted preparing to hug him and she was too close to back off. Goodbye, she said, and reached around him. He remained straight. It was like embracing a tree. She stepped back, unnerved, pretending it hadn't happened. She turned to look for her bag and went quickly to the door.

Take care, he said under his breath. He sounded weary and sad.

You too, she said brightly, out the door, her heart knocking her ribs. In the elevator, she thought, Ah, so something cold follows. That was a new thing to know.

She sat at the table, with her ink and paper, her attention tilted down seventeen blocks away to where he was and to the room he was in. If she was lucky, for a part of the day she could still disappear into the world on the page, writing line after line, crossing out half, adding to the margins, crossing out more. Writing was more crossing out than keeping.

Then in the afternoon she arrived at the blue doors. Inside, the hallways were already teeming, the stairways a waterfall of children with petal faces being urged forward by proud-chin mothers, fathers with tired eyes, lackadaisical minders. Nicky's face appeared as a cutout in the stream. She could tell his mood in an instant. Fluttering eyelashes signaled distress, a parted mouth the possibility of a plan. Today he had his one-eyed skeptical look, as if to say, You, a mother? She suspected the attitude had been picked up from his father who, near the end of their marriage, often looked at Ivy with an expression of, In what way will you disappoint me today?

Having lovely thoughts of Ansel Fleming—shoulders bearing down on her, blotting out the ceiling—kept her spirits from being deflated.

Shall we hit the park? Ivy said.

I guess, Nicky said.

Does *I guess* mean yes?

He suppressed a smile.

Later walking home Nicky held her hand.

We had a substitute teacher today, he said. She told us to shut our traps.

Having something of her own to occupy her, Ivy feels an extra heft in herself. She thinks Nicky senses it, too.

Nicky had been the one to suggest the wrestling. It had to be on the bed and you had to have your shoes off and he would start on top and she would pretend to fight the little hands, flipping him over periodically, noting how each time she could feel him actually stronger. They would laugh and threaten each other and he picked up the trick from her of using his knees to pin down her arms. Nicky's enthusiasm always outlasted hers; he was never discouraged to be pinned down, as long as it wasn't too long, then would muster all his strength, grinding his back teeth, to push her off and get onto her. The triumph in his eyes had a small degree of fury, when he was hovering over her, finally having power over his mother, and she would think one day he will be a large person, a man. Then he would start the torture: tickling her throat. It was, they had decided, where she was most ticklish. Or she would go for his feet, his worst area. She would laugh with a mounting helplessness that Nicky never saw otherwise. Perhaps that was the real reason he liked to wrestle, to see his mother laugh hysterically. Afterward, when she finally escaped, they were flushed and sometimes bruised and happily complaining.

John and John put great effort into their dinners in their yellow rooms. Something *en croûte,* something marinated, something just harvested. John with his cropped haircut and clean white T-shirt would have four burners going. He was trying something new with navy beans, or cod. John One talked about all the things he loved. I love to cook. I love Christmas. I love John. He'd been a theatre critic for decades. John and John had three dogs, one named Kitty who was blind, a small brown rescue who wouldn't let anyone but the Johns pat him and a fetching tan young mutt with mascaraed eyes. We hear there is a man, said John Two, holding fluffy Kitty on his chest. John Two was born in Nigeria and worked at the UN. He kept track of genealogies and business matters. Everything at the Johns' was cherished and cared for and mattered.

Ivy thought, One wants to share secrets with enthusiasts.

Sleep over used to be a verb, now it was a noun. In Ivy's time it was called spending the night. Not all of the children Nicky's age were ready for sleepovers, but Nicky was. Ivy had worried it was because she did not provide him with *enough* so he was seeking more at another house. But she also saw it as an indication that he was sociable and confident enough to be away from his mother.

On Saturday afternoon she got a call from Mike's dad—that's how he introduced himself. Hi, it's Mike's dad. Did Nicky want to come for a sleepover tonight? Dads, Ivy noticed, often did not plan ahead. He told Ivy he had Mike for the weekend, and though he himself would be going out that night, their sitter Sabrina who knew the kids well would be in charge, along with Mike's twelve-year-old brother, Alan, who was also having a friend over. And what's your name? Ivy asked. Oh, he laughed, Cliff. He also said, apparently to advertise his engagement as a father who was going out on a Saturday night instead of staying with his children, that Sunday morning he planned to cook them all pancakes. Ivy held her hand over the phone and hardly was the invitation out of her mouth before Nicky was nodding tightly, with a frightened expression, as if any delay would break the deal.

They walked through the dusk. Ivy carried Nicky's backpack which contained his pajamas, a change of clothes and most important his knot of rags which had once been a stuffed animal, a rabbit named Enny without whom Nicky did not sleep. They turned down a quiet street with sandstone stoops layering into the distance. Nicky walked with his small pointed chin forward, his expression of trust and interest—in life, Ivy thought. She wished she had more of that.

The door was opened by a jumping boy with hair covering his eyes. Behind him came the dad. Cliff was bonily thin and handsome with close-cropped dark grey hair and darting eyes. Ivy kept on her coat while Cliff reiterated the evening's plans. She asked if he'd lived here long and he explained he only half lived here now. He and his wife switched off since their separation and were "nesting" here where the kids had grown up. He came in every other weekend, and Cindy left. That was their mother, did Ivy know her from school? They were both lawyers. Sometimes he was there during the week also. We're figuring it out, he said. Ivy wondered if Cindy went to where Cliff lived, if they each had a separate place to go. She knew of other couples doing both.

Do I get a goodbye? Ivy said into the living room where Nicky and Mike were on the floor examining a castle of Legos. Bye, Mom, Nicky said and raised his hand.

Okay, have fun. To Cliff she said, You have my number, if anything.

They'll be fine, he said. Just put them in front of a screen and we're done.

Ivy chuckled, then realized he was not joking.

Walking home, Ivy found her thoughts slid off to the black-and-white room. Should she try? There could be a no. Or, worse, no answer. In that case she would be wriggling on a pin for the rest of the night.

Her small phone flipped open in her palm as if by magic and she tapped out the words. *What are you doing tonight? I am suddenly free.*

Yes! The bubbles of response were moving.

Then the message. *Out and about.*

Her heart fell. *Out and about.*

She decided she would go to a movie, to be out and about herself, or at least be out of the apartment when she had the chance.

It was a documentary about the Andes plane crash of the Uruguayans, with the rugby team. The survivors were famous for living months in the snowy mountains and for how they had managed it: by eating the frozen dead. Now thirty years later, five of the survivors—they'd been in their twenties at the time—were, with a few family members, hiking to the site of the crash where they'd spent seventy-two winter days. It was summer, not winter, and the men—all were men—were accompanied by some of their offspring. They were all professional men, educated, some doctors. We had to be united or we would never have made it, one said. They'd slept in the makeshift shelter of the fuselage. One night they woke to a rumbling which turned out to be an avalanche. More of them died that night. One man described it. Dying felt wonderful, he said. Extraordinarily peaceful. I've never felt that peaceful again. Another spoke of his wife who did not survive the avalanche. After she died, she was laid alongside the plane for three days. I talked to her there, he said, *con amor.* Then, he said, one day a storm came and covered her. I never saw her again.

At home Ivy took a bath, a place where she always found peace. The movie had given her some perspective, and her longing for Ansel was less strong. She was grateful not to be sleeping in a fuselage in snowy mountains. She was drying off when the phone *tinged.*

I'm in the village with my dear friend and the father of my goddaughter.

The text was a happy surprise, with an extra bonus of personal information. Before she could answer there was more.

A seven-minute walk from you.

Replying, she hit the wrong button and dialed his phone and, not being prepared to speak, immediately hung up.

From him: *Saw you just called. Loud in here. Where are you?*

Home, she wrote. *Come.*

Be there in ten minutes. A minute later: *All well?*

She thrilled at the unnecessary comment!

All fine. Waiting for you.

Be there shortly. What number apartment again?

The apartment sprung alive and she lowered the lights as if to quiet it down. She put on a slip and light robe, lit a candle in the bedroom. Lamp on or off? On.

Be there shortly. How a phrase could be so thrilling.

The knock on the door was an egg cracking, tapping into the universe of him. She went to the door as it creaked open. Now he knew it was unlocked. He came in smelling of smoke, in a black wool jacket with breast pockets and across it a wide leather strap to a soft briefcase. A colored woven scarf was wrapped a few times around his neck. He greeted her without a smile, but Ivy was smiling, everything about her was smiling.

You notice I never lock the door, she said.

Is that safe?

It's so I don't lock myself out.

The hall was dark and he followed her inside.

I'm not sure if that's a metaphor, she said.

The bedroom was glowing with the yellow lampshade and the candle on the dresser a foot from the end of the bed.

He looked into the room as she settled herself on the bed. I don't stay the night, he said, unbuttoning his jacket.

Oh? Why not?

I have to get back to my place.

Okay, she said, unconvinced. He unwound his scarf as she watched him. But why?

I snore. He kicked off his boots one at a time.

That's all right.

He pointed to the window which was open a crack. And I'll get cold.

She got up, and pushed the window down. There, she said.

Standing in the bedroom doorway he lifted his briefcase strap over his head and took off his jacket, glancing around for where to put it, and hung it carefully on the closet doorknob. Do you want a hanger? she said. He considered this, but shook his head, he'd adjust.

She patted the bed beside her and he came over and settled back against the pillows. She thought about how these were now her pillows, and they were in her bed, and was amazed at how happy it made her.

Want to see the video?

Definitely.

He told her to pass him his leather bag and she got back up and found it on the hall floor and gave it to him. He took out a screen tablet and handed her back the bag which she put back out in the hallway and turned out the hall light. She curled up close beside him and he propped the screen on his chest, his square thumbs on either side, and they watched.

The music started. A figure in a sheepskin coat was at a distance walking underneath old subway tracks, with bars of light over him. She wondered if he meant it to be a jail reference, but did not ask. The colorful striped scarf he'd just taken off was wrapped thickly around his neck. The song played, the one he'd played that first night, but not one which was on any of the CDs. He sang as he walked. It's wonderful, she said, and he frowned, meaning, Don't interrupt. Sorry, she mouthed. He walked slowly toward the camera, beside a graffiti wall, through an iron gate, singing. She thought of how this had been filmed the day after they'd first slept together and wondered, watching him walk and sing, if any thought of her had been in his head that day, as it certainly had been in hers. He walked by a boy banging cans like drums, went past a curvy woman in a fur collar and hoop earrings walking the other way. He glanced sideways after her. His face singing was radiant. Near the end of the song, he walked up to the camera and past it and his back kept walking. The song ended and the music stopped and he kept walking with the sounds of the city tinkling quietly around him.

He closed the window on the iPad. Now she was allowed to speak.

She said she thought it was fantastic and that she loved it. She was relieved she could be thoroughly sincere. She asked him if he was happy with it.

He nodded. He took the tablet off his chest and slipped it on top of a row of books in the full bookshelf.

He put one arm around her. Tell me about Nicky, he said.

About his personality or . . . his history?

His history.

As she talked, he listened by looking off, which it occurred to her really was a more pure way to listen to someone, so you weren't trying to read a person's eyes or have to show back what you were thinking. You could take in the story. She wondered if not looking meant you had a less probing interest in what you were being told, and thought of how she was assessing him even as she spoke and how strange it was really all the many levels one could be thinking on, even if it was barely thinking and more like gathering impressions. And, too, how one probably gathered more impressions the more engaged one was, as if more parts of you were activated and alive, and how with the man she was often aware of riding a wave of strange engagement, and knew it wasn't going to last at this intensity but here it was in its rarity so she had to note it and couldn't stop from assessing it in some way, even checking when the last time was she'd felt this delighted, and feeling it had been so long, or maybe not ever exactly like this, because she'd never been this age before or in this same circumstance so all that was in her up to now contributed to how she was seeing everything . . .—had she ever? exactly like this?—and overall basking in the luck of it, and grateful for the feelings she had and for the person here making them.

As she talked his hands moved lightly over her back. Then they wandered, wider, onto her shoulders, down her arms, up her arms, over her neck. By the time they'd moved to her lower back and her rear, she had stopped talking.

She reached over and turned out the lamp, leaving the candle flame like a light underwater.

You like that? he murmured.

He was behind her on his knees, holding her hair like a rope. She felt a slap on her rear. Really? It was the first wrong note from him. She glanced back flatly and let the moment pass. In a sliver of her brain she thought, Ah, others liked that.

She pulled him onto her.

Don't you use protection? she said.

Usually.

But not now?

Should I?

Well, you won't get me pregnant, she laughed. If you're thinking of that.

You don't have birth control?

I am rather past needing that, she said. But don't you worry . . . about disease?

I'm careful, he said.

How do you know I am?

You told me you've been with only your husband for ten years.

It thrilled her—even as she felt it somewhat pathetic that she did—to hear that he'd registered something she'd said. She knew a normal person expected attentiveness, particularly from someone in one's bed, but she was not normal that way.

She felt the secret of no one knowing they were here together and the protection of that.

Later their bodies lay still. It hovered over them, his saying he never stayed the night, and she wondered when he'd go. Meanwhile she stretched down to the foot of the bed, blew out the candle and drew up the covers. She straightened the sheet and fluffed the comforter, bringing it over their shoulders. He resettled his arm by her neck and shoulder and continued to lie there, eyes closed, mouth regal. She waited for him to stir, with an animal alertness, watching from dark bushes a lit house to see if anyone leaves. But he did not move. His breath grew rough, then she felt that tremor, the shiver she waited for so many nights from Nicky, as he slipped into sleep.

She lay awake.

His breathing was quiet. Then it changed. A low growl at the back of his throat became the low rush of traffic in a tunnel, then opened full force into the in and out of a foghorn. As he said, he snored. She was amused. The sound mounted and every now and then he would seem to be climaxing and with a cough would be suddenly silent. And the gentle rasp would begin again.

She did not sleep. She was too happy and something in her did not want to miss a moment of having him in her bed, of being alongside this body. Her head lay on his shoulder, her palm on his chest, her leg hung over by his, pinning her hip. The position dazzled her. She knew her feeling—of intimacy, was it?—was here faster than it ought to be. It was the sex cheat. But there it was, the miracle feeling. The skin of her cheek, the muscle of his shoulder, it all amazed her. It was as if a wand had passed over them and there was new color in the air. The window cast its usual shadows on her wall with the cable cord shaking in the wind and the radiator ticked. Somehow they'd become miraculous.

Careful not to stir and wake him, she inched a pillow over to tuck under her head. He was not *not* spending the night.

She didn't want to assume his staying meant anything special, but she still felt the victory of it. Why not feel victory? She'd dismissed victory.

Dawn came, lighter grey. *Sleep over.* The phrase now had another meaning: no sleep. The corner lines of the room bracketed her happiness. Already she was thinking of how she would revisit this moment, and the moment wasn't even over.

But sleep did find her, in its mysterious unannounced way.

When she woke in the white morning, he was still there, breathing quietly.

I like the sound of the radiator, he said, holding her in a familiar way, his eyes still closed.

He looked up at the bookshelves which covered the wall to the ceiling. Have you read all these? he said.

Not all. A lot of them. Maybe most. Or at least perused most of them.

He nodded solemnly.

I don't always read the whole book, she said. You can get a lot from a book in only a few pages. People are overly pedantic about finishing books. I think they're like rivers you can step in and out of.

I wish I could write, he said.

You kidding? What about two songs a day?

Songs are easy, he said. I mean on the page. That's hard.

Then you're a writer, she said. A writer is someone who finds writing more difficult than other people do.

He chuckled.

Thomas Mann said that, not me.

Mildly he said, I should go.

Not yet.

She was relieved he did not leap up immediately. In fact, he pulled her onto him.

Now I'm going, he said.

Okay, she said, lying back. I'll let you. As if she could let or not let him do anything. Why did she say these idiotic untrue things? Ansel Fleming did not seem to say idiotic untrue things.

After he dressed he came out to her in the living room where she was opening the white curtains with the red poppies which got pulled closed each night. As she whisked the curtains open she thought of how she had a woman's brain after sex, demented and magic. She heard him behind her and said, I've felt so happy since I've met you. This was easier to say not looking at him.

She turned around to see him buttoned snugly in his jacket, scarf around his neck, long hair wrapped up, looking compact and handsome.

I'm just going to float around all day, she said.

At the door she reached up to the hall bookshelf and took out a book. Would you like one? she said.

It's by you, he said.

It is.

Of course, he said. You'll have to write your name in it.

I will, she said. Next time.

He opened the door. Thank you for the book.

Don't be a stranger, she said.

I'm as ephemeral as the wind, he said after he'd turned his back to her.

Yes, I got that.

She watched him descend the stairs past the curling grate, through the glass of the elevator shaft, and heard his footsteps going across the quiet lobby.

But did she really? Well, nothing was going to poke through the cotton swathing her. Later she'd wonder why they went their separate ways that morning when they were both otherwise alone. But she was still accepting any new thing.

At noon she met with her AGW group—Assisting Girls Worldwide—which met twice a month at Irene's. Most of the women—the group was all women—had substantial means and Ivy was one of the less flush members who tried to come up with nonfinancial ways to support the cause. Write articles, tap celebrities for fundraisers. Today they had a guest, a woman from Sri Lanka who spoke to them about her work with sex-trafficked girls in India. The New York women listened, rapt. Like everyone, Ivy was both gutted by what she heard and ashamed at being better off.

After, Ivy walked home through the clear November day. Couples passed her, each carrying a coffee cup, women wearing new fall fashions. In her mind were images of young girls locked in cheap apartments, being fed drugs. She sometimes reasoned that thinking of these things, girls having horrendous struggles, added to an odd kind of solidarity, an internal gesture that they were not forgotten, even by a stranger, but she also felt it crushing her spirit. Her thoughts went to a tender place closer at hand: to Nicky and she felt his absence like a stab. Being with Ansel had lifted her away from worries about Nicky, and despite the relief of that, she felt neglectful. Or perhaps she just missed him. In an hour and a half she'd pick him up. Was there time to try to work a little? Yes.

She thought of how inside her there was a space, she saw it now like a cube, a block which was always grateful to be alive. It was always in her, but her awareness of it came and went. Ansel reminded her of it, or maybe it was the sex reminding her, but she felt it now. Writing could sometimes remind her of it, though it was not as intense as with sex. She stepped off the curb, a bus whooshed by, and she quickly stepped back, startled. She was a cliché. Hit by a bus. Less rattled than amused, she texted. *I nearly got hit by a bus. I blame you.*

He wrote back immediately. *Be careful.* He wrote—a long text!—how he'd gone for a run and, at his usual turn, decided to keep running and ended up running across the Brooklyn Bridge. *Full of energy,* she wrote back. So he'd also felt happy after his night with her. Then she saw its opposite: after their night together, he needed to run, run, run—away.

She understood the urge, of wanting to run.

Life with a child was standing at the counter with a knife and wooden plank, puncturing tomatoes, peeling carrots, it was the stove with a spoon, stacking dishes, upending cups, sweeping, sponging, folding socks, plumping pillows. You filled the laundry basket, unzipped the coat, heeled off boots. There were sounds of the dryer, the cartoon whistling, the water filling a soapy pan, burners lighting with a puff, wrappers tearing, crinkling, rain through the open window. It was glancing up and seeing all the places one was not and herself there in them—tilting on a dusty hill, hauling ropes in tumbling surf, weaving through dark crowds in a moonlit square. She was not kneading bread on stone, examining a patient's bones, not guiding the lost through a mountain pass. No, she was putting napkins under forks and setting eight plates around the table for the people coming to dinner. It was scrubbing, refolding, crumpling, hugging, pouring, wiping, heating, brushing, corking and always the thought splitting in: Is this really my life? Is this the best I can do?

Ivy saw how much she'd been dragging herself along, dutifully plodding to the store, dazed as soon as Nicky was asleep, turning to the blue screen to disappear into a movie, to fill her stupefied brain. This new joy made her more patient with Nicky. She felt the love for her son like something sharp, and also something she would never be able to express.

That night Ivy was brushing her teeth when Nicky called from his bed, waiting to be tucked in. I'm feeling neglected, he said.

Coming, she laughed.

She climbed up onto the loft bed and lay beside him in the grey dark. Mommy, he said, did you know that God is everywhere in the air?

That's what people say, she said, hedging.

In the evening she often heard his ruminations. Do mermaids pee out of their bosoms? Why does your brain disappear when you close your eyes?

Nicky made his fingers like scissors cutting the air. That means I'd be snipping God's hair right now.

Ivy smiled in the dark.

And, Nicky said, he's as long as you want him to be.

. . .

She keeps returning to the black-and-white room. She lifts off the bed, swims to the ceiling, kicks off, flips. There's no gravity in the black-and-white room, it's a Milky Way.

People referred to sex as a drug, as if it were, like a drug, manufactured, giving one feelings not real. Yet it was, like the body was, solid and real, the most real thing there was. Her mind was a glassy sea, with him lolling in it, indifferent.

Patience. That was the thing. It was easier to be patient after she'd seen him and windy fields were blowing in her. Maybe on Tuesday morning she'd text him. Or wait till Thursday. Maybe Nicky would get an invite on the weekend.

In the headline she thought of Ansel Fleming. "Cast Adrift in Milky Way and All Alone, Billions of Planets Wander in the Void."

It was a birthday lunch for Tina and Amy. Along with Bridget and Ivy, whose birthdays were also near, they had a tradition of birthday lunches. The restaurants chosen for the birthday lunches were airy and pleasant and pricey. Ivy went with her usual qualms, ordering the cheapest salad, feeling mortified not to be on equal financial footing with Tina and Amy and Bridget, familiar though it was. She felt they must look down on her in the tiniest way. They never showed it; they were loyal friends, they often picked up the tab for her. They knew each other well and teased each other. Amy would always arrive late. Bridget could never decide what to order. Tina was overextending herself and working too hard. Ivy was unrealistic and stubborn. She loved them. Going to lunch meant you were cutting into work time and further undermining finances, but one needed people and these were friends she'd known for decades—she'd known Amy and Bridget since high school—and she would feel better after having seen them.

Then Irene asked Nicky over after school because the twins—they were in private school—had a half day, and Ivy's day opened further. Rather than seeing that she now did have more work time, she reasoned that the day would already be lost with lunch, so maybe she'd try to see Ansel Fleming in the afternoon. She'd texted in the morning, not wanting to spook him by planning too far ahead. He had texted her to stop by after lunch.

The restaurant was loud. It was one they had not been to before. Ivy noticed there were far more women than men. Though the four of them were all writers—Amy wrote about politics and had spent a lot of time living abroad, Bridget was a poet and Tina a journalist and writing teacher—they rarely talked about writing. Ivy had noticed that female writers talked less about their work than male writers did.

Since they'd known each other so long, they talked mostly about their families, their children, gossiped about other friends, listed movies they'd seen or books they were reading. If someone had something in particular new—an ailing parent, a new therapist, an accident—they would be the focus of the meal. Over the years Ivy might leave the lunch feeling that she was not keeping up with Amy, Bridget and Tina, though they were always warm and loving toward her, but she felt she was sliding to another place from where they were. Today Ivy gave a very short version of her new, as she put it, not exactly romance, but thing, whatever it was, and her friends, all being solidly married, both teased her and congratulated her and with astute humorous comments reflected on the unlikeliness of this going anywhere. Tina filled them in on what she knew and Ivy was riveted to hear that she'd seen him one weekend with a girl that summer. She had tattoos on her hands and was in med school. They were together, but I don't think it was anything official, Tina said. I never saw her again. Good for you, Amy said. For getting out there. Ivy always felt that these lunches ended just as the friends were relaxing into their old rhythm. When they were younger they might have stayed together after lunch, a couple of them maybe, walking home or stopping at a store, but now everyone had to get back and get going. Each went her separate way.

Outside the restaurant Ivy unlocked her bike. You're going to him now, aren't you? said Tina. Ivy nodded, as if caught in the act.

I think I've seen that idiotic smile before, Tina said.

I'm sure you have, Ivy said.

Well, he's awfully cute, Tina said. Can't argue with that.

Down the carpeted hall the door was ajar.

Hello? she called, going in. From deep in the apartment came his voice, In here.

She passed through the quiet living room into the empty bedroom. The bathroom door was open and she went in. He was stretched out in the bath.

Well, that looks nice, she said.

How was your celebration? he said.

Very nice. I brought you dessert. She held up a white box.

The water in the tub was still as glass, rimmed around his chest.

Thank you. I'll have it later.

They're little brownies, she said, and sat on the toilet top.

I love brownies, he said.

I love baths.

Then come in.

Again her body thrilled at the lack of usual preliminaries.

She undressed and stepped in. Beneath the clear water, he was shiny and dark against the white tub. With her back to him, she settled between his legs as if he were a canoe. She lay back on his chest and his arms folded over her. Her heart was beating madly. Through half-closed eyes she watched his hand move on her body, pale and rippled over by water, sending bolts through her. She arched her back into it and reached one arm above to cradle his head.

His fingers kneaded her shoulders. You like that?

His hand reached between her legs. And this?

She felt as if she were being twisted, wrung out like wet fabric.

For some reason she thought of the avenue outside the building where she'd just been, of the figures walking by not knowing each other, the taxis riding the bumps like waves, and of how she was here in the center, of this universe, at least, her ribs felt both brittle and bendable and his hands were finding the solid places which needed cracking and he was breaking her open like a birdcage. She felt him as a thickness between her thighs.

No, he said decisively and lifted her at the armpits.

He handed her a towel and she took it, keeping her gaze blurred not to break the spell. He pulled back the covers and they slid onto the smooth sheets with their clean dry skin. Yes, this was wider, now they could move. He pressed himself along her length, grounding her with his weight. He splayed out her arms holding her elbows. She freed one arm and pressed his chest, pushing him up. Wait, she said, I need to breathe . . . He propped himself up in a push-up. They were both smiling.

Okay?

She looked at him as if he were joking.

Yes. I am definitely okay. Except for breathing . . .

His eyes were low, regarding her, slightly merry, slightly formal. Again she was awed by how naturally and expertly he moved, turning her, sucking her, sending spears between her legs. Or were the spears shooting like rays out from her?

You like that? he murmured. For some reason this seemed to be the most intimate thing a person could say. It spotlit that attention missing for her.

He did not look long at her face. He looked at her body. She wondered fleetingly if it was shyness or avoidance. She looked often at his face, thrilled by the different angles, curious of what she might catch in his eye.

They lay half under the covers in the foam of the sheets.

What are you doing today? she asked. After sex she felt more bold about asking him about himself.

This and that, he said. I have a meeting later.

Can I ask you something personal? She moved around to put her face in front of him.

You can always try, he said.

Weeks later, months later, years later, she would flash back to that moment, his chest in the peaceful light, his watch on the bedside table beside the white cube lamp, his head resting on the twisted ropes of hair and the pillow, feeling herself both safe and unsure, but secure enough to ask what she wanted to but hadn't dared, as if one needed to have slept with a person before you were allowed to ask certain questions. She felt herself going out on a limb. It was a risk when you showed interest.

Are there, she said, others like me?

He answered right away with a gesture, opening his hands a little, lifting his arms. Did she mean this here, lying there in this particular configuration?

She nodded she did mean that.

Yes, he said in his deep voice which still seemed so honest and commanding. His lack of guile continued to stun her, as if he didn't know that this was a matter about which people usually lied. His admitting this so forthrightly made her feel, ironically, how close she was to him.

So she could ask the next thing.

What happens to them?

Some fall away, he said. His eyebrows indicated that this had to be. Some go into a wider orbit. Some come back.

She studied his face which she could do because he wasn't looking at her. She was not yet lost in his face; she was still in herself. He hadn't hurt her yet. There were no stakes yet. But she could feel it starting to matter a little more. She said, I've never had it like that before. With someone.

He nodded, then shrugged. He wasn't going to entice her or try to convince her. He didn't need to persuade her of anything. She was here, after all, naked in his bed, with her arms crossed over his chest. She pushed herself up, rolling off his torso, but kept her legs alongside his.

I'm starting to get attached to you, she said keeping her tone light.

That's not a good idea, he said in the same tone.

It's not?

No.

Why? she said with the inflection of Tell me again, though he had not in fact told her this yet.

It's not what I'm interested in, he said simply. Some people are good at some things, and not good at others. I'm not good at it. A relationship is not in the cards for me.

Ever? she said. Her hand touched his chest, as if to test the nearness of the heart under there.

Way in the back of her mind, in the observation tower where she viewed the future, she saw this as possibly being a dividing-line moment, the moment with a straightforward statement about himself and his intentions, and she ought to pay attention. She also had the more wafty thought that he might not *really* mean what he was saying.

Her *ever* did not hover long between them. He hit it back like a tennis ball.

Maybe not, he said.

His eyes were nearly closed. If she'd not been slumped near him, her hip grounded by his hand, she might have heard the certainty in it. She had been here before, hearing a person talk of never.

But we all want love, she said. Don't we? To love. Be loved.

It was as if he'd gone deaf.

If she had believed he meant this, she would have said to herself, Okay. This has been interesting. We've had a lovely moment and it has given me a real boost. She would have removed herself from his stretched-out legs, and away from his dense dark arms and have sat up. She would have thanked him and would have said goodbye.

But she did not move.

She felt a new self in her, peering down into an unknown canyon. Maybe this canyon would suit this new self. She wouldn't know if she didn't try.

She'd always believed in fidelity as a given in a relationship. But what had that guaranteed, finally? Maybe it was time to learn different ways.

People generally measured the success of a relationship by time. Endurance was valued above all. But was that the most important thing? Shouldn't the measure be how much love there was, however long that lasted? But then how could love even be measured?

Ivy had not sustained an uninterrupted partnership with a man. She had left each one, or he had. Her stories always veered off the road. Being with someone in a different possibly undefined romantic relationship might teach her something. Maybe this was where she'd been working to arrive at all this time. She was older now. That should make her more discerning about her body's enthrallment. She'd known pretty many men, in various configurations: as boyfriends, flirtations, intrigues, crushes, even affairs, and it made for a long line of sentimental education studded with solid posts of more substantial relationships. Her first longtime boyfriend, Tommy, whom she'd met at fifteen, had lasted four years, like a mini-marriage. The ones after were mostly solid and polished, like pearls on a string, one at a time, official boyfriends, this one for six months, this one two years, two months. At one point she noticed a pattern, not so surprising, of alternating intensity. If she had a boyfriend she'd really liked, then the one after was more likely, as the phrase went, to *like her more,* as if after a painful breakup, she needed a pause in intensity of feeling, if no pause in having a boyfriend at all. There'd been a lot of boys and men around in those days, when they were young, always a new one entering the door. But now the men were mostly gone, into families, into longer commitments.

But if you didn't keep with the commitment, you failed. That was how people put it. People rarely said that a relationship or marriage *came to its conclusion,* or that it ended, like a good story, in the right place. No, if a marriage ended, it failed.

Of course there were the varied geometries of relationships. A parent and child, for instance, had a relationship with the goal of ending. For a child, leaving the relationship was the goal. This relationship succeeded *when* it ended.

What if people could think of love that way? Once lovers no longer had the same interlocking need for each other, then their time with each other was done and they would be encouraged to move on. But that wasn't the common wisdom. The common wisdom was that after the first spark of love, love would grow and change, and become something else. All of this was considered in a matter of seconds.

Most of these thoughts were not new.

The part of Ivy that believed in fidelity, in one's body remaining reserved strictly for one's lover, stayed tucked back in the shadows where it had never questioned itself, so certain an aspect of love it was. It may even have slipped behind the dividers in her mind, not needing to see what might happen next.

She did not get up, she stayed.

When it was time to leave, she rose sluggishly from the bed. Ansel had gone into the other room in sweatpants and T-shirt, and was standing at his computer. She pulled on her jeans reluctantly and reentered her thin socks, the things of herself she would have to go back to, aware that some decision had been made by her, even if it was backed into. But she would try this different way. Why not? He had cracked her open. How much harm could it do?

Should I sign my book? she called. She'd gotten used to it, people not saying anything about a book you had written. Why should they? But, with Ansel, she was curious to know what he thought.

Please do, he called from the other room.

She wrote an inscription to him, in ink.

He was in the kitchen, getting something out of a cabinet. She would not try to hug him goodbye today. I won't be needy, she thought. I will just drift out, happy. This was not difficult to do. Because she felt it—happy.

When she got home, entering the hallway, she saw her

reflection in the small mirror above the mantelshelf where she put her gloves and the keys. The old self looked back at her, the usual self. Oh no, she thought. Being back home inside her own walls she felt the usual self had a new feeling. Oh, boy, said the feeling. Here we go.

Music took on a new power. It seemed now a thing spinning out of the darkness at her like a meteor. It had always been there, in the sky, like the moon, beautiful, loved, basked in when luminous. As a teenager she had, as teenagers do, played music continually, playing records over and over again, always turning on the radio.

Ansel Fleming's voice hit a particular new frequency in her.

Words on the page were quiet; you had to seek them out in a book. But music could just find you, driving by in a car, emanating from shops into the street, to grab you by the throat and strangle you. It could hover over you like a cloud so you could live in its shade. It could move in and out of a person. She had not tried to understand music as she had books and paintings. Perhaps that was why it was extra intoxicating now. Though the glow was also a reflection of the sex. Each song was a seduction.

She thought of Ansel Fleming's *Songs are easy.* It seemed a miracle, and his ability amazing.

She was walking down Broadway, headed to Old Navy to buy winter clothes for Nicky who'd grown out of nearly half of his other Old Navy clothes—at Old Navy no item cost more than twenty or thirty dollars. He needed a parka, sweatshirts, pants, socks, winter hat. She had as usual seen no one all morning; most of her writing that day had focused on all the new feelings about Ansel Fleming, not on real work. But these new feelings were a welcome relief from the recent feelings of grief, self-recrimination, worry and doubt. Okay, doubt still lingered, but it had an added texture—of longing, and hope!

Uncertainty lay like a shadow alongside her joyful feeling. She saw how unlikely they were: a single mother nearly fifty-three and a musician only thirty-five, never mind that he was free out in the world after seven years, with that wide world waiting. She crossed Houston Street and a plastic bag spun up in front of her, twirling like a genie.

The signal came with a *ping. You over there making magic?* It was late morning, and though at the table, she was decidedly not making magic.

The charge hit her body in her chest and in other places he'd activated.

Trying, she wrote back. *You?*

Just had my cereal.

How easy it was sometimes, like hooking fish in a stocked pond.

It was raining lightly as she rode on her bike in the shine of wet traffic.

The door was again ajar, pleasing her. Did they have a routine now? She entered, pulled it closed, toed off her damp boots. Passing through the living room she noticed a number of burnt-down candles in shallow holders, and a couple of brass candlesticks. He'd not lit candles with her. There was a full ashtray.

He was stretched out on the bed in soft sweatpants, surrounded by newspapers and books, wearing the black glasses he'd had on the first night they met.

You look happy, she said.

She hung her coat on the doorknob and crawled onto the bed like a cat. He had one arm out, relaxed against the pillow. She settled against the solidity of his chest. She saw her book was on his bedside table.

This time they did not kiss right away. Instead they talked, like normal people. They talked about the news. The war. He asked about Nicky. She said he wanted to get a dog. Ansel said he wished he could have a dog. She told him Nicky was joining a soccer league.

I'll come watch him, Ansel said. Internally she did a double take. Something alerted her that this was perhaps his first lie, his first false promise.

But she also believed in the normalcy of it and her body filled like a vessel with his warmth. He took his glasses off his forehead and placed them on the bedside table. Expressionlessly he pulled her shirt up and off. Books and papers slid off the bed. He picked up a handful of books and placed them deliberately on the floor, then returned to her.

It was a Friday afternoon and Ivy had an extra two hours to work. Nicky had gone home after school with Oscar. Late afternoon was often the most productive time, since it took her that long to dispense with logistical things and finally focus on the other world being created out of air. Before she left to pick Nicky up, she got a text from Padma saying they wanted Nicky for the night. Ivy packed his shark knapsack, the precious Enny, and with a spring in her step thinking of a night of freedom she walked across Washington Square, past the circular empty fountain, to one of the university high-rises off Bleecker Street.

It was Padma's parents' apartment and she'd grown up in it. Her father had worked at the university and was entitled to the housing, while his wife mostly managed their Indian restaurant in the East Village. The parents now lived in semiretirement in Port Jefferson. Oscar's father was not there. Ivy did not learn till sometime after knowing Padma that the father was in Russia. It was complicated, Padma told her, when she finally told her, having takeout coffee at the panini place next to the school entrance before Padma left for work. She was a film editor, going freelance from project to project. She had met Oscar's father while working on a documentary about corruption in Ukraine. She rolled her eyes, which Ivy saw nevertheless sparkled. It is not worth describing, she said, and pinched the corner of her black glasses as if reviewing one of her film scenes needing to be cut, as if to decide which images to keep. Ivy listened, fascinated. Let's just say we had an amazing two weeks together and a motorcycle was involved.

Ivy was buzzed into the glassed-in lobby and rode the elevator up to the twenty-second floor. There was a particular sadness one felt in the windowless halls of apartment buildings, silent yet occupied, with each shut door a thin membrane to each set of rooms with each their different smells and different voices, different histories and different vibrations, all closed off to each other.

She pinged the black dot of 22B. Padma was directly inside the door in the square kitchen area, placing chicken nuggets on a baking sheet. Water was on the boil and beside the pot was a sealed plastic tray of tortellini. Padma wore a long loose dress, light grey at the top, black at the bottom, and seemed to be only half cooking. She had a languid manner, as if her mind were elsewhere, in a place of contentment, a manner which didn't exactly square with what she'd told Ivy about her struggles with insomnia and anxiety. Did Ivy want to stay for supper? Padma asked sleepily. She could make them a salad, she also had some leftover curry. Ivy said thank you but she was going to take the opportunity to zone out. Padma nodded knowingly, understanding. The small moments of understanding that mothers gave to one another were not, Ivy thought, always acknowledged as the precious coin Ivy felt them to be. Where were the boys? Padma gestured vaguely down the short hall. Ivy walked past the wall of small framed photos—Oscar at various ages, Padma holding a newborn, her parents in cloth sun hats by a bridge, a pair of Persian miniatures of people sitting on the floor by golden walls and persimmon trees. Ivy pushed open the ajar door to Oscar's room. The boys were on their stomachs on a blue rug printed with train tracks, staring at a screen.

Ivy had the sinking moment of pause she often got visiting more spacious living spaces—that is, pretty much every apartment one visited—and was speared with her inadequacy in not having provided her son with a room where he could stretch out and languishingly play, as he'd once been able to in the house she had with Everett. Oscar had a large bed with a comforter covered in stars and rocket ships, shelves of books and bins for toys and a window that looked over the trees of a tiny park to other residential towers, and up the avenue to a half slice of the Empire State Building, its needle lit tonight white and orange. She set down Nicky's backpack and hugged him goodbye, checking his open face for signs of happiness and, finding them, was relieved. It would carry her spirit for a few hours at least.

She returned home across the now-darker Washington Square Park. The white arch was flood-lit, showing in sharp relief its molding and curves and recessed blocks. She thought of the real Arc de Triomphe and the Champs-Élysées, of the parade after the liberation of Paris in 1944, the women in shoulder-pad dresses in the flash of associations which studded off in the mind like skipped rocks. Her hand palmed the round phone edge in her pocket.

It was standing at the cliff edge, deciding to send a message. Your toes in the tufts of grass, inches from the drop. When you pressed SEND you had the leap in the chest. When it mattered, you argued with yourself, and practiced restraint. When it mattered less, it was easy.

Now, in one of those carefree moments of indifference, she wrote, *Am suddenly free.*

You were rewarded when you didn't care too much; he responded.

I have something later but you are welcome to come now.

His high building met the sidewalk like a vault, its steel-lined black windows looked tonight like a grid of turned-off television screens. She was aware of the protection she felt that no one knew where she was, that no one knew what she was doing. She didn't want to have to explain. But more than that, she had something of her own. As she could melt into Ansel Fleming . . . well, she didn't think much beyond that now.

She'd see how it would go. Though something in her felt she knew.

. . .

She was down in the canyon, in the blasted hole of down there, the crater of his comet. Around her she felt the rubble of all that'd gone wrong in her life. But above her was an open night sky and if she climbed up to the lip she felt as if there would be a survivor's vista of shimmering sea with birds swooping and suns rising.

Now that her body had been entangled with his, she found, when alone disrobing, the sex would come back to her. In the bathroom her female smell now somehow belonged to him, and his face and body and heat would seem to materialize before her. Stepping into the bath, her leg was more interesting now, now that it had been his.

So, she said, lying on her side, loosely clasping his shapely arm. Had arms always been this beautiful? I've been thinking.

Yes?

About you.

Oh, he said with a drop to his voice.

She made herself continue, I was wondering when a person gets attached to you, what is she supposed to do?

She should do whatever she wants, he said.

Oh, she said. Right. She smiled.

They were silent for a while.

She urged herself onward. The thing is, she said sputtering like a motor not starting, one starts to, I don't know, inadvertently starts to expect, well . . . when one feels things.

Sometimes when you spoke, a rush of blood spread pressure to your forehead, often accompanied by a blockage to the throat, signaling either that you were saying something challenging, perhaps a breakthrough of emotion, or you were saying something ill timed, ill conceived or inappropriate.

She felt this flush, uncertain what it was signaling, and with even less confidence went on to say that she didn't always want to feel the way she did, but feelings just seemed to come when one got close to someone and this was—She turned onto her back, and covered her face with one hand.

I don't know what I'm trying to—

I know it's not fair to you, Ansel Fleming said.

She felt a surge of hope. If he could recognize this, surely he would recognize other things.

She looked above her to his profile.

You're like this comet, she said. One that has streaked across my radar. And I don't have a lot of things streaking across my radar. While you, you have all these planets orbiting, and a lot going on . . .

He didn't say anything to that.

I mean, she said, what do you think of all those planets?

I care about them, he said. They all matter to me. But his tone of voice told her that he had gone into himself, at a remove from her.

And they—?

They either understand me, he said. Or they don't.

She wanted to be one of the ones who understood. Maybe she would understand him better than anyone had before.

I never forget about them, he said. His profile was still against the white ceiling; he was often still. She thought of the clips of him playing music and how his body moved to the beat but even then he seemed to keep to himself, subtle and alluring.

I just put them up on a shelf, he said. I put them in a cabinet.

A cabinet, she said. For long? She half laughed.

He blinked and let his lids lower. Maybe, he said and paused. He added, I never forget about them.

That's good, she murmured, and she pictured all of them, the girls inside his cabinets, a wall of cabinets filling the room.

When she left him—he to his meeting, she to free space—she felt strangely clear, as if washed by his candidness, as if the truth of himself whether difficult or not was still an elixir if he shared it with her. The air was mild and her body matched it. She felt as if her feet had been untied and were soft on the sidewalk. It was rare not to have to get back home, so she walked. Tonight she understood him better, and maybe since she had spoken, he understood her better, too. Whatever it was, she felt closer to him, and not only in the body, though she felt it there the most. She thought again of how he'd been unfree for seven years. Seven years. She tried measuring the time against her life—around when Nicky was born. Just after. She thought of all the places she'd been since then, of all the different days there would have been with Everett, with Nicky. All those years had been the same day for Ansel, wearing the same uniform, sleeping on the same bed, the TV loud in the air . . . no, one couldn't fathom it. She thought of what he had said. The point of prison is to remind you that you are no longer a human being. The point is to erase you. Some people in the joint operated there the way they did out in the world, organizing workers, or hiding everything they did. Or you leave that person you were out there and have a funeral for him inside your head and do your best not to think about him, because there's no place for him in here, there's nothing for him to do. This isn't any place for a human being.

In the East Village people were out, swirling around. She turned down the street where her friend Bruno lived and miraculously spotted him in the light of a bodega, his familiar figure in a light T-shirt and paint-spattered pants looking into a plastic bag. He walked toward her under the shadowy trees. Hello there, stranger, she called. He smiled as if he'd expected to meet her right here.

Bruno lived in a few places. He had the studio here in New York, he had an apartment in Berlin, there was a family house in Hawaii. He was always traveling for commissions, or for fun, and was one of those friends you ran into and it was as if you'd just spoken the other day.

A kid'll eat Ivy too, Bruno said, lifting her hands and dancing her waltzlike, humming the song. Bruno never remarked on something being a coincidence; he even seemed to expect happenstance. Isn't it a lovely night, he said. Shall we walk? He hooked his arm in hers.

He said he was just taking a break from the studio but they could at least circumnavigate the block. They asked after each other and Bruno said he did have some news. He'd met someone, when he was in Hawaii. Yes, he was a little younger but as Ivy knew Bruno liked them younger, except this one was different, because he was also successful—an architect this time. He lived in LA, however, so they were dancing around each other and talking about where and when to meet next. I have a commission in Buenos Aires, Bruno said, so maybe he'll meet me there. This one is actually smart for a change, Bruno said with a wiggle of his shoulders. He asked Ivy if there was anyone. Well, actually, she said. Sort of was. But it was new. Not anything yet, but it probably wasn't going to be anything. It was someone not interested in anything more.

Bruno nodded, understanding it all. So just enjoy yourself, he said as they reached his door.

I will, she said.

He squinted at her in the shadows cast by the trees. I can see that, he said. You look like you're on crack.

On her block the topaz streetlights illuminated the yellow ginkgo trees. The gutters were piled with the fallen leaves shaped like scalloped fans. Ivy shuffled through the yellow leaves, layered like pastry, ankle deep. Remember this, she told herself.

Remember the feeling and how everything looked. Remember the lift, the padding around her connecting her to the world. Remember the glad body of invisible limbs and the miracle of dotted lights and paved streets and dark figures looming. Remember the pity she feels for those not in this frame of mind, the limping man with the sideways foot humping into the deli, the woman slamming the taxi door, harried. Remember the awareness at a distance of some remorse for not being this happy more often, and further remorse for not giving her son his father and more stability and happiness. Remember even so the bliss as it flashed slow motion by, with her certainty of all being as it was supposed to be, had to be, even the mess and the tragedy lining alongside, especially the mess and the tragedy, encroaching. Remember how the feeling comes from Ansel Fleming and that whatever else happens, this makes it worth it. Whatever fallout there might be and she was pretty sure there would be fallout, she must remember this, this night of the yellow leaves.

3

Certainty

The advantage of the emotions is that they lead us astray.

—OSCAR WILDE

She did not hear from him. She felt chunks of cliff breaking off and puffing into a rocking sea below.

Nicky sometimes wrote notes, in imitation of the notes his mother left in various stations about the apartment. She found one. *Mum, what about calling a book Marbles?*

When Ivy refused him a midday viewing of *Shrek,* she found a note on her bed.

to MOM:

I'll only like you
if you let me watch
a movie.

Not at all love,

Nicky

A week passed and nothing from Ansel Fleming.

Not at all love.

Thoughts of him and their hours together ballooned. Where had he gone? Possibly out of town. Where was he this moment. Where would he be. Would she be there with him. She wrote, *Thinking of you. Hoping all fine there.*

If you didn't ask a question, you were less likely to be answered, but she feared questions made her look needy. She was determined to remain cool.

She tried to write of the night of the yellow leaves but could only gesture in the direction of its exalted feeling.

She wanted to manage the swirling emotion by writing it out, both the good and the perplexing, so she could turn to her work. The writing came out in a nonstop stream, and she was riveted by the new feelings he inspired, bowled over by the level of her desire. Interest in sex wasn't new, but this felt more enormous.

In ink she reminded herself not to expect anything from him, he had promised her nothing. Though she did suggest a counterargument: people often found surprising configurations with each other. Then she'd note reality, the impossible future, barely able to put down the exact number of the difference in their ages. Seventeen years, eighteen depending on when. He had a whole life ahead of him. In no time he'd find a beautiful *young* woman to give him babies. But what if he were truly one of those people who did not want a young wife and family? Maybe he was. She used to be like that. But who would want an older woman who already had a child. Even Ivy could not picture that delusion for long.

So she would turn back to her view of him, to the pleasures of him, the glacier of him, and in this way, the morning would pass. She would stand, dizzy, to make more tea. Waited for water to boil, her head careening.

Stay away from the portal. But the lure was too great. A month ago she'd not even known what Twitter was. She looked at his feed. People messaged him comments. How did one do that? Not that she wanted to, but other girls did. More girls than boys. Who were they? SexyiNiKnowit. Blue_Sunset. Cupcake69. Funkfuk. They knew how to manage the portal. The more she read, the more her nerves sagged. Well, if this was how he liked interacting with people, then he and she really were ill suited. She read an old comment from EzeeBreeze: *Looking fly in your white shirt Ansel Fleming.* An icicle went up her spine. Wait, that was her white shirt! She noted the date, that day he had his appointment. The day they had eaten eggs with the kitchen sunlight.

Soon she'd dropped from her height and was back on the ground ruled by the age-old complaint of lovers since the beginning of time: Why wasn't he calling her? Well, that's it, she thought, exhausted by the preoccupation. This has become unmanageable.

Then a text. *It's a beautiful day to be alive.* At first, joy, then a hardening. The days of hearing nothing had been too trying. What kind of a message was this anyway? Impersonal. It could have been a message sent to anyone. She did not respond. Now she would give him a taste of what silence was like.

Then on the ninth day—she didn't mean to be counting—he called. On the phone. His name appeared on the screen, surging electricity through her body. She was reading on the couch, editing a manuscript, rain filling the wide windows with the red brick beyond.

His voice mixed with the street sounds. I'm out in the rain, he said. He told her he was crossing the street. He was laughing. Something about his umbrella. He said he'd seen Maira—he'd seen Maira?—who'd asked him about Ivy and, Ansel said, he'd taken it as a sign to check in. Excuse me, he said and she heard his deep laugh far from the phone. He was ordering coffee. Ivy had conflicting feelings—delight that he was calling her, appalled that he'd needed to give her a reason and wonder that Maira had seen him . . .

She mentioned none of this. What had he been up to? As often when she was nervous, she sounded more happy than she was, coming up with banal things to say.

Working, he said. I don't need to talk about it. Get into all the details.

It hit her like a board, all the days he didn't give her details.

It seems you don't want to get into anything much, she said, and immediately regretted it. I mean, she said in a lighter tone. I've been wondering where you were.

I'm not a checker-inner, he said.

Yes, I got that.

Now I'm checking in, he said. There was a pause. And you're making me feel as if I'm doing something wrong.

Something evil in her liked seeing him on the hook for a change and she didn't let him off it. Not yet.

I just wanted to hear from you, she said.

I texted you, he said. And you didn't answer.

Yes, he had. The nonquestion text. She was too embarrassed to tell him she'd felt it insufficient. *A beautiful day to be alive.* Suddenly she saw it as a splendid text and became confused.

You did? she said, lamely buying time. Oh, right, she admitted. She felt herself losing more ground, as watery as the streaking rain.

I don't want to complicate your life, he said. You have things to do, I have things to do.

But she wanted complication. She pictured him on the splattering street under an umbrella, holding his cup of coffee, simple.

Sorry, she said. I didn't mean to . . . sorry. I'm just trying to I guess get used to you. I want to understand what's going on. I don't want to be pestering, I just want to know how to do this.

There was the sound of motoring tires on the wet road. He did not reply.

You going home for Thanksgiving? she said, changing the subject. They could have normal chitchat, too. He'd mentioned going to see his grandmother.

Yes.

That'll be good.

It will, he said.

She was thrashing in high waves. I'd just like to see you, she said and the truth of it felt like landing on a raft.

We could make that happen, he said. Then he was talking to someone passing on the sidewalk, and laughing again.

It's really raining out there, she said. He said his umbrella was only half working. He was heading for shelter.

There was a pause. She waited, wanting only everything.

So, he said. Work well.

Okay. She saw his figure vanishing. She threw in, And about seeing each other . . . ?

Try me, he said. I'm busy. I'm busy the next three days. I don't want to tell you all the shit I'm doing. I mean, not shit, but I don't want to explain. If you're free, you let me know. If I'm free, then . . .

Okay, she said. Maybe after Thanksgiving then? Nicky and I are going to Virginia.

Everything is possible, he said.

She wanted to stay on the phone, but thinking from a lifetime of habit that what she wanted was probably not the best to do, she told him bye and ended the call.

She realized immediately that she'd done exactly what she'd coached herself not to do—complain about his behavior. She'd completely lost her grip. For the second time in the past few days, she felt she simply couldn't do this. She didn't get how. How were you supposed to tell what you wanted without criticizing the other person. The more she thought about it, the more mortified she became. He'd called her! And instead of showing how happy she was—frankly she was shocked—she'd upbraided him for not calling, that cliché of complaint. It was beneath him, beneath what she'd envisioned for them.

. . .

At Thanksgiving she and Nicky drove to Virginia so she could deliver her son to his father. They arrived after dark, and Ivy parked the car between the house with its windows lit in the kitchen and the barn with no windows or light. This was a place she returned to with new versions of herself.

It had been here they told Nicky. It had been under discussion for more than a year.

It was early spring, the leaves light green and see-through, draping the trees in lime chiffon. The three of them sat in the truck, Everett in his weathered cap behind the wheel and Nicky between them. They'd just returned from the small lumber place two towns away, supporting the independent place instead of the more convenient chain, and had stopped as they did on Saturdays at the Stir Up Diner for tomato soup and BLTs. In the booth, bracing herself, Ivy had felt like one of the pickling jars that lined the back wall. Nicky and Everett both got ice cream in the small silver bowls and she watched Nicky eat not knowing what was coming. The truck parked in front of the barn and the three of them sat there, not getting out right away. It was the last time they would be together intact, Ivy thought, and wished she could escape from the truth of it.

There'd been other bad periods which they'd gotten through. The move back from Tanzania when Everett's mother had become sick, Ivy's occasional trips to New York for work which Everett never minded in the planning, but would resent by the time she returned. Nearly always she'd bring Nicky with her, not to add work for Everett. But a complaining air rose up. Bickering became their biggest trap. In Arusha, in the early days of their love, they'd seen the hand-painted words on a *matatu* bus floating in a blue ribbon THOSE WHO BICKER LIKE EACH OTHER and often invoked it. Then, years later, Ivy would catch the expression on Nicky's face if he rounded a corner to see for himself was this really his parents acting like children? She withered with shame to think she was creating this rancor. She could withstand disturbance, but when she thought of her son, her standards were higher.

They'd seen not one but a few therapists. One in Virginia, two in New York. The Virginia doctor was actually named Dr. Fine. Sometimes after a session of tears and revelations, Ivy and Everett would leave feeling tender and hopeful, but more often Ivy felt even less understood than before, and Everett, when not silent, expressed the same.

But when the option was raised of being done with each other, it was too big. They would agree, Let's keep trying. They would remember, I do love you. They saw it would be too awful. Sometimes all that was needed was to say Nicky's name . . . and impetus would lag.

As a kind of solution, Ivy started to spend longer periods of time in the city with Nicky, even enrolling him in the public school down the street for a couple of months in the fall and, when they visited the farm, Everett, instead of being bitter, would have felt lonely and missed them as a family and be tender at her return, renewing their hope. With hope, Ivy was able to be more patient and less reactive, Everett made an effort, and for a while the separation made them appreciate each other again.

One weekend Everett came to visit them. He never stayed more than two or three nights, not liking the city, but she appreciated the effort. He arrived on a Friday afternoon and she roasted a chicken, chilled the beer he liked, and they all went to bed early. In bed she and Everett still met best.

The decision having been made not in a fight but quietly in the playground, the agreement to split up was now more real, though it went into yet another suspension, of relief, as if the problem had been solved, and for another five or six months through winter into spring, Everett and Ivy clung to each other, in a kind of premourning, and spoke little about the future. But eventually the well-worn tracks of rancor, laid down who knows why—incompatibility, circumstance or stunted growth—were traveled on again, with nerves more raw and frayed than ever.

Inside of each union is the possibility of its undoing. Marriage vows deny the option of undoing to be considered. Ivy met a woman once who'd told of how when she'd been young, almost on an impulse, she'd married a man she barely knew. When they woke up the day after the wedding, both of them looked at each other and thought, Who is this person? They said to each other, What have we done? It wasn't that they didn't like each other, but more that neither believed it would work. Suddenly it looked ridiculous. Well, they thought, we're married, so we might as well see how it goes, and agreed that whenever one of them wanted to end it, they'd end it. They would leave the possibility open and take it day by day. They'd been married now for twenty-eight years.

Dad and I have something we want to tell you, Ivy said. The thought flashed that it was actually: *don't* want to tell you. Nicky glanced at his mother's hand on his favorite blue sweater, the one with a chicken on it that his aunt Margaret had knitted for him and which was getting too small. Nicky, noting formality from his mother, sensed danger and instinctively drew in his chin.

What, he said in a dull voice.

Everett flicked his gaze in Ivy's direction over Nicky's messy dark hair and kept facing forward. Ivy would have to be the one to say it.

Dad and I love each other, she said, but we have decided that it's better if we don't live together anymore. She heard the person saying this, already having drifted out of her body, bracing herself, putting emotion at a distance for Nicky's sake and, let's face it, for her own.

Nicky's bowed head snapped a little as if hit. Maybe he would need a moment to process, maybe he would find it hard to understand. Maybe he wouldn't believe it until it started to happen.

Everett, never one to mince words, followed up. So we're going to get a divorce.

Nicky did not wait to react. He immediately understood. He burst into tears and dove onto his mother's lap. She started to hug him, but he wasn't wanting a hug, he was trying to get away, scrambling over her and grabbing the door handle, his head down as if under fire.

My love bug, she said, and offered soft arms, but he wriggled away and full-out sobbing in an unselfpitying way pushed open the door and jumped down. He ran, then walked, then ran again toward the side of the house and they watched him disappear around the corner toward the backyard.

Ivy looked to Everett. His handsome face was bland, but somehow crumpled. His slow eyes slid over her and away; he had nothing to give. Come on, she whispered, or maybe didn't even say it out loud, and only mouthed it. But was thinking, Now what?

They each slid down from the truck and followed their son.

When they rounded the house they could see Nicky standing with his back to them, knocking his hip against the bottom of the slide. Everett had built him a wooden jungle gym with an aluminum slide and monkey bars, and just the previous fall they'd gotten a small round trampoline which stayed out all winter despite the snow and was now tangled in the new grass. Nicky would jump on the trampoline for hours, cracking the plate of ice in the middle, going up and down, then shooting at a slant like a wayward spark, his face lit with the joy of surprise.

It was to the trampoline that Ivy moved.

Come here, Ivy said, as if it were Nicky's idea. She sat on the bright blue bumpers and swung her legs onto the springs which radiated from the black disk. Everett sat sidesaddle opposite. Nicky walked toward them with swollen eyes, no longer outwardly crying, and climbed on with them. What a relief it was to have him position himself so obediently between them, even if he continued to ignore them. He slid onto his stomach, his head on his folded arms, refusing them.

They sat with time falling in a trance around them.

Ivy touched his back. Sweetie, she began, and he jerked up, electrocuted, and slithered to the padded edge and spilled off. But he didn't run away this time, he stayed underneath them.

Ivy faced the dense black trampoline fabric as if being able to see through it to where he was. She did not try again to share a look with Everett. Then the trampoline's surface erupted with the shallow imprint of sneakers pummeling from below. Everett and Ivy lurched as if on a wave. This was good, she thought, he was expressing his frustration physically. He could kick the trampoline instead of them. Or himself.

Beneath the black mesh came his voice, thick in his throat. Why can't you just get along? he said.

Everett looked to Ivy. She was the talker, she could answer.

Nicky . . . , she managed. We've . . . it's hard to explain—But what words could follow?

She had written down the impossible moments between her and Everett in order to examine them after, or to refer to them when they happened again, as a way of trying to figure them out. But it hadn't figured out anything. They could not reach a consensus, that was the final thing. They had not agreed on what love looked like. Everett had felt that if there was irritation or hate, then it wasn't love. Ivy expected love could embrace everything, but then what did you do with lack of respect?

All you have to do is stop fighting, came the voice from below.

We can't, Everett said immediately.

Each moment seemed to chip away a piece of her. Each kick from his small foot was another chip. How many pieces could be chipped off a person?

Everett's dead gaze said, I'm not going to suggest we try it again. We're done with that.

A strong bump from below hit her palm and knocked her off-balance. She tipped back on the springs, laughing an empty, yet real, laugh. That one got me, she said.

It was supposed to, said the voice below. Nicky continued with his earlier point, Then all you have to do is when you're about to argue you just decide not to and you won't fight.

That's true, Ivy said.

Everett appeared to be shaking. He was being pummeled from below. Am I sitting on a jackhammer? he said. He looked almost grateful.

No, said the voice. It's a machine gun.

Goodness, Ivy said. Fuck, she mouthed to Everett.

The chickens wobbled near, wondering, in their nervous head-swiveling way, if perhaps they were going to be fed. The bolder chickens straggled in front, followed by a hapless but unified formation behind. The chickens stuck together. They pecked the ground, seemingly unaware of each other, but always within a few feet. No chicken wandered off on her own.

Here come the chickens, Ivy said blankly, needing to say something not loaded, then immediately regretting it. They needed to stay on subject. They needed to stick with Nicky and go however he needed to go.

Nicky, able to distinguish the shadows above him, was alternating kicks to his mother, then his father. Hit me, she thought. Hit me harder. I ought to be smashed to bits. She felt numb and yet in pain at the same time.

The fleeting thought came, Nicky would never again be able to look at his parents together and say, They love each other; I am safe.

She'd seen another change, in the suspended moment on the trampoline. Looking at Everett as their son banged them from beneath she saw through the cyclone that Everett was changed to her. He was no longer hers. She'd tried at other times to see him that way, but she hadn't quite managed. He was hers after all; she was his. But now, now that Nicky knew, she was able to picture him no longer hers.

The chickens streamed by, daring quick glances in the vicinity of the trampoline. They'd hatched them a few weeks before, having taken ten fertilized eggs from the coop of neighbors with roosters, slipping them out from under the warmth of the broody hens. They'd set up an incubator in the living room, leaving the light on all night, and after twenty-one days on the dot watched in amazement as they hatched. You could hold an egg to your ear and hear the unhatched chick chirping inside. She thought of Nicky's face listening. Chirping before it was born! Then you heard the tiny tapping on the eggshell from inside till a crack showed and the shells broke and the chicks emerged wet as rags. One of the rags remained curled in a half shell, looking drier than the others and not moving. Everett matter-of-factly got some vegetable oil and rubbed it over the tiny twigs of feathers till there was some movement and a head lifted and the chick eventually trembled out onto its feet. That chicken went by now, the one with the crooked neck walking a little sideways, the one Everett had matter-of-factly saved.

There was a pause in the pummeling. Then she felt a smack on her rear. Oh, she said. Ouch.

She knew Nicky must be getting tired. She spoke, We're not going—but stopped herself before *away*. It wouldn't be true. They were going away. In fact, one parent would pretty much always be away. If Nicky was with one of them, it would mean he was not with the other.

We're always going to be your mum and dad, Ivy said, clutching at straws, wanting to say something positive yet also true.

She was about to follow up with, We'll always be here, when the black smoke which seemed to churn over all the knee-jerk positive things people said at difficult times obscured the view. It will be okay. It's all for the best. They were not true. Love offered false comfort. Did comfort have to be true?

How could she say, We will always be here? She and Everett would not always be there, not with each other, not even in life.

Nicky crawled out from beneath and got onto the trampoline lip. He didn't meet their eyes but crawled onto the black circle. A child didn't have the choice to go anywhere else, not really. He came back to them. She thought of how above, from where the eagle soared, the trampoline would appear as a bull's-eye.

How could she say it? Then she said it anyway. Nicky, we will always be here.

Now what. Now nothing. A new feeling of grief—like water rising—flooded her throat. She pressed it down and a trickle of water escaped her eyes. This may be the worst moment of my life, she thought. Had she thought that before? When her parents died. When her heart first broke at nineteen. It had felt like a worst moment, but she'd not put those words to it. So maybe this was it.

They lingered on the trampoline.

Then Everett had surprised her. He summoned a voice which somehow had normalcy in it. I've got some rails which need to be taken out of my truck, he said and slapped the blue pads. Nicky looked up, relieved to return to something regular.

Everett stood. Anyone want to help?

Nicky nodded, not enthusiastically, but with something grateful in his eyes. He slid off and joined his father. Ivy was left on the platform, as if on a once-sacred place.

Want me? she said as they walked away, then was immediately embarrassed at the phrase, certain Everett would roll his eyes and slap it down.

But he didn't. Breezily he said, I'm going to need all the help I can get.

They arrived late to a dinner cold on the stove. Everett was more impatient than usual. Is there any reason you parked your car there? Is Nicky supposed to wear these city sneakers here? Ivy, now a guest, stayed in the guest room. She had redecorated this room after Pamela died, getting rid of the wooden armed love seat and brass lamp, replacing them with a kilim-covered hassock and curtains in the window, a flowered linen tablecloth found at a thrift shop, cut in half and hung with wooden clips. In the chest were still old sweaters of Ivy's.

On Thanksgiving Day in Dover, Ivy, Everett and Nicky went to Karen and Andy's who lived on a creek in a converted millhouse with vast iron-paned windows. Karen and Andy had twin boys Nicky's age and had been close to Ivy and Everett, but now were closer to Everett. Everyone was still friendly, cracking jokes, but Ivy felt placed at a remove. That is, she was aware of having placed herself at this remove. She looked at the pounded-copper counter in the kitchen and saw where she'd been with Karen over the years, filling small glasses with wine and talking about their children, the town, their bodies, their husbands. Then Ivy had left. To curb the discomfort, she withdrew into thoughts of Ansel Fleming. She had something separate to think about now, something hers.

That evening Ivy took the train from Dover into D.C. to make way for Rebecca, who was coming after visiting her parents in Florida for the holiday. Ivy stayed with her high school friend Rosemary, a lawyer married to another lawyer, Don. They had a teenage son, plus older stepchildren from Don's first marriage. The household was steeped in D.C. politics, though Rosemary and Don, both witty, never took themselves too seriously, even if they were invested. They cared, but were not duped. Ivy saw Rosemary rarely now—maybe once a year, if that—but told herself that this didn't reflect the love she felt for her old friend. They had been through some important things together. Though Ivy had to admit that the longer you lived the more you saw some friends less, and if time was the measure of a friendship, then less time spent might allow a friendship to grow thinner and less robust. On the other hand, one saw that if a friend remained longstanding regardless of the less time shared then that love was the more robust for it, tolerating the extended periods without interaction. Like many things, it could go both ways.

Rosemary and Don lived on a tree-lined street in a yellow house with a porch and a short walkway, side by side with similar houses with slightly different walkways and slightly different porches, some bigger, some smaller. Ivy liked Rosemary's by far the best. Inside, the house was clean with uncluttered surfaces and walls of books. A low table had only the newspaper spread over it. Framed prints and paintings which one felt had been selected with care were scattered along the hallways, and the sofas and armchairs were comfortable and wide.

When thoughts of Ansel came to Ivy in this airy, laughter-filled house he seemed more of a dream to her than ever, and rather easier to manage. Whenever a guest, Ivy would feel that other people's lives, the ones belonging to her hosts, were more real than her own. After dinner the next night, Ivy stayed up with Rosemary on a back screened-in porch with a mock fire behind a grill and told her about this unformed affair with Ansel. The more she spoke about it, the more idiotic she felt, as if she were sliding backward down a muddy hill. Rosemary listened with eyebrows raised in encouragement. But Ivy seemed unable to capture the intensity of the thrill, the amazement of the boost. She said instead that she knew it wasn't going to go anywhere, but, well, what could she do? Rosemary shrugged. Ivy felt the sting. Her wise friend nearly always had something to say.

Back in the city, ruminations continued.

Whenever she thought of the phone call she flushed with shame. Finally she wrote him an email that she was sorry, she'd expressed herself badly. She wanted to explain, though everything she wrote felt like an understatement. She was trying to learn the ways of Ansel Fleming. Maybe he would illuminate her, even though she had picked up on the idea that he didn't seem to like particularly to illuminate himself. Maybe he didn't want to be known by her. If that were the case it would help if he'd tell her so. No, she thought, cross that out, it was complaining and demanding. But seeing the words describe her frustration so well she was unable to delete it. Maybe he ought to see some true feeling, she thought, even if it looked unreasonable. She knew she shouldn't send it, so she did.

He did not respond.

. . .

She felt there were things she must ask him and tried to prepare questions in her mind. What do you want? Well, he had answered that. Not a relationship. But there was more to learn. Once she raised the subject, then surely a clarifying discussion would follow.

A ticker tape in her brain now helplessly kept track of when she'd last heard from him, last seen him. She thought of her small attempts to drag him out—inviting him to skate, another time to the movies—being met with quick refusals, then of his appearance in the portal out in the world, with his arm around women smiling in a flash, of the clips he posted of concerts with looping stage lights, of him standing next to a benefit sandwich board.

Monday morning, wrung out, she spent a long time composing a text with the attention of someone writing a ransom note, stripped of any character or defining elements. She wished she could go with the straightforward *Are you free?* but she'd barely had contact for two weeks and shouldn't that be acknowledged? Maybe not. Maybe just start in with *Run this morning?* Or go directly to *Come warm me up.* Eventually she decided on the factual. *You up yet? It's cold out there.*

And in she stuck the pin, of waiting.

But there was a *ting* right away. Rays of light flooding the horizon after weeks of monsoon.

Still in bed. You?

Bed! She did not pore over composing what next to say.

On her bike ride down, her old worries become a distant low-lying mountain range an inch high. What did she need so badly to say? What did she need to know? The closer she gets to him, the hazier the worries become.

Today he's at the door to meet her, but his face is weary. This concerns and touches her. He's wearing a dark long-sleeved T-shirt and soft grey sweatpants with a tweed pattern. The weary face is new. Looking off, he gives her a hug. It's nice to see you, he says. Come in.

In the bedroom she notices a book on the sparsely filled bookshelf by an author she knows and how normally she might mention the author is a friend and would talk about the book, but with Ansel, she doesn't, not wanting to break the separate-from-the-world feeling she has with him. She is reluctant to bring him into the world she knows, liking how it feels separate in this one, maybe uncertain where and how he would fit. It is the same reluctance she's had about asking about prison, not wanting to invade his privacy. She wonders how did he manage without sex. Did he have sex with the other inmates? Her interest feels sensational and obvious and she does not want to insult him by being nosy and intrusive, even if she is. Why does one refrain from showing interest? It seems to do with respect. Ansel seems to be a person not concerned with trivial things, one of those people who doesn't take the low road shortcut of just blurting one's story. She admires his reticence, another quality she wishes she had more of.

She notices her book is no longer on his bedside table.

Taking his place on the bed, he holds out his arm. Bring it in, he mutters and she sinks into the contentment of being again on his chest. She asks him about going to his grandmother's for Thanksgiving.

It was great, he says.

Were your sisters there?

Yes, with their families. I love the babies.

Does your family ever argue? Ivy said. Mine would. Little squabbles.

I don't notice it, he says. I don't go there.

He is above all that, she thinks. Not spoiled.

Then he says, I'm not feeling so great today. Tired. Feeling tired.

So she had read his face.

Why? she says. What is it?

He takes her hand and puts it on his soft tweed thigh. In her happiness, Ivy feels two colliding urges—to hurry and to be slow.

Dimly she recalls the questions she's promised herself to ask. But she prefers his questions when their clothes are off. Is that good? What do you want?

What you're doing is what I want, she says.

And how does it feel?

I . . . I can't say.

From the word maker? he says.

No, she says. That's the beauty of it.

Later he says, You like doing that.

A lot, she says. She is thrilled to see he almost smiles. She adds, Maybe too much.

Can't like something too much, he says.

Well, she says, I don't know, but I think you may have something to do with it.

I think you'd be that way with anyone, he says. You know how to let go.

She thinks this an astonishing thing to say. That seems to be the furthest thing from herself she can imagine.

She lay across him with the sheet pulled up. She said how odd it was the first time she came there, how she'd wished for no talking and that's just what happened. It had seemed like a miracle. Or, she said, at the least a nice turn of events.

How did you know you wanted to have sex with me?

Good question, she thought, because she didn't have an answer right away.

I just felt it, she said finally, vaguely. She saw herself that night moving toward him on the couch, strangely out of body, felt again the pause before they kissed.

But I was still surprised, she said. It quite blew my mind, you know.

Maybe you feel so much because it's been such a long time.

Maybe, she said. I thought that at first. Now I don't think so.

. . .

He had appeared when she was stuck. She thought he was amazing, she said with a catch in her voice she hoped wasn't heard. She saw his face listening, but not revealing any thought. Feeling encouraged by no reaction, she kept talking. She found that she didn't need to ask him anything so much as to tell her side of things. She said she understood he was not in the market for a—she paused, wanting to avoid the overused *relationship,* and came up with—whole sort of thing with someone, and that had been something she thought might suit her situation better now. For a while it did. It was a wonderful busting open. But, the more she saw him, the less fine it felt, in a certain way. That is, she felt a little less freewheeling. Feelings started to come up. I mean, that happened. When the body was so engaged, it would drag feelings along after it, whether you wanted them or not—

I don't think I misled you, he said mildly.

No, she said. You didn't. You didn't at all.

His face was still and smooth.

It's my own . . . , she began. My own dilemma.

But she found she did want to explain it.

When I didn't hear from you, for those days whenever—as if she hadn't been keeping track exactly—for that week and a half, I started to think, Oh no. I'm waiting for a man to call. And I thought, I don't want to be waiting for a man to call.

She felt her delighted state of mind darken. Shit, she thought, Am I in that trap already? She had appreciated his telling her there were others like her and was waiting to see if she could handle it. Maybe it would be good to try to handle that. It wasn't something she'd tried before. And at first it was okay. Surprisingly. She figured she'd stay with it as long as it felt okay. But now, she said, it was starting to not feel okay.

Outside, the morning was bright with a large shadow bisecting the building across the street.

There are some things I'm good at, Ansel said. Some things I know how to do. But other things, like wanting what other people want—well, I think, maybe that's not for me in this life. I can only stick to what I can do. I was away a long time. I have a lot of issues, trust issues.

When he first got out he had a girlfriend, he said. For about five months.

A girlfriend! Since prison. She'd like to ask about that, but he says nothing more.

I did feel a strong—for some reason she cannot use the clichéd *connection*—thing with you. She is surprised to feel embarrassed and hesitates. Vibrationally.

She would like now to close her eyes and stay on top of him, but she feels she has to push on. Why does she feel that?

So I guess I want to know where I stand with you, she says limply.

I'm not sure what you want to know, he says.

I guess where do I fit in . . . for you?

I don't take you for granted, he says. Even when you don't hear from me, I am not taking you for granted.

That's nice to know, she says.

There is a silence and she feels more things between them.

I appreciate it, she says. I'm trying to figure out if I can do this. But I'm getting the distinct feeling that I'll start to want more.

Of course this has already started to happen. She has even pictured it. Ansel at the apartment with her and Nicky on a Sunday evening, watching a movie, on the couch, Sunday papers, plates of pasta in their laps. The unplanned time when people fall back on each other.

Do you mind being asked all these questions? she says.

No, he says. I just don't volunteer information.

I feel like I talk too much. And ask stupid questions.

I'm like one of those teachers who believe there are no stupid questions.

She kisses him.

She says she's told Nicky a little about her new friend Ansel. You know what he said?

What?

Not a good match, Mom.

Ansel laughs. He said that?

I know.

Ansel sits up. Want to hear some new songs?

She lets the rest of the morning go, sitting on his lap, in front of the keyboard. The computer screen is covered with a mixing board and Ansel pulls up songs, opening and closing squares, moving bars along graphs, mixing melodies. One song is called "Your Love for Me Will Grow."

You shouldn't play that for me, she says, laughing. But she's not feeling any worry.

What's that sound? she asks. It sounds like an animal growling.

Just something I made up.

He hums a little, takes out a notebook and starts to sing the lines on the page. He picks up the white guitar and Ivy moves to a nearby chair while he plays and sings. When he finishes she stands and hugs him from behind. It's beautiful, she says.

Just trying to change the world, he says. Even if I don't go out in it.

She will manage this, she thinks. He is magnificent and glorious and inspiring. She puts on her coat to leave.

Thank you, he says, for hanging out.

The birthday party was at a gymnastics place called To the Stars. Ivy and Nicky walked up a ramp into the echoing bouncing space, carrying the shopping bag with the wrapped present, plus his knapsack. After the party he was spending the night with Oscar. Ivy caught sight of them reflected in a wall of mirrors and had the stabbing worry she wasn't looking after her son well enough, sending him to someone else's house. Ivy tried to return the favor and invite Oscar, but Padma mostly waved away the offer. With work she didn't get to see Oscar enough and besides she had more room at her place.

A few gymnastics instructors were practicing among the stacked red and yellow cushions, on the crossbeams or trampolines or pits full of blue sponge cubes. A woman was flipping her waist around a parallel bar, then landing like a statue, knees bent, stiff arms upright. Wow, Ivy said. Nicky's face took on the intent disapproving gaze it got when fascinated.

The party room was located past a small shop area with racks of tiny sparkling leotards and shelves of Ace bandages, a blindingly bright room with pink and white balloons hovering at the end of a ribbon. Nicky entered eagerly, shouldering out of his parka, not looking back. Children greeting each other standing close and looking toward each other's necks. The pile of presents was gathering on a table. The birthday girl named Charlotte wore a white leotard with a sequined pink peace sign, a pink ballet skirt and a diamond tiara. Grown-ups stood against the wall, and Ivy recognized a few of the parents, but could not remember all their names and was relieved to see Padma, her lustrous hair dipping over one eye.

Are we supposed to stay? Ivy murmured.

Don't think so, Padma said, still in her trench coat. I have to work anyway. Till it's over.

A trio of dads stood with green bottles of beer at their chests, as if badges of manhood.

Who're the parents? Ivy said. She knew she should know, but couldn't always keep them straight.

Padma tipped her head toward a small athletic woman adjusting the presents curling with ribbon over the pink plastic tablecloth.

Becky's a doctor, Padma told her. The dad—they're divorced—is over there. She indicated a beefy fellow in a fleece zip-up. He's a journalist. But now Becky's with—her head tipped toward a thin man—Mike's dad.

Oh, I met him, Ivy said, proud to be in the know. Cliff. Nicky had a sleepover there.

He did? Padma looked surprised.

Yeah, why?

The kid is weird, she whispered. I think a little sadistic.

Jesus, Ivy said. Nicky didn't say anything . . .

Padma said, They don't like to tell. Sometimes they don't even realize—

A perfumed woman came up and Padma introduced her as Violet's mother. Violet's mother had a handsome unmade-up face and gazed about coolly, interested in what was happening, but calm. She wore a long patterned dress which Ivy recognized as being by a hip designer, whose clothes were made to look not expensive, but were.

Nicky is adorable, Violet's mother said in a honeyed voice. I think Violet is crushing on him. She seemed to be amused by a private joke; Ivy wondered if she was on medication.

Which one's Violet? Ivy asked her.

Over there, Violet's mother said and pursed her lips in the direction of a small girl with cropped hair and huge eyes.

She's gorgeous, Ivy said.

She's a bitch, Violet's mother said happily. But I still love her.

Ivy thanked Padma again for taking Nicky for the night—and Padma waved her off as if bored. Violet's mother turned her glittering gaze to Ivy. What're you up to tonight? she said.

Ivy smiled and shrugged.

I can see you're going to get into trouble, Violet's mother said, elbowing Ivy. If you're lucky.

Ivy had the strange feeling that some depravity showed on her face and Violet's mother could see it. She smiled without feeling it.

Ivy called Nicky over to say goodbye. She adjusted his curls and he jerked his head away. This looks like fun, she said encouragingly.

Obviously, Mum, he said, regarding her with pity and shaking his head. It's a birthday party.

. . .

But she didn't get into trouble that night. Ansel Fleming was not free.

She thought of the other girls, their heads lined up on the shelf, or curled into a cabinet, one waiting behind each door. She told herself, Don't make anyone so important.

Monday, rain was running in the gutters. A rainy day was a good day to work and she knew she ought to stay at the table. But she wanted a different kind of disappearance. She texted him and he was there.

She arrived to him damp. He didn't care. On the coffee table she noticed a cluster of candles, white, red, burnt down. She saw a brass ashtray full of cigarette butts. There'd been a party. Bottles were lined up on the floor in the kitchen, wine and beer bottles, mouths open like drains. She felt the slap of it, how she was not one of the people he saw. She wondered who had been there. But bed was what she was here for and they sank into it. She was conscious of a new mixture of feelings. She felt a bit of herself hardening, which was a relief, as if she was reclaiming something of her discernment. It meant she wouldn't keep sinking. It was good to know what was what. She wasn't going to be a part of his life, of his beer parties late at night. She didn't want to be, really. The people were probably all twenty years younger anyway. She was past that. She would kiss him and enjoy his body, but she would not be as susceptible to him now. She was wising up, recovering a clear frame of mind. She took in the black-and-white room past his smooth shoulder, and thought, One of these days will be the last day I'm here.

She sent Ansel a text inviting him for dinner the following Thursday, giving him plenty of lead time. So far he'd said no to a few invitations, but she'd given them offhandedly and thought to try something planned. Just to *see*. She invited a few people for dinner, not her closest friends, but one degree away, six people, not too many. One worked in music, scoring films. One was the author of the book Ansel had on his shelf. She would surprise him with that, wanting to bring him to something of her life.

He answered right away, *I don't do dinner parties*. She did not point out that she had met him at one. *Never?* she wrote back, trying to joke, but stunned by the power of his refusal.

He replied, *Never say never.*

Despite feeling nonplussed, she tried for a light tone, not always picked up in texts: *Well I think it's mean of you not to come.*

He wrote, *I'd rather be absent than mean.*

It was a strange statement she couldn't puzzle out.

He added, *Sorry*.

The *sorry* was like a guillotine.

Okay, she thought. So that is how it is. Good to know.

But there was nothing good about it. She felt gutted. And rejected. Plus idiotic for having tried, then idiotic for her feelings. The sharpness of the pain seemed to call up old pains, increasing it. Why did some pain call up more? The older one got the more pain there was to recall. Doubled over in the living room, in a ball, she thought, Just get it out of you before your son finds you this way.

The weight of him changed from being ballast, to being a thing she was dragging around. They were not matched. Even her nine-year-old thought so. She thought, Better get out while you can. Sooner better than later.

Then she thought of T. S. Eliot. Wait without hope, for hope would be hope for the wrong thing. But still she prayed—was it praying if you didn't believe in God?—Please, let me be patient. Let me accept him. Let me live without needing an agreement.

Then, maybe let there develop an agreement between us? No. Let me just accept this as it is.

The dream woke her at 2:00 A.M., at first out of reach, but she understood it had an important message. The darkness was thin as grey water, her bed a pool covering her in sleep. Tell me, dream, come back and tell me what to do. There'd been a radio station, she was behind glass, broadcasting about women. They needed to be advocated for. This was her mission. Then, somewhere else. She knew not to concentrate too hard or the dream would recede. Sleep waited, heavy and purple, but first she wanted to learn what the dream had been after. A shoreline, flat water. She stood at the curve of a cove, knee deep, seeing, dotted off in the distance, scores of couples in the calm water, head beside head, each a pair, with their bare shoulders above the waterline. She, in shorts and a T-shirt, was the only one unpaired, the only one dressed. She waded in, wanting to join them, keeping her clothes on.

The next morning she sat in her parked car for alternate side parking. She kept the secondhand Volkswagen so she could drive Nicky as often as possible the six hours to Virginia to see his dad. A garage was too expensive and she'd gotten used to the twice-a-week tyranny of an hour and a half requested by the New York City Department of Transportation that a person be in her car, pull out of the parking place for one minute so a street cleaner could pass by, then sit another hour and twenty-five minutes just because. Her diesel engine was loud and rumbling and now and then someone, always a man—he was being helpful—pointed out to her that she might need a muffler. No woman ever decided she needed to be told this.

In the container of the car, she idled the motor to run the heater and not drain the battery, then turned it off for silence. His refusal to come to dinner had upset her far more than it should have, she knew, and Ivy took it as a sign that things had to change.

She had reached the point. Feeling strength in her decisiveness, Ivy decided to call him. It was easier for some reason to phone when not in the apartment surrounded by herself, but still her heart thumped.

Hello, he said, as always never surprised.

She asked him how he was and he said all good.

I've been thinking about you, she said.

Good thoughts, I hope.

Yes, but.

Silence waited on the other end.

I mean, she went on. I shouldn't have given you a hard time about not calling me. I'm sorry.

Silence waited.

But I think I had . . . I mean you know how I said I was worried I'd start having feelings and maybe getting too . . . well, I think that has started to happen.

She talked on. She felt as if the words evaporated as soon as she spoke them. She didn't seem to be able—she wasn't sure she could—she blah blah blah. It sounded to her like blobs of words even as she kept on. She had hoped, but now she saw. She thought she had to blah blah before it got worse. Before more time blah blah. It was like being in quicksand. She felt she'd only sunk. Had she described what she meant? She stopped talking and hoped he'd say something to carry them along.

Okay, said his deep voice agreeably.

I mean, it's my problem, she said. I just—

But she'd gone as far as she could.

There's a lot you don't know about me, he said. And that's by my design. But one thing about me is that I hate mean people, and when you wrote me that I was mean, then I realized this was taking on a bad dynamic. I know you said you meant it in a playful way, but it still makes me picture you over there feeling bad because of me, and me not giving you what you want, and if that's the case I don't want to have any part in making you feel that way.

No, she said, astonished. I mean, okay.

The rain came lightly down, dotting up the windshield.

So if it's a bad dynamic . . .

I shouldn't have criticized you, she said. You've been clear. Really. I should have just stuck to how I was feeling. And realizing that I'm having a hard time managing it.

A pale girl with a spout of hair lugged a bag of laundry out of a nearby entryway. She looked for the car picking her up.

I guess the thing is, Ivy said, I see it's getting too . . . I mean, I think it would be better if when I see you I kept my clothes on.

Finally she had said something substantial.

I think that's a good idea, he said right away.

The car pulled up to the pale girl and she opened the door and got in with enthusiasm.

So that's okay with you? Ivy said.

I said okay. His voice was calm even if he had to repeat himself. You do what you have to do.

Okay . . . , she said. Yes.

The rain seemed to have stopped. Two handsome men in crisp trench coats were strutting by hand in hand.

But I still hope I can see you, she said.

I think we can make that happen, he said.

She felt she'd stepped off a cliff into air. Being decisive wasn't giving her much relief.

And you still don't want to come for dinner?

Why did she say that? She was clutching at straws. This was totally beside the point but she couldn't stop herself blurting out, Not even if the writer you like is coming. She mentioned the writer's name.

No, he said. What kind of an asshole would I be then? Listen, I appreciate you including me in your circle.

You're hard to lure out, she said.

I'm a hard nut to crack.

Well, I think you're great, she said. And that's how you are. And if that's how you stay great, then . . . This was a relief, saying something she believed.

If it's meant to be, then maybe one day, he said.

Okay, she said, flooded again with hope. A hooded woman

with a sad, pulled-down face followed a feathery Pomeranian who walked before her on a leash, jauntily lifting her white paws like a drum majorette.

By the way, Ivy said. It's my birthday today.

Happy birthday, he said, never surprised. How old are you, twenty-eight?

Ha ha, she said. No. Old. So old it's sad.

No. It's a blessing.

I'll try to think of it that way.

How are you celebrating?

Some of my friends are taking me to a spa in Queens.

Spa Castle? he said. I love Spa Castle. My people go there.

I haven't been, she said. I don't really go to spas, but my girlfriends think it will be good for me.

Well, have fun, he said. Stay safe.

Thank you. She didn't want to hang up, she never wanted to hang up. Therefore she was the one first to say, Okay then, bye.

PART II

There is no crime greater than having too many desires.
There is no disaster greater than not being content.

—LAO TZU (*TAO TE CHING*)

4

The Open Door

> Perhaps the feelings we experience when we are in love represent a normal state. Being in love shows a person who he should be.
>
> —ANTON CHEKHOV

They had lived at the top of a steep escarpment in a mud-thatched house where the sky started at the floor of the open door and flowers were tangled around the water tanks. A flat savanna stretched out below with a dusty haze over it. The sky at that height was more huge. The view drew her outward, and she felt small on the escarpment. In a foreign place you felt yourself less keenly.

She carried Nicky against her ribs, a kidney shape slung in a kikoi, taking the footpath along the top of the cliff. It was like walking on the spine of an enormous dragon. Smudges of smoke rose from hidden dwellings. The expanse of the hazy plain had a godlike presence. Maybe it was the view you imagined God had, seeing the contour of the earth, far away.

She had liked how the clouds would drift up, then engulf them on the hillside.

After a few months the view became familiar and she was paying more attention to the baby against her chest and her sneakers below creased with red dirt. Thin and see-through were the quick thoughts of clicking boot heels worn out at night in New

York, and of the years before Everett, and the other men she knew and how you met new people who flung back the curtains onto other worlds, and the ones whose entrance changed your life in an evening. Because there was always another life from the one you were living there, and no matter how much you loved it, your mind looked to other places, if for no other reason than you knew about possibility, about change and how nothing was permanent.

At Spa Castle they took off their clothes.

Ivy, Harriet said, handing Ivy a towel in the changing room. You're too skinny.

The three friends walked barefoot down a beige hall to a dark room with four different pools of water, some circles, some rectangles, set in the floor. The other women there all seemed to be Korean. Ivy let herself imagine she was somewhere else in the world. This could be her cleansing. Then she thought she didn't really want to be cleansed. She was still thinking of Ansel Fleming, not altogether sure about where he would go, even if certain that it would only become more painful the longer she stayed attached to him. Which is why she had acted, even if now she felt uncertain about that.

Irene and Harriet had congratulated her for making the right decision. They were not only wise and solid, as far as their relationships went, but actually happy with their husbands. Irene had been married for fifteen years. Her husband, Josh, was someone she'd known in college but remet after he got divorced. Harriet, who was British, had been through periods of difficult romance, though Ivy had never seen her in them, since she'd been married now for nearly twenty years to the cinematographer she met on a movie shoot. Kevin was a solid person, full of humor and industry, and they had three children. Harriet and Irene were talking about school. They'd met each other when their youngest children had attended the same preschool. Ivy was bored to tears by talk about children's schools. She taught on and off and felt she ought to be more interested, but institutions and logistics were not the part of teaching she was interested in. She loved Harriet and Irene, who both worked in production and now and then on overlapping projects, and was deeply grateful to have them on either side of her today, like each end of a hammock. They surveyed the pools. Irene explained how each one was different. She was going to the icy pool, wanting to get refreshed. But there was a warmer one, a salty one, a menthol etc. Ivy sank into the warmest pool up to her neck and felt the pain in her chest and hoped it would not stay too long.

You want a massage? Harriet said, scrubbing her feet with mud. It's great. They have switches. If you want, they give you a good bollocking.

Any English word Harriet said was like a bonbon for Ivy. Snog. Jumper. Knackered.

Later they walked still in their towels up three flights of stairs to the roof level. There was a sauna on the roof and an ice room. On a landing Ivy paused at a small window to look at the December world of grey and brown framed by the pink wall. Snow was falling through the air in flakes thick as ash.

On the way back in the cab Ivy felt soft and pampered. She was grateful to be taken care of and thanked her friends. She also felt a dread of returning to her apartment, as if a corpse were waiting for her there to deal with.

Harriet and Irene exchanged a look. Tell her, Irene said.

What? Ivy's body was suddenly hollow, like a let-go balloon.

Well, I wasn't going to tell you, but now since—Harriet said. They were all in the back seat of the cab. Ivy was by the window where the bridge suspension was flashing by.

It's something about Ansel Fleming, Irene said.

A realtor that Harriet knew had shown Ansel Fleming an apartment in Harriet's building. Harriet's sister-in-law had also looked at the flat, as she called the apartment, with the same realtor, which was how Harriet knew about it. It was pretty pricey, too pricey for her sister-in-law.

Wow, Ivy said. She knew Ansel planned to move out of the apartment eventually but had not mentioned he was looking. If he had, she thought she might have given him some suggestions, even helped.

Harriet looked to Irene for encouragement.

Irene said, He was looking at it with a woman.

Really? Ivy said.

Yes, a blond woman, kind of young. They were looking at it together.

Oh, Ivy said. So she was helping him.

No, Harriet said. They were definitely a couple. Mona said they were definitely a couple.

Well, who was she? Ivy said.

Harriet and Irene again checked with each other. Did Ivy really want to know?

Apparently a law student? But older, like she'd gone back to school. But she was still young, in her early thirties probably. Pretty, blond.

Right, you said that, Ivy said.

Harriet and Irene regarded Ivy. They were waiting for her reaction.

Well, that's interesting, Ivy said.

They were looking at the apartment to be in it together, Irene said, as if she had not gotten the point. We just thought you should know.

Yes, Ivy said. I guess.

There are things about me you don't know.

The cab was humping up over the bridge, and the iron girders flashed by the window, slicing the flat grey river beneath them.

I mean, I can't say I'm surprised really, Ivy said. He keeps his cards close to his chest.

But her body felt otherwise and the tires below them thumping the expansion joints hit like one punch after another.

Well, then, she was well out of it.

. . .

So why did she feel this flattened? No longer preoccupied with when she would next see him or hear from him, her attention was occupied by surprise at how devastated she felt.

She'd been the one to make the decision. It wasn't as if this had been done to her. The choice was supposed to be healthy and strengthening, but almost immediately it felt the opposite, as if she'd harmed herself, the precise thing she'd been trying to avoid.

She went through the day robotically. She gave the planned dinner party, going through the motions. Her guests were lively though half of them apologized because they didn't eat lamb. People stayed till 1:00 A.M. and after they left she washed the dishes, weeping.

Not at all love.

Perhaps she'd been too abrupt with it. Too determined to control. Ansel was, if nothing else, a new friend. He had appeared like a beam of light in her life, opening the air. That was worth valuing, wasn't it? If he could be her friend, she would be able to keep him in her life and maybe keep some of the happy feeling and not feel ripped down the middle. If he was going to be her friend, she should establish that friendship sooner than later.

He kept as friends his old lovers, he'd told her. Ivy did, too, though the change in relations with someone she'd split from usually occurred after a period of time and, nearly always, after an initial total break in contact. But time was different now in her life, having a different measure. Mainly, there was less of it.

So after a week she texted a breezy hello. He texted back, breezy, too. The reply gave her that nervous thrill.

Don't be a stranger, he said, saying what she had said.

A few days later she texted she hoped they could see each other and he texted back that they should make that happen. But didn't suggest when. She felt she was dropping crumbs, not so much to catch a bird, as to mark her trail in case she needed to retreat.

It had been nine days. On a Friday she texted him she had a movie screener and did he want to watch it with her? Sure, he said. He was free. She got a sitter for Nicky, making it a sure thing she would have to come home that night. But that wasn't so much of a danger. She wanted Ansel to know she had meant what she said, and to be able to see each other this new way.

Ansel greeted her with a hug at the door and she returned the hug, holding back on her side, keeping her word, even if he probably couldn't tell. She hung her coat up on the hook above his shoes. He brought out two bottles of beer from the fridge. The apartment was different, with her resolve, as if the edges had become sharper, more in focus. Ivy found herself different, too, talking more than usual, with a newfound buoyancy, as if words might take the place of sex. She felt more like the Ivy she was familiar with, the one less likely to get swept away, the one to her more tedious.

Ansel handed her a bottle, took the DVD out of its envelope and slipped the disc into his player, getting right down to business. She sat on the couch, bracing herself for the new eerie space between them. She reminded herself about being grown up and even wise, and tried to ignore the nervy air. She was adjusting to these new relations. He sat down beside her as the movie began. Then facing her, he tucked his feet under her thighs, surprising her. That was what a close friend would do, wasn't it? How relaxed of him. It would be okay. And something relaxed in her, too, not having to endure the nervy separateness. Because now they were touching. She felt vaguely she was breaking her own rule.

The movie was good—luckily—about a girl with a wayward (single!) mom living in the projects in Scotland, or estate housing, as they called it in the UK. A few minutes into watching Ivy made a comment about estate housing being an interesting term, and Ansel said, You're not going to talk, are you? Ivy thought he was joking and playfully asked if it bothered him, and he replied earnestly, Yes. It did. Ivy was in the camp of liking to talk while watching a film, liking to include whomever you were watching something with. Everett was not in this camp and had complained about her talking also. Maybe her camp was small. When he walked her to the door after the movie to say goodbye she put her arms around him in a hug. Thank you for having me, Ivy said, and Ansel somehow expertly slipped both hands down the back of her jeans onto her bare skin and gave her butt a friendly grip. She laughed and said, No, no, as if this was outrageous. Though she did not feel it was outrageous. She liked it.

The door closed and she walked weakly down his hall, proud of sticking to her resolve. While what felt like the real Ivy was shaking her head, thinking, You idiot. You have no idea of the right thing to do.

Nearly all of her adult life, Ivy had slept with a person beside her in bed. Night had been the time for comfort and communion, the bed the reward at the end of the day. Now, being alone, night became the time for worries, the bed a plateau from which she surveyed coming storms and receding storms.

Suddenly worries were everywhere. Perhaps they'd always been there, behind the protecting wall of the warm body. Now the worries lay beside her, they sat on her chest like stones. Most had to do with Nicky. But there was also Everett.

She'd ripped her son out of a happy bucolic life and dumped him into a land of concrete and noise where he never touched grass or climbed a tree, but swung on freezing iron bars. He had no siblings. How lonely he must be. At the top of the list was the unforgivable: she'd taken him from his father. He did not get to see his dad every day. She made herself focus on all the elements of this, as penance. He saw his dad less and less. And it was all because Ivy had not been able to stay with and find happiness with Everett, the man she had married.

. . .

What was the reason again? Why didn't it work? She would have to go over it and remind herself why.

She felt the crack in everything, the kitchen floor splintering, the trembling of the avenues. The base of her stomach was continually unsettled, with fear.

Did a child need consistency above all or might it be a gift to give him early the lesson that not everything is constant, that not everything continues as one might hope, that things only change. That maybe change finds something better.

Or, if the new version may not be better, at least it is the truth.

Ivy was now one of those divorced people who say those justifying things that divorced people say, up against the steep rift she had not only allowed, but perhaps also caused. *He sees his father sporadically.*

When did the rancor first appear? After a year? Or was it there from the start? It had not been easy to parse out. It had not been easy to separate. When was that ever easy?

Wanting to stay in touch with her city life, after they'd first moved to Virginia, Ivy would take trips back to New York for weeklong stays with Nicky while Everett stayed on the farm.

In a different relationship, spending time apart might reinforce trust and a desire to refresh, but it had not suited Everett. She should have realized that sooner.

Each time she returned to the city after being away, she would thrill to the vibration in the air. Even known well, the city could strike you anew. Again she was amazed by the mathematics of so many people together, making a particular feeling in the air, of movement and numbers and variety. But she couldn't add it up—no one could. You didn't find it in the country, the awe of walking in a strong wind down the avenue, the buildings rising around you in triumph, or what it was to be in a cavernous old movie theatre, alone, watching a movie from another era and another country, in a city with millions of other souls. In the country you could not stand in a winter sweater and look at a Bonnard painting of summer with its purple shadows and red-checkered tablecloths, crimson faces and plates of oranges by a green open window. The city was the place to be if you were interested in humanity.

In one glance you saw the well dressed and coddled, next to the wrinkled and the wrung out. The crisp beside the bland beside the flamboyant. On one block, twenty faces passed, each with its own wisp of despair or hope, radiating beauty or disappointment.

But try to fathom the actual populace and you'd be stupefied by the density.

Initially, after weeks apart they would both miss each other and Ivy would return to their house on the farm and be welcomed back into their safe and satisfying bed, and they would wonder why they ever fought or thought about splitting up, and it would not take long before the bickering started again. Why was she cooking the vegetables in that pot? Hadn't she followed the news story about the budget hearing? Why had she used that tone ordering something on the phone? Was she wearing that out? She felt the need to stick up for herself, and would point out how critical he was being and ask him to stop griping. I'm not griping, he said. You're just impossible. She had to contradict him on that. We are different, she reminded herself when fighting. She knew she ought to *not engage,* as the phrase had it, but she couldn't let *that* comment go—it was disrespectful and critical—and did not want to live with a person who would say that sort of thing to the person who . . . etc. again.

When their bickering increased, Ivy made the trips longer.

. . .

Other worries were general. Death was coming. It had come, would come again. Had she made her life worthwhile? Where was the money coming from? How could she get more steady work and still stay near Nicky? Then the worries zeroed in on the specific. What had that person meant by that look? She'd forgotten to call Y. What had happened to X? What about people in prison? What about children ignored? She hadn't written enough. What if the water on the planet dried up? What if there was no longer fresh air? Who would ever love her now? Had anyone really loved her? Had she really loved anyone? Why did she let people go? Had she ever really shown herself? How could she love if she hadn't shown herself? How could anyone love her if she'd never appeared? Could she teach and still give enough time to writing? Could she teach and truly help anyone? How was it being a good mother to sit vacant at a playgroup? How could she be a good mother if she didn't always know how to live? Why wasn't she more fun and cheerful like the mothers who talked about how much fun they had with their children, effusing how happy they were with the small cute things?

Each morning the newspaper was at her doorstep, a small offering, despite its layers of distressing stories. She read of others, she read the weeping of the world. Headline this morning: "Comet Gives Earthlings a Reason to Look Up."

At times the small space of their apartment felt like being in a tree house. She always kept the windows open—even if it was in the winter—a crack, needing to let the outside in. On warm evenings she could hear the fountain gurgling in her neighbor's back garden, and being close to others was like being a bird in an atelier. Other times the room with the table and the stove closed in on her, the floor corners dusty and Nicky whining and a trapdoor opened beneath them.

. . .

Sometimes alone all she wanted to do was just make things all day. Things on paper. She liked to draw and paint, with ink and watercolors, and kept them nearby, as treats, something she soothed herself with, because that wasn't her real job. Making something you became absorbed and inhabited an alternate world. The absorption was not like sex, because you did it all alone, and sharing absorption with someone made it a little more valuable.

But you could not live a life of being otherwise absorbed if you had a child. And having a child was what she had longed for and it kept her attached to the world just as she had hoped and without Nicky's level assessing stare and the immediacy of his needs she might have drifted into the ether, with only a transparent thread connecting her to others, and she did want to stay attached to the world in this one and only life, she did. Look at the radiance it had!

But how many lives might one have had. If she'd not been a mother. If she'd not married Everett. If she'd loved that other man. If she'd stayed married to Everett. If she'd dared to be how she had sometimes half wanted to be. One image she had was living in a huge room, bright and airy in the day, window open or at least wide, with art being made, or some atmosphere of industry and invention, of explorations undertaken, even important problems being solved, like a laboratory and an Italian villa combined. At night the enormous windows looked over a sparkling river or cast light on a snowy field banked by black woods. And down on the flowery path laughing people would arrive for dinner, in red shoes and rumpled jackets, carrying bottles of wine, on their way to her.

That life was somewhere. This was her life just now.

Each day she faced the steely resolve to work. Sometimes she obeyed it. She circled which chair to sit at, which area to set out papers. Whether to face the window, or put it at her back. She opened books, fanned out papers. If anyone came over, the papers had to be put away, piled on chairs, stacked under a table. The next morning she'd set the arrangement out again like floating rafts in a pool. But the surface would have iced over, and she'd have to chip at it to break the blocks, to make enough water for things to float. Sometimes she vanished into work. Other times she stayed just this side of it. There would, she told herself, be other better days.

Having handled her body he now had the power to—what? Make her feel real. Why was that?

Using the coming holidays as an excuse, she told Ansel she wanted to drop off a present, the memoir of a musician she knew he hadn't read. Ansel had plans to go out, he texted, but she should stop by before. Good, she thought, she wouldn't need added willpower. He was sitting in front of the computer monitor when she came in and patted a spot next to him on the swivel chair. She perched on the seat edge and they watched footage of some videos he said he was putting together. This was more like it, she said to herself, not being expectant of when they would be in each other's arms, not waiting for the next moment, but staying in this one, just beside him. She still felt a wavering air alongside her body, but that was the effect he had on her, that was just her liking him. The video he'd recently made was a medley of three of his old songs, but played acoustically with only his voice. They played over a film of a young blond woman blinking at him over a glass of red wine, sitting on his couch, with the dark windows behind her, sipping the wine, then looking down embarrassed, then her staring at a slightly different angle into the camera for a long time with no self-consciousness, the way actors can do, when being directed, confident of their face. Ivy immediately flushed as if thrown on a bonfire and felt queasy, but she stayed on the edge of Ansel's wide chair, feeling his leg against hers move in time with his beating foot. She said she liked the music, loved the songs, and said nothing about the girl. Walking home she debated with herself whether not commenting on the girl had been cowardly or wise. She decided both. But not being straightforward about her feelings widened the gulf between them. If you didn't reveal yourself with a person, he would not know who you were. He never mentioned opening the present she had left him, or if he had ever looked at the book.

Now not taking off clothes was increasing, not lessening, misery.

At Christmas Ivy and Nicky made the drive to Virginia, leaving early in the morning as the light came up on the quiet streets, and swooping up ramps onto salt-streaked highways. The air was warmer where they arrived. Everett had waited for Nicky so they could go together into the woods and cut down a tree and drag it back over the patchy snow. Before dinner, Ivy carried down from the crawl space the lightweight boxes of decorations that sat there unseen all year. She took out of the scrunched tissue paper spangled pine cones and cookie reindeer made by Nicky in happier times. Many decorations were Ivy's, ones she'd bought in antique stores or at tag sales, painted birds and glass bells and red balls with stamped snowflakes, ovals with indented spaces, and many had belonged to Everett's mother, Pamela, the elegant and reserved woman who divorced Everett's father after Everett was grown. Pamela had loved Ivy and welcomed her at first into the family with a warmth at odds with the rest of her, and Ivy often felt that she was mistaking her for someone else. Her illness later had encouraged their move to Dover. In a collapsing white box Ivy even had a few decorations inherited from her parents. Seeing the ornaments each year, she would be hit for a moment with the fascination she'd had for the velour pear, and be back as a child, with her earliest feelings, then the impression vanished. A torpedo icicle was caked with glitter, a cardinal had real feathers, a walnut held a snowman. Seeing the ornaments this year had a new strangeness. She used to take it or leave it, the holiday celebrations. But having Nicky made these rituals important again, and recalled to her the excitement she had felt when she was young. Everett had a place to store the ornaments, so they'd stayed here in his house. Were they hers? Or theirs? Must she care? Anything she'd left here was for Nicky, so he had parts of his mother still in the house where he'd grown up, a house she wasn't a part of anymore. She'd felt she was playing a role, decorating the Christmas tree, but now it was a role she actually wanted to have because now she didn't really have the same claim to it as she did before. The stupid angel twirling inside a glass ball became a little anchor for her, something she could say was hers that actually belonged there on the tree.

Again Ivy stayed in the guest room where not a thing had moved since she'd been there last month—the china dish with the rabbit on it left a circle in the dust when she lifted it off the table, her hair clip still beside the lamp. Clothes of hers hanging in the closet were ones she'd not wanted anymore, but Everett didn't keep track of things like that and hadn't bothered getting her to clear stuff out. On the chest was the same Hudson Bay blanket with the stripe folded on top the way Pamela kept it, but the curtains were ones she put up, light pink linen from a thrift shop in place of Pamela's yellow-and-green chintz ones.

They'd first come to Virginia when Nicky was ten months old, not long after they were married, to visit Everett's mother. She lived in the house where Everett had grown up, horse country, on land which had been the Scott family's for generations. Everett's father had been a horse breeder, dying of cancer when Everett was just a teenager—so he and Ivy had that in common. His longtime stepfather had died eight years earlier, leaving his mother still healthy and active. When they arrived home, Everett was shocked at the state of his mother's health. Having finished the project on the escarpment, Everett discovered he could work at the home office in DC, and, by the following winter, they had moved out of Tanzania and were living in Dover. Once again Ivy felt that the changes were like riding a wave, and with her arms full of Nicky—she'd not been working, their expenses were being shared, they now lived without rent—it was as if her husband were carrying them in a boat, and she would drift wherever he took them, as long as she was with those she loved. Changes made for a kind of adventure; things not planned were challenges for discovery.

In the fall Pamela had a stroke, needed extra medical help. They had a nurse come in every day. For privacy Ivy, Everett and Nicky moved into the guesthouse across a tangled rose garden, and the world shrank down to a plot of green field out the window and Pamela's upstairs bedroom with her small tables crowded with medicine and a circulation of nurses. Ivy attempted to work on some short stories while Nicky napped, but with Everett gone in the day, she was often needed by her mother-in-law. She didn't mind it; she was fond of Pamela. While the idea of moving back to Africa hovered, they were going to stay as long as Pamela needed them. In the spring they went camping a few times in the rolling blue hills and she felt again the freedom of traveling the world. Summer was sultry and they swam in a neighbor's pond. Pamela became more frail; her memory more foggy, she had difficulty speaking. Small strokes, the doctors said mildly, ominously.

In October they found a nearby "home," as it was ironically called, where she could be better looked after. The big house remained empty for a month, till it became clear that Pamela would not be returning and Everett and Ivy and Nicky moved in. Ivy saw afterward that this was the moment Everett threw down an anchor he was not likely to pull up. Everett's putting down roots felt to Ivy strangely as if a trapdoor were opening. Staying in one place was a challenge Ivy had not yet faced. Because this worried her, she took it as a sign that it was something she must face.

Settle. It had an appealing calm meaning, settle in. Settle down. There was the other meaning, too, which was a kind of giving up, giving in. But when you loved a person, you would go to places you would not usually have gone.

Everett visited his mother every other day at her early dinnertime and tried to coax her, thin as a rake in her blue cashmere sweater, to eat from the tray over her chair. She tried to talk, and you could make out a yes or no, but mostly it was sounds and moans, then she would stop, shake her head fed up, her eyes hooded and discerning, with an expression of *Can't be done.* Once a week a hairdresser came and puffed her white hair up in the high coif she had worn all her life. Ivy and Nicky often came along. Watching her grandson move about the railed bedroom made Pamela smile, though the smile looked to be a painful grimace. In fact, it was only when she looked at Nicky balancing on his front toes or patting her knee with his rubbery fingers that her face did not look haunted. In a room with a sick person, things become stilted, thinned down, and no one is happy. Nicky was the one person who could still behave naturally, well behaved and still when placed on his grandmother's wheelchaired lap, as if knowing the importance.

One rainy Sunday in November Everett and Nicky stepped out of Pamela's room to go look at the fish tank in the common room and Ivy stayed. Pamela's bone-thin hand reached out and clutched Ivy's arm, her fingers fixed and intentional. She stared into Ivy's face and made a distressed animal groan from the back of her throat, her mouth open and frozen.

You don't—Ivy suggested, hearing complaint—like it?

Pamela frowned in agreement and shook her head.

No, I see, Ivy said. It must be so frustrating for you.

Vigorous nodding. Then another groan in which Ivy was sure she heard *Help me.*

What can I—? Ivy started.

Stop it, came the words from the back of her throat.

Stop it? Ivy repeated.

Pamela nodded again, her neck thin and straining.

I don't . . . I'm not sure . . . , Ivy stammered. She kept holding Pamela's hand.

Then Everett and Nicky returned, bringing life into the room.

On the car ride home, after Nicky fell asleep Ivy told Everett in quiet tones what his mother had said and wondered if there wasn't something they could do.

Like what? Everett said curtly. You want to kill her?

Pamela lived on this way for another three months—three months too long, in Ivy's mind—and died one frozen evening in February just twenty minutes after Everett had left her on a visit.

By then Everett did not want to leave Dover. It felt familiar being back in his hometown, and Everett liked familiar. Quiet roads ran along fields seamed with fences and occasional lumps of forest. He was in his childhood house; he'd reestablished old allegiances. The work in DC was now part-time which suited him. His taste for wandering the globe was gone. Ivy wondered if he'd ever really had it. He talked about farming himself. If he sold off some land, it could finance revitalizing some of the old farmland. It would be good for Nicky to have roots. Ivy agreed with that, didn't she? She did. Was it what she would have chosen for herself? No, but it was probably right for most people, to have a hometown. She had not felt she had one. She and Everett were a team, and if he wanted to do that, why not? She was flexible. He had already led her to places she would not have gone on her own and here was another place to explore. Staying in one place. That was a challenge. She believed Everett's instincts might be better for raising a child. Roots etc. Because the thought of it was so foreign to Ivy, she saw it as a new challenge, as a new thing she ought to try. She could write wherever she was. Wasn't life for trying all its different ways? Having roots and settling in one spot seemed like the most challenging thing she could do and therefore she accepted it. They would settle.

Everett sold a portion of the land, bought a tractor and volunteered for the local fire department. In a small town one's involvement mattered. Ivy liked that, and appreciated its value in contrast to the anonymity of the city. She appreciated the quiet of rural life, and how at the end of the day after the birdsong abruptly stopped the air turned blue and there was not a sound. The night was dark green velvet. The stillness was in contrast to all the moving she'd done in her twenties and thirties, and sometimes while Nicky was napping she found herself staring out the window at the flattened winter grass or the spidery branches, stunned by the pause. She had been traveling about as if she were in a moving car, passing blurred houses on the side of the road, out the train window, always wondering at the lives inside, and thinking how most people in the world chose to settle. Now she was one of them.

So she settled down, into the life in Dover, where you woke early and went to bed early, where she walked with Nicky through woods and swam in ponds, growing vegetables and cooking not feeling really embedded in it, but she'd never felt truly embedded in a place, had never felt she belonged somewhere, so feeling slightly foreign was a natural feeling.

She attempted to stay in touch with her friends in the city, or in Europe, or Africa, but everyone including herself was settling into a more embedded life, many with children. She spoke on the phone with Margaret, with Irene, with Harriet, but soon the intervals of speaking became longer and longer. She brought Nicky north every few months to the city but each time felt less and less a part of the lives there, which was true. Her life was elsewhere. The friends they had now in Dover came through Everett. His childhood friend Andy brought back a wife from Brooklyn; the Stewarts had never left Dover. She missed Daphne, she missed Tina, but everyone was busy. She discovered that if you were not side by side with a person, in a place, having many of the same day-to-day concerns, you grew apart from them. She learned, too, that not to have a trusted friend was perhaps the greatest hole a person could have in her life.

Ivy felt in the right place when she felt love. And love was certain when it came in three dimensions, holding Nicky in her arms, being held in Everett's. The body was proof. That was as much of proof as she could find.

They got through Christmas Eve doing last-minute shopping and wrapping. Each Christmas Everett worried how he hadn't done any shopping in time and didn't know what to get anyone, then always seemed to appear with excellently selected presents: a red sleigh for Nicky, rugged hiking boots for Ivy. One year he made her an enormous wooden salad bowl, another a new dining room table. Both were still there in the kitchen. On Christmas morning they watched Nicky unwrap his presents. Everett had gotten Ivy a cookbook; she'd bought him a shirt and socks. She knew he hardly ever bought clothes for himself. Their friends Karen and Andy came over in the afternoon with their children and they all walked on the frozen grass blades over the hills, Andy carrying the new baby in a sling against his chest. The children poked sticks into the paper-thin ice formed in field divots and footprints. Again Ivy had the impression which came and went that Karen and Andy didn't know quite where to put her. Karen's smile was just as beaming, but her voice went into the higher octave Ivy knew she used when making an effort. And Ivy noticed Andy's glance slide off her as if she'd become see-through. She thought, There's nothing I can do about it. She had in fact become less substantial.

After their walk Ivy gave them tea and toasted slices of the stollen cake which Karen made every year and gave as gifts. Sitting in the living room where the four of them had sat so often Ivy noticed again how the room was less cluttered without her. It perhaps looked better. She looked at her parents' Christmas decorations on the tree and thought they would always be Everett's now.

The night sky was dark blue and bright.

She went to a tall party at Harriet's, in a tall room with tall people. Many were from London, the girls wearing long belted dresses and the men in jackets. Ivy wore a velvet dress she'd borrowed from Daphne and had pinned at the back. She sat on a low eggshell-blue couch between a couple she'd not known long.

How do you stay so tiny? the wife said.

Heartbreak diet, Ivy laughed.

What's with the man then? the husband said in a kind tone.

He's not there, Ivy said. She avoided the worn-out word *available.*

Married? the wife said.

No, said Ivy.

Other girls? said the husband.

Well, yes. He says he's not good at intimacy.

Oh well, said the husband. Then you're better off letting him go.

I guess, Ivy said. That's what I did.

Don't let his limitation stop you, said the wife.

Ivy's heart leapt. You mean, I should try to keep him close?

No. If he's gone there's nothing you can do, the wife said.

He wasn't always gone, Ivy said.

A girl in crimson satin came over and crouched at the knee of the wife who bent toward her, smiling—possibly, Ivy thought, relieved.

Why do you want to do that to yourself? the husband said, staying sunk back beside Ivy. Why do you want a man who doesn't want you?

I liked how it felt, she said.

That's just sex, he said. You can find that around any bend.

You can?

Sure. You're just not open to it.

It's as if I couldn't believe the stove was hot, so I kept touching it to make sure . . . , she trailed off.

You're better than that, he said.

Ivy shrank inside. She appreciated his kindness, but thought, He doesn't know. He doesn't know that I'm not better than that. She tried to lift it to a philosophical level.

She said, Why can't I just take him as he comes and be glad when I see him and ask for nothing else?

That's not love, said the man.

Maybe it's the biggest love there is.

Do you want a man who doesn't care?

He cares, Ivy said. Somewhere.

Sweetheart, the man said, he may say he cares but where is he now?

No, Ivy said. He doesn't say he cares.

You take your good love, the man said, his voice quiet in the loud party room, and you leave this man behind and keep it to yourself until you find someone who will know how to give it back. Listen to me. I know.

He spoke without insistence, which made it more convincing.

She thanked him for being so nice.

No one was telling her, Keep trying. No one was saying, Be patient with him. No one was saying, like the song did, Be prepared to bleed.

In January on a Saturday night with Nicky at a sleepover, Ivy had dinner with Bruno at a Thai restaurant in the East Village. He'd just returned from Rio and looked tan. Let's order a lot of dishes, he said.

They talked about art shows they'd seen and why Bruno never liked a certain painter everyone loved and what Brazil was like. She asked him about the architect love affair and Bruno talked about how it was going weirdly well.

He asked, How's the crack habit?

Ivy told him she'd gone cold turkey. Bruno was not one of her friends who tried to solve problems or gave her suggestions about how to live her life, so she was able to admit that it was making her miserable. He then asked her to describe what had happened and who the guy was and as Ivy talked about Ansel she felt a buzz in her limbs.

Ah, Bruno said, not a nester. A flame in a small clear jar threw footlight shadows on their faces and on Bruno's dark sweater which had holes showing the white shirt underneath.

No, Ivy said. Even though he spends a lot of time in his own nest. Doesn't go out in the day . . .

Prison habit? Bruno said.

The plates on the table had last bits left on them, a thick-lipped platter with flat noodles of pad Thai, a black bowl piled with green edamame pods looking like tiny deflated balloons.

I'm still stuck on him, she said.

Wait, what's stopping you again? Bruno said.

I'm old?

Bruno stared at her dully, refusing this. It doesn't sound, Bruno said, as if he cares about that.

Ivy laughed. Because he doesn't know any better. He isn't the one in danger, she said. The older person in this situation is always the one more in trouble.

Bruno pinched his lips, showing he was thinking. Not with me and Roger, he said, beaming. Roger's the one in danger.

I wish I could be you, Ivy said.

It's pretty fun being me, he said and stretched out his arms, yawning.

Listen, if it's making you more miserable not to see him, Bruno said matter-of-factly, then see him. That's what I'd do.

After having two glasses of not-very-good wine, Ivy saw how reasonable this was. If both choices gave her varying degrees of misery, why not choose the one that at least had moments of pleasure alongside it? The logic of this was so solid, she marveled she'd not come to it before.

So, what, I could just go see him? she asked wondrously. Now? She looked at Bruno for permission.

As long as you know that you're licking honey from the razor blade, he said.

Ivy picked up her phone.

She attempted a sort of preparation on the way over in the cab, her head flung back on the scuffed seat, the lights of the city streaming in one flickering river. But how much did it matter really? Was he in town? she'd asked. He was! It was so simple . . .

Look at how close he was. She texted *I want to ask you something,* wanting to have a reason to appear. What did she want to say? The wine had given the courage not to worry about it, the courage to be going to him at all.

She was back, in the now-usual spot on his couch, turned toward him, the wide black windows icily behind her. Now that he was before her in three dimensions, in the dark sweatpants, in a long-sleeved T-shirt, she simply wanted to look at him, she no longer felt the need to ask him anything. She also wanted to touch him. But the memory of the hours she'd juggled on her own so many questions about him insisted she say something. She would make it offhand and uninsistent. She made herself speak. She'd been wondering. Often wondered. What did he think of this? That is, of them. Of her.

The question did not faze him and he answered immediately.

I like you, he said. I like fucking you. But I don't need it.

The simplicity of it was stunning. She felt as if a sword had sliced down her torso so smoothly that both sides remained seemingly connected.

Well, that was said clearly. Ansel Fleming and the thwacking power of his straightforward statements. He was not trying to say the right thing, or the thing to let her down easy. Even as it hurt, she still admired it. He said he knew it wasn't fair to her, but that's what he was offering. She said that she just wanted to know and that described it. She said how she was reluctant to say certain things or reluctant to know certain things and that she probably could represent herself better and be better at communication and felt as she spoke her abstractions become thinner and thinner like smoke disappearing upward. He said he wasn't very good at those things either.

She knew this was a bad idea. She ought to be home. But she couldn't move. The white rug and the counter and the couch where she sat were weighted with magnets. Thoughts seemed so deep in her, like birds diving into steep valleys, and the indecision was itself hypnotic.

He picked up a camera from the table. Can I? he said.

What?

Take your picture.

Okay, she said, still feeling stunned—by what he'd said, by being here. As always happened when a camera lens faced her, she felt her face tighten. Why did that happen? Self-consciousness, yes, but what was that? Was it having your thoughts turn objective, because you were thinking of another's gaze, of another's perspective.

He was clicking the shutter.

What should I do? she said.

He stood up and clicked from a different position. Nothing, he said. You're good. This is good.

I feel embarrassed, she said.

He pretended he didn't hear—one way to handle embarrassment—and kept snapping.

Then he looked around. Come stand over here.

She liked him telling her what to do. She liked obeying.

In a parking garage, when you leave you pay your ticket and the mechanical arm lifts to allow you out. At the same time, behind you on the ground rises a low line of sharp spikes to deter you from reversing back into the garage. If you backed up, your tires would be punctured by the spikes.

Stay there, he said and positioned her against the white wall of the bedroom. She felt foolish, as she always did in a cliché, and knew the wine was dulling her embarrassment.

This is me communicating, he said after a while, clicking the shutter. He said, I wish you could see what I see.

Soon he was kneeling and unzipping her fly. She put her hand on his shoulder, and watched it as if unattached to her. Was the hand going to push him away or keep him there? She was leaving it to fate. His studied manner made her want to laugh, then his fingers found her and the sensation flooding her stopped those thoughts.

In a very short time they were in bed.

A time would come when his radiance would not be the most alive thing inside her, she knew that. The coals would no longer be a secret warming her. No, eventually they would crack off, burn a hole through the floor.

But now, beauty.

The world looked beautiful again.

5

The Snow Arguments

'Twas my one Glory—
Let it be
Remembered
I was owned of Thee—

—EMILY DICKINSON

She was returned to herself. She had not let herself down; she was victorious.

She simply wasn't done with it, with the beautiful fact of him.

It was now clear that all the reasoning and arguments she had with herself were not going to decide this. Time was the only thing that would bring this to its conclusion. However far or near that was. Not much else was clear.

At work she could now concentrate.

She organized her files, thumbed through the draft of the long-simmering work. Her eye flew swiftly over the pages, saving these, crossing out those. Crossing out so much! Now it was clear what worked, what didn't. No mulling was needed. Her mind was as sharp as a child's. She imagined a difficult march through rough country. She wrote about a murder at a roadblock, and rewrote it and rewrote it. She picked up two assignments, one reviewing Japanese short stories, one an article about an undiscovered female photographer who worked as a nanny on the Upper East Side in the 1950s.

Why be strict with herself? Throw yourself into life, she thought. Interact with another adult human being. Be alive. He thrilled her; let herself be thrilled! On her deathbed she would never regret him. She would regret if she stopped it. When she had, she'd felt the machine of herself stop humming. When it had just started to hum. Yes, her life as a mother needed to be careful, but other parts didn't. Experience required abandon and risk and was past logic.

She would manage it, somehow. She would take in the good parts; that's how she'd manage it. She'd take in the beautiful afternoons when they came and bask in them when he disappeared. She'd accept his elusiveness as being integral to what made him compelling.

Steel yourself not to care, Bruno said. She would not care too much.

In the days after she saw him, his face would sit on the inside of her skull, and she would find herself looking at the world imagining how he was seeing it. Trees, for instance. They were something she'd always liked, but now with his extra perspective of them trees were more fascinating than ever. The enormous trunks, the rings of wood inside, all from a tiny seed, and the way branches spread in a perfect but unplanned design, with each unique leaf perfectly placed yet random, dropping off in the fall etc. etc. The miracle of trees. They had never spoken of trees, but somehow Ansel had given her increased amazement about trees.

She continued with dinner preparations, measuring water for rice, cutting broccoli into thin trees. Often, chopping broccoli, she thought of live oaks with their thick trunks and ruffled leaves.

This would make her think of Audubon Park in New Orleans where she'd gone when Daphne had an art show there thirty years before and she'd swiftly remember the canopy of oaks over St. Charles Ave and a party they'd gone to in a white house with sparkly entrance windows and high creamy ceilings and a balmy garden in back with yellow lights behind large black leaves and men in pale suits, drinking and drawling, ties loosened. There'd been a man named Boyce, someone Amy's brother had gone to school with, and Ivy got a crush. One night she was close against Boyce in the back of a crowded car spiriting off somewhere and she waited for him to kiss her, but nothing had happened—there may have been a girlfriend—and now Boyce would cross her mind this way thirty years later when she chopped broccoli because of the live oaks in New Orleans.

Behind her in the living room she could hear the looping sounds of Nicky's cartoon, then a jagged villain laugh, then more looping sounds. Every now and then Nicky would laugh himself, giving Ivy an outsize lift of joy. If he was laughing, how bad could watching be? Everyone warned too much watching was not only bad for the children but harmful.

Voices near her on the radio reported on states passing same-sex marriage laws. Then an assessment of Obama's State of the Union speech. At least there was some happy news, she thought. For the moment.

To an outside eye, she appeared the same. She sat at a dinner, hair untidy but clean, wearing her black shirt with narrow arms, worn boots, dark jeans. The easy uniform. She observed people with genuine interest, laughed with gratitude at jokes, passed the pasta bowl, helped clear the handmade dishes, while the ticker tape running along the floor of her head, or strangely across her lungs, was keeping track of Ansel Fleming and the vibrations between them, or not. She looked past whatever green candles were lit on the candlesticks to when she'd see him next.

. . .

Are you in the city?

I am.

See me sometime?

You bet.

Then, eighteen hours later. Or three days. Or nine . . .

She wondered how many people around the table, or standing in line for coffee the next day, or coat flapping past her on the sidewalk, had, like her, a secret they carried, warming them.

Ivy knew how to appear as if she were part of the world, even when she felt an eerie lack in common with those around her. But everyone felt that, right? She was aware she'd dragged her feet in tending to "adult" concerns. She stared a little longer at things, to puzzle out how it all worked. Why was it wrong to be rude? Why was it inappropriate to talk about one's sex life? Sometimes she saw herself sitting at a firepit in the rainforest studying a foreign tribe. Her need for society wavered. Much more strongly occupying her was a low-level burn like coals buried in ash, waiting to be stirred. She hid it mostly, the shame of wanting her life to be otherwise. Ansel seemed to exist in that other life, where the less talk there was, the more appealing. She didn't tell him what she wanted, not sure anymore what that was. She knew only she was drawn to him as a shivering person to heat.

One night he arrived late. Why do you ask me over if your son is here? he said.

Later his hand was over her mouth, him murmuring, Let it go. Soon he was coming by when Nicky was there, but only late at night, when he was asleep.

Each time she noted new things about him, to keep for review. The thrust of his fist entering a sleeve, his straight back when he picked something off a low table, squatting, his low voice in a guffaw. After she'd seen him, a wand passed over the day making her more interested in life, in herself. She thought of his leg thrown over hers, of his round shoulders and heavy arms. She went over the things he said. I'm such an idiot, she said once. You are the furthest thing from an idiot, he replied flatly. She thought of his lidded look which seemed to say, I have some things I might share with you or not. You won't know till you're on your back.

. . .

She liked simply thinking of him. It took up the slack hours. Also the hours she should have been working.

She knew she was idealizing him, but there it was. She felt he had things lined up right and when he was nearby, whether on the other side of the room or lying beside her touching, she felt close to those things, things which mattered to her, things hard to grasp out in the world, and staying around him she was able to keep the sense of those things in mind and have all the crap clinging to her fall away. For some reason it was hard for her to keep those things always in mind on her own.

His attitude seemed to be, I'm in no hurry. I might go there. I might decide to check that out. And whatever he decided would be alluring.

Yes, it was idealizing. The waterfall of him, the eddies before, the eddies after. Her ear on his chest, receiving messages from this new world of his.

She recognized her fascination with him was romantic, that it was based on little more than instinct, on desire, on something undeveloped in herself. It was strange though how she couldn't exactly describe it when it felt as real as a stone in her hand.

A night alone in the apartment changed from that of a pause in having to look after a child to one with possibilities. The phone stayed within reach. On the sink edge while she bathed. On the bureau while she dressed where there was space in the hallway, on the bedside table at night.

The yellow lamp threw smoky curves up the walls. The bed took up the room's floor space, so the high ceiling was like a dome. She picked up her book. She kept reading the page. After a few attempts the river of the words took her along and at least part of her brain was taken up with the story of a boy on the diving board, the girl who had to measure her marriageability, or the family trying to get to a lighthouse, and she was lifted into another place. When she looked up back to real life she found herself in a new state of expectation. Somewhere out there was a dazzling new person who might let her know when he was finished with work.

She touched the phone screen, it lit, no new messages.

Prepare yourself for no arrival, she repeated to herself. Prepare yourself for nothing.

She went back to her book. After some time the phone shivered.

I am done. Shall I come over?

Her pleasure unfurled up the yellow walls. But one should hide it.

How would one even be able to show it?

Yes. Yes!

On my way.

She did not meet him at the door. She thought, I will be simply as I am when he comes in. But she was not *simply* anything. She was as lit up as the yellow lampshade.

He came down the dark hall and appeared in the bedroom doorway in an overcoat.

I don't know what we're doing here, she said in a happy tone as he took his coat off.

I do, he said, moving onto her.

Later, with both of them trying to catch their breath, his body was collapsed on hers. Without planning to say it, it just came out. I love you, she said. She said it panting into his cheek. Ansel Fleming did not move. She was not sure he'd heard. It seemed to hover above them suspended and she couldn't leave it there; she was embarrassed. She pulled it down with a comical tone, That's why I'm here, she said, and pretended it hadn't happened.

One afternoon, swept under the dark wave of writing, she glanced up at the clock. Two-fifty. Pickup was five minutes ago. She ran.

One often saw mothers running. After a toddler heading off the sidewalk. Late for school pickup. Or they were jogging at dawn or dusk on the street, headed for the river, holding on to sanity. Ivy wondered if they were still adjusting as she was to the time warp of motherhood, to how time shrank here, expanded there.

She ran through the blue doors still open, up the empty stairwell to the second floor where children were brought to the administrative offices if they had not been picked up. She had not been late because of forgetfulness before, but remembered this from the early days of orientation. Opening the heavy swinging door, she saw Nicky across the hall in the first doorway, sitting in one of the five chairs against the wall, banging his heels on the metal legs. He caught sight of his mother, and kept his head in profile, not sure if he was glad to see her or forlorn at being forgotten. Ivy came in breathless, brightly apologizing. The office was crowded with desks all piled with papers and wire baskets and folders about to slide off, and perhaps because the people in there were women, the chaos felt inviting. Behind the first desk sat a secretary named Marlene in front of a giant beige computer which she tapped at with blue and green nails. Ivy thanked Marlene and also apologized. Ignoring her, Marlene said, Nick and I have been having a nice chat, haven't we?

Nicky nodded, but he was regarding his mother with interest, as if he'd just seen new information about her of which he ought to take note.

The song she listened to most was the one he'd played for her that first night, the one he sang walking by the river and on the New York streets in the video. She watched again the video, examining his face, examining the eyes, and did not see anything of the night before with her in them.

Large then small parts of herself swung in and out of focus. In him was a life she had but did not know. She was in it, both unrecognizable and more real than ever.

The blizzard in her head made it impossible to work.

. . .

The vibration which came when she heard his voice; it struck her in the chest, toward the back of her spine, then spread across her shoulder blades like wings opening. After seeing him her body felt it had just emerged from a seaside storm, or thrashed through weeds in a bog—her senses alive and challenged and vibrating.

Always the vibration . . .

The world was suddenly saturated with sex. She walked by the window of a lingerie store. The perfect coned breasts of mannequins with red lace bras, a black garter strapped a thigh, dotted stockings covered a leg kicking up out of the platform. Ivy was amazed at the people walking breezily by, unaffected by the sex dripping in the window while she was all trembling wires.

Her body was too receptive, outsize, as if she were a giant walking over a diorama of the city, too big to fit anywhere. She wished she had another layer of skin to cushion her from the vibrations. She read about sexual assault in the newspaper and felt a sick thrill at the sex part of it, horrifying herself. She was losing her mind.

Washing the evening dishes with rain falling and Nicky home all day sick, she reminded herself, You have no more important job than your duty as a mother. Other days she would think the most important job was as a citizen. Then, it was the job you had chosen for yourself, as an artist, being the work only you could do. Work is the thing, Hemingway said, the only thing that counts.

She read a book about death row, a world so far from hers, which made knowing it seem all the more important. Feeling powerless was one kind of surrender which did not appeal to her, even if in the grip of obsession she wanted to vanish. How could she justify that as living a good life?

After the holidays returning to the city, she signed up with a group that visited prisoners, people who might not have anyone visiting them. In this case, it was the Women's Correctional Jail in Brooklyn. When it came time to pick a scheduled day—Sunday morning, any afternoon—she realized there was not guaranteed cover for Nicky and on the weekends she needed to be with him and had to bow out.

Afternoons were the times she went to Ansel's. Usually she had to be gone by two-thirty, but one day Nicky was being picked up with Oscar, so she could stay to see the light draining from his rooms, and see in the building across the street the windows light up yellow as the air turned blue.

They never spoke of their both having lived with relatives not their parents, but it was something which made Ivy feel closer to him, even if he remained an enigma, at a distance even when she was clutched in his arms.

When she closed his door, her last view of him was an arm bent, putting in earbuds turning to his computer screen. It gave her a sinking feeling, with him turned away, the dusk gathering behind him; he was going into his evening on his own.

She rode her bike home alongside sidewalks talced with salt. Her wheels thumped in the ragged potholes.

In her small lobby she walked past Hector sitting at the wooden desk, below the grid of wooden cubbies, and saw nothing in her box. Afternoon, Hector, she said, and realized she always said this with the same tone and in the same way. Hector said, Hello, in the singsong friendly way he always did.

Up she went on the softened marble stairs, and rounded the glassed-in ironwork of the elevator to her landing. In the center of her door was a metal art deco eyehole, something Nicky liked to look through from inside, lifted up so he could surprise a visitor with his glinting eye.

She entered the narrow hall and switched on the light. After two steps the hallway split into a T shape, left to the back, right to the front. Straight ahead was the small mirror above the shelf where the keys were left, plus sunglasses, and gloves, a picture of Nicky cradling a chicken. Her face looked back at her. After fifty years you'd think one would be used to one's face, but no. You were never sure how pale or how scattered or how fleeting you looked. And now there was the extra version of looking old, a new development.

Usually after seeing Ansel, she'd come away feeling improved. His face would be superimposed over hers, lighting it up, while hers looked happily pummeled. But today her face looked only messed with, and his face wasn't there. Her reflection was a slap, the end of the unsettled bike ride home, of each heavy step up the stairs. *I like it but I don't need it.*

What though but keep on? She'd tried once stopping and that had been worse. It would last as long as it had to. Eventually it would alter. It would—what?—have the cold water of reality smack her to her senses.

The weekend was a series of hurdles with Nicky: making lunch he didn't want, drizzle in the park, a meltdown in the aisle of the corner bodega. She felt the knife of motherhood stabbing her hand to the table.

She dreamed she ran into a poet friend she'd not seen in years. They were at a crosswalk and the poet languidly ignored the traffic signals. What I'm really interested to read, she said in the thoughtful way she had, is this new collection *The Snow Arguments.*

She had managed to buy her apartment with a publisher's advance, after the success of her first book. You're on your way, said the seasoned editor with his rimless glasses and nicotine breath. She was single then with few expenses. The purchase of the apartment with its crumbling plaster and shadowy interior had been nerve-racking, with the mortgage agreements, and lawyers and contracts, all things she had never wanted to be a part of and only half trusted. Yet the purchase gave her, for the first time, a base of her own, and she no longer had to rely on the cloud hopping from one empty apartment or sublet to house-sitting for a friend of a friend. Having her own place did not encourage her to make any further plan for her future; she would just go as she had, always writing, juggling jobs, spending little, making money intermittently. She took travel assignments abroad to Barcelona, to Umbria. She rafted down a river in Idaho, climbed the Needles in South Dakota and hiked in New Mexico. Then came the stories in Africa, where she'd become particularly transfixed, going to Zanzibar, to Lesotho, to Kenya, which led to the work on the film in Tanzania where she met Everett.

With Everett sharing her life, costs overlapped and the burden of finances was slightly lifted. It was never discussed, but naturally understood, that each would carry him- or herself and this was straightforward till Nicky came along, and expenses increased, but that was to be expected and not a surprise if perhaps more layered. But when she and Everett split, finances were thoroughly altered. She had Nicky, her time had evaporated, and the cost of living which she had managed by cobbling together as needed, now increased with her seeming to have less say in the matter.

She had met these fluctuations by addressing each change as it came; she would similarly manage matters with Ansel Fleming.

It was late, the visit was brief. He was headed to LA. Candles in the dark living room, the pocket doors closed, she straddled him on the couch. For the first time in their few months of knowing each other she did not feel gratified after he'd left.

. . .

Puzzlement persisted. The fluctuations went between certainty and perplexity. Why had this person become so quickly crucial to her? Was it only the sensation of sex? The last gasp of eroticism? Was it because he took her to the other end of the spectrum from Mother? Was it his youth mesmerizing her? His coolness? His having paid a price? His music? His mouth? Why did she want to disappear into him? To vanish from herself. Was this only ridiculous lust, relieving her from everyday tedium? Was he the last offering? The last chance? Or had she actually become more herself than ever before?

Up to this point she had always waited, waited for the man to approach. She seemed to require that he look at her in a certain way and indicate desire and that would ignite something in her. She waited for that to happen, even when she liked someone, she would wait for the move. She loitered in the shadow of the wide shoulders and the maleness, waiting. Or you might, as someone had described it, put yourself in their line of vision. Come interest me, come try.

But now there was a new electricity driving her, she was not waiting to react. That is, she wanted to instigate it, she didn't need the warm-up. It was hard not to recognize this as an advancement sexually.

Her instinct tells her he's back in town; the dark tunnel opens.

Will she try to find him? No, she'll hold out. She'll work. Plus she was the one who had made first contact the last time and she lived in mortal fear of it not being balanced, and of appearing to chase him.

But maybe her instinct was wrong.

. . .

Most ruminations eventually concluded that life was too short and she would, after restraint, text. Half the time, no answer. But sometimes she got it again, the joy of the ellipsis dots blinking . . . it was the needle in the vein.

Hello, it would say. He was busy now, but is she around later?

Yes, she replies. *Anytime.*

The radiance, as if radioactive, lasted for shorter and shorter spells.

Soon she is poring more over the ways he troubles her than over his charms. Why doesn't he want to spend more time with her? Well, that's obvious; he's young and free, with life to catch up on.

She sees the parts of herself he is right to avoid. But that was another good thing about Ansel Fleming; he was not looking too closely.

The periods of absence become more acutely felt. Ha, she thinks ruefully, he was hardly ever here in the first place. It becomes more difficult to think only of the good parts. Absence tilts her. Too long away and the certainty of what has passed between them fades. She picks at her puzzlements like thorns on her sleeve.

The obsessed brain does not tire of rumination.

Ivy's friends were now lit depending on their view of Ansel. Maira's light was the brightest, with her magical proximity to Ansel. Others had a cooler cast. At lunch, the girls who'd once cheered his appearance, now pronounced him an asshole.

Music had a powerful new dimension. Songs sliced through her like wire. Music playing in a shop as she entered chopped her at the knees.

Music always conjured up old feelings, ambushing you as you put the silverware away, or in an audience chair, or snapping the light switches, filling you with an old feeling of love. And you might think, Enough love has come to me; then in the next moment you want more. Music now bombarded her, blasting the message: Here is the important Thing, you have till now missed it, this saturated vitality, the intensity of life. You have perhaps ignored it with knee-jerk expectations, with your packing of conventional boxes, which you believe will keep you from being left out and ignored. But, music said, if you come *here*—difficult to say exactly where here was, a sort of outer-limits place—this is where the real stuff of life is happening.

So it was going to be a roller coaster.

She couldn't call it a relationship, she could barely call it an affair. It was a thing. Okay so it was an unreal thing.

It was like tending an opium crop on your back terrace, and you had to make sure your guests didn't look out there. So you invited fewer guests over. She believed that age had led her to this understanding, that her erotic life needed to be apart to flourish.

Protecting this unreal thing was a far more interesting activity than many more mundane things she might have been tending to. Health insurance, the credit card bill—she could barely look in their direction, like not wanting to see the blood of an accident. The dread of the restaurant bill and the toss-up between the shelling out of cash she couldn't really spare and the mortification of letting kind friends pay for her, both infantilizing, as was the acceptance of this being how it was. But these dilemmas became less oppressive when she gave her attention to the unreal thing whose fabulousness was ever bountiful. She gathered evidence in poetry to support the unreal thing. Rumi was especially good. *Gamble everything for love, if you are a true human being.*

She observed people trying to improve themselves and felt

she'd tried with the standard elements but was suspect about where that road led or if that was the road she wanted to be on. The strange road pulled her to extreme feeling and to places of beauty, even if it was unreal.

To the emotionally underfed, the motto is *I can manage*. She was, she told herself, hurting no one.

Each night a moment of reprieve, the peace of getting into bed. She pulled back the blue flowers at the sheet's edge below the white pillow, yellow lamplight casting shallow dents in the wall plaster, wearing her black slip, her legs sliding between the sheets. All of it wished for him. She reached for her book and saw his hand with its sturdy smooth nails. She looked at the words on the page, but saw him, bent over his keyboard, writing a song. Then she saw someone behind on the couch, someone holding a glass of red wine—the blonde with glittering eyes.

She woke in the darkness. It hovered there.

The Thing. Like a pillar in the corner, or a tree's shadow on a wall. Doors opened in an empty room to the Thing. The Thing was a sort of see-through movie with the days passing normally and this movie playing over them. The Thing was down the hallway, waiting. It hovered at the windowpanes, throaty as a hummingbird. A car drove by and she sensed the Thing inside, watching her.

Was it love? Well.

I think we all want to disappear from ourselves, says the rock star with stiff white shirt cuffs and swept black hair. This happens in song. You become someone else and get away from the shit that is you.

. . .

Mostly they met in the dark.

The first dinner in Brooklyn became a dream.

She spent far more time with him in her mind than she ever did with himself.

He did not see what had happened to her. In candlelight, his face stony with sex as she lifted her slip, she watched his face watching hers in the pleasure of lowering herself onto him. No, he had no idea. Later, buckling his belt and finding his boots under the low heavy table, he would leave, as if what he'd gotten were something normal.

Sometimes departures were like having the tips of her fingers sliced.

Or she'd feel she'd run through a tangle of bushes and trees, feathered by leaves, ripped with thorns, left scratched but ravaged and invigorated—part of the natural world, pooled on the sofa in a lozenge light, liquid as runoff, done for.

The day after was not unlike being at a fairground in the bright daylight after being there the night before with its moving colored lights and piped music and fried dough in the air. Now you saw the wire skeleton of the Ferris wheel, the trampled yellow grass and the flimsiness of the shooting booths.

Take it as it comes, she would repeat to herself, like a mantra.

If he kisses your hair, don't wonder why.

Initially, she talked about Ansel and her situation with her friends. She said, Still no word from him.

No, Irene said. But you knew that.

I did?

It sounds as if he was pretty clear about that, Irene said.

Yes, Ivy said, painful as it was to say. Yes, he was.

Years later, Ivy would flush with shame at the amount of time she had spent trying the patience of her friends, wanting them to reflect her hope rather than describing reality. Soon she stopped discussing it.

On the walk home from school there were two puppy stores waiting like unexploded mines. Both were closed in the morning on the way to school, but open on the way home. One was a quaint independent establishment with a thick wisteria vine wrapped up its iron entrance and the other generic and sharp edged, part of a chain, with bright lights and inside a grid of cages with animals pressed back into corners, with all the elements associated with animal trafficking—an ammonia and urine smell, unhappy dog expressions and signs of malnutrition. People argued that purchasing animals from the chain only perpetuated the horrific animal factory. Nicky, actually understanding the charge, argued that if you bought there, at least you were saving a puppy.

The stores were a block away from each other, on opposite sides of the street, so it was possible to avoid at least one of them. One might even pass the glass windows to find no puppies on display tumbling over each other in shredded paper, or sleeping blissfully in a mound of fur. But more often the puppy eyes were open and looking out much interested at a child's eye level. One often saw children in a standoff with another parent outside the puppy store, the child often in tears. Why can't we? you would hear the outraged cry.

I'll look after it! a six-year-old boy might scream, replying to his mother's murmur. It was the valley of tears outside the pet shop.

Mum, Nicky might say sweetly as they approached, knowing that gentleness helped him get his way. Can we look? Please.

They would stop.

One afternoon staring in the window, Nicky announced, It's always been my *dream* to have a puppy. Ivy knew that *Follow your dream* was a phrase sprinkled through many of the cartoons and movies he watched.

He looked up at his mother with especially mournful eyes, which then flared open in shock.

What are you smiling at? he cried. This isn't funny!

Ivy told him she didn't think it was funny. Not at all. She was smiling because she knew how much he wanted an animal. But, she told him as she had often told him, they could not have a dog. She could not look after a dog.

But today his face crumbled with the truth of it and tears began to fall. She saw that he was accepting the decision and was weeping not in order to get his way, but because of genuine disappointment. He was not arguing with her. He turned to walk bravely on. His forbearance made her suddenly so sympathetic to him that she spoke without thinking. Maybe though, she said, they could get a cat.

He glanced at her, stunned. We could? he said with a stuttering breath.

His eyes shone with hope and desperation and she saw in them all the loneliness she worried he suffered. Being up close to animals had been important to Ivy when she was young—meeting dogs at other people's houses, or patting the velvet nose of a horse above a fence was mesmerizing, and when she got a cat to look after, something alive that was hers alone, it had been like a miracle. She slept with its dark fur draped across her neck each night and even the terrible case of poison ivy which ravaged her chin did not diminish her love for Petal. Ivy immediately realized that there were certain sentences one could not utter to a little boy without consequences and this was one of them.

That weekend they traveled uptown to where Ivy had located an animal shelter on the East River. The shelter was many long empty blocks away from the nearest subway stop and Nicky walked the long blocks uncomplaining. Inside the sandy building on the entrance floor was a woman with a spray of frizzled dark hair at the desk. They told her they were interested in kittens. She stood slowly and led them nearby to four cages. The room was carpeted and grey and soothing. Nicky looked at the cats on their long thin legs with their narrow ribs. They were a few months old, and technically kittens, but not the round balls of fluff Nicky naturally had in mind.

Did they have any ones younger?

Only some newborns, said the woman blinking as if waking from a dream. They're too young to be in cages, so we have them down in the office. Would you like to see them?

Ivy and Nicky followed her down a narrow staircase to a room with a square desk at each corner and a lot of colorful folders.

Miss Nadine has been looking after them, the woman said and indicated a desk where a foldout iron cage curved around a chair on rollers. On the floor was a pink blanket and two black earmuffs. Nicky stared, speechless.

The woman leaned down and picked up one black muff. In the black fur foggy blue eyes opened. They had been brought in a week ago by a homeless man, she said, right after being born. They'd named them Genevieve and Lancelot. Of course, the woman said, we feel littermates ought to stay together. Do you want to hold him? she asked Nicky. Nicky looked amazed. This was too good to be true. He held out his hands in a cup, accepted the kitten and drew it in under his chin.

Oh boy, said Ivy. The woman reached down and like a giant swooped up the littermate and offered it matter-of-factly in Ivy's direction. Ivy took the kitten; it was light as an egg.

Nicky faced her, holding the ball of fluff with pale eyes next to his cheek. Mumma, he said, see the resemblance?

They kept the name Lance, and Nicky named the female Air. At home Ivy cordoned off an area with plastic bin tops, so the kittens wouldn't vanish in the crannies under piles or disappear in the no-man's-land under the Balinese bed, the apartment's main storage area. That first week Ivy went to bed with added worry. Nicky paid attention to them as a child would, that is, intermittently. The longer the cats were there and the bigger they grew, the less surprising they were to him, and the more Ivy became fascinated and attached.

He set two green bottles on the counter.

I heard you were looking at apartments, she said. In the two months since her birthday she'd resolved not to mention this to him.

He froze in the position of opening a bottle top. How did that come up? he said curtly.

Ivy flushed, wishing back the resolve.

My friend Harriet lives in the building, she sputtered, not sure why this was wrong. And she knows the real estate agent.

That means you were talking about me, Ansel said.

Ivy remained frozen on the couch.

Well, yes . . . , surmising it might make him feel spied upon. Why couldn't she shut up?

He cracked the bottles open and carried them to the couch. He handed one to her, staying sideways.

Was that—she paused—bad?

He sat down, elbows on his knees. He took a long swig from his bottle. He kept not looking at her. Finally he said, I don't like being talked about.

Ivy waited a moment. This was something to respect.

Then she said, I'm sorry. A small note in her tone indicated that she'd not been aware it was wrong. Though this maybe was not altogether true. If she had thought about it for a moment she would have surmised this for Ansel Fleming would be an invasion of privacy.

Do you . . . , Ivy began, searching for where to go with this. Do you want me to keep you a secret?

I can't control what you do or say, Ansel said. But I don't like being talked about. I don't talk about other people and I don't want to be talked about myself.

Okay, Ivy said.

I don't know what you say about me, he went on, but I don't

say anything about you. It's no one's business. I don't like that, people talking about each other. I can't control it, but the other night Matt comes back and he asks what's the story with Ivy? What's it to him? Why should I say anything?

Matt Morgan was a musician friend of Ansel's and Ivy suppressed a thrill that he might have heard anything about her.

You shouldn't if you don't want to, Ivy muttered.

I don't, he said. I don't talk about myself a lot. I do in interviews maybe. That's it.

Ivy nodded, studying the top of her bottle.

There was a lot of talking about people. Probably too much. Did one actually feel better after minding other people's business? One would feel better if it was true about the treachery of the human heart—who made up that phrase?—the phrase describing the feeling of relief when we feel we are above people . . . she thought of Rumi. Speech is a river. Silence is an ocean. Once again Ansel Fleming took the higher ground. She wanted to be like him, not needing to relieve her heart by speaking of others. She wanted to be better, as he was. So she asked nothing more about looking at the apartment or about the blonde who was with him.

Later in his arms she was relieved they felt as welcoming as ever, but she sensed the partition which he must have pulled up in him, blocking her full view. This was part of getting to know a person, you hit new edges, you hurt the person. The disturbance smashed her contentment of moments before. She was right to have been reluctant to speak. She didn't want to keep making mistakes, she'd just shut up. Afterward she thought of how he never really answered her question about the apartment, but that's how it was.

The morning winter sun was low on the fast train to Boston. She sat on the eastern side watching the light flicker through thin leafless trees on her way to a university to speak with a writing class. After the three-hour visit she would take the evening train back. Leaving Nicky and the city made her uneasy, though she knew he was safe with Oscar and Padma. Having to patch in helpers to look after him reminded her that she had no one she could automatically rely on to take over. She'd not taken a teaching job for that reason—to be unavailable even for three hours a week was a risk. What if the sitter canceled, as often happened, and Ivy was unable to get one of the dozen or so sitters she had in rotation? But debt was mounting. A job was necessary.

Nearest the train she looked down to a blur of grey, above it to chunks of rock and rubble. Every now and then the woods stopped and a sparkling ocean opened beyond tawny marshes. The sun on the silver-platter surface sent its rays into her and she thought of him—standing in the doorway, bending to step into his pants. The beauty of the landscape streaming past seemed to match her feelings for him. The sea was more glittering than ever. She felt euphoric, zooming along, having nothing to tend to in the moment but this rapture. How can this be bad, she thinks, if such feelings come from it?

She walked down the aisle, swaying, to the uncrowded café car with its wide windows flashing onto leaf-strewn forest floors, panning the backs of houses streaming by, with the quiet talking of men on stools and the floor vibrating through her feet as she ordered a coffee, with the miraculous invention of the thundering wheels, feeling it all belonged to him.

Friday nights were the worst, with the road tipping up and widening to the weekend. Or midnights were the worst, any midnight, reflecting black windows. Or 3:00 A.M., waking with something stabbing her upper lung. Though a Tuesday afternoon could be the worst, when she'd not spoken to anyone all day, and the net which connected her to others and to the world seemed to dissolve.

Sunday mornings were a version of the worst, the sidewalks frozen planks beneath leafless winter trees.

She'd put Nicky in front of a screen—or he'd put himself

there—and she'd read the paper beside him. There was the column about what New York people did on Sundays—couples working out together, families always going to *their favorite brunch place, browsing* antique markets, frequently walking their dogs, visiting the Botanical Garden, doing an hour at the gym, having friends over for roast chicken or homemade soup, checking emails, *catching up on* TV. Sunday was the day each week she felt most deficient as a mother. Her cousin Margaret, happily married since she was twenty-four, had said of her wonderful husband Ted, Every Sunday afternoon I think about divorcing him.

Sundays one felt most caged. She missed nature. She missed hills, she missed tundra she'd never even seen. What could she offer her son? She would drag him to museums—another thing the Sunday-activity people seemed to do—and sometimes it would not be too tedious. But it wasn't his favorite thing and they both felt it forced.

What to do? Must get out of the house. Stroller. Boots. Nicky would push the old stroller with Enny in it, and not refuse it later. They went to the park, even in drizzle. The slide's all watery, he would say. The sand's too wet to dig. We can still go on the swing! You saw more fathers there with the children, looking into their phones. Occasionally they glanced up, then continued texting. How many were having affairs? Ivy wondered. How many loved their wives? Their husbands? Then Nicky would come down the curving slide tipped back, checking that she was watching his fun, and she would latch on to the glinted moment.

She thought how nearby, or a neighborhood away, or a state or even a county away, her friends with families of more than one child—and more than one parent—saw this as valued family time. Occasionally she would tag along with these more robust units. Nicky's petulant streak sometimes caused a scene, and while her friends calmly withstood it, she didn't blame them if they chose to avoid them. Why should she be trying to cram herself into another family anyway? It was less intrusive relying on a real relative, so they would often take the train on Saturdays to New Jersey to Margaret's. Ivy and Margaret, though cousins, considered each other more like sisters. Margaret had worked in publishing in New York, then fell in love with Ted, a history professor at Princeton, and moved there after marriage. In her thirties when she wasn't traveling Ivy would visit Margaret often; her house was the closest thing to a home Ivy had. There were many Christmases Ivy spent with Margaret and Ted, who had a happy marriage and four daughters. But then, Ivy, away across the country, or across the sea, only half registered each time Margaret had a child, so foreign was it to her life. Ivy had never envisioned that family scenario for herself. Was it the trauma of having lost her parents? She didn't think so. The bustling house full of children had been something she wanted to get away from, if only to think.

Margaret's was a light blue house at the top of a steep street, with a chocolate dog barking at the door and Margaret telling him to cut it out. Nicky would disappear up to the second floor—a second floor!—with his four older cousins, or they'd straggle over the backyard—outside!—while Margaret made another pot of coffee or threw quesadillas on the pan at lunchtime so the kids would swoop in, take a plate and swoop out. In between Margaret was putting the laundry in the dryer. Ivy tried to help cook or fold, but Margaret had the tempo of her duties in an uninterrupted rhythm and despite having four children was both calm and quick to laugh. Ivy was grateful that Nicky could join this tumult, which she couldn't offer him, and was aware of sucking familial energy from her cousin without feeling she could give anything in return. Ivy also learned how to be a parent. We don't do that in our family, Margaret would say lightly and Ivy would be mesmerized, never having thought to say such a thing.

Her impatience with herself only added to her self-loathing. Honestly what was her problem. Her life was fine. Think of the unspeakable things that people endured. I mean, honestly. She thought of a man she knew distantly who had lost his wife and two daughters in a car crash. Ivy had been at a dinner with him, in a cheerful kitchen. She knew he'd continued working in a law firm. He was passing a bowl of pasta to the person beside him and laughing at the story being told and Ivy was amazed to see a gleam of joy in his eye.

Then 5:00 A.M. could also be the worst in the dove-grey bed. Had he really even been there? It seemed too wonderful. She saw herself in a life which made only occasional sense and longed to lay herself alongside the calmness she saw in his, cooling the nerves.

At Daphne's birthday at a Moroccan restaurant she met a painter named Sherry who had known Ansel back in the day. Sexy man, Sherry said, her champagne sloshing in the shallow glass. Tell me everything. Ivy told her a lot. Sherry shook her head, leaning on a pillow, then nodded, then shook her head. Worth it all, said Sherry in conclusion. A new friend! Ivy stayed in touch with Sherry after that.

Lovers leave traces of where they've been.

A person in repose could look so still. One could never see the riot of thoughts in the skull, or the electric need zigzagging through the body. Nicky's sleeping face had always transfixed her, so beautifully calm, worthy of worship.

Watching Ansel's sleeping face was almost more intimate than sex. His lower lip was relaxed to the side and the looseness changed his features. His face was like a still pond and the shut eyes made him more approachable. When his eyes were open they were watching, sometimes with a flirty brightness, sometimes with lids lowered, unconvinced, not going to be taken, or bored.

On the street she passed a man with Ansel's wide shoulders, causing a zing in her spine, all things associated with him having that vibration. How was it a person could feel lodged at the bottom of your spine like a bullet. Or shot up through your nervous system through your head. It seemed his bed was filled with explosions in the quiet afternoon, like warning shots going off over a neighboring hill.

Inside the hall she closed her door and her legs buckled beneath her and she slid down the wall. A sob burst out of her and she began to cry. Her insides seemed to be shredding themselves. A whirlpool churned inside her, then gradually moved outside of her and circled the heap on the floor. Soon all was quiet. She felt exhausted and relieved. With blurry eyes she glanced at her wristwatch, only four minutes before she had to leave for school pickup.

She pulled back the bedcovers and slid onto the sheets, missing him. She thought of his hand with its sturdy smooth nails, his fingers fastening a watch around his wrist. *I'm going to be watching out for you.* She imagined his room lit low with a person on the couch, a girl holding a glass of red wine.

She was a blur, then she was ebullient. What had happened to her?

The intensity of the Thing was itself fascinating. Well, it wouldn't keep going on. Nothing did. A time would come when the Thing would not be so important. She'd lived long enough to know that things which felt absolute did change. In fact, change was guaranteed. She would be the lively girl with enough gumption to laugh after he was gone.

In bed she put her arms around herself and pretended the arms were not hers.

C. S. Lewis noted how the sexual appetite, like our other appetites, grows by indulgence. Everyone, he wrote, knows this.

. . .

On the radio she listened to people sobbing.

Late at night when the streets were quiet she'd hear a truck backfiring and think he might have heard that same sound. He might have seen the same moon.

Then the recognition smacked her: if he was nearby, he was choosing every moment not to be with her. The smack was part of the Thing.

Snow appeared in the still air, wide flat flakes floating down like tiny magic carpets, filling the air as far as one could see. Did everyone feel the same emotion seeing them? A sort of release? Both happy and sad.

Sailing home in a cab after wine, slightly drunk, she texted without worry.

Yu home?

Yes.

Want to visit?

Still working.

He was there! Alone, quiet, diligent.

Late?

Probably.

Am heading home now. If y done soon, come. if you want.

Will do.

Then asleep in the dark comes the vibrating trill on the bedside table. She reads the glowing rectangle.

You still up?

She types. *Barely.*

I can be there in five.

Yes please.

It's past midnight so she goes down the stairs in her robe to let him in the outer door.

Are you ever going to let someone matter? she asked him.
I have a lot of people who matter to me.
A woman, I mean.
Maybe, he said. Maybe not.
So you just take whatever passes by?
Something like that.

Watching him sleep, she felt the closest to him. Only one of them was conscious. Once she lifted his arm and placed it over her heart and laid her hand on top of his. She recognized it as a position she'd been in before, with someone who had loved her, and tried to make the thought disappear.

The aftereffect of him spread wider and rather less specific; her mood swings became steeper. When alone, she found a backlog of things she'd wanted to ask him, or feelings she wanted to explore. But really, she'd argue with herself, why did one need to tell a person one's feelings? What difference would it make? Feelings were hers to stay in herself.

Didn't it take her into the deep universe? Didn't she disappear through him into a feeling of being at one? She did. She did.

She washed herself in the bath with a pale green soap the size of a mango. As she shaved herself she thought, This is his. I want this body to be his and not keep it myself. Giving it away is the way I like it best. So many thoughts were embarrassing to her and she kept them to herself. She also kept to herself the thought that maybe if one day the embarrassing thoughts were brought out into daylight they might not be as mortifying as she thought they were.

You here?
I am.
Good trip?
Excellent.
Find me one of these days?

Will do.

Then days would pass.

My love is my weight. Because of it I move.

She thought, Maybe I have been here before, and maybe it's not a good place to be, but I feel it's where I belong.

Willful blindness, Ansel had told her when describing his trial, is not an acceptable defense.

On the radio she heard, Obsessive thinking signals that we are not telling the truth either to ourselves or to another person.

Now and then she'd recall that early version she'd had of Ansel Fleming, boyish, sexy and . . . harmless! She looked back at that earlier version of herself when she still had skin. The truth of the matter was he had not done this to her. She had. She'd made him into a spear and was using him to stab herself, over and over.

But of all the little ways I've found to hurt myself
Well you might be my favorite one of all

So she would resolve to stop. Enough, she would think. She would coach herself to focus away from him, stick with work, give more time and attention to her son, seek out friends. The first days of these withdrawals were always painful and she would apply her habits of discipline to keeping herself busy, to exercising, to staying at the desk. A great deal of internal energy was spent talking herself out of him and soon the missing of him would change and go through its normal fluctuations and become less fraught. Then without the need to be scrupulous and manage her agonies her thoughts of him became lighter and looser and no longer the dangerous minefield they had been and she would think, really, what's the harm. One day we will be dead.

In the evening was it procrastination or refueling—to leave the attic of one's head and disappear into a movie, a book, to let other images in, other people, other stories. When does a break become self-sabotage, the avoiding of what you've pledged yourself to, the picking up of tools for the work only you Ivy Cooper will be able to do?

The humming city is quiet and the hiss of a car on the rainy street is rare but the ground has gone soft and even the small chores of neatening feel as steep as mountainsides and you are thrown back to a hollowness you thought you had escaped. But it is here again. There is nothing poetic in it. So she would turn to the swelling of the soundtrack and the floating of the credits over the bright images and vanish from herself while at the same time weirdly also feeling up close to the window of her soul.

Wendy Cope's poem *Seeing you will make me sad. I have to do it anyway.*

Was he around? Well, yes. But not sure. He'd let her know later. But he did not let her know and she went to bed.

Sleeping?

Not yet.

Should be there by 12.

Tonight she decides to say something. *I really wanted to see you very much but I am not feeling good about it after not hearing from you till now.* That described it, now what could she add. It took her some time to come up with *Can you help me out of the mood?*

Do you want me to come by? I am finishing an edit that was due hours ago.

As always he goes directly to the point. She waits, trying to find refusal in herself.

I do want to see you.

See you shortly.

I hear you have a new friend, he said.

She looked at him with surprise. What?

Not so?

She scours her brain. Ah, the date she went on. Maira knew of it. His face was bright with interest. She wanted him to believe it, so she would have something apart from him, but it wasn't true and she told him so.

You seem happy when you think I'm having sex with someone else, she said.

Yes, he said. It's great. It's fun.

Do you want to know how many people I've had sex with since I've met you?

It's none of my business, he said.

She held up her thumb and finger, making a zero.

As he fell asleep she touched the parts of his body she had not yet felt. She thought, I have not covered a person's geography with this kind of intention before. It's taken fifty years of life to get here.

Each morning she opened the paper and went first to the obituaries. Before wading through the world's disasters, she would examine an individual's life. You never saw the headline "Mother of Three, Devoted Her Life to Children's Well-Being."

In the day she circled the chair and the table. She set out her pen and ink, opened books and unfanned papers, and for a few still hours if logistics didn't keep her from it, she swam in the pond. Each morning the pond was iced over and you had to chip at it to get back in.

The blizzard in her head made it difficult to work.

Her throat was definitely sore. It was Thursday evening, so if she was getting sick she would at least have the day tomorrow to sleep while Nicky was at school. Padma and Oscar were away visiting her parents this weekend, so she wouldn't be able to ask Padma for help. She woke in the night feverish, her throat seared. Okay, here we go. The thought of *him* came—the wish for his cool hand on her forehead—and was immediately dismissed. No time for dreaming if you were sick. Enough of that, she said to herself, and got up to take medication.

In the morning, with her throat plugged like a bottle, she heated soup for Nicky's thermos, cut carrot sticks and celery. Could he ride the laser? Not today, she said, I can't run after you today. I'm getting a little sick.

They walked to school in the gusting cold, Nicky's mouth set tightly.

At home she made some tea, but collapsed in bed before drinking it. She woke at one, heated leftover chicken. She wouldn't be any good writing today.

You can always call if you need help, friends said. And they meant it. But that was for emergency help. Meet me at the hospital! But the help she needed was simply for a person to be in the other room. It was what the husband had been. He would have picked Nicky up and fed him dinner. He could take him out on Saturday and even Sunday if she was still feeling rotten. By then, the cold would be lodged in her head like packed straw and she would be on her way to the cough which would keep her up most of the night leaving her wrung out in the morning. She knew what to expect and braced herself for it.

That afternoon in a cotton-thick delirium she fetched Nicky. No, darling, no park. It was freezing anyway. Yes, they could get French fries on the way home. They picked them up at the French café on the corner. Seeing this opening—of her saying yes to something—Nicky chose then to stop and lodge himself adamantly in front of the puppy window. Inside two grey-and-white puppies were tumbling over each other in a sea of paper strips. Three other animals were flat and sleeping. Couldn't they go inside and play with a puppy. Not today, Nicky, please. The *please* was another mistake, widening the tear in the fabric of her parental authority. He looked defiantly at her, then burst into tears. I'm never ever ever ever ever going to get a puppy, he wailed and fell against the glass window.

What about Lance and Air? she said.

They're not a puppy! he cried.

Illness put you in a state of mind most difficult to keep your spirits up. How did sick people manage? Where did they find the resources to put one foot in front of the other, not to mention to take pleasure in life? When ill, you floated with a vague despair, apart from everyone, thrown back onto yourself, viewing your weaknesses which you now had the clarity to see had been there all along—you'd just been distracting yourself! How had you not appreciated every second you could sleep without coughing, could taste your eggs or a sip of wine?

How underappreciative you'd been of the ease with which you breezed up and down the streets. The longing for health flooded the brain when you were sick, and there was nothing to do but be patient. It was hard to believe you would feel better. At night, strung out from no sleep, lying in the dark, you felt the tickle come in your throat. You coughed your lungs out.

You worried you would wake Nicky and knew you'd be in pieces tomorrow.

You promised the God that you did not believe in that when you were better you would value each simple and yet miraculous breath. If you sat up, it was less likely that the tickling would start, so you propped yourself up with pillows like a tubercular patient, and tried to sleep. You think of Elizabeth Barrett Browning who was sickly when courted by her husband, Robert Browning. Still the tickle came. Nothing to be done.

Irene dropped off some soup. Nicky sat in front of movies and cartoons all day. In the evening she made macaroni and cheese and they watched *Shrek* together and Nicky laughed at the same places he always laughed.

Two people were kissing beside a tree on the leafy street. The woman's hands framed the man's head, his were lightly at her ribs because she loved him more.

. . .

It was a windy April evening and Maira had organized a small dinner, a small dinner for Maira being twenty people. Ivy put on a dress, one Maira had encouraged her to buy. The dress had thin straps with a plaid pattern and she felt not like herself in it. She put on a pair of high ankle boots and walked to the nearby restaurant, with wind swooping pear blossoms across the dark sidewalk. When she opened the restaurant doors a huge roar met her in the creamy light.

Maira was at the end of a long wooden table. Ivy knew some of the people sitting, some she'd only met. She kissed her friend hello amid the clatter. Ansel may stop by later, Maira murmured. He said he was busy, but I told him to come if it wasn't too late. I hope that's okay. Ivy wasn't surprised, but the mention of his name still hit her with a thwack. Ivy found a free chair. The din was so high, Ivy could speak only with the person on either side of her, and even then had to shout. On her right was a Persian woman with parted dark hair and a French accent. She lived in London, was a barrister and by the end of dinner had offered Ivy her flat in London if she ever needed a place to stay. On her left was a man Ivy had met a number of times with Maira. He was a brooding fellow whom Maira thought fascinating, whom Ivy thought a poseur. Ivy drank glass after glass of wine, nervous about seeing Ansel, and decided the fellow was less arrogant and simply shy.

Out of the corner of her eye, she saw the two people weaving through the crowded tables toward them. Ansel was with Fred Brown. Fred was an Irish musician who often played with Ansel. He was a little older than Ansel but to Ivy looked like a youthful street boy, with a chipped tooth and small-brimmed fedora. She knew his music; he had a beautiful voice. When Ivy learned Ansel knew him she'd wondered aloud why Fred wasn't more famous. Ansel said there was a longer list of musicians who ought to be famous than ones who were. The question ought to be, Ansel said, why were the famous musicians famous?

Maira stood up, beaming, greeting Ansel and Fred, and

pointed to chairs to be moved around, and Ansel and Fred were engulfed. Ivy didn't dare look down the table.

She looked at the time. It had gotten late; she was already past the time she'd told the sitter. Still she did not leave right away, hoping, but Ansel did not come.

She stood to leave after leaving four twenties—for the squid appetizer, side of spinach and wine—and scooted between chairs toward Maira at her end of the table to say goodbye, passing in front of Ansel, feeling him see her. He was wedged between two women and couldn't have reached her, even if he wanted to, but he smiled at her, seeming to be surprised at her there. It did not feel personal. She waved, gesturing she was on her way out. Fred Wood stood up in his dark vest and rumpled white shirt and kissed her hello, filling her with gratitude. You're not leaving? he said. We just got here. Yes, she said, but she had a sitter at home and had to go. She gave Maira the half-shoulder hug and thanked her and ignored the look she felt of Maira's Are you okay?

She walked home with deliberate steps, not to tip off her boots. Already she regretted not speaking to him. She would text him when she got home. After the sitter had gone. He was so close. She had not seen him in over two weeks and couldn't leave it like that, as if he was nothing to her, nothing but this wind blowing by. Then she remembered him saying, way back, I am like the wind. Were those the words? Or maybe it was I am as ethereal as the wind. At home she paid the sitter, slipping out of her wallet three twenty-dollar bills she had left. She went down the hall and into the peace of Nicky's room and gazed at his sleeping face.

She texted Ansel she needed to tell him something. She wasn't sure exactly what she wanted to say, but blurred and encouraged by the wine, she figured she had so many thoughts and feelings, something would surface.

He answered that he would text when on his way.

She deliberately did not fluff up the apartment. She didn't want to give attention to caring. She did however go back down the hall and quietly click Nicky's door shut and she did close the pocket doors for more privacy and turned off some lights and lit a candle, but she kept a living room lamp on, not wanting to concede to too much atmosphere.

At the door they didn't hug each other hello. They'd just seen each other. He followed her into the living room.

You wanted to tell me something? he said. He sat on the couch, summoned.

Ivy sat down on a folded leg. I met a guy one summer I spent in Colorado, she said. We were camping with a whole group of people and Stanley and I got together. It was only that week, but I was crazy about him.

Ansel listened.

After she returned East, Ivy went on, she assumed they'd see each other again, but Stanley ended up traveling in South America and living there for a while. A couple of years later when she returned to Colorado for the wedding of two people from that summer Stanley was there and they had another week together, as if no time had passed. They went rock climbing, and slept under the stars. When it was time to leave, Stanley suggested how they should say goodbye. They should both wave to each other. It was a sign of good faith . . . to wave. Then you would have that image in your mind, and be able to picture the person waving and see it as meaning both goodbye and hello. It was actually on the side of a mountain when they said goodbye, so she had that image of him waving. They stayed in touch with letters now and then. Stanley told her when he had fallen in love. I can't wait till you meet my grandchildren, he said. Then one day she got a call from the bride of that wedding telling her that he'd been killed in an avalanche. He was twenty-six. Ivy said, I'd been so sure I'd see him again.

So when I go you want me to wave, Ansel said.

She made a rueful embarrassed expression.

I'll try, he said.

Thank you. She leaned close to him. It's nice to see you. She shifted her leg against him.

In a quick motion he scooped up her legs and flipped her back onto the couch.

She laughed and reached to slip off her boot.

Keep it on, he said and reached under her dress. His hand felt around, then she heard the sound of her underwear ripping and a small dark bat was tossed in the darkness. Like the movies, she thought, feeling hilarity inside. She pulled him onto her.

Later, she walked him to the door loose limbed and mercifully not herself anymore. Or was she back to herself more than ever? This was often difficult to tell.

He went down the stairs and a hand fluttered up over his shoulder. Waving, he murmured.

This time she did not announce to him that she was done. It was up to her. What did it matter if he knew? Besides if she went back on it, only she would know how indecisive she had been.

She had noticed from an early age a decisiveness in her son. Nicky was amazingly quick when making choices. Which balloon would you like? The answer came immediately. The black one with the yellow bat. Which stuffed animal did he like? One five-second glance at an enormous tower of animals in the airport gift shop grid and he would point to the black-and-white leopard, as if this were the obvious choice. Ivy wondered if this clarity of mind made his worries sharper, trying to find the reason for his waking in the night screaming.

Did you know lions are a kind of cat, Nicky said on the walk home from school, even though they have round ears.

Ivy forgot John's birthday and called two days later. Oh, no worries, John said, perhaps mildly. John made me a layered *dulce de tres leches.*

Sounds delicious, she said.

Yes, he said, it was. And we got a new puppy.

Ivy exclaimed and said how Nicky would be jealous.

Well, it helps after Kitty.

Oh God, Ivy said, did I miss that?

Yes, we had to put her down.

Oh, John, I'm so sorry.

It was, he said, as always reasonable and deliberate, her time to go.

But Ivy also heard the note in his voice: she'd been neglectful.

The less said about them the better, the unendurable evenings when solitude is not a warm fire or a yellow light on the page, but instead the shifting and hard-to-endure reminder you are alone. And harder still the evenings when there is someone you long to be with who is choosing, minute after minute, not to be with you. The less said the better about the empty minutes unmoving. All your planning and planting and sorting—it cannot protect you here. Friends, tried and true, are deep in their lives. Many may even be alone like you, but you are each finally in your own room. And in those moments you lose the thread connecting to them. It is more than blankness. It seems a shutter opening to negative space. Each time it seems you were never as alone as this.

She thought of the initial blaze when her friends had said, Fun. Good for you. And of how now it was, You don't want that, smiling at how obvious it was. But she did, she did want that.

They didn't know the glacier of him when she opened the door.

Awake in the night she would go over it: the winter air on his coat, his cold cheek, the apartment dark with points of light, the slit by the curtain, the cable box, the flame in a jar, the spaceship of the apartment zooming. Afterward she was amazed he'd been there, as if he were a hologram, but reviewing the elements kept them real. Till the waking in the night changed, no longer a sublime contemplation, but a sinking.

. . .

Though her body remained with people in normal life, with Nicky, with her friends, she felt the part sectioned off, tethered to the place Ansel was, or to the place she'd been with Ansel or the place she wished they both might be in the future, that place being more desirable than where she was with the rest of herself.

In the dream she was trying to steer a car which kept banging at the sides of the bridge she was crossing.

6

Occupied

All men know the utility of useful things;
but they do not know the utility of futility.

—CHUANG TZU

While she was sweeping the wooden floor, she thought, Really all that I want is someone to sleep beside. That's all. She was trying to boil it down to the main elements. Just have skin beside me, and some arms. A heart beating. A solid body. It was that simple. Okay, if she was going to be honest with herself there would be a little more. She would also likely want the body to appear upright she supposed in the day. That was normal to want. And for that appearance not to be unpleasant. In fact, for her to like the person. But the person could do whatever he wanted, just be sometimes nearby. Like at the end of the day, while she was doing what she had to do. Maybe the person would be sitting near, while she was reading. Or maybe they were watching a movie together. That's all. He could do whatever he wanted otherwise. Well, not everything. Obviously. Not awful things out in the world. And not loving other people more. And, yes, it would be nice if he were working, doing something worthwhile. For his sake. Okay, so maybe she wanted someone who was her person, and she would be his person. They'd be most important to each other. He could go away on his own and come back. And he would be cool with her doing the same. He also should probably be a person one could have a good conversation with, if she was really going to enumerate the important things. And funny. Dear God, he must be funny. And his mind, she'd have to be interested in his mind. She would want to like the way he moved. Because the way he moved would embody what he was like. And she would need to believe in him. She had to believe in him. It would be great if he were someone who knew how to look after himself, so she could continue to learn better how to look after herself, and knowing each other would also help them both learn it, even as they would be counting on each other. They would help each other out the times when each needed it, and would understand when that would be. If they didn't understand, they would let each other know. They would learn what mattered to each other and be both open with each other and trusting. That's all, she thought, sweeping the dust into a dustpan. That's all I want.

Mumma, Nicky called from the living room. Where are you?

Right here.

Are you going out tonight? He was drawing at the low table, his cheek pressed down beside a large pad of paper.

No. I'm not going anywhere.

It didn't look as if he could even see what he was drawing, but the pen remained poised and moving and he stayed in the position for a long time. Afterward he showed her the finished picture of an ocean liner with hundreds of carefully drawn square windows in a grid on its hull and an upper deck with a line of people, each figure with its hand up, waving.

On the first night they'd met, Everett had told Ivy he was not particularly anxious to have children. He'd seen too many problems caused by overpopulation. Besides his father had been an asshole and he thought he wouldn't know what to do. Ivy told him she used to feel the same, though in the last few years could see the possibility moving toward her—like a grey storm cloud—to at least consider a child. Perhaps she should check it out before she lost the chance. The air of discernment and steadiness around Everett seemed to Ivy a safe and inviting place for a child. One time she saw him carrying the baby of a friend, his hand covering the back and propping the head with assurance and ease; his glance to Ivy said, Not so bad actually. After she and Everett had been together only a short time, she asked him if he was adamant about not having children and he said, in the dry straightforward way he had, that if a child were something she needed to have and if he and she were happy together, he didn't see why not.

Nicky was not exactly planned, and frankly Ivy had not expected to conceive at her age. Luckily Everett accepted her pregnancy as if he'd expected it.

A few weeks after Nicky was born, Everett was relocated, as he had been expecting, to a rural project, and they moved onto the edge of an escarpment in a small house made of tree trunks and cow dung with a stunning view overlooking the savanna. The isolation was just another thrilling chapter for Ivy and it felt surreal to be walking along a path with a baby in her sling, in a land she did not know. One night, washing the dishes in the plastic tub on the deck with the sun setting miles away behind the blue hills, Everett said, So I think we should probably do it. His back was to her and she had not heard what he said before that, but when he turned around looking frightened, she understood that he meant getting married. Her heart went out to him. Ivy had never longed for marriage, only to be one in a couple, but a child upticked a number of things she now thought best. Security, safety, health, were all things she'd not particularly cared about with only herself to look after. They were married at the town hall in Arusha while she held Nicky in her arms. Ivy was far from the world she knew, and liked feeling she was a new person, far from old concerns.

Nicky had been an alert and active child, with a deep belly laugh, always trying to get ahead of himself, as if aware he was older than his toddler body. Everett seemed surprised at his paternal ability, though he found it hard to tolerate moments of mayhem. Ivy did her best to take on the child's volatility and spirit, seeing how it disturbed Everett. Perhaps he was reminded of his own father's temper which Everett said had been wicked. In this and other ways they would find their balance and Ivy soon learned that they got along best when she adjusted to the world as Everett saw it. She didn't mind doing it, why did she need to assert her will? She saw the surrender as yet another challenge, even an adventure.

Nicky's curls were loose and thick, his cheeks round and his chin came to a point like Everett's. A discerning look often appeared in his eye, as if he'd observed the world and had taken its measure, but was now double-checking to make sure he was right.

As a mother Ivy did experience moments unshadowed by thoughts of her son, but not many. As with most parents, concern for the well-being of her son was continual and pervasive. She had expected this, but it was more pervasive than she'd envisioned.

Ivy had regarded being a mother as an instinctive thing, and when Nicky was born had full confidence in her ability to care for and raise him. In the early years, this proved generally to be true. A small person needed to be fed, clothed, hugged, played with. He cried, you fed him, you put him to bed. He laughed, you kept throwing the puff ball at his face. This attention did take up the bulk of one's time, and she rarely put him in the care of others. What was the point in having a child if you his mother were not going to look after him? Only when he was asleep was she off duty.

When a child got older, he naturally became more willful and oddly less reasonable. If he did not want to put his jacket on to go build the snowman, he now stiffened his arms and refused. When a small person was stubborn, he could hold out; he had nothing else to attend to, had all the time in the world. One had to summon patience and determination, but even then skirmishes often had no outcome but exhaustion.

So far in her life when she'd felt extreme discomfort or unhappiness, Ivy's instinct had been to flee. When Nicky was brooding, or bullying her, or seeming deliberately to try to do everything possible to alienate her, the same instinct kicked in. But at this late stage of life she had encountered a situation she was unable to leave.

The more Nicky got older, the more Ivy's instinct as a parent started to scramble. Indulge and you will spoil. Be too strict and you'll dampen his joy. Show intolerance and crush his spirit. Things were no longer so clear. Though Ivy's interaction with her parents had been kind, it was formal and distant, and having felt a lack of acceptance and warmth she feared passing it to Nicky. But the hardest thing was being a rule maker. She had always mistrusted rules and did not relish enforcing them, much less deciding which ones were valid, and it was quite likely that this was not lost on her observant son.

When she found her instinct unreliable, she turned to parenting books.

In many of them she encountered the phrase *good-enough mother.* It was meant to take the pressure off the anxious parent. Somehow the concept did not console Ivy. It made her even more determined to be better, the qualities of "better" being firmness, calmness, discernment—all things which required she have another personality not full of doubts and conjecture. Being a parent had seriously—another parenting-book phrase—*reduced her self-esteem.* She wanted Nicky to have the best. She is a great mother, one heard said of a person. Ivy fretted this was not likely to be said about her.

Well, she was the mother he had. Nothing could be done about it. Even if she made the wrong choices of what might be *best* for Nicky, she loved him. If only love, she reflected, were all that was needed.

Love, said her friend Rosemary. The oldest excuse in the book.

But now, with her attention taken up with matters of her son, her writing work was secondary, even if it was her livelihood.

Being a mother was not a job you could do just sometimes. And Ivy found that a single parent had it more than twice over. The single parent did not have the option of handing over care to another. She could not discuss this puzzling new venture with that other person, and parse out the perplexities with a fellow parent, who would be as invested in the child as she.

When Ivy had moved back to New York, a place she'd lived not as a mother, she noticed the contrast. Mothers were not considered interesting—except perhaps to other mothers.

When you became a mother, people stopped noticing you. Except for your children, of course. You had a captive audience in them. Perhaps too captive. A mother has, for each child, a splinter in her heart. A fan always opening.

She noticed how she often saw them running.

She noticed on mothers' faces a nervous jerk to their gaze. Those were the attentive mothers. Not all mothers were attentive. Simply having a child did not make you an attentive person necessarily, and did not make you necessarily suited to be a mother. The nervous jerk was the eye either checking on the child, or, Ivy thought, looking for an ally. In all the fear, Ivy also saw perhaps the fear of being discovered unable to find peace. When Ivy measured herself against the more robustly maternal women who observed their children with a knowing air, certain to their bones of what was right or wrong, she felt more inept than ever.

One mother had a child with anxiety attacks. Another had daughters who fought. One's son didn't have any good friends, another was a bully. There was trouble with schoolwork. Each mother was distressed in her own way, but all had distress.

She feared his discomfort; the thought of injury to him was unbearable. This throbbing worry was a kind of ache. It was not joyful, even if it was love.

The love was solid as a wall of granite, not a feeling contingent on character or beauty or behavior, on whether Ivy felt understood or not, all those elements which inspired love in a man. This was a whole different brand of love.

. . .

The encampment had been there a month before she stopped by on her bike returning one day from the East Village. It was pathetic she'd not at least checked out what was being broadcast all over the world. At an earlier time in her life she might have been there, smoking cigarettes, righteous. The sitter had to leave at five-thirty, so she hadn't much time. She pictured Nicky at that moment.

She chained her bike to a parking sign and crossed the street toward the patch of park with its fluttering orange trees surrounded by a compressed wall of sleeping bags and blankets.

Plywood barricades at the end of the block hid the crater of perpetual rebuilding still going on after—what?—more than ten years. You could not be in this neighborhood and not think of that day. She flashed yet again on seeing shopkeepers outside their doors with crossed arms, of standing in Washington Square among a milling group of baffled people, observing the smoke down Broadway, wondering how many people the towers held—how many floors were there?—when before their eyes the building simply dropped down as quiet as a ghostly soufflé, and vanished in the haze. The vision had been very like a hallucination, and yet at the time, her brain registered that the vision was indelible. Which it had been. Out of the thousands of images one subsequently saw of that morning, none had been from the precise place where she had been, knees buckling, dropping as the building dropped.

Afterward she'd felt weirdly a sort of custodian of the deaths. But, really, what kind of custodian could one be and what could one do? She wondered how many people had, like she, witnessed the towers going down, the murder of thousands of people, and how many kept the vision inside them and felt as she did, to be a custodian of it.

Near one entrance a figure in a Darth Vader helmet and black cloak had a sign around his neck: I AM ONE OF THE 99%. Ivy wandered on cement pathways choked with boxes and tied plastic tarps and yellow police tape draped on the box shrubs. She looked at the faces, a girl with dreadlocks, a dog in a red bandanna and a young man sewing, passed signs I AM HERE BECAUSE I AM SCARED FOR MY COUNTRY. The movement had been both criticized and praised for its lack of definition, no leader, no clear agenda, but at least, she thought, these people cared, and she remembered the lure of feeling that purpose.

She thought of her purpose now: Nicky probably at that moment on the living room rug intent on a train, or an ambulance. Recently, she was playing with him, making the ambulance sound as he asked, describing again the person who was hurt . . . No, Mama, you said he broke his arm. Mama, do that part again, you forgot to say the person coming out of the store, you forgot the dog etc., asking for the scenarios to be repeated exactly, as she was also thinking, I am the same person whose brain goes white light as she's pushed against the wall inside the man's door, still in her winter coat . . . She shuddered. She thought how Nicky—

Shit. She looked at her watch. She was late. She half ran to her bike.

At the traffic-jammed crosswalk she saw an area across the street sectioned off by orange cones in front of a building under construction and pedaled manically across the street to honking horns. She didn't care, she was in a hurry. She had a son. Around the corner she was surprised by a patch scattered with sharp gravel. Surely she would skid if she tried to slow down on it and without thinking she squeezed the hand brake that worked. The bike stopped and she pitched over the handlebars, aware in the microsecond that either this was going to be really bad, or she'd be okay.

Her chin landed with the sound of two rocks hitting.

A white, then black, strobe swept through her head. She crumpled onto the cold tar. A fizzing numbness spiked through her body at the same time that a burning pain raked the left side of her face. Shakily she pushed up on one arm, relieved she could move and sort of sit. The wind was knocked out of her, but her neck didn't seem to be broken, though there was an unnerving ache across her jaw. Was her throat closing up? She turned her torso in slow motion to see the construction worker striding toward her. She touched her chin, felt wetness and saw red-black drips on the front of her olive-green jacket.

I'm not maimed for life, she said to herself. The sky around her widened.

In the next few moments she felt the clarity one has after an accident or a near miss. She would never have been this reckless with Nicky, yet with herself . . . well, it was easier to care about a person not oneself.

She was not looking after herself; it was time to make the break. Again. She didn't need to tell Ansel Fleming about this. It was simply up to her. She felt clear. Looking at her face in the mirror was a good reminder.

She deleted all his texts. She regretted it immediately. She'd just wiped away the history of her heart. So what if it was the history of something made up, it had been a parallel universe where she had liked living.

In the quiet week after Christmas Ivy stayed at a nearby cottage belonging to one of Everett's mother's friends. This was Nicky's time to be with Everett, so she left them alone.

There was a cedar tree across the lawn which she watched through the kitchen window when she worked there. The tree took on different aspects of character, a guard, a friend, an indifferent god.

She ran each afternoon on the soft side roads and often, veering off to the rise of a hill or seeing the bruise on evening clouds, might feel euphoric. Life, she felt, having no better word to articulate the feeling. Life. Hours later drinking beer and cooking dinner, listening to music, she would be weeping.

It was New Year's Eve. Everett and Rebecca would be at the

bonfire with all her previous friends. She'd gone to the Christmas Eve bazaar in the church basement and seen those faces; she'd had tea with Karen. But she had left those people and was here alone by a small fire in a large fireplace.

With an hour to go before the year changed, she was looking into her phone and dropping again all the strategies of self-coaching and protection, sent a text to Ansel Fleming, telling him happy New Year . . . wherever he was. The answer came back immediately, warm and friendly.

He was up the Hudson. With friends. She thought probably at Clover Johnson's, the heiress's mansion, where she knew he sometimes hung out, though he didn't say. How was she. And how was Nicky. Things were good. They texted back and forth. Ivy always found text conversations strange—why weren't they speaking to one another instead?—but this time felt protected. She had vowed not to contact him; this at least was only words. Not as close as it might be. Also if they had been speaking she was certain he never would have said what he wrote. *You occupy a warm and secure place inside me.*

It was a freezing day in January and Nicky had been home from school two days, sick with a sore throat. The world fell like a curtain outside the window; life became only tending to him.

When Ivy spoke on the phone to Padma she found out Oscar too was home and strep was going around. Ivy called the doctor, hoping to avoid a visit, but the doctor needed to see him if he was to get antibiotics. Dr. Qualley was an affable man who, while feeling the glands at Nicky's slender throat and swabbing for a culture, talked about his recent trip to Colombia. It wasn't dangerous there at all, the doctor said. You just have to know the right places to go. They waited for the test to show strep, and the prescription was called in. Ivy tried not to wince as the assistant took her card and charged the two hundred fifty dollars for the fifteen minutes. Ivy bundled Nicky back in his parka, brought him back to the apartment where she tucked him in bed with the portable DVD player and headed out to the drugstore around the corner. As she waited for the prescription near the tall lit shelf of designer soaps, she heard, Is that Ivy? and turned to see a beautiful young girl who looked vaguely familiar. Zack, the girl said to remind her, and Ivy vaguely remembered the time Daphne's nephew Zack had stayed in the apartment with a friend . . . The girl, then with dreadlocks, now had a pixie haircut, and was wearing a shearling coat with a colorful threaded pattern and dragging a suitcase on two wheels. Her name, she reminded Ivy, was Cleo. She bubbled out that she was living in Denver now, she said this as if surprised at herself, her eyebrows lifted above sparkling eyes. She was here visiting a friend in the city, then laughed. Actually, she said, she'd just gone to the friend's apartment and the friend was not there. So she'd come in here to get warm. She did not appear worried. Ivy tried to remember if Zack had gone out with the girl, but thought not. Ivy said she would offer to ask her back to the apartment, but that Nicky had strep throat and she really didn't think—Oh no, no, said the girl breezily. She was fine. She had a girlfriend in Brooklyn; she was waiting till the girlfriend finished work. Ivy asked about Zack and the girl said, He's much better, I think, and Ivy said, What happened? and Cleo said, Oh, I thought you'd know . . . it was a—well, I probably shouldn't say, then. No, Ivy said, no you don't have to. And they said goodbye. She picked up chicken soup at the corner deli where Nicky liked to get it, preferring prepared food to the exact same food she might have cooked him at home, thinking she must call Daphne and find out if Zack was okay. She sort of carried with her the air of the beautiful hip girl, recalling that feeling of being young and loose, relying on friends, but without a place to go, and felt relieved she was not there, but also the opposite envy for that open feeling of being young and lost and relying on friends with a new place to go. Then she remembered the girl was an aspiring singer, and thought with a small nauseated pause how she was just the type of hip beautiful girl Ansel would be writing songs with and who would probably fit far better into his life than she.

She had not seen him in months. She'd known he was going

abroad—across the pond, as he put it—but she never got the exact time line and was careful not to pester him about dates. She had sliced into the internet a few weeks ago, saw that he was in Berlin. She knew he was also going to London. Maira, who had become an involuntary information portal, yesterday on the phone said that she was pretty sure he was back. He never tells me, Ivy said, doing her best to sound matter-of-fact and not complaining. Call him, Maira said, breezy and expansive. Ivy said she wouldn't. She would rather he find her if he wanted to.

Nicky was settled in her bed and later, instead of going back to his room, to the high bunk bed, he stayed in hers.

After he was asleep she ate the leftover chicken soup, reading the paper she'd not gotten to yet, and was still hungry. She was scrambling some eggs and cheese when her phone rang. It was the girl Cleo. Zack had given her Ivy's number. She was so sorry, she said, but it had fallen through with her friend in Brooklyn, it was a misunderstanding which had to do with something that wasn't her fault, but her friend was—she broke off—anyway she was supposed to meet another friend and it had been an hour, or something, Ivy couldn't really follow it, and since Cleo was speaking in the fast manner of the young people, Ivy did not catch every word, not to mention every reference—the Ubo? what?—but she quickly gathered that Cleo did not have a place to stay tonight and she had looked into cheap hotels but because of the cold they all seemed to be full—because of the cold?—and she was so so sorry to bother Ivy but wondered if she could just crash on Ivy's couch and be gone in the morning—if Zack had stayed in the apartment when Ivy and Nicky were in Virginia, Ivy realized that if Cleo had stayed there once this would be a natural possibility—and went on to say that she was actually a few blocks away now which was why she thought of it and it was pretty cold out tonight. It was the last thing Ivy wanted, having to see to someone else, particularly a stranger, and particularly someone who appeared to be more wayward than she'd realized. But how could she say no?

Ivy dug the bedsheets out of the big Peruvian basket and made up the couch. When Cleo arrived, bright eyed and red cheeked, bustling with a fluffy scarf and mittens, Ivy felt less put out, and was glad she'd said yes. She gave Cleo a bottle of asked-for water and said she herself was going to take a bath and go to bed. She drew closed the pocket doors and stood in the narrow space, saying good night. Totally good, Cleo said. This is great. Ivy closed the door, figuring that *This is great* was probably a new way of saying thank you.

In the bath she read Angela Davis's *Are Prisons Obsolete?*

Nicky was sound asleep and she lit a candle to continue reading in bed.

At the foot of the bed on the bureau her phone rang. She scrambled up and with a shock saw the name: Ansel Fleming. She moved quickly out of the room, pulling the door almost closed, and in another step was in the bathroom, closing its door.

Hi, she said.

Hello, came his voice. Beyond was the sound of the streets. You home?

Yes, she said.

I'm nearby, he said.

You are?

Want a visit? It's cold out here.

Yes, she said. I mean, I'd love it, but, actually, I have someone sleeping in the living room, a girl who's the friend of my friend's nephew, anyway, I mean someone I barely know who needed a place to stay . . .

That's a problem? His voice sounded a little thick.

She laughed, feeling giddy. Well, I'm not sure where I could receive you.

Why not your room? he said.

Well, the other thing is that Nicky is sick with strep throat, so he's sleeping in my room. So it's not the best moment. It's not ideal.

I wanted to ask you something, he said. I don't need to stay long.

Oh, she said. Was he slurring his words? She'd never seen him drunk, so that was a surprise. And even more surprising was his wanting to ask her something. It rather stunned her. Okay, yes, yes. Where are you now?

Two blocks away, he said.

This also so immediate.

Okay, she said. Okay, yes . . . come up. But come quietly in the door.

Will do, he said.

Where could she put him? Not in the kitchen . . . it was practically the same room with Cleo. They couldn't just stand in the hall. But she certainly wasn't going to turn him away if he was *asking* to come and was only two blocks away. She waited in the unlit hallway by the door.

He came in all darkness, wearing a black wool beanie. The cold could still be felt on his black overcoat which he wore over a black parka. She smelled the alcohol before she kissed his cold cheek. She whispered to him to follow her, shutting the door to her dark bedroom as she went by and leading him back to Nicky's crowded room. She snapped on a small light under the bunk bed and moved some piles under the window so Ansel could sit on the small bench wedged between the bureau and the bins of clothes and toys. He sat and pulled her standing in her robe to between his knees. He had taken off his cap but kept his coat on.

This isn't ideal, she said. Sorry.

He slipped his hands under her light robe to her waist.

Cold? he said, looking at her face but seeing what his hands felt. He appeared unfazed by the cramped space.

I'm happy to see you, she said. When did you get back?

It had been months. She didn't point out that she'd had to concentrate on not contacting him. He'd been in and out of town. She tried not to keep track, to blur time in her mind, but she knew pretty much where he'd been. He told her he had a show in the city in a few weeks. Yes, she said, she knew. She had a ticket.

He looked surprised. So you're coming?

I finally get to see you play, she said.

I'm glad, he said. He sat her on his knee.

I want to ask you something, he said thickly. His black wool coat still held the cold from outside. She saw his eyes were swimming and inebriated. It was both repellent and exciting. Usually he appeared in command of himself. This was new. Could she trust less what he said because he was high, or because he was high might he be more revealing?

You say you want all of me, he said thickly and looked at her.

It was as if melted silver were being poured into her body. It seemed to be the first time he was reflecting on something she'd said to him, and yet she couldn't remember saying that exactly, even though she had felt it.

What if I don't have it to give? he said, speaking quickly and looking past her. What if my work is too important and it takes too much of me so there isn't anything left over?

She put her arms around his shoulders. This is what he came to ask her. She couldn't believe it. Her heart was banging dumbly.

Is that what you think? she said.

I don't know if I can do it, he said. His profile gazed with a round eye to the dimness under the bunk bed where Nicky's plastic tool belt hung beside yellow Lego bins and sweatshirts on hooks.

We deal with it, she said. We try.

She shifted to the small space his knees made and looked into his face. He blinked slowly, as if he'd already decided it was impossible, but the watery look in his eyes had a kind of morose feeling she'd not seen before and it gave her a weird hope.

Ansel, she said and kissed him, tasting beer. His hand thrust between her legs, and nice as it was, she pulled it back.

We can't, she said. Here there's no room . . . and . . .

He nodded, looking almost relieved. She slid off his knee to kneel in front of him, and kiss him. She parted his coat layers and slipped her arms under them close to the body underneath and pressed against him. She felt light and fluid against his protective bulk. Baby, he murmured.

He said it as if she were his.

The awkwardness of having him back in Nicky's room and the oddness of his being rather drunk alongside this undercurrent of urgency that he could not stay and needed to be gone soon all went against any likelihood of her feeling happy, but happy was what she felt.

She felt a sort of *at last* feeling. It was as if a younger version of herself had sort of fluttered up and was here and he was seeing it. She felt as if this had happened before, long ago, and she'd been trying to get back to it all this time. She reached for the top of his jeans. Here, she said and unzipped.

He waited a moment, as if unsure this was happening, then shifted himself, lifting his butt so she could pull his pants down which sort of trapped him so he pushed one leg farther so his knees were free. His arm knocked something and it toppled—a pink three-legged stool she had for reaching things on the high shelves—and they both ignored it, shifting to reassemble themselves, to put themselves in the best position for each other. He had to slide to the edge of the bench and brace himself with one hand against the bureau and she bent over him, applying her mouth firmly around him and moving, not quickly, but not lingering, since this didn't want to take a long time. From deep in his throat came a cutoff grunt, acknowledging they had to be quiet. But he never did much moaning. His sounds were rare and well chosen.

There was a sound. Then the word, *Mama*. The door clicked open and Nicky stood in the dark opening.

Ivy looked up and immediately placed her body in front of Ansel. In the split second, she was *pretty* sure that her body had blocked Nicky's view of the man his mother had in his room. Also in the split second she knew that in the future she would review it and decide if she could be reassured, or mortified.

She tossed Ansel's black coat over his lap and stood, moving toward the door. Nicky, sweet, she said, taking she hoped any breathlessness out of her voice and sounding, she thought, normal. Hi. I was just back here with my friend Ansel, because we have Cleo sleeping in the living room . . .

Mama, Nicky said interrupting her. It still hurts. He wasn't interested in explanation; he was sick.

Oh, my love, she said. Come. She said they would get him something to make it better, turning him around docile as a doll—nearly sleepwalking—and steered him back to her bed. She poured medicine into the small plastic cup. As he drank the sweet stuff, the color of lilacs, he stared at her face, as if binding her to him. She tipped him back down, and pulled the covers up. He swallowed and winced, making sure she saw. I know, she said. I know. She brushed his forehead a few times and waited. He closed his eyes and she stood. He grabbed her arm. I'll be right back, she said. You go to sleep.

Mama, he said.

I'll be right back.

She went the short distance down the hall. Ansel was standing. Fuck, he whispered. His face looked truly worried. That's not good.

I don't think he saw, she whispered. I think I blocked his sight.

Fuck, he said again.

She put her hand on his chest as if to feel the moment they had lost. I know, she said. Sorry.

Okay, I'm going.

Will you say hello to him on the way out? Ivy said. Since you're right here. I think that might be less weird.

You want me to?

Yes. Please.

Ivy went first and stood in the door. This is Mum's friend Ansel, she said into the dark bedroom. Remember, who wrote the songs?

Hey, Nicky, Ansel said and tipped his head into the room. I'm sorry to hear you're not feeling well.

Hi, came Nicky's scratchy voice.

Listen, you rest up and get better, he said.

Okay.

Ivy was amazed at how relaxed he sounded. How nice he could be to Nicky! Your mother tells me you like to skate, so maybe one of these days we can go skating.

Nicky said nothing.

That sounds fun, Ivy said.

Okay, Ansel said. You take care. Nice to meet you, Nicky.
Bye, came Nicky's voice even smaller.
At the door she kissed Ansel goodbye. I'm sorry about tonight.
Let me see before I go, he said. She saw where he was looking.
She lifted her robe and slip.
He looked, as if to memorize and take with him, then turned.
She watched him walk down the stairs.
Stay warm, she said. But maybe he was too far away to hear.

She turned out the light in the back room and slipped into her bed. Nicky pressed his foot against her leg, as if to keep the anchor. She now reviewed the moment of Nicky's opening the door, and felt pretty sure she'd been at the right angle for him not to see anything to unnerve or damage him. Though she did always wonder at people thinking they knew what was damaging to a person or not, as far as seeing things. Nicky had the surprise of a man in the house which maybe was disturbing. Though, if Nicky was to be believed, one which he had hoped for. You should get a boyfriend, he often said. Then she thought of what Ansel had said to her. He was drunk so maybe he didn't mean it. Or he was drunk and finally saying what he really meant. Either way, his having spoken of the possibilities of them for even a split second was a flash of what it might be like if he were actually considering her for something more than their one-offs. And she let herself for the moment forget the list of things she'd accepted as what must keep them apart—her being older, being a mother, having a thoroughly different life. She felt for a moment she was a person he found worth considering and she nearly wept, except that she was smiling, beaming in the dark.

Soon she felt Nicky's body twitch, then twitch again, and his breathing thicken. Whenever he was asleep, she felt a pause in the maternal vigilance, allowed to be a slight degree less alert on his behalf.

So you want all of me? he'd said. Was that what it was? Where to put this. She wondered if it was a passing moment, or if it was a turn in the road to something else. Again, time would tell. But she felt a new hope, as if he'd given her something new to consider.

The phone hummed. She picked it up. Ansel! She crawled to the end of the bed, knowing that in the immediate time after Nicky fell asleep he would stay out.

Hey, she whispered.

Can you come out? he said.

She laughed. Ansel.

I mean it. I need to see you.

Are you still on the street?

Almost home, he said. Come to my place.

Ansel, I can't. I have a sick boy at home.

But you have that—isn't there someone there? She can look after him.

She can't look after him . . . he's really quite sick. I have to be here for him.

Just for a little while, he said.

She had an odd flash of a man needing simply to get off, and that drunk he'd become weirdly determined that Ivy would do it for him. But she knew he was perfectly capable of getting himself off. What was he up to?

Fleming, Fleming, she said. I can't.

The sound of feet clopping, cars going by.

I'm sorry, she said. But I hope you understand.

Just for a little while, he said again.

I wish I could.

Yeah, thanks, man, she heard him say and a whoosh, then the street sounds were gone.

Are you home?

I am.

I'll see you tomorrow or the next day, Ivy said. I just can't leave him. Can we do that?

Certainly, Ansel said.

Okay.

There was a silence.

I'm glad you came, she said. Sorry.

. . .

The next morning Nicky was still weak and Ivy congratulated herself that she had stayed with him. She wasn't the sort of mother who would leave her sick child to answer a booty call.

His still feeling lousy gave her the excuse to encourage Cleo's departure. Cleo went obediently, though Ivy detected a slight aura of rejection when she stood in the doorway saying goodbye as Cleo waited for the elevator. Honestly, thought Ivy, I helped her out.

By the afternoon the antibiotics had kicked in and Nicky looked more normal. The throat was not so sore. All the morning Ivy had floated, warming herself around the thought of Ansel's gesturing in this so surprising way toward her and of her sense that something more was happening.

Feeling this new confidence and no longer wrangling with doubt or second-guessing, she texted him.

You free later? She felt the text itself almost smiling.

It was two and a half hours later before he replied.

No.

It was a slap. Okay, she paused. He'd put himself in a vulnerable position; she'd not come through. She had not, the only time he'd pleaded with her, responded by doing what he asked. But she had a good reason. Surely he understood. Was it his ego that was wounded? Did that mean he didn't care, or that he really did? She felt slapped, but managed to see encouragement in the curtness.

What about tomorrow? she wrote.

This time the answer came back right away.

Can't. Busy.

Yes, she felt slapped. Maybe she'd misunderstood. Maybe she was misunderstanding the slap. It felt decisive, but she wasn't sure in which direction. Don't think. Making dinner, she heard high inviting sounds coming from the corner of the living room and saw Nicky's tangled hair and profile in silhouette against the brick building out the window across the street. Each hand clasped a Dalmatian which fought with the other. What's happening? she called from the kitchen. They're getting a divorce, he said. She's moving to Paris.

That night she was not in a hurry to leave Nicky, alongside him in his bed.

Any other questions? she said.

Yup, he said. This might be a hard one. When the world was made, how did all the animals get there?

She sat with three hundred people in the dark. Along one wall the bar was lit in red pieces and small candles dotted the tables crowding the room. At her table were people she both knew and strangers. When the spotlight hit the stage Maira, beside her, squeezed her knee under the table and the applause clattered as Ansel walked out alone. He picked up a guitar and sat on a stool. She had told him she was coming so she had.

He started singing right away and one felt the dimension of the room change, filled up with voice and guitar. As he played and sang, the band members trickled onstage. The drummer, the bass player, the guitarist, and as each added his instrument the music thickened. Ivy felt the eyes of everyone there at the tables or in booths, on the stools of the snaking bar, like the multiple eyes of a bee, but felt she was the bee, watching him, separated from everyone because, she thought, he meant more to her than he did to anyone else there, and even thought she knew the music as well as anyone, every word, every beat. In between songs Ansel spoke a little and she noted when he was nervous, and when he was confident, and when the laugh was genuine or half put on. He gave a shout-out to some school friends and there was cheering from the other side of the room. Mostly he looked glowing.

After a number of songs sprinkled with enthusiastic clapping he said he was inviting a friend out to sing with him—she was from Serbia—and asked for everyone to give a warm welcome to Ziza. A pale girl with stark red lipstick in a short orange ruffled dress came out, carrying a guitar. She wore a long brown braid over her shoulder and boots laced up her shin. Ivy recognized her from some of Ansel's videos. The girl sat on the stool beside Ansel and rested her guitar on her bare knees. She started to sing, her voice rich and cool and unhurried, not a song Ivy knew. When Ansel joined in they looked at each other, he smiling, she not smiling. Ivy's body felt pricked with a hail of needles, and a wave of nausea swept through her. She gulped her beer, feeling her fingers shaking. She caught the glint of Maira's eye in her direction and, with no idea how to return the look, continued to gaze with a sort of horror toward the stage.

Outside, the March night was gusty and cold. The air hit her grateful face, a smack of something fresh and real. She had stayed for all the songs. She stayed for the encore and clapped, and smiled, because she still felt the thrill of seeing him and still loved to hear his music, even if it ripped her heart out. She told Maira she had the sitter and kissed her goodbye—Maira who looked at her with a bright smile as if to say, That wasn't so bad, was it? On the sidewalk she stepped around some broken glass—or was it ice? She would walk home and breathe. At the end of the building was the stage door and as Ivy passed she saw a pale figure leaning against the building, with a screen of cigarette smoke lit up by the parking lot light next door. It was the Serbian girl out here freezing. Ivy walked slowly by. The girl was in her same dress with bare thighs and a short matted fur coat which would hardly keep her warm. She held her cigarette up near her mouth, puffed at it quickly, then exhaled a long plume. She did not look self-contained and happy, as she had onstage. She looked forlorn and far from home. She looked like she was fretting. Ah, thought Ivy, he got to her, too. Maybe she would write some beautiful songs about it and look beautiful singing them. Sadness on her was becoming, not the sadness of someone old.

Ivy walked by and the girl took no notice of her, remaining absorbed in her own lovelorn thoughts, without the least idea that the shadow going by in this foreign city might have some thoughts more identical to hers than she might ever imagine.

It was beautiful, she wrote him in an email so as not to expect the immediate response. But he wrote back right away, *Thank you for all the support beyond the words.*

Maybe she just needed to be patient. She heard from Maira that the concert was so successful, he could now move forward with a number of irons he had in the fire. Hadn't he told her? No, Ivy said. He hadn't.

He was always going away, always gone. Always coming back. Mostly now she did not know, and tried not to find out.

At the end of the phone call Maira asked Ivy if she wanted to hear the news about Ansel.

I don't know, Ivy said. Do I?

Maybe not, Maira said.

Oh great, said Ivy. So now of course tell me.

He got some girl pregnant and they're getting married.

Wow, Ivy said.

I know, Maira said. He barely knows her. It was more of a one-night-stand kind of thing.

Well, that is news, Ivy said.

I know, Maira said.

Who is she? Ivy did not want to be feeling what she was feeling.

A party planner or something. Sort of a Euro girl, but actually Asian. No one really knows.

Wow.

Yeah. He's the one who wanted to get married. So the child would have a father. You know, because of his . . .

Right, Ivy said. Yes.

No one has really met her, except Fred and Matt. And Clover. Clover thinks she is a fortune hunter.

Ivy knew from Maira these were Ansel's closest friends. She had seen Fred Brown and Matt Morgan in some music videos.

With Ansel?

I know. I don't know. I guess famous musician?

Well, that is news, Ivy said again.

You okay? Maira said.

Well, Ivy said, trying to keep her voice steady. Would rather know than not.

A month later Maira let Ivy know that the party planner was no longer in the picture. The whole thing was off. Maira wasn't sure what had happened. Either she lost the baby, or who knew if she was even pregnant in the first place.

Other times she would go to the portal. One says we *enter* the portal, but we never actually go in. We stay outside, looking in, watching. And yet what is on the screen seems to enter us.

He was sitting in a chair on a roomy stage in Texas or in a blurry Berlin bar lit blue. He sat on a red couch in a radio studio, his voice hoarse. He looked tired, had not shaved. He was wearing the caramel sweater. Her heart got a punch each time a woman's profile came into the frame, a singer watching him as they sang a chorus together, smiling catlike. One girl with crushed eyes blew cigarette smoke toward the camera, and the shot pulled back so you saw her, in jeans with a belly button showing, lying on a white rug beside the familiar glass coffee table.

A hot day at the end of May. He was back for a moment. She'd heard he was leaving again soon. Best not to text. Less to recover from.

Then like a string snapping she thought, Maybe I will never see him again. Maybe like Stanley he would be suddenly gone. Or like her parents, there one minute, gone the next. So you ought to catch at any chance. She messaged him, when was he leaving?

The answer right away. *Sooner than planned.*

She said she was sorry she couldn't see him then, and he'd surprised her with *What are you doing now? I'm nearby.*

I have to pick up Nicky in twenty minutes.

Let's fit it in.

Instead of being insulted that she was being fitted into such a narrow sliver, as she figured other prouder girls might be, she was thrilled.

Okay, she wrote.

On my way.

She opened the door. He was wearing that white shirt. How long had it been since she'd first seen the white shirt?

I haven't had lunch, he said. The first thing after not seeing her for months. She leaned on him, her forearms Sphinx-like.

Your heart is beating so fast, he said. Why is it beating so fast.

I'm seeing you.

You didn't miss me, he said and backed her out of the hall.

He set her onto the stool at the drafting board and kneeled down, pulling up her black skirt and pulling down her underwear.

Wait, she said and brought his shoulders up. Over here.

She moved to the couch and laid herself back holding her arms out to him.

Why are you looking at me that way? he said.

What? She had no idea what the look was. She was thrilled to see him. Perhaps it looked alarmed.

Are you angry with me? he said.

No, she said. But she wasn't thinking it through. She had been angry many times, though she wasn't feeling so now. So how was he seeing it?

Come here. He came toward her, then glanced at the windows with the curtain pulled open and the brick daylight of the leafy street.

He pulled her up by the arm and into the kitchen. Things are about to get primitive, he muttered. He looked around for where to put her. His gaze slid past the table to the counter near the door. He backed her against it and with one lift hoisted her onto it. Her breath was lightly socked out of her. She felt some magazines under her sliding. He entered her, filling her thoroughly.

Do you remember how I feel? he said, looking at her face.

If only I could forget it, she said.

He stayed in her, then began to move without hurry, yet conveying great urgency. She thought, Maybe this is the last time. She tried to register it as the last time, feeling her eyes melting, her lids being torn off.

It was both very quick and very long.

Who knew how much fun could be had in fifteen minutes, he said as they left the apartment together.

She followed him down the stairs. Usually she watched him go, and she was aware now of not watching, like entering into a painting and being part of it. They went through the open door of the lobby together and down the red stone steps to the sidewalk—together! She was walking beside him, past her usual wrought-iron grates, past the low stoops. She was floating. The May shadows feathered onto them. You've got a glow, he said looking down at her sidewise. She felt unabashedly blissful. Well, yes, she said. From you.

They crossed the avenue and he said he was turning there. She leaned onto his white shirt again, the cliff and raft of it.

Go on, he said, laughing her off. Go get your son.

Was he embarrassed? She didn't care.

She actually skipped away from him. She thought, I will never regret anything, and went running over the clouds.

All was clear. Was she suffering? No, she was fine. She accepted it. But it took only ten hours for the plug to be pulled and the heart to lose its gladness and swirl down the drain. And it began again, not letting him matter.

. . .

No traces of him were ever left, so afterward, when she found on the kitchen counter the accordioned magazine creased into tiny pleats like a Fortuny gown, she had to stop herself from saving it as a memento. Though her last text to him hovered on her phone and she did not throw that out. She could stab herself with it whenever she chose to look. *Have you left yet?* she wrote on her right side of the text column and the left side showed no answer.

During the summer when she was out of town, considerations of Ansel needed less management. There was no chance of seeing him, so she could not wonder if or when or how. She could remain suspended between her usual two attitudes, the resolve to keep away from him—*I like it but I don't need it*—and acceptance of taking what came along. *You occupy a warm and secure place inside me.*

Upstate, August.

Maira had a compound up the Hudson where she spent weekends. Her daughter, Bibi, from her first marriage, was often there, and her present husband, Tony, was in residence there. The property had a large barn with an internal balcony and sectioned-off sleeping areas. A carriage house of whitewashed beams had an outside staircase leading to a second-floor apartment, and Tony's woodworking shop with a garage door took up the floor below. There was a yurt back in the woods and a couple of small cabins—one Bibi's, one for guests—and at the top of the dirt road was the main house, a stately Georgian beauty of faded pink brick and perfect proportions. To make ends meet Maira rented most of the dwellings, usually to friends, and in the summer she and Tony lived in the yurt or even rented a place near the sea. The rest of the year Maira went back and forth from their penthouse on the edge of Chinatown, purchased long before it became a fashionable place to live, and Tony lived upstate full-time, working as a bespoke carpenter in nearby Red Hook when he wasn't working on their property, building additions or renovating a greenhouse or working as maintenance man and landlord to the shifting population of renters. Tony had an easygoing nature and never seemed bothered that Maira came and went. Ivy admired their marriage. They seemed to love each other, giving each other an extra look when something was funny but extra funny to them, and speaking appraisingly of each other in absence, a sure sign of love, and yet not to miss each other when they were apart. It was a combination Ivy couldn't quite figure out, still needing the three-dimensionality of love. Recently Tony had bought a second-hand Airstream and set it up as a pool house near the pond he'd dug after they'd first moved in fifteen years before. In the pond he put a canoe he'd made out of birch bark, and lily pads choked the shady end.

Maira's birthday was mid-August and this summer she had cleared the compound of renters so guests could come and she could throw herself a birthday party, since the best present for Maira would be to have as many friends as possible be with all the other friends. The country ones could meet the city ones. The ones she'd met last week could meet the longtime ones. Tony would grill steak and chicken and sausage and there would be platters of her favorite hard and soft cheeses, with fruit and fresh bread, and bowls of nuts. It was a potluck feast so people would bring everything else—red pastas and white pastas, lettuce salads, quinoa with raisins and cauliflower, rice with peas and mint, corncobs, asparagus vinaigrette, tomato and basil, coleslaw and bacon.

Ivy traveled up from Virginia. Nicky was going camping with his father and Ivy was glad for the excuse to leave the sweltering South if her son was not nearby. She planned also to visit her cousin Margaret in New Jersey and, if there was time, Irene on Long Island. Being single she was more often a guest now, as she had been in the old days. She slept in the guest rooms and felt the odd disorientation of not being where she belonged, not a completely foreign feeling, while she also felt the kindness of the friends who had her. Ivy had purposefully not asked Maira if Ansel Fleming would be coming. She'd noticed a wary look appearing in her friend's eyes when she'd raised the dilemma of Ansel Fleming and took the warning. Even Maira was tiring of the repetition. Ivy put herself forward as having turned a corner with Fleming. Maybe not speaking of him would also help his power fade. Mostly she was not in contact with him. Ivy had been on a few dates and told Maira about them to demonstrate her interest elsewhere, even if it wasn't much felt.

In the field below the barn was a firepit with granite slabs for benches and cushions scattered in groupings under trees strung with garland lights. A line of tin Moroccan lanterns had candles flickering inside them, marking a path to the barn. Music played from speakers, thumping. Figures were shadowy, then faces lit up near the firelight, drinking from bottles. Hands carried wine in short jelly jars, in plastic flutes. A long table of tea candles had dishes glistening in the two lines with Tony's wooden carving platters of meat flecked with black. Now and then out of the chatting hum, laughter bubbled up, softened by the night air. Now and then the speakers were quiet and real guitars took over and played.

Ivy saw him coming down a slope from where all the cars were parked by the main house. Slow stride. He was with Fred Brown and Matt Morgan, the heartthrob musician whom Fred toured with. Matt Morgan, punky and careless, had his elbow interlocked with that of a wide-faced woman, Clover Johnson, his best friend, who lived nearby in a mansion overlooking the Hudson which had belonged to her family for generations. Clover Johnson had fashioned it into a sort of unofficial artist colony, where there were concerts and art shows, and where both lost souls and famous ones took up residence, often for years at a time. Matt Morgan was one of the famous ones. Ivy had years ago been to a party at the Johnson house, having gone with Daphne, who'd been in art school with Clover's brother Jordy. Ivy had been running into Clover Johnson for years and Clover never remembered meeting her. Clover was wearing a long white dress with red cowboy boots kicking at the hem. Her face was plain, but projected a beauty she seemed convinced by. Word was that she was in love with Matt, but he wasn't interested in her that way.

The three amigos, murmured a voice in Ivy's ear. She turned to Maira's sparkling eyes, a pleased hostess who reflected every soul there.

The figures drew near. Maira, in a green skirt shimmering like a mermaid, walked in stacked sandals over the grass toward them. All kissed hello. Then Ansel saw Ivy behind and held his arms out wide, as if greeting a mischievous child. Ivy came forward into the hug and felt strangely blotted out.

Look who's here, he said breezily, furthering the blow.

Never know where I'll be, she said, aware in the following seconds of it being one of those stupid things one said, meaning nothing and conveying even less.

But after that, she was speechless. He was here. She wasn't surprised, but she was stunned. Then Ansel was engulfed by more shadows and carried off. I'll find him later, she thought. There will be a better moment. Her heart was all askew.

To steady herself she found a place to sit back on a Turkish pillow arranged around some lanterns, beside two people chatting closely together. Just be, she told herself, just be. A pair of boots darkened the space next to her. Her heart sat up.

This looks like a good place to be, said an Irish voice, and she looked up to Fred Brown, in his hat, crouching to sit beside her.

Hi, she said, genuinely happy it was him. Yes, not bad.

Nice to celebrate Maira for a change, Fred Brown said.

Well, I'm not sure she's still not celebrating everyone else, Ivy said. But, yes. What have you been doing today?

Fuck all, he said. A good day.

You going to play tonight? Ivy asked him.

Didn't bring my axe, he said.

That's a shame. You ought to be celebrated, too, she said. Fred's songs were beautiful, she thought, melodies which sounded just the other side of familiar, so that you were moved by something rare. His lyrics were simple and clear, which Ivy knew was a lot harder to do than complicated and vague.

I'll leave it to Matt, he said. He's the showman.

Do the Irish have that expression *hide your light under a bush?* Ivy said.

I think it might be from the Bible, said Fred Brown. And possibly it's *bushel.*

Ivy turned to face him, surprised. You're right. That is where it's from.

She looked to where she'd last seen Ansel, talking to their mutual friend Casey, holding a beer bottle against his chest in a priestly way as Casey talked, moving her hands around and making him smile. But he was not there now.

She asked Fred Brown what he'd been up to recently and he told her he'd spent the winter touring with Matt and then had gone back to Ireland for a short trip to visit his parents, then ended up staying longer in London when he saw his old girlfriend and things started up again. Ivy said that was nice and he said yes and no, and Ivy asked if she would come here and Fred Brown said she was a working girl and couldn't get away, so now he was thinking about maybe moving back to London for a while so they could see about it once and for all. We keep coming back to each other, Fred Brown said, and I'm not sure if that means we're bound to end up together or if we're too fecking stupid to let go.

Love is hard, Ivy said. She immediately added, Wait. Do I think a cliché is helpful?

Fred must have thought not, but allowed, I don't know. If it's hard I have a feeling it's not really love.

Good things don't come easy? Ivy suggested. Let me see if I can come up with some more clichés.

Fred laughed. You're funny, he said as if it just struck him. I like you. Maybe we should get married.

Ivy blushed, glad no one could see. Fred Brown was one step away from Ansel, that's how it felt. She wondered if Fred Brown knew anything about her from Ansel, but figured not given Ansel's attitude toward talking about people. She wondered if Fred Brown felt the same kind of adjunct feeling.

Is that what you're after, Ivy said keeping the playful tone, getting married? He shrugged. She then asked what it was like staying at Clover's. He said sometimes they jammed all night.

A well-known melody reached them, one of Matt's songs. His silhouette holding his guitar blocked the fire which lit eager watching faces.

Ah, said Fred. There he goes now. But Fred did not stir.

It must have been past midnight. She was in a dark part of the lawn looking at a distance to the fire and Matt still playing, watching a young woman in a strapless black top singing. Should she go find Ansel? She had hoped Ansel would find her, but he had not ever really done that before, so why would he now? She'd have to find him. Now? Or wait longer?

She'd last seen Ansel in silhouette, unmistakable tonight, his hair curled out at his neck, in front of the barn with the candlelight behind. Okay, she thought. She walked on the black grass to the side of the barn and entered through a sticky door. People were strewn on the couches, and tall candlesticks dripped wax on a long table scattered with flowers and three birthday cakes in various stages of annihilation. Out the wide barn door she saw a group of people passing around a joint and made out Ansel's figure in between Fred Brown and Clover Johnson. As she watched, Matt Morgan appeared out of the darkness with the young woman beside him and seemed to be suggesting that it was time to leave. Clover Johnson looked at the girl up and down, half smiling, half dismissive, unabashed in showing her curiosity.

Ivy stepped into the light as if onto a stage and waved toward the dark audience of Ansel, right away catching his eye, glinting and friendly.

He came toward her.

You're not leaving, are you? she said.

It looks like maybe, he said.

But I haven't seen you at all, she said.

Easy come, easy go, he said.

She brushed his arm. I haven't seen you in so long, she said, surprising herself at how straightforward she was being. Will you give me a minute?

He laughed.

Come, she said and took his hand. She picked up a candlestick from the table and felt hot wax on her hand. She had not planned this.

Come see where I'm staying, she said. They stepped off the dry planks of the floor back onto the lawn. The cottage was on the other side of the driveway tucked in woods. 'Scuse me, said handsome Matt Morgan, his eyebrows slanted, a joint at his lips. Can I cop a light? Ivy stopped, holding Ansel's hand, watching while Matt Morgan lit his joint on the flame, fixing her in his gaze as if to say, He's not yours and never will be. But look at you.

They crossed the packed-dirt driveway.

Where you going, chum? Matt said.

I'll be right back, Ansel said over his shoulder.

Ivy heard Clover Johnson murmur, We'll see about that.

Ivy was aware of how they must look, the candlestick in front of them on the still night, walking up the outside steps processionlike to the door on the second floor. It occurred to her that this was the first time she and Ansel Fleming had been seen together outside of their rooms, outside of the city, in public. And like so many things with Ansel Fleming—that is, her *thoughts* about Ansel Fleming—she found herself in a place she hadn't thought she would be in.

The room was small with heavy beams and a slanted roof which reached to the floor, so that one could stand up only in the middle corridor of the room. Nice home you've got here, he said.

A bed was at the other end, her suitcase on a chest near the door, a small closetlike bathroom and a sofa facing it.

I have to pee, she said. Excuse me.

She set the candle on the floor and he sat on the sofa. He watched her through the open door to the small rough wood bathroom where she sat in the dark on the compost toilet. The bathroom smelled of cedar.

She stood up.

Leave them off, he said.

She dropped her underwear and stood in front of him.

How have you been? she said.

He looked at her. His face wasn't interested in small talk.

Come here, he said.

She lowered herself onto him, not looking away.

Feels like old times, she said.

Hey, chummy, came the call through the screen. It was Matt Morgan in the driveway below. You coming or not?

Chummy? Ivy said, staying on his lap.

I'm going to miss my carpool, Ansel said. His eyes were like black jellies with white points of light.

Stay, she said. I can drive you home.

His expression was unreadable. He moved her off him gently and stood up.

He went to the screen door and, without opening it, called not loudly, Nyet, he said. Okay, she heard from down on the driveway and a car starting and Ansel came back to her and the happiness under the slanted black beams.

Are you real? she said.

For the time being.

Do you ever get your throat rubbed? she said.
No.
She showed him how it felt.

It was late and after the wine she'd had over the long hours she did not feel drunk, just loose and vague and suspended, and even with his face again in front of her, she also had images flickering by of the faces of the people she'd seen tonight and their unprocessed impression on her and saw again the house and the slope of lawn earlier before the sun went down while they were setting out the tables and the sky going colorless and the trees black, then the sky suddenly black too with its sprinkle of stars. Wrapped around her was the warp of seeing him after so long and the pleasure of him being led by the hand across the driveway in front of his friends making this somehow a new meeting, even if it would not mean a new thing in the future. Nothing was changed, this was always the reminder she had to repeat, and she saw how it was and determined not to hope it would be any other way and was not going to watch for him to show any sliver of love or be different than he had been and felt the strength of that clear-sightedness and even surprised herself by savoring what was unfolding minute by minute as if she'd stored enough in the vault of wondering about and thinking of him that she did not now need to review it further. His eyes regarded her with a mixture of merriment and desire and her body filled up on sensation and pleasure, feeling even a little playful, even accepting.

Look at you, he said, as if he could see it.

I don't know what came over me, she said. I mean, I do . . . but . . .

He said, You look happy. He said it appraisingly, and also sad.
Did you know I was going to be here? he said.
I wasn't sure, she said. I thought maybe. But.

. . .

She picked up the candlestick and brought it to the bedside table and pulled back the sheets. She never knew if Ansel Fleming would suddenly shy and bolt and was relieved to hear him following her. They lay on the wide bed.

Did you know I was here? she said.

Not telling, he said.

I was just fishing, she said. She shook her head. I'm really taken up with you more than you know.

You mean missing me? he said. He seemed genuinely baffled.

She nodded. I even miss you when you're here.

How do you mean? he said.

She was beside him and still, in the stillness that was like a pocket of oxygen in her vacuum life.

I'm not sure I should say.

Please do.

She turned onto her back, looking up at the eaves, dark against the whitewashed ceiling. Well, she said after a silence. I love you.

There was silence again but she did not feel rushed, she felt like all bets were off, and what was there to hide now and why hide.

She said, And I know you don't want it.

More silence contained his response. What could he anyway say.

So he asked her about Nicky and she said he wasn't in the best shape. She thought that his having to go back and forth between her and his father was getting to him. At least that's how she explained to herself his increasing defiance, his stubborn attitude of not listening to her, of not doing the smallest things she asked without a battle. Ansel told her about his niece, his sister's daughter, and how when she was little before he was away he used to look after her sometimes and take her to the park. She was willful too and rude whenever she felt as if she was being told what to do. He said he told her that he loved her and whatever she did was okay with him and after that she stopped being so rude.

If only it were so simple, Ivy said. But you make it sound possible. Not sure a mother can do that.

You're a good mother, he said.

I don't think I am, she said. But that's nice of you to say. I don't like having to tell someone what to do. And that's what a mother does. I don't like rules.

I'd like to see him, Ansel said. And really meet him. Ivy had coached herself to refuse all hope where Ansel was concerned, but this gave her a jolt.

That would be nice.

I've never said that before, he pointed out.

They talked more. For the last year on and off Ansel had been working on a documentary of being on the road, collaborating with other musicians. It looked as if it had finally come together, he said. She said she couldn't wait to see it, and meant it, knowing that it would have extra power for her. When Ansel dozed off she did not try to sleep also. She didn't want to miss a minute. Expect nothing, she kept saying to herself. Expect nothing. Soon the black windows turned a deep blue.

He didn't need to say that he wanted to be home before sunrise. When the air was still light green, without shadows, they were up, walking down the steps of the cottage, she barefoot, in a slip with pink beading, Ansel in his clothes of the night. Ivy's car was hemmed in by other parked cars so they took Maira's old green station wagon with its red cracked seats and Ivy drove.

Bessie Smith was in the old tape machine and sang scratchy and full. They passed few cars. Ivy was weightless, in that see-through state she was often in after a night with Ansel, glad to be herself, and yet after the communing thoroughly freed of herself and occupying instead the wideness of the world which passed through her and filled her, with what felt like a total acceptance of existence. She knew the state did not last, but how good to know it even once.

She turned off the curving road at a vast iron gate with a carved stone crown and flaking bars, up a winding driveway in a manicured forest with no brush on the ground and majestic thick tree trunks and was surprised how well she'd remembered being here, though it had been only once and the party she'd come to with Daphne had been more than a dozen years before. They passed through the same avenue of stone columns choked with vines and a huge statue of an Indian chief, his head bowed. The party had been at the same time of year so that was part of it and Ivy remembered an enormous room with French doors open to a long terrace the length of the house with marble stairs leading down to a sloping lawn and the wide Hudson beyond. She remembered sitting on a hassock.

Down here, Ansel said, pointing to the right and a white gravel road off the paved one which led up to the stone mansion. They pulled up to a dark green house which looked as if it had once been a stable. This is me, he said. She stopped the car.

I liked listening to you last night, he said.

She smiled to hear it, about to make a crack about him meaning sex, but feeling so loosely strung did not find it hard to stop herself, to let it go, to let everything go. As always with Ansel she was relieved by his not having to make a crack about everything.

He opened his door. Get some sleep, he said.

Then thinking of sitting on that hassock she had a strange flash of sitting beside another person. Then she remembered before the person sat down Clover Johnson had introduced him.

Wait, she said, and faced him with a look of wonder. We met before.

I know, he said, stepping out of the car.

You do?

Yes. He looked down at her.

It was here, she said. I just remembered it. At a party here we met. You had short hair then. And I just now remembered it, where you were sitting, where we both were.

Yes, he said. I know.

You remembered that?

He nodded.

But you didn't say anything.

His face never surprised, still not surprised now.

I didn't remember till now, she said, ticking her head in amazement.

He did not comment.

What was the lesson he was teaching her now? That she really didn't know anything at all. That all the time she'd spent thinking of the man she had not even remembered an actual real-life meeting. He lived so much more in her head. She did know that. But like so many things she knew, she was learning it again.

She drove out over the crunching gravel. Yes, it was coming back to her if she concentrated. They had talked a little. Oh, and there was a moment, she remembered now, when he had laughed at something, but something she didn't think very funny, and she had thought, This guy is trying too hard. And now here she was thinking him one of the most important people she would ever know.

She drove home, still drugged, a warm and dewless air blowing in the window around her neck. How strange she had forgotten meeting him, and only remembering now. It had been more than two years since the first time she saw him at her door, arriving early, looking familiar. It turns out he was. He was not, after all, a stranger.

What she had seen so long ago as trying too hard now looked like making an effort. Ansel Fleming making an effort toward her had a whole new meaning now.

She went back to bed and woke midmorning thinking first of the feeling of his hands. She went over it slowly, his eyes and his face, his arms and his back, holding on to his back. She thought of his *I liked listening to you,* of lowering herself on him. She thought of the configurations on the bed, of both of them on their sides facing the same way with Ansel's arm holding her down like a shadow.

Expect nothing, she repeated to herself, driving under the dripping rags of green on the Taconic Parkway. Expect nothing. Her car rode the swells of the hills and swept the curves and it was easy not to expect anything right away, while he was still glowing on her. Her next stop was Margaret in New Jersey.

Margaret brought her with the kids to the town pool and in between Margaret calling to her children and drying them off and giving them money for snacks and putting on suntan lotion and firmly saying no, she and her cousin talked and laughed and Ivy watched as always with wonder Margaret's decisive manner and tried to take notes for later use. In the evening they made margaritas on the back patio with some neighbors, and Margaret's husband, Ted, had them laughing so hard the children called from the high windows to be quiet. Ivy often felt like a spy at Margaret's house, misrepresenting herself as also a mother, when Margaret seemed maternal one hundred percent of the time and accepted it without complaint and a solid wife one hundred percent of the time, seemingly happy with that, too, while Ivy when she went upstairs to the guest room under the eaves checked herself internally to see if she still was gratified by seeing Ansel and continued to savor the hours. When Ivy said goodbye on the plump walkway in front of the blue house, Margaret did not meet her eye when she said, I don't want you wasting energy on someone who doesn't love you.

From there Ivy drove to Long Island to Irene's beach house. Ivy and Irene walked the dogs beside the swirling surf; Irene's husband made supper. One night they went to a cookout at some friends' shack on the inner bay where a white-haired man flirted with Ivy, telling her he wanted to read her book though he did not usually read anything contemporary, and told her how he rarely went out and when he wasn't working he spent his time alone and was only here because his friends had dragged him here tonight. I liked talking to you, he said when they said good night. Ivy had hardly said a word. Afterward Irene laughed and told her the man was actually married and lived occasionally with his wife but was famous for not mentioning it. Listening in the guest room to the surf's low moan across the potato fields Ivy continued to feel the spell of Ansel Fleming and tried to ignore whether it was wearing off or not. So far it lingered. Truly expecting nothing was the trick.

He who binds himself to a joy
Does the winged life destroy
But he who kisses the joy as it flies
Lives in eternity's sunrise.

Ivy drove the long hot drive back to Virginia and its heavy dark foliage. She felt she'd restocked her reserves and with Nicky was able to be more aware and patient. The usual frustrations did not rankle. She hugged him tight. She was more playful. It was a reminder to have experiences separate from being a mother, and so be a better one.

When she saw Everett, she wondered if he could see the change in her, with the spell and the acceptance of it, but if he noticed, he did not show it.

Ten days passed in the suspension of the end of summer and still she was not suffering. Maybe her suffering had been caused by her inability to truly accept how things stood with Ansel. Well, she seemed to have a handle on that now. Her energy boosted, she got up at dawn to run on the quiet rural roads through fragrant air which grew heavier as the day went on. She kept the joy in a secret box. When not with Nicky, she got back to work and the writing came steadily.

. . .

Edith Wharton had married in her early twenties, having had no sexual experience, to a husband who didn't provide her with much more. In her early forties, divorced and living in Europe, she had an affair with a sophisticated diplomat, a well-known lover of women. After a rendezvous with him she wrote rapturously how such afternoons were enough to illuminate a lifetime! She was aware he was not a man to be tied down, and would therefore simply bask in this new experience of passion.

Two weeks later however her diary noted that she had spoken too soon and actually one afternoon was not enough.

Ivy had accepted no word from him, until day fifteen when something shifted. Her spirits took a dip. It was a tiny prick in the raft, deflating the firmness in her. Ah, she thought, here it comes again. She did not know how to fight it. She told herself it wouldn't be as bad this time, now that she knew what to expect. Wasn't she getting used to it? Then the old creaky reel started up, playing in her head, and it didn't feel better, it felt the same, only more so.

She decided, though not for the first time, Enough.

She kept thinking of him. Though the decision had been made, he did not go away. The first few months of being apart were always the most excruciating. When she returned to New York the city still vibrated for her, depending on if he was there or not. But that wasn't supposed to be her concern anymore.

In New York with her son for the first time—after she'd moved from the house in Virginia—Ivy had felt the roots of her heart being ripped out of a deep ground, deeper than she'd realized. She stood by the decision they'd made, but she still thought of Everett.

There'd not been many times that Ivy had glimpsed a controlled distress on Nicky's face as he watched his parents fighting, but once was enough for the expression to be seared into her, and it was to that face she returned when she faltered in the conviction that she and Everett were best off living apart. Nicky was her guidepost for what was acceptable.

To solidify the move to New York, Ivy had worked at resettling into the apartment, buying new chairs and getting a better bed for Nicky. Her office was now his bedroom. She moved around boxes, sifted through their contents, then shoved them into new places under the bed, or onto closet shelves, as if the rearrangement of stored things should reflect the new rearrangement of her life apart. She found it harder to get together with Irene and Harriet and Daphne. She had left the rhythm of their lives, she had left the rhythm of hers.

She was at the edge of all kinds of missing all the time. She missed especially the slowness of their life in Tanzania. She missed the childhood she didn't have.

She kept her eyes closed though awake, so the rest of her body might not know it, and as long as her eyes didn't reveal it maybe her body would be tricked and sleep would come. The insomnia was a new thing. The room didn't know it; she *could* have been asleep. Maybe she even was. Sometimes feeling at the edge of sleep one did wake up and find that one had gone there after all. If you opened your eyes the insomnia would have won. The room would know and have to admit you were awake, watching at the watery shadows near the window on the wall.

She was still thinking of Everett.

Because it hadn't really severed things even after they'd made the decision. That was just making the decision. In fact they had made the decision a few times. The first time they'd backed out on it, the prospect of being apart seeming to be more unbearable than the staying together. So the decision could be gone back on. When had that been, that first decision? Her memory was dark at the edges, and this line of thought was the least conducive to sleep, but she slipped off the soft shoulder, and remembered again the playground. Everett beside her and not looking at each other. The silver gumdrop and the dangerous spinning carousel they let him go on because no one else was there. What had been the words? We don't even live together anymore. It can't go on? She remembered Nicky in the dirty sandbox picking up a broken shovel and trying to dig with it, then his triumphant face flashing by on the dangerous ride—Look at me!—having no idea that twenty feet away his parents were deciding whether to rip his life in half like a scenery backdrop.

How, she thought, would she ever make it up to him?

How how how.

The nights she lay there, tears leaking from closed eyes.

The place where Everett had been was like a gouge taken out of the earth with Nicky standing at the edge of the hole, baffled. When Ivy saw Nicky's figure that way she'd make an extra effort to engage him, as if distraction could keep a boy from noticing that his father was gone.

Nicky brought home compositions.

a year ago my dad and mom fighting
I tried to stop them
but they wouldn't listen
they stoped after 5 minutes
they stomped into different rooms
I just stayed where I was
with a waterfall of tears rushing down
my face they wouldn't stop until
my mom and dad stoped then
after a while my tears stoped

But the city was not welcoming to the lonely, as the country could be. The city did not sympathize with loss. It zoomed past loneliness, a bus bypassing its station stop. Indifference paved the busy streets and shut doors felt more cruel than the obtuse trees swishing their hair in the wind or clouds moving off without ceremony. Despite its indifference, one felt that nature saw you, was more forgiving. It regarded loss and death matter-of-factly, accepting it. Up came the daffodil—fresh, yellow, trumpeting—then in a blink, it was a brown piece of rolled paper, shriveled.

On the subway Nicky curled over her lap, laying down his head and shoulders. Variety was here in the city, she told herself. Good for a child to see.

One day Everett called Ivy on the phone and said, I've started seeing someone.

In an unguarded moment, depending on her mood or how porous the hour, Ivy would be overtaken by a most expansive shatterproof worry—for her son's happiness and well-being, so that she might, if she gave into the tender hollow feeling in her chest, weep.

Relief came at the end of the day when Nicky's weight sank against her arm, growing steadily heavier as he fell toward sleep, and the wonderful certainty of peace when she felt the twitches and final spasm of his falling into sleep. They had made it through another day, he was unscathed.

Nicky stood at his desk area in the corner of the living room with an expression of horror. Where are my math problems? he said.

Ivy told him she'd been cleaning up and probably threw them out.

Those were my math problems! he cried.

I'm so sorry. I thought it was old homework.

It was old. But I still wanted them.

Oh, sweet, I'm sorry.

It surprised her when he began to cry. Why did you throw

out my math problems? His voice rose. You don't even know how hard I worked on them.

She saw other thoughts moving across his face, one fear leading to another.

I didn't know you wanted them. I am sorry.

Would you ever throw out Enny? he said through his sobs. Would you ever throw out a picture of Dad?

No, she said. No, I would never throw out Enny. Or Dad.

But he was not looking to be reassured. He had other injustices to address.

And why does Dad live somewhere else when he should live here with us? Why?

Ivy could not answer.

Nicky, seeing her hesitation, grew even more outraged. Why do you throw out my math problems? he screamed. They were *my* math problems! Nicky did not cry often, but when he allowed himself, the tears could flow and flow.

It was September and she returned to teaching. The students in the class looked at her with either blankness or worry and, occasionally, interest. The class met in a room near the apartment in a tall university building off Washington Square and she'd gotten a commitment from a sitter named Katia for every Thursday afternoon to pick up Nicky from sixth grade and to stay till she got home at five.

They'd met inside so often in the dark that when she ran into him in the daylight out on the street it was like an arrow hitting a bull's-eye.

She was leaving the huge university building. After dismissing her class she did not stand with the students waiting on the seventh floor for the elevator but walked as usual down the stairwell. Today she was joined by one student, Janine, a slight willowy girl with a streak of green at the back of her head, visible only when she wore her hair twisted up on her head, as she had today. She and Janine reached the bottom of the stairs and stepped out into the building's enormous evening shade on the sidewalk where other students changing classes streamed around them, entering the lobby, crossing to the coffee shops and pizza places or heading east to the green cloud of Washington Square Park with its checkered evening light. Janine asked Ivy if she thought her recent story was strong when Ivy was shocked to see a familiar figure in the crowd, only two feet away, passing near her like a slow arrow. For a dizzying moment, she thought he was there to find her, then realized in the same instant he could have no idea she was here. No one but her students even knew where she was.

Hey, she said before he passed by, not seeing her. Seconds later and he would have walked by the building. Seconds earlier, she would have been across the street and on her way home. They had met like the intersection of shooting stars.

Hi, she said, somehow making it three syllables. She put her hand on his shoulder, as if testing his three dimensions. He was here, in her day, in her world. Where are you—-? She smiled. She turned awkwardly to Janine. Oh, this is my student, she said, not introducing them further. Janine was motionless, eyes ticking, as if waiting to finish her sentence which had been interrupted. Ivy, her head blasted open, managed to blurt out, Okay. I'll see you next week.

Janine nodded and swung her head like a colt, the green streak leading the rest of her body to tilt away.

Ivy turned back to Ansel. He was wearing his snug dark coat and the woven scarf of striped colors wound thickly to his chin. It was not cold, but he was protected.

He said, That wasn't very polite, in a flat tone.

Oh, she said. No, she's fine. Denial always the knee-jerk response, but she knew immediately he was right. Ivy had cut Janine, unceremoniously casting her off. Damn Ansel, she thought, slicing her in half. She had been too surprised. Once again she was not equal to him.

Where are you off to? she said.

Movie screening, he said. More press. I need to introduce. Then I do a radio thing. He spoke robotically, as if not wanting to show that it mattered.

That's exciting, she said. Come on, you must be excited. It's great.

I am, he said deadpan. He faced forward, as if not to lose sight of his destination.

Well, the movie's fantastic, she said. As I wrote you. Really great.

A week before, she'd gone to the premiere with Maira, who'd organized the tickets. Through Ansel.

They'd met for a drink before the screening at a new slightly inconveniently located place Maira knew, being a person who keeps track of new hip places, and sat at the bar, Maira in a moss green velvet jacket, fingers glittering with gold, telling her people's news. They got seats in the center of the audience and, waiting for the movie to start, Maira leapt up to greet friends. Ivy, having come to demonstrate a supportive friendly attitude, nevertheless looked at every woman walking down the aisles or showing the back of her head and imagined them Ansel's lovers—the old, the young, the pale, the shiny. She was fascinated to see him out operating in the world, and was seeing it demonstrated: his life so apart from her.

When he stood, dressed in a three-piece suit, tightly fitted as was the fashion of the moment and which she thought maybe wasn't the most flattering—to any man—his gratified expression remained patient as the audience quieted down, and he thanked with sincerity the indefatigable film team, and welcomed with sparkle his family and friends. He pointed out his grandmother—a silhouette with a strand of pearls, who waved off his words and refused to stand up—and if the clapping and laughter were any indication, everyone there was a friend. Then before the lights went down he saw Maira and blew her a kiss, and noticed Ivy beside. He pointed a finger at her, the gesture you saw politicians do, on a stage, acknowledging the volunteers gathered on their behalf.

. . .

On the sidewalk, with the young people like water around them, Ivy told him she hoped he would get a lot of attention for the film.

He nodded one slow nod. This is where you teach? he said.

Yup. Up there.

He looked up the building's side which towered above them like a canyon wall. She felt the bright evening lighting her, not to her advantage, her hair like ragged straw over her ears. His face looked more beautiful than ever.

I can't believe you walked right by at this exact second, she said. She didn't say, Something was bringing you to me.

I didn't know this was where you worked.

No, she laughed. No one does. Except my students.

How is Nicky? Ansel said.

He's great. I'm heading home to him now.

Good to hear.

At the premiere, Ivy had sat and watched Ansel's face huge on the screen, watched him performing on red-lit stages, watched him singing in booths with earphones on and walking through airports, watched him in a train compartment writing music with a Hungarian girl, in a hotel room with an Italian girl, in a park with a Japanese girl. It seemed to her each girl was looking at him with adoration.

When the lights came up after the applause, Ansel answered questions, leaning on the stage edge. He was humble and earnest, radiant with the attention, and after a great last applause, the audience ruffled itself out of its seats. Maira waved at Ansel, making the unmistakable and yet never-defined hand gestures which mean I'll see you at the after-party. Ivy followed Maira out to the third-floor lobby and saw at the top of the escalator a young woman lying on her side on an unused table, in leather pants and a bustier top, one arm printed with tattoos. Her lizard eyes coolly regarded the crowd filing out, as if she were security. Ivy recognized her but couldn't remember from where. Was she famous?

Then she remembered the face with less makeup, with smoke wafting like cream from her mouth, lounging on Ansel's white rug. Ivy did not go to the after-party and would not have even if she'd been invited.

Well, I better get going, he said on the sidewalk. Meeting Fred first.

Say hi to him, Ivy said ridiculously.

I will, Ansel said.

Ivy, stunned by the encounter and, despite having so easily placed her hand on his thick scarf, was nevertheless unable to say more. And off he walked, through the crowd. So radiant was he to Ivy, she was amazed that everyone he passed didn't look at him, struck by his beauty.

She walked the four blocks home and saw nothing. She felt she'd been hit by a bus.

She climbed the stairs, taking the three different directions around the elevator bank, walking as if on her knees.

When she opened the door to the apartment, Nicky came running down the hall. He was not usually there to greet her. She felt his hyped-up energy and saw the sitter Katia behind him smiling.

Is it okay if I go? Katia said, slipping on her shoes and hoisting her shoulder bag. I've got a thing.

Yes, yes, Ivy said. Is it okay if I pay you next time?

No problem, Katia said. She clearly had assessed Nicky's mood.

Nicky grabbed Ivy's arm. Let's wrestle, he said and pulled her toward the bedroom.

Hang on, hang on, she said, but letting him pull her. She dropped her bag and managed to slip off her jacket before he pushed her down on the bed. Wrestling meant that he was feeling loving and wanted to be close to her, or it meant he was mad at her. Either way it meant he needed to express it to her and this is how he had figured out how to do that.

Ha ha! he said, pinning her down right away. He straddled her at her hips and pressed down on her wrists. She rocked him side to side, trying to ignore the slab of steel across her chest, a walkway across the bottomless feeling below, trying to catch his spirit with his twitching face showing the intensity of his purpose. She heard the shallow tone of her protest, unable to rise to the occasion. He was wired and laughing and she looked at the determined face above her, the spit glistening on his lip, delighted he was actually able to keep her down, and felt how far away she was from sharing in his delight, which was the best thing she could do. He bounced her up and down. Her mind went mortifyingly to the man doing a different kind of pinning her down, here on this same bed, pelting her throat with shame and she tried to blot out the image, but the thought had come. She steeled herself to keep back tears.

The shame was choking her. The tears leaking out might look like part of the tussle, and she tried an extra laugh to show she was enjoying herself, knowing she should be, but it sounded off, and there was a flicker of awareness in Nicky's dark eye, that something was going on with his mother. Well, she thought, something was. How could she protect him from herself? She must not live this way anymore, being here and yet otherwise consumed. It had to stop.

The wrestling session did not last long.

She picked up her bag and put it down unthinking in another place on the floor. She'd learned to expect indifference from the man, so why had this been like a grenade blast? Perhaps because she was more out of it than in. She walked into the kitchen and faced the mantelpiece and the mirror on it. Her skin was flushed and her hair a mess.

She heard Nicky's footsteps padding back to his room and in

the space before he reappeared felt the moment expand as if the kitchen was suddenly underwater, a fishbowl with no bubbles of air. She looked at the mantelpiece, but saw instead the inside of her head as a slab of slate and the words on it I WANT TO DIE.

She waited a moment, then tested the words again. They were still true.

PART III

If you are not building rooms where wisdom
can be openly spoken, you're building a prison.

—RUMI

7

The Rooms

Deep experience is never peaceful.

—HENRY JAMES

The world seemed sealed off, as if covered in shrink-wrap. Withdrawal, again.

Her head felt thick, giving her vertigo, as if she'd taken a painkiller which didn't kill pain. Her feet hit the ground just off from where she estimated they would. She took steps on faith. She wondered if she had ever been truly adjusted. Maybe she'd always pretended.

The music which had been humming in her brain, the enticing soundtrack blotting out the mundane, dropped to a low groan, a tuba, and a starkness she saw she'd spent her life trying to avoid.

The more days that went by, she reminded herself, the less her mind would turn to him. It had to happen. It would get better. It was like quitting anything. Cravings didn't go on forever.

As in other times of withdrawal she repeated this to herself. All preoccupations fade if you starve them out. There had been a life before without the cigarette, without the person. Other times of heartache had been different with each different person, yet the feelings were eerily similar. I have been here before, she thought. It feels where I belong.

But this time it had to be different. What could make it different?

She went to the rooms.

In the Brown Room it had a few names: neurosis, delusion, fixation, grief.

In the Pink Room it was *dukkha*.

In the Grey Room sickness, addiction, disease.

In the White Rooms its definition cast a wider net—being out of touch with reality, lacking empathy; it was an undiagnosed condition, sexual warp, political division, economic inequality, social inequity, racial bias, universal chaos, environmental deterioration, species extinction, fantasy thinking, ignorance, the human condition.

In the Red Room they called it love.

In the Brown Room, with the brown sofa, brown pillows with woolly brown stripes and brown rug, you met with the Professional.

In the Pink Room a teacher sat cross-legged and guided you.

The White Rooms offered a carousel of different people often with microphones speaking to an audience. These were the experts.

In the Red Room you watched the gods and goddesses. You observed the wide world and the microscopic, all beamed to you in light and shadow.

In the Grey Room, you listened to strangers off the street, your fellow populace.

When you found a handhold in the rooms, you told yourself, Remember this, it will help.

. . .

The Brown Room was on the Upper West Side in a prewar building with two entrances and a long lobby with a black-and-tan-checkered floor.

She pressed the brass buzzer next to the other doctors' names and was clicked into a windowless waiting room with a couch and an armchair and a stack of magazines under a lamp. She sat. What if it turned out, at the end of the world, that these moments of waiting, not moments of action or interaction, were the ones which held the true meaning of life?

In the suspension of thought, and pureness in being.

The Professional then appeared at the top of two carpeted steps, whippet thin, intelligent face, sweeping his hand and inviting her to precede him. The Brown Room had a brown upholstered armchair waiting for her to sit in it. The Professional, too, a swivel chair facing her, his back to a desk and a window shielded with venetian blinds.

What is it you hope to get from our work here? the Professional said.

Ivy had been considering this very question on the walk up—going on foot the one hundred blocks to demonstrate her commitment, though the protracted approach could be seen as expressing reluctance. She would describe her dilemma, as wanting to be with but not being able to stay with a man. As she began to put words to this for the Professional, something else was swelling up in her, making her want to cry. She knew the Brown Room was where you came to cry, and this was happening more swiftly than she'd envisioned. What she wanted, she found herself saying before the sob choked her, was to be able to live—not just with another person, but with herself.

The Professional nodded, a choking sob being standard procedure. He then listened to her talk about the man—the man at present—for some time, then interrupted. Okay, he said mildly. But I'm not so interested in him. I'm interested in you.

A liquid feeling spread across her chest and she looked off, into the corner, down at the lower bookshelf, up to the dangling pull of the blind, anywhere but at the Professional's face. I don't even know who that is, she thought and a yawning canyon opened at her feet.

No thoughts in the Pink Room. That is, thoughts were to be left behind. When thoughts drifted in, swirling, you were to let them keep flying up and away.

In the Pink Room, you stretched out on a blue mat. On your left was a stranger with long legs, toes painted scarlet and a life you'd never know. You would never be that person. Why do you even think that?

In the Pink Room there were body parts barely mentioned outside the Pink Room. Sitz bones, hip flexors, thorax, heart center, perineum. Initially the positions—twisting, balancing, being upside down—all things, Ivy reflected, children did naturally—blasted the tightness in her body, sending a fizzy energy to her head. But sometimes the contortions, her chin on her knee, started the sex thoughts. That huge engine. The idea was to take out the sex thoughts. *Clench your perineum.* Without her conjuring it, his body would materialize alongside hers, under her, with sex tunneling to the soul. In the airy room full of willowy women in tank tops and the occasional T-shirted man, she would feel herself pressed into his upper arms back in his bed. She wondered if anyone in the room was as sex flooded as she.

Up the stairs they trudged into the Grey Rooms—the heartbroken, the reluctant, the bereaved and the furious, up the worn rug off the sacristy, past a security guard sitting at a small school desk, through closed doors, the abused, the pummeled and the speared, into a grey room with grey unfolded chairs set in circular rows like a Greek theatre.

The adults were all ages, with different accents and different skin tones and different sizes, mostly dressed as you would see them on the street. Everyone was here because of pain and often because of another person. That other person was the reason for your suffering—you thought—and you were likely blaming that other person for your anguish till it began to dawn on you that the other person was not to blame. Guess who is.

There is no conversation in the Grey Rooms, yet someone is always speaking. A person with raised hand is called on. Ah, one thinks, seeing the face collapsed and forlorn, here are rancor and despair. Then out of a ragged crushed face comes a story with layers and texture, articulated clearly.

Most stories were riveting. The narrative might meander, getting into unnecessary details, or lapse into self-pity, but when the Grey Room has its effect, then truth would be spoken. And truth always makes for a stunning tale. When a story wasn't stunning, everyone still listened. In the Grey Rooms you spoke and had an audience. So mostly in the Grey Rooms you listened.

There was the girl with Botticelli hair who did not like sex. Her brother had pestered her when she was young, always invading her space. It wasn't sexual, she said, but it was physical. He'd throw me around. Later she recoiled from any contact. She was hoping to get over it.

A man said, My parents were always yelling at each other and I grew up telling myself, I'm never going to do that. And I don't. Now I'm the one who sits back criticizing everything. I'm above it all. And am alone.

Occasionally an irritating person would surprise you by making you cry. You felt ashamed for having thought you knew better or that your problems were worse. This is how it is with me, they said. And there would be nodding, for this was how it also was with many.

A girl talked cheerfully about having no self-esteem. Legs crossed, stiletto heels, a narrow business skirt, silk shirt pressed etc. She looked sparkling, described her Greek family and said in a commanding tone, I never had anyone tell me that I was worth a thing.

Ivy listened, checking internally, was this like her or not. In the Grey Rooms you learned along with everyone else how, despite your best intentions, the central part you play in your chaos.

The phrases repeated were a chorus of laments. They were clichés, but here clichés might have a powerful impact. *I felt I wasn't good enough. No one told me I mattered. I never saw a healthy relationship. If I could just be with him everything would be perfect.* Things you thought unique to you turned out to be standard behavior in the Grey Room.

The man in a dark blue suit and a loosened tie was rounded forward like a skier ready at the gate with one arm raised. He was called on, and his arm dropped. His face tilted up shooting out rays of pain. I cheated on my wife, he said starting right in. She's a wonderful person and I'm . . . I'm such an idiot. He started to cry.

His palm was pressed like a starfish across three-quarters of his face. I don't know what I was doing, he said. I mean, I do. Fuck. I was looking for excitement. I wanted to feel like a big man—he spat out the words *big man*, as if that were the most abhorrent thing in the world anyone would be enough of an idiot to want to be—and I've gone and fucking broken the heart of a kind, caring person and I'll never be able to take it back.

Everyone in the room sat silent while the man with his pulled-up dark socks and long black shoes wept with heaving shoulders. She doesn't ever want anything to do with me now, he said, catching his breath. She's right, I don't blame her.

The timer gave him the three-finger sign which meant he had three more minutes. You were allotted ten minutes, got the finger sign at five, three at three. Everyone could see he had more to say.

I just don't know how I'm going to live with myself, he said.

It was a conclusion reached by many people in the Grey Room and it was always amazing and strangely consoling to Ivy how the audience would let the statement lie. You never tried to talk a person out of what had been said, or felt. Outside of the Grey Rooms people tended to say, You won't always feel that way and That's not true and even You don't really mean it. But not here.

Next to the man in the suit, a large guy—grizzled face, flannel shirt, work boots—listened, gazing down at the floor. A woman in the row behind was slowly chewing gum. Near her a bald birdlike fellow in a windbreaker gave his attention with eyebrows raised. Everyone kept listening.

Sometimes a darkness lowered itself behind your eyes, then other times you felt screws loosen from the band around your head. You learned how most complaints directed at others might better be directed at oneself.

In between the rooms she ran.

In a free hour she wove down the blocks—on the sidewalk, off the curb, back on—to the river. The wind, grey waves, figures strolling. On warm sunny days the cement walkways along the river streamed with people. When it rained the river was deserted, air speckled with mist, and she could run for blocks without seeing a soul. The buildings stacked inside along the West Side Highway were full of thousands—millions—of people and none by the water. She ran along the railings and turned onto the old piers jutting into the Hudson, now park areas with lawns spotted with male couples and people doing leg crunches. Children ran like chickens from their parents. At the end of one pier on Sundays, a Victrola played mazurkas under concrete parasols and couples danced the tango, thigh to thigh, stiff heads swiveling, serious even when they were smiling. The women wore thick high-heeled shoes and dresses fluttering at the calf, the older men stepped with a suave glide. Sometimes the wind raked over the microphone.

Many people held a rope with a dog at its end.

On windy days the waves slapped the concrete along the promenade sending up a longing splash. On sultry days the water undulated like mercury; on bright days it glittered in sharp pieces. The silhouetted skyscrapers in New Jersey and the LACKAWANNA sign were occasionally sliced by sailboats or ocean liners passing like buildings five stories high. As she ran she listened to music, the same songs again and again. Mostly she did not listen to Ansel Fleming, then sometimes she did.

Some days she'd get a hit of euphoria and return to the apartment, leaping up the stairs, eager to see Nicky, to hug him, to love him and need no love back at all.

Other days returning, she stood at the whizzing crosswalk of the West Side Highway. One would, she reflected, have to time it precisely to step in front of a car so it would not have time to brake. And it would be difficult not to cause other accidents unless the car was not near any other cars. But one also wouldn't be able to choose which car, with a driver who was not too sensitive a person to suffer lasting trauma if she hit a person. Ivy thought of a famous writer who had hung himself and, though she did not know him, nevertheless felt a sharp pain in her chest whenever she thought of it and, reminding herself of this, tried to keep the thought that one did not want to cause that kind of sharp pain to anyone if one could help it. Though, in certain states of mind, Ivy was not always convinced her absence would matter so much.

In the Red Room you are still. You sit in soft red chairs unmoving. The Red Rooms are large with rows of bolted seats and a huge glowing rectangle casting light on upturned faces like sunflowers. Sometimes you are the only person there. In the rectangle it is silver or lead, it is rainbow colors. Sound hits your sternum. You watch images moving, the faces huge. You experience love affairs, fistfights, snake along a mountain road, sit at the dinner table with the argument, watch the avalanche, and yet none of it happens to you. You live the stories and yet none of it is happening to you.

In the Red Rooms there is a focus on behavior—tolerance and cruelty, the beauty of sacrifice and the paltriness of arrogance. You see how terrible humans can be and how full of integrity. How full of surprises. You visit places on the planet you will never visit. You laugh, you cry. You remember what love feels like or what it could feel like and imagine what death might be like and how good animals are and how astonishing people can be.

Ivy studied the women, and how they were with men. In the '50s they wore pointed shoes, pointed bras and short hairdos making them appear old, and especially different from men. In the '40s the women had mystery and elegance and even smarts, but their worth was still measured by their allure to men. In the '30s women seemed more playful and stylish and even self-possessed, but men still held the power.

You feel what the figures on the screen feel, but only while watching. You come out of the Red Room and reenter the world, stepping onto the sidewalk with its real sound, momentarily disoriented. It has become dark. Everything feels slow, distant. But you feel that you have more in you than you did before.

Later you recall what you saw, less vivid, though you remember its impression. You experience it as you do dreams, not real, but powerful.

Don't recognize self. Where are all the cabinet selves?

Disconnection from body. Body felt solid when outlined by his hands. *Drop your head to find stillness.*

Loss of self is a goal in the Pink Room.

Scattered across the city were the White Rooms. At the front of the room were people at lecterns, or sitting in chairs with microphones. Sometimes a few people along one side of a table, some speaking rather more than others, those speaking less usually more interesting.

A poet stood on the stage reciting, his body swaying and his feet stationary like a tree in the wind. It wasn't quite a song, but close. It made Ivy want to—what?—just live.

A scholar read transcripts from the trial of Jeanne d'Arc. What do the voices sound like? they asked her. Ask me on Saturday, Jeanne d'Arc replied.

A lawyer with a cropped beard described his client on death row. The man was deluded by obsession, he said, so his logic and reasoning became corrupted and increasingly dangerous. The lawyer said this as if everyone knew this about obsession.

A neuroscientist explained love as it appeared in the brain.

Love exists below cognitive thinking, she said. She wore dangly silver earrings.

The ventral tegmental area registered the emotions of love. This was also the home base for motivation, cognition and several psychiatric disorders, including addiction.

The cells where pleasure is felt lack clear anatomical boundaries. That sounded right to Ivy.

Also, the firing pattern which encodes reward expectancy is in error, the doctor explained. Therefore rejected love will stimulate the amygdala, the place one feels pleasure.

Ivy walked home in a cheek-speckling mist. *Rejected love stimulates the place one feels pleasure.*

In the rooms you picked up what you liked, like shells on a beach. Often a fragment was just as beautiful. The Buddhists defined the different forms of suffering: *sankhar-dukkha,* the suffering of existence, *viparinama-dukkha,* the suffering of change, and *dukkha-dukkha,* the suffering of suffering!

You noted how fear permeates all anxiety. You saw the different ways people work overtime not to think of death, to try to live a good life, to figure how to be a person.

A soft-spoken man in the Grey Room says, I know I might sound like I'm together, but it's just a show. Inside I'm a shit show.

When we live our lives from a place of integrity, says the

teacher uninsistently in her pink sweater in the Pink Room, we do not doubt ourselves. If you have to convince yourself you are acting with integrity, you are likely wrong.

In the Red Room a man in a suit embraces a brunette in a negligee. She snaps at him.

Hey, he says, that doesn't sound like my girl.

She snarls back, her upper lip dark as a plum, I'm a lot of girls.

She would arrive at the Brown Room windblown after pedaling on the bike path along the Hudson's choppy grey silk water, feeling refreshed and mild, and within five minutes of sitting in the brown chair would be sobbing. Often as she talked, sometimes more tediously than others, it would be as if her voice were coming from the heating vent or under the brown bookcase, not from herself. But sometimes she felt like a stone. This was called resistance.

Ivy had been in other Brown Rooms over the years. It turned out that the talk in the Brown Room in your twenties was different from the talk ten years later and again ten years after that, and yet when all was said and done, it was somehow the same. Other times in the brown chair, she had been talking about a frustrating man who was out of reach. Of course the common denominator was herself.

She'd had to borrow money to pay for it. Daphne didn't look surprised when Ivy asked her, nor hesitate to say yes. I know you would do the same for me, she said.

The Professional asked the usual questions. How does that make you feel? And you thought what? They still slid into her like saber blades. One question baffled more than pierced her: Why do you think that's so?

. . .

Part of the Professional's job was to steer his patient's attention back to herself. Ivy learned—again—how often one wriggled away from oneself and how paradoxically this steeped a person more densely in herself. This took a lot of energy. Again, too, she discovered how distress and fear in present events were likely rooted in past original events of distress and fear which had more potency. What she'd learned in other Brown Rooms turned out to be difficult to hold on to. One needed to be reminded—again and again.

The Professional said, You'd be surprised how many people come in here, in terrible distress, wanting truly to change. But the majority of them would rather continue in a painful way that is familiar than to try something unknown. Fear of the unknown turns out to be worse than suffering.

She thought of Flannery O'Connor's It's easier to bleed than sweat.

You were mimicking intimacy, the Professional said.

I guess, said Ivy. She did not like undercutting the intensity of all she'd been through and guessed this was a sign she still clung to it. Could one still admire the high even viewing the rubble it caused?

Sex can do that, he said.

She said she knew. She thought how that was yet another of its marvels.

But it's not real intimacy, the Professional said.

Ivy nodded obediently, but she had a flash of greeting Ansel Fleming at her door after an absence and falling against his chest, not being able to breathe.

She said something about the intensity of sex.

Well, said the Professional, not everyone goes there. It can be frightening there, and very powerful and chaotic. Not everyone dares.

He added, Which is why you might want to put yourself in the hands of someone who will care about you.

They talked about her father, about his being gone. How even when he had been in front of her he'd been gone. The Professional suggested this was a hole which would never be filled.

So how does one get over it? Ivy said, then laughed at the stupid question.

The Professional did not laugh with her. You don't, he said.

Plates shifted in the Brown Room. This was one of the reasons she was here.

Speaking of certain things might set an anvil on her chest or give her a choke hold. She'd read somewhere that grief was lodged in the throat. Sometimes this aching would burst like a pipe and tears would fall. Insights came, seeming to beam down from the corner above a framed '60s poster of a Parisian street, causing warmth to fan out in her upper intestines, where strangely she felt her soul to be, halfway between her genitals and her heart, but closer to her heart.

Then other days she would leave the Brown Room having lost all bearings.

The Professional said, As you make progress, you also necessarily regress.

Part of the effort was to untangle the ball of knots and see how each had been strangling the rest.

Was it the hole which caused the suffering? Or what you randomly threw into it? Was it possible to avoid suffering? Not if you kept your eyes open. Not if you considered what was at the end of the line.

When will the anguish go away? she asked the Professional. Or even will it?

It will change, he said. Nothing stays the same.

She half laughed. Except me.

The thing was to change her perspective. Didn't Abraham Lincoln say, Folks are usually about as happy as they make their minds up to be. Maybe she hadn't made up her mind enough. Tom Stoppard: Happiness is equilibrium. Shift your weight. The mantra in the Pink Room: Lead me from the unreal to the real.

She read Toni Morrison: Love is or it ain't.

In the night she would wake and try to steer her thoughts away from the man, and it would be like pulling a giant steering wheel on an ocean liner in high stormy seas.

She thought of Nicky. How she was supposed to be ushering this small person into the world, and teaching him how to live, when she hadn't figured out how to do it herself?

If you circled something long enough you saw different angles. Truth shimmered. The desire to connect with another—so acceptable in her romantic view—now appeared with a creepy predatory aspect. Why did one need to *penetrate* another? She thought with shame of the times she'd busted into people's business in the name of connecting, of being friendly, when they might have preferred, she saw now, to remain private. Did knowledge always come with shame beside it?

Now was not the time to think of the night of the yellow leaves. She had to coach herself to think instead how she had no more important job than looking after her child, being a mother. Even if she felt herself an artist. No one needs you to be an artist and no one will notice if you are not, though someone would definitely notice if you stopped being a mother. She reminded herself of the foolishness she felt in some roles and the purposefulness in others. A prayer in the Pink Room: Lead me from the unreal to the real. Here washing the bathtub, scrubbing the wooden floor, was the real. But conviction of what was real wavered in and out of sight, like an undulating image in a '50s movie with a wavering melody, indicating that the action was going into the past, or that a character was losing her mind.

You became familiar with the faces in the rooms. In the

Grey Room you might nod, in the Pink Room might smile. But mostly everyone acts invisible to each other. It is a city agreement. The holy sadhus allegedly walk through the streets of India and say no one sees them, because they've achieved a level of enlightenment.

Sometimes Ivy arrived late when the pink door was shut and the person signing her in at the desk would shrug at Ivy's lateness, cracking a joke about being hungover herself. These forgivenesses could choke up a person.

Some directives were heard nowhere else but in the Pink Rooms. *Soften your knees and squeeze your ears. Dome your upper back.*

Others were metaphors for living. *Stand loosely. Slow the breath. Soften your tongue. Lower your gaze. Lift your gaze. Try not to let your eyes harden.*

The Grey Room, too, had its particular language. Adages came spilling over the hill like a flock of sheep. *Don't just do something, sit there. You can't buy donuts in a hardware store. You can't make someone love you.* For those in anguish, clichés were life rafts.

There were descriptors of Grey Room behavior: Acting Out and Bottom Line. There was Not Respecting Boundaries, Not Having One's Own Boundaries. Eroticizing.

The people in the Grey Room Beat Up on Themselves and Feared Abandonment. They Lacked Self-Esteem, or Respect for Others. They Avoided Feeling, Retreated from Intimacy. They Ran from Responsibility. They Became Emotionally Attached to people without knowing them.

They, i.e., you.

In Nicky's room, each night, a long goodbye.

Can I ask you just one more thing? he said.

Okay.

You know how your favorite color changes every day? Well, what was it today?

I think . . . red.

It was?

Yup. For a change. You?

Green.

Oh, St. Patrick's Day.

Yup, but watery-blue green like the ocean.

Okay now, she said. You nod out. She shifted to sit up.

His stiff arm barred her from moving. Stay, he said as he did each night and she plunked back softly. After a while, she whispered, All right, and again stirred. Five more minutes, came the words, drugged, eyes closed, and she'd wait again till his breath slowed, then roughened, and his body twitched as if electrocuted, indicating true sleep.

You may have gone to the Grey Rooms for relief, but you ended up learning to listen.

If you were in the Grey Rooms it was likely your social radar needed tuning. You misread others, as well as yourself. You assumed things about people. But when you listened, you saw how wrong assumptions often were. At first this unseated you and you thought, How can I ever trust my instincts again? Then you recognized that not trusting things to be true which were being decided in a knee-jerk way was perhaps an advancement. Another handhold for the trek up out of the crater.

I got sober in yellow pajamas on Thorazine, said the man with an eagle tattooed across his throat. So that's who I am. Everyone laughed.

It was never not interesting to hear each story, each person's version.

In those years there was a marriage, there was a kid, there were accidents, people died, all the shit you hear about . . . No, Ivy thought, I don't hear about it.

The stories were compelling even when they gave it all away up front. You listened not to see what happened, but how it happened.

What Ivy heard washed through her and flushed things away and gave her valuables to discover, but Ivy still kept apart. In the rooms this was called being One Up on people. She was not surrendering to being like everyone else. You were encouraged to speak, to give your time to service, to the meetings.

One night she made herself speak. Her raised hand was called on. She felt a flush go through her to the folding seat and her throat swell. The words teetered out, faltering, a new voice, wobbly and inarticulate, groping its way forward, unable to keep from crying, a voice she'd never known. She thought if this voice didn't speak she might perish of loneliness.

Having strangers listen to her, many she'd listened to herself, was like an oven door opening, scorching her. This sort of earthquake feeling was not rare in the Grey Rooms.

No one in the Grey Rooms quoted Rumi: What's the lover to do but humiliate himself and wander your rooms?

It was only in sex that I would feel safe, said a glassy-eyed girl in a dry voice. It would last for ten minutes, maybe an hour, then be gone. But it was better than nothing.

One man had described how he'd managed to go twenty years without picking up a drink, but in this room it was different. How do you not pick up a thought?

Trees no longer full of wonder.

I was living in a shitty place then, said a pretty woman, fists jammed into a little jacket. Into drugs, pretty much always high. I'd get guys to come over in the middle of the night, fuck me—excuse my profanity—remind me how worthless I was in various insidious ways, like calling me by someone else's name or stealing my wallet, or beating me which I was actually sort of into, but more than I wanted them to—anyway . . . Ivy watched the woman's bobbing boots and thought it sounded sickly alluring, a sign to Ivy she still had a ways to go.

In the rooms you think, Wait before speaking. Wait and listen.

In the Marble Rooms she stood in front of a painting. A girl in white on a bridge at dusk recalled another way she had thought of herself, a better way.

It was so crowded in the White Room, Ivy sat in the aisle on tiered shallow steps. Alice Munro wore a scarf headband low on her forehead holding back curly hair. She spoke quietly, as if not expecting people to listen to her. When you're a writer you're never quite like other people, she said. You're in a secret world.

The Call-In Doctor on the radio says, Shut up about him. I don't want to hear about him. She also says, Rehashing old things doesn't help a person move forward. Ivy considers this re the Brown Room.

The Professional soon became a human with a name, Dr. J. One day Dr. J. appeared with a cast. Ivy asked what had happened and Dr. J. told her he'd broken his wrist. How? He'd fallen. But I'm fine, said Dr. J., in a tone which meant, We are not here to talk about me. Then in another pointed tone, It will heal.

One day Ivy thought of another room, the front hall of a house. The sun coming through tall windows made bright trapdoors on the white floor. There was the sound of a TV, of dinner being made in the kitchen, of someone coming down the stairs. Alone in the hall of the house where she'd grown up, she had the feeling of being the one person there who did not belong.

The empty room. The beauty of an empty room.

There was also the Dark Room, where you went each night. Into sleep.

In dreams rooms would expand—the apartment suddenly added onto with ballrooms and balconies and terraces. Or rooms shrank and you crawled through passageways fitting your head but not your shoulders.

When the radiance reached her now, she measured its power by how much it pained her.

The older woman had an Irish accent, Mary Poppins haircut, corduroy slacks, tidy cardigan, powdered face. A small crisp mouth described how she was in love with her boss. He was fifteen years her junior. Being at work was difficult, she said, any interaction with him triggered her. *Trigger* was a favored word in the Grey Rooms. It had been going on for a couple of years. Then, at the end, she added, as almost an afterthought, that nothing sexual had gone on between them; the boss didn't know anything about it.

There were the Clattering Rooms with forks on plates, talk swirling around tables, clatter in the kitchen.

Her brain was a room which could not be entered since it was inside her. It was sometimes an attic, with shoebox-sized windows near the floor and a round cathedral window at one end looking onto rolling landscapes. Or it was large and dark, a subterranean cave, filled with overlapping images, some moving, some still. Places, people. Many were things she'd not actually seen. But most were from the past. The past, the past.

In the Grey Room a girl was screaming, I want my head back!

A man said, I'm not going to tell that story anymore. I've been telling that story too long a time.

Maira had left messages. Ivy meant to call back, but days passed. She told herself she had bothered Maira enough with talk about Ansel and would give her a break—but really she had backed off as if from something radioactive, to avoid the association. A lethargy settled around her, convincing Ivy that no one would truly care if they heard from her or not. Anyway, she wasn't good company, she was a drag. When she finally returned Maira's call she got voicemail, which was a relief, and left a message. She did not hear back anything right away and she didn't really notice, being too self-absorbed. When it occurred to her, she felt vindicated. See? Maira hadn't called her back either. They were in an out-of-touch period. It happened; it didn't matter.

Then one night at an art opening Ivy ran into a friend of Maira's who asked her with a concerned face how Tony was doing. Ivy asked her what she meant. Didn't Ivy know that Tony was sick? It was cancer. A hot mortified flush spread through Ivy, as if she'd known on some level it might be something like this and was only now admitting it. The cancer wasn't in the last stages, the person at the cocktail party didn't think, but it wasn't in the early ones either. He was doing chemo.

As soon as she got home Ivy called. Maira answered the phone in a quiet voice. Oh God, Ivy thought. Sorry, was she asleep? Hardly, Maira said. In an uncharacteristic robotic voice Maira filled her in on what happened, how Tony had felt perfectly fine, but when he had a checkup they'd found it, and it wasn't good, and how he was feeling shitty now but they trusted their doctor who was terrific, a friend of a friend, and they felt they were in good hands and how great the kids were being. Ivy kept repeating how terrible it was and how she was so sorry. There was a pause and Maira said straight-out she'd been hurt not hearing from Ivy. The truth deepened Ivy's mortification. Maira was right to be hurt; Ivy had let her down. One should always answer a friend, she saw, no matter how low you feel. They might actually need you, for a change. Ivy had let down her friend, this person for whom friendship was golden, this person she cherished. She felt doubly guilty even to feel bad about having been lame, when Maira and Tony had a lot more things to feel bad about.

One did want to be able to stand being oneself.

You're doing all you can, said Dr. J. Pat yourself on the back.

In a peacock-blue room she sat at a dinner party. Cherry blossoms on branches, actual literary conversation, which often happened with strangers. A few people at the table Ivy knew only by reputation. A journalist in a collared shirt with a blunt haircut had decided there was a major flaw in *Anna Karenina*—the deterioration of the heroine.

Here was a strong vital woman with a discerning intelligence in her personality, the journalist said, setting down her wineglass. Tolstoy never convinces us that this vibrant person could deteriorate into someone with the weakness to throw herself under a train.

Ivy did not point out the journalist must never have known the devastation of love and sex taking over her life. Plus, suicide always seemed to Ivy to require great bravery.

. . .

On the subway, Ivy noticed fewer people holding books. When she saw someone reading she thought how they had entered into someone else's room. They were communing there with another person's consciousness in the room of words on a page.

In the living room she walks by Nicky intently watching a movie. He doesn't glance up from the screen, but says, I love you, Mama.

8

The Operation

Sometimes the cold and dark of a cave
give the opening we most want.

—RUMI

The hospital was uptown on First Avenue, big, pale and brand-new, its atrium lobby with windows two stories high. Ivy held her son's hand crossing bright squares on a white floor. A guard with a long shadow directed them to a turnstile and they passed through it and up a silent elevator to pediatrics on the third floor where there was a similar wall of windows keeping out the June heat. Inside it was cool. Mother and son sat waiting on low grey sofas, as if on rafts in a marble sea. Now and then figures in pale coats and pale trousers passed—male, female, dark, light—casting soothing looks toward the small boy clutching a ragged rabbit.

They had waited till the school year was finished for Nicky to have the operation. Today it was finally happening. It was a simple procedure, the handsome Dr. Rosencrantz had told them. He would take out Nicky's tonsils and he'd be able to go home that same day. He'd have a pretty nasty sore throat, Dr. Rosencrantz said, tilting forward a sympathetic frown, but then he'd be good as new. A person didn't need his tonsils, especially if they gave him extra sore throats. After the consultation, when they left the examination room, Nicky said, Mum, you should marry him.

. . .

He was given a fresh room with grey-blue walls, glinting machines and the one bed perched on metal legs. Nicky sat against the pillows in a tied-at-the-back hospital gown as one young medical person after another entered breezily, stood officially bedside, and asked his name—Nicholas Cooper Scott—and his age—eleven—and why he was there. Each then repeated: he would be going to sleep and waking up without his tonsils. Nicky's gaze flicked toward his mother with each new person, checking with her the way he still did when they were out in the world, trusting and relying on her, unlike back home, where he'd begun to express a new swagger of opposition and suspicion.

A compact male figure entered the room. It was Dr. Rosencrantz. He calmly said hello and patted Nicky's arm and repeated the information he'd given them at their first consultation. He did this operation all the time, only one out of a hundred people ever had complications, Nicky was going to be fine.

A small woman with a needlepoint hairband and stout neck appeared and cheerfully described that she was going to put an IV needle into Nicky's arm. He looked with alarm at his mother, then immediately accepted his lack of agency. He flinched at the poke, then relief rose in his face. Not so bad. Rattling wheels passed the doorway, and a small figure in pajamas drove by in a go-cart, making engine sounds. Nicky's face showed dismay he did not get a go-cart, then immediately owned that he was too mature for such childishness. Later a table glided by with the presumably same child under a thin blanket, on each side a parent, one mother, one father, leaning in.

Once again she was the only parent. Everett had not understood why Nicky couldn't have his tonsils out in Virginia and Ivy explained this was where they'd found the doctor covered by New York insurance. One of the positive things about divorce, Ivy thought, was no longer feeling you had to cave into what your partner wanted. The flip negative side of course being no father present for the son.

Soon Ivy was leaning beside Nicky's bed as it moved down the gleaming floor past brushed steel, around a corner and through a doorway into a cavernous operating room with soft walls. Deep within six or seven people in pale hospital garb, their shoes covered with plastic bags, milled about, checked monitors sprouting wires, muttered to each other. How polished and efficient money could make things, Ivy thought, not wanting it to comfort her, except now when her son was about to be cut into. Thank goodness they had the insurance; before Nicky, she'd never paid attention to insurance. She did not see Dr. Rosencrantz. A child in a shower cap came forward and a man's voice came out of him saying he would take over from here. He then asked Nicky for the fiftieth time his name and what he was there for. Ivy squeezed her son's small inert hand. I'll be here when you wake up, she said, her voice catching.

Mumma, Nicky said.

Bye, Mum, said the child in the shower cap and the bed wheeled away.

You'll do great, she heard the voice say to Nicky. Feeling tears rising, she hurried down the hall to the nearest restroom and, once inside, mercifully alone, sobbed as silently as she was able.

While he was being operated on Ivy thought of the day on the trampoline. She had considered that the last day she and Everett were tied together in their marriage. Telling Nicky had been the severing moment.

Nicky lay, eyes shut, head sunk on the pillow. She sat in a chair close to the bed. When his slit eyelids opened she saw pupils as black as beans. I feel funny, he said, his swollen lips barely moving.

The anesthetic's still in you, Ivy said. You feel a little loopy.

Are my tonsils gone?

Yes, they're gone. She thought how she could tell him anything and he'd believe her. Luckily she had his best interest at heart. But what if she didn't? A parent could do so much damage. And one did lie to one's child. Nicky was beginning to discern when she was lying. For his own good. She wondered if it was yet another job for a parent, to teach a child to lie. That is, when it was advisable to lie, and probably how.

His eyes closed. He muttered, Did they take out my adenoids?

She half laughed. They'd not discussed his adenoids, but she and Dr. Rosencrantz had. He'd told Ivy that if the adenoids looked enlarged he would, while he was in there, take them out.

No, you still have your adenoids.

His eyes opened heavily. What are adenoids?

They're a gland in the—

But he didn't want to know. He murmured, I want Keanu Reeves to come visit me.

You do?

Yes. Maybe he can come over, Mum. Do you think he could?

I don't know about that. Why do you want him?

Because he's Keanu Reeves.

She held up a cup for him to take a sip of water.

Is that a caterpillar? he said.

No, sweet. It's a straw.

I had some crazy dreams, he said.

You did.

But I don't remember them. Should I?

He frowned as if he'd just received a bulletin. Mumma, he said. Do you think that somewhere in the world a lion is chasing an antelope?

She suppressed a laugh. I don't know. Do you?

No, he said. It's a good day for antelope.

The plan was for Nicky to spend summers with his father on the farm. Everett had been annoyed that his arrival was being postponed.

Why can't you bring him down now? Everett said on the phone that evening, back from the hospital. Nicky was flat out in her bed, sleeping.

Ivy, still irritated Everett had not come to the city for the operation, repeated the doctor's recommendation that Nicky not be moved for two weeks after the operation. In case there were complications.

Two weeks! Everett groaned. Don't you people think we have hospitals in Virginia?

The city was hot. Last week Ivy had hauled the air conditioner out from under the linen curtain cover and it was rattling in the window. The unit was old and dripped down the brick façade of the building, getting her in trouble with the building management. She jimmied a tray underneath it on the sill and hoped for the best. The day after the operation Nicky settled on the couch in the cooler living room and slept on and off. He even allowed Ivy to sit beside him and watch a movie, usually preferring his independence while watching, and even slumped against her, grimacing when he had to swallow. In the afternoon he slept back in Ivy's room and she sorted papers and drawers and slowly packed up for their summer departure. A person named Wendell, a friend of a friend of Daphne's, was unofficially subletting for the summer. Many of Ivy's friends had left town for the country. The ones who stayed worked in offices or were by their own air conditioners in their small apartments. Ivy would go to Virginia and stay in the cottage. How could she not be in the place where her son was? And even if Everett didn't acknowledge it, Everett often needed her help.

She had put on some music and was separating files into piles on the table in the living room when she looked up to see Nicky standing in the pocket door entryway in his oversize T-shirt, startling her.

Mumma, he said tremulously.

His loose shorts made his legs look especially frail and thin; on his outstretched palm was a red splash of blood.

Oh, sweet, she said and stood. In the bathroom she washed his hand at the sink; she looked at the back of his throat. They'd been told there might be some blood, but not to worry. It's okay, she said as reassuringly as she could muster and folded him back into bed.

Ivy did not like calling doctors. Many of her friends—the mothers—seemed always to be taking their children to the doctor, but Ivy dragged her feet. Mostly, she felt it unnecessary. Also, she didn't like asking for help. And mainly she dreaded the stomach-thwacking bill of the visits not covered by insurance.

She did not hesitate now. She phoned Dr. Rosencrantz. But Dr. Rosencrantz was not the doctor on call, the answering service said. A Dr. Estin answered. He sounded as if he was outside. She heard a bird singing. Dr. Estin was decidedly unconcerned, and even over the phone she could tell he was bored. It was perfectly normal, he explained, to cough up a little blood after a tonsillectomy. It was nothing to worry about. He seemed irritated that she was even bothering him. If it happened again, Dr. Estin said practically yawning, she could go to her nearest emergency room, but he doubted that was necessary.

It was a pretty big amount of blood, Ivy said. And he says his throat really hurts on one side.

Yes, said Dr. Estin. You do get a nasty sore throat.

Afterward she sat beside Nicky and told him this sometimes happened, hearing a hollow note in her reassurance. He took another shot of the liquid purple Tylenol.

That night she slept suspended with concern beside him, feeling his small warmth, his goodness, his innocence.

In the morning as she scooped yogurt for him, Nicky's voice called plaintively from the bathroom. She rounded the corner and saw a large bouquet of red blood splattered across their old standing sink.

Come on, she said calmly.

. . .

The nearest ER was only a few blocks away on Seventh Avenue, an unusual structure with a white-and-black honeycomb façade, but they took a cab. It was 9:00 A.M. on a Saturday morning and inside the doors was quiet as a library. Ivy saw no other patients. Wide cubicles spread out past the reception area.

Soon Nicky was propped up on another bed with a surrounding oatmeal-colored curtain hovering a foot above the floor. Eventually a young man with a dangling earring said hello, called them honey and said someone would be with them shortly. A while later a small nurse with a braid said a doctor would be with them shortly. After fifteen minutes, Ivy let go of Nicky's hand and pulled back the curtain to the stillness of the huge room. A couple of heads showed above a maze of dividers. Now and then one saw a part of a figure move.

Ivy ventured out and stopped at the nearest person, a woman holding a phone receiver to her ear. Not seeing any other humans, Ivy waited till the woman hung up. Ivy explained she was with her son . . . The woman blinked as if telegraphing Morse code, not unkindly, but not sympathetically, and when Ivy finished, the woman said the doctor would be with them soon.

Ten more minutes passed. At last a thin-necked man in a white coat entered the curtain and set his hands in his pockets. Sorry, he said without feeling. We're short staffed this morning. I'm Dr. Cord.

He looked into Nicky's open mouth, pointing a small flashlight he'd taken from his pocket.

I see the stitches, he said. It looks okay. A little bleeding happens after a tonsillectomy.

He says it really hurts, Ivy said. In a sort of sharp way.

Yes, the doctor said, in league with them all. Getting your tonsils out hurts.

Ivy and Nicky exchanged a look of defeat, but she was the parent and had to remain upbeat. Okay, my little, she said. Then we're good.

The doctor turned to go.

So we can leave? Ivy said. She suddenly felt how drawn and frizzled she must have looked, her wrinkled black sundress, her stained canvas bag.

Well, yes, he said. As soon as I write you up, you're good to go.

They remained undisturbed for another fifteen minutes.

Ivy ventured again out from the curtain. One ought to feel reassured in a hospital with help within reach, but she felt the opposite, oddly invisible and her son not truly cared for. The woman on the phone was gone. Ivy walked farther to a woman in a floral shirt standing at an open file cabinet. Ivy began by apologizing—always a woman apologized!—she and her son were waiting for the doctor's . . . what, release form? The woman half turned as if hearing her voice across the valley from a distant mountain. For the first time in the last three days, Ivy felt the thought of the man she was trying to forget wing by over the room, as if testing if it belonged here. As if reminding her she had been seen at one point. Then it swooped off. This was no place for allure. An urge to weep rose up, and her throat ached in sympathy with her son. He was in that dimension where illness put a person, a dimension where the only thing one wanted was tenderness and care.

Eventually the man with the earring arrived. Ivy signed many papers and they were free to go.

For most of the day Nicky slept, conking out after two spoonfuls of chicken soup. Ivy turned off the air conditioner and opened the window to let in a breeze, to lessen the trapped feeling. She sat legs on the couch with her computer.

Nicky's voice woke her, asleep on the couch. She got up. It was late afternoon. He was in the bathroom leaning over the sink which looked like a murder scene. His chin was smeared with blood.

Jesus, she said. Then added less dramatically, Poor sweetie. She washed the creases of red at the corners of his mouth, and brought him back to bed. His skin was the color of an oyster shell.

She took a picture of the sink and called the doctor as she washed it. Dr. Estin was still on call. This time she said simply, I want to bring him back to the hospital. Can you admit him? She had walked to the far end of the living room so that Nicky would not hear the deep panic which might be heard in her voice.

Okay, said Dr. Estin in an oddly finicky tone. But you will have to go to the outpatient emergency room. It's across the street from where you had the operation. They'll assess him and admit him if necessary.

I've never seen him so pale, Ivy said quietly.

They'll take care of him, said the doctor. Ivy had decided he was on a slanted lawn in Connecticut with flowers blooming, pillars at the door, a stone wall, pond. She did not feel kindly toward him.

Come on, my love, she said to Nicky. She grabbed a hooded sweatshirt for him, a long-sleeved dotted shirt and a book as if she would read and threw them into the canvas bag. She added her sewing pouch—there was a tear in the dotted shirt and maybe she would sew it—along with a suede purse for her wallet and keys and phone. What else did they need? Help. That was all.

The cab ride up First Avenue seemed endless. Nicky's head lay in her lap. The turbaned driver, an older man, had a calm aura about him and Ivy thought how usually she might chat with him, but today she couldn't. He glanced at them in the rearview mirror but said nothing. Perhaps he was at the end of his shift and had his own worries. Perhaps he was respecting their privacy by not commenting. Outside the cool windows the buildings looked bleached in the heat and shadowless.

It really hurts, Nicky mumbled.

She knew, she said, and told him how brave he was being and that they were going to get him right away to the doctors who would fix him up. It was awful to feel so rotten, she said, and he was really hanging in there. She called Everett as they rode the potholes and briefly filled him in. His voice was as infuriatingly calm as everyone else's. He'll be fine, he said. Keep me posted.

. . .

The cab pulled onto a turnaround of bricks patterned in scallops and dropped them at the base of a building with a wall of glass windows which looked eighty stories high. Good luck, the driver said looking ahead. They entered the cool shadowy lobby and were told by a guard that this wasn't outpatient, this was inpatient. The man's dark face had a white mustache. Outpatient was another building, he said and pointed toward the river.

Oh, she said, crestfallen, but spellbound. The man's voice was calm and warm and he seemed to be the first understanding person they'd found today. Her arm was pressed around Nicky, who was literally swaying. She noticed a line of three wheelchairs against the wall. Is there—? She didn't need to finish the sentence. The man answered, Certainly, and moved to get them a chair.

You sit right here, my friend, the man said. Nicky plopped down, dazed.

The man took hold of the handles and pushed. Allow me, he said.

Thank you so much, Ivy said, feeling gratitude swell in her body, and nearly toppling at his feet.

Back through the sliding doors they rolled into the searing heat. The guard pushed the wheelchair along a white cement walkway with grass edged alongside it like a rug, past young trees growing out of circles of pink impatiens, off one curb, over a road into a garage entrance disappearing underground, and up over another curb to more walkway, till they reached a smaller entryway where doors reflecting their image—Nicky in a wheelchair and Ivy beside him, leafy trees behind—parted and received them.

It was past four in the afternoon and Ivy was relieved to find the emergency reception area empty. Crying could be heard from a child they couldn't see, but no other patients were in evidence. What day was it? Saturday. The guard left them and Ivy thanked him. So much, she said.

The reception desk was breast high, as if to keep children from reaching. Ivy related the facts. A moonfaced woman with drawn eyebrows wearing a sleeveless white shirt listened. Was it possible, Ivy asked, for him to have something he could cough up the blood into? The woman rolled her chair to another desk, opened a drawer, closed it, reached toward another handle, couldn't quite reach and stood. She returned with a square of blue plastic which Ivy unfolded into a plastic bag. She asked also for paper towels and was handed a few, along with a clipboard to fill out. Ivy parked Nicky's wheelchair a few feet away in a yellow waiting area where a wide-screen TV played a loud cartoon. Nicky did not look. He was fumbling with the blue bag; Ivy widened its mouth. He coughed a little, as if he'd been holding back, and a long red worm dribbled down the plastic. He looked to his mother, as if to say, How is this happening?

It's okay, she said. That's why we're here. They're going to help us. She wiped his mouth, which had crusty dry blood. The baby's crying was coming from behind a door connected to the waiting area. The crying had increased to a gasping rhythm. Ivy filled out the forms, keeping the wheelchair close to her chair, and her leg touching Nicky's.

When she handed the clipboard back, she tried to make eye contact with the moonfaced woman, but failed. Ivy said nothing further, thinking to pace herself with how much pestering she did.

They waited. Nicky dribbled more red spit into the blue bag. Ivy thought about texting, but there was nothing yet to report; they were in suspension. Yet time was passing. From the TV came irritating crash sounds, manic laughing sounds, mechanical curlicue sounds and annoying pop music. Ivy looked toward the small window in the door where the baby was crying but could see nothing. Now and then the door at this end of the corridor would swing open and a medical worker with a stethoscope around his neck would exit. Or a woman carrying towels would enter. Ivy glimpsed another reception area which seemed to have much more activity. Were they in the right place? One time when the door opened Ivy was at the counter asking the moonfaced woman if there was any update and saw a row of curtained-off areas. Ivy waited another fifteen minutes by the clock on the wall before going again to the counter.

We have to wait till an examination area is available, the woman said, ticking her eyes toward the big grey door. They will let you know.

Mum, Nicky said when she sat back down. When are they going to help us? The blue plastic bag was streaked with blood, which inside looked dark purple. He looked at her with his doleful face. Usually his doleful face appeared when he was appealing for a present, or an ice cream. But this doleful face had no artfulness to it. This doleful face was sincere.

Ten minutes she waited before returning to the counter. I'm just worried about him, she said. He's spat up a lot of blood and really looks so pale. I've never seen—

They'll see him when they can, the woman said.

Okay, Ivy said, feeling the opposite. Thank you. Inside she was begging and screaming and weeping. Why wasn't anyone helping them?

Out of the speakers came motor collision sounds and looping gurgles. The crying also continued, high and frantic, muffled behind the door. This was Hell.

I wonder what's the matter with *that* kid, she said almost to herself. Then, Why do they leave this TV blasting if no one is even watching?

Nicky frowned at her. He never liked when she complained in public, it embarrassed him.

No one can hear me, she said, lowering her voice.

I can, he said.

I just want them to help you, she said. It's frustrating.

A pretty slender woman in a white lab coat came walking from down the corridor toward them. Ivy sat up expectantly, but she walked past to the door of the crying child. She entered, leaving the door open, and Ivy saw a young woman with curly peach-colored hair in a plaid halter and an older man—her father? husband?—wearing a windbreaker and a baseball hat. The woman sat on a table holding a toddler now at that stuttering stage of weeping when one attempts to steady one's breath. The pretty doctor spoke coolly in a low voice. Underneath the TV sound, Ivy heard the mother answering in an accent . . . Eastern European . . . Polish? Hungarian? The woman muttered, something about a picnic . . . the child had eaten . . . something indecipherable . . . but only . . . something else . . . then a long time later she'd starting crying . . . the slender doctor listened. A picnic, Ivy thought, a tree, shade, children's shouts . . .

According to the clock, thirty-five minutes had passed since they'd arrived. Ivy stood again. She'd been relatively patient till now, but honestly. When would something happen?

At the counter she said, with perhaps a little less apologetic tone than before, I am really worried about my son. I understand we have to wait, but—The woman at the counter calmly regarded her face and yet seemed to look through her.

So it was a surprise when the woman said, They'll take him now.

Really? What if Ivy hadn't stood up just then? Would they have come and gotten her? Never mind, no point in asking.

She gathered her bag. A woman in a crimson sweater sloping off downy shoulders stood at the handles of Nicky's wheelchair and pushed him forward. The wide grey doors opened for them at last. The inner room. The TV no longer assaulting them. People were moving purposefully around a more populated nurses' counter. Ivy felt as if each door they entered today brought them deeper both into illness as well as into the ability for care. At the third curtain was an empty bed into which Nicky was moved to be propped against a nearly vertical back. Ivy noticed his lip trembling. You cold? He nodded. Would it be possible for him to get a blanket? The woman nodded, as if expecting this, and walked away to disappear past lockers and tables on wheels and down a parallel corridor out of sight. Ivy left the curtain open feeling they'd be less likely to be forgotten. Also she could keep an eye out for who was going to help them. For not the first time today, she thought, My son's life could very well be in the hands of the people here and I have no choice but to trust they can be relied upon.

The woman appeared with a stack of thin blankets with black piping and gently laid one on Nicky—Oh, Ivy said, helping to spread it out, it's warm! She thanked the woman, wanting her to know her appreciation. She really was grateful. And to Nicky, This'll warm you up. The aide asked for Nicky's hand and placed his middle finger in a plastic pea pod attached to the wire of a nearby monitor. She looked at the flickering lines and digits, green, yellow.

His vitals look fine, she said.

Vitals. Only here did you ever hear that word.

Nicky's face looked to his mother like it was made of marble.

I've never seen him so pale, Ivy said. She delivered the words to the aide mildly, blandly, not wanting to alarm Nicky.

His blood pressure is a little low, the woman said. But nothing to worry about.

Nothing to worry about. The phrase floated above them, a mocking balloon. This isn't his usual coloring, she said.

The aide mysteriously turned to leave.

What—? Ivy said, not wanting her to go. She found herself cleaving to each person they encountered. What happens now?

She knew it was best to stay calm. But she couldn't help but scan each person for any extra signs of humanity, any personal acknowledgment that Nicky would be looked after, that he was going to be all right. Never had kindness seemed so precious.

A doctor will be in to look in on him, the woman said. She said this as if it was obvious, or that she'd said it already. Perhaps she had. They seemed to assume that Ivy knew the routine. But how? One wasn't in emergency rooms every day.

Okay, Ivy said, trying to stay obedient, determined to be patient. Thank you. Thank you.

She smoothed the curls back from Nicky's bleached forehead, his hair still the same from an earlier time. Lately he'd started to jerk away when she did this, but he was not jerking away now. He spat more red drool down at the edge of the bag.

She turned to scan the room. Who here was a doctor? Were they all nurses? Medical aides? She'd watched enough medical shows to know all the love affairs and power struggles and moral quandaries which lay within the scenes. But, truly, she thought, all had real worries themselves. A sick mother at home, a brother in trouble again, the jerk boyfriend—and yet watching them, Ivy envied each one for being in a workaday world, going about a job. Not in a crisis.

Nicky sat forward beside her, as if preparing for a big cough. He opened the bag wider near the side of the bed and leaned over it and without warning out of his mouth came a gushing red waterfall of blood.

Oh Jesus, Ivy said, holding the bag which was now bulging and heavy. Then Nicky threw up another half bucket.

Help, she said, letting urgency into her voice, not being hysterical but needing to be heard. Please? Can someone come in here? She wasn't leaving Nicky's side.

No one appeared. She stood up and called out from the side of the curtain. Can someone—please! Come help . . .

A young man in white nurse's pants and a T-shirt walked calmly over.

He's just thrown up . . . Look! The man glanced at the bag which Ivy held up, but turned to study the monitor.

His vitals look okay, the man said.

But—Jesus, Ivy said. She could feel her son's gaze on her searching for reassurance. Look at all the blood.

His blood pressure is a little low, the man said. Is that all anyone could say here? Then he said, We could give him an IV.

Yes, please, Ivy said.

Her son had thrown up two gallons of blood. Why wasn't anyone rushing him into an operating room?

But—he's—I mean, that's okay?

It looks as if there's been some bleeding, the man said. The doctor will check.

Ivy couldn't believe it.

Nicky lay back, his face frozen in terror.

It's okay, she said. They're doing everything they need to. But she didn't believe it.

The doctor will be here soon, she said, not believing that either.

Nine and a half minutes later a strapping man wearing a white medical jacket over a crisp blue shirt appeared. The shirt opened at a sturdy neck. Hello, he said in an African accent. I am Dr. Mankattah. We're having a little bleeding, is that it?

His elegance was illogically reassuring. Something to like! Ivy began to explain all that had happened, the operation, the ER visit etc. He seemed only to half listen and asked Nicky to open his mouth. He took his iPhone out of his top pocket and shone the flashlight into Nicky's throat.

I find these work better than the hospital flashlights, he said under his breath. Then more forthrightly, I can see where the suture is not healing. That is what is causing the hemorrhaging. The tear has formed a scab which prevents it closing up.

She did not like the word *hemorrhaging*.

He needs to go back into surgery, the doctor said. So we can redo the suture.

Ivy felt the balm of understanding for the first time in two days what was happening. She could now give Nicky a hopeful look. His face was frozen in terror.

The doctor was checking the monitor and the IV. Because Nicky had received medication, he told Ivy, he would have to wait a half hour for surgery. But, the doctor said, there probably wouldn't be an operating room available before that time anyway.

Let's see, what time is it. He looked at his iPhone. Ivy looked at the clock on the wall: 9:33. They'd been here for five hours.

And it's okay to wait? Ivy said.

His vitals look fine, said the doctor. In league with the rest of them! He will be okay, he said. I will speak again with Dr. Estin. I spoke to him earlier.

You did? she said, full of wonder. How had they found one another? Sometimes efficiency amazed as much as lagging. Oh, that's good.

The doctor tucking his iPhone in his breast pocket. Don't you worry, he said to Nicky. We'll fix you up.

The doctor left and Nicky closed his eyes and seemed to sleep.

While Nicky lay motionless, Ivy texted. She texted Everett. She texted Irene. She texted Margaret and Harriet and Daphne. Daphne answered immediately. *Do you want me to come?* She was still in Brooklyn, had come in for the weekend. *No,* Ivy wrote, it was all right. Who knew how long it would take. But she thanked her, it helped to know she was there. Then Irene texted. She was out on the island. *Tell me what I can do. Keep me posted. Yes,* Ivy said. And no, there was nothing. Margaret texted, *oh god.* Harriet texted, *I'm here.*

Ivy wrote down *Mankattah.* Or had it been Maknattah? Mantakka? She didn't want to be caught not knowing the doctor's name.

Nicky opened his eyes. Mum, he said in a whisper.

Yes?

Mum, he repeated.

I'm here.

At 10:10 P.M. the doctor returned with a bed on wheels. A hefty orderly wore a hoodie and yellow aviator glasses. Ivy read the label on the doctor's white coat. MANKATTAH. *Man, cat, ta.*

Okay, said Dr. Mankattah. We are ready for you. Are you ready for us?

Nicky nodded. He was moved onto a bed. I can't swallow, he whispered.

That's just what we're going to take care of, the doctor said.

Ivy followed. As the orderly pushed, the doctor kept one hand on the bed. Out the wide grey doors, past the reception counter and the yellow waiting room, familiar to her now and nearly quaint, TV sound still blasting, down a long hallway to a turn at the end, into another long hallway with occasional empty beds along the wall and occasional handholds. They came to a T and went left, wheels rattling.

Is it far? Ivy said weakly.

Operating rooms are in another wing, said Dr. Mankattah in a reassuring tone. It is a big hospital.

Another hallway, another turn. Fewer people appeared—a figure split by a door, a leg turning a corner. Then no one. Fewer doors, less light and only the sound of the wheels wobbling. It felt like an airplane hangar in the '50s at an army outpost. Walls grew more dingy, baseboards seemed to curl.

Almost there, the doctor said.

They pushed through double swinging doors—another hallway! another circle, mustard walls, olive-drab trim—and neared a dark doorway open like a scream.

The operating room was like a garage. Crumpled balls of paper littered the floor beside curls of tape and torn plastic. Three figures in the gloom, shower capped and short sleeved, looked up blankly when the bed entered.

Can I come in—? Ivy asked.

Just to here, said the burly orderly, suddenly militant, but with a lisp.

Ivy pressed her hand on Nicky's chest, kissed his hand and told him she'd be there when he woke up.

I can't swallow, he said, both panicked and resigned, and his eyes filled with tears.

He says he can't— Ivy began, but the bed was wheeled away.

Ivy watched the doors close.

Where should I wait? she asked.

The orderly, striding off, not turning, said, Take two lefts, then a right and a left, and you'll find the waiting room.

Two lefts, then a right, then a . . .

Ivy stood like the Minotaur at the end of the maze.

What if they were incompetent in there? Who had she just surrendered her son to? What if he died? A sob choked out of her.

She moved down the dingy hall.

If something worse happened it would be her fault. She had chosen to do this. If she hadn't chosen *the elective surgery* her son would not be in there now. He would be in Virginia, wisteria curling at the windows, his feet under a sofa cushion, watching a stupid movie. Both of them would be in Virginia. No, at this time of night, he would be asleep, unharmed, holding the scraps of his rabbit, the peaceful linden outside the window.

One left, another long hall. Then a left here at this sort of half hall, or left at the next?

She made a few turns, backtracked. She passed a woman lazily walking a table with a clattering lower shelf. Then it was quiet again. A fellow pushing an empty wheelchair pointed her back to a corner and amazingly at the end of a hall she saw a door with narrow glass windows on either side. She entered into a hushed carpeted area with a quiet elevator bank. Everything in here looked new. There was a glassed-in lounge area with empty mahogany shelves and a glass coffee table and modern upholstered chairs with black iron arms and no one in it. Nicky's knocked-out unconscious face in her mind's eye.

Her phone told her it was 10:34. At the end of the hall a black window to the outside reflected her figure. She walked toward it and through her silhouette saw a dark wall a few feet away. Which way was she facing? She'd long ago lost her sense of which direction was south or east or west, never mind where she was from the hospital entrance.

She sat down on the carpeted floor. Staying in the corridor, she would see the door when it opened and not be hidden back in the empty lounge. There was no one here to ask, How much longer? Please please please, kept repeating in her mind. As in,

Please let it be okay. She thought of the littered garage of the operating room and how Nicky's mouth must have to be propped open—was there a contraption for that? And the hands of the surgeon—Dr. Mankattah? Dr. Estin? She didn't even know whose hands were reaching a needle down her son's throat, hooking it into his soft throat skin with black or clear gut. She remembered Everett, trained as a volunteer EMT, saying that the word *stitches* described the treatment, but the result was, she should know as a writer, suture. Nicky had gotten a badly done suture and was getting another one. Who said this second suture might not be bad? What had they pumped into his small body? Who was the suturer?

And in the quiet now came the clichés of wisdom which rose up like signposts in times of distress. *Things can change from one moment to the next. Without our health we are nothing. You don't value your health till you lose it.*

She was at the end of the line now, nothing to do but wait.

The elevator doors opened and a bent wire of a man emerged clutching a walker. He wore a heather-grey sweater over a collar shirt and khaki pants. Over his shoulder was slung a dark green bag with a bookstore logo in white, which was indeed filled with books. Even at thirty feet away she could recognize an orange cover and see part of the title: *The Stories of John Cheever.*

What was this man doing here at this hour? He actually looked like John Cheever. But older. He appeared lost. She was grateful to see another person, not unlike a god of wisdom, carrying books, carrying knowledge. He passed her, headed to the door with the narrow glass windows from whence she'd come, where she knew there was nothing but endless corridor. She tried to catch his attention, sitting on the floor practically in his path, but he seemed determined not to see her. He was concentrating on taking steps and went by her as if by a ghost. That is, an invisible ghost. Not all ghosts were invisible. Perhaps she was a ghost. Perhaps she was dead. He went out the door.

11:02.

For one moment the ancient thought of Ansel Fleming swept over her like a shadow, a relic of another era. She remembered how the need to disappear, the vanishing into him, had been one of the strongest feelings she'd ever had. Now it was hard to imagine any place for that here.

The bent man appeared again in the hallway, retracing his steps, passing her again as if blind.

Good evening, she said this time.

Hello, he said ceremoniously, bowing a little. His head tipped in her direction below as if unable to see who was speaking. Then, having completed his reconnaissance of the hallway, the man pressed the elevator button, leaned on the handles of his walker waiting, and when the doors opened, stepped in to disappear.

11:11.

11:17.

Nicky's heart was still beating. Of course it was. She did not need to discover new reasons why illness was so bad, but had gathered some. Illness limited your mind so it was not able to meander over things in a loose, easy way, and that meandering was the real pleasure of life. Illness distracted you with worry, the kind of worry which allowed for no other thoughts.

11:20.

She heard a click and turned to the door leading to the corridors. Through it came a bare-armed man in pale green scrubs with pale green baggies over his shoes.

Nick's mum? the man said, approaching her, a white shower cap set like a bonnet on his head.

Ivy scrambled up off the carpet.

Hello, he said. I'm Dr. Estin. Early forties, eyes slanted like a sloth's. The familiar voice so irritating on the phone belonged now to this kind and sympathetic man. His vibe was more nurse than doctor. Your son is doing fine, he said. I stitched up the suture.

This doctor knew the correct term. Nicky, he told her, was on his way to post-op and she could meet him there. He'd had a lot of fluid in his stomach, Dr. Estin said, and they'd drained nearly three liters.

Ivy refrained from pointing out that he'd been the doctor who had not offered help early on. He threw up a lot of it while we were in the emergency room, she said. Was that all blood?

Mixed with water, he said. Blood from the suture was dripping down his throat. Blood makes a person pretty nauseous. He added, Must have been awfully uncomfortable.

Ivy put her hand on the wall, suddenly faint.

You okay? Dr. Estin said, and took her elbow.

Just a little tired. It's been a long day.

He walked her back out the door. Ivy mentioned how they'd continually been told the one-in-a-hundred statistic and how she guessed they'd won the draw.

It's even less than that, Dr. Estin said ominously. He strolled beside her for a few hallways till he could point out far in the distance the double doors of post-op.

He'll meet you down there, said Dr. Estin. It'll be very sore for a while. But he'll do fine.

Thank you, Ivy said. Thank you so much. Her gratitude speared her in the throat.

The post-op room was as empty as everywhere else. The tops of two women's heads could be seen over a circular console of desks and file cabinets, barricading them in the center of the low-ceilinged room. She could hear the light banter of the women chatting and rounded the corner to see two rather young women, late twenties, early thirties—weren't they awfully young to be in charge of post-op? Their faces lifted like flowers to Ivy as she said she was looking for her son.

He's on his way, one woman said breezily. She had the air of a cheerleader, or maybe it was her high ponytail. You can wait for him to come in over there. She pointed to another set of double doors, from which Nicky would enter.

Ivy crossed the room and set her bag on the counter. The women continued chatting as if they were at a slumber party. Ivy heard bits: . . . it was pretty nice, a place that Sharon likes to go to, but they don't serve you unless . . . Ivy was half reassured by the normalcy and half worried they weren't being serious enough.

The door opened and a bed came wheeling in. Ivy went forward, but Nicky wasn't in it. A white-haired woman lay flat on her back, bird profile upward, eyes closed. Behind the bed came the tall bent man with his book bag and his walker. The bed was wheeled to the opposite side of the room around the barricade and out of sight. One of the nurses stood and followed with a high ponytail swinging. Ivy heard her teenage voice now, warbling. The orderly walked past her heavy footed, out the way he came.

Ivy wondered where they'd put Nicky. Was there a pre-post-op room?

She shivered. It was cold in here. Ivy walked over to the seated nurse humming to herself and asked if she had an extra blanket. The nurse stood, her thick eyebrows raised in thought for a moment, then moved uncertainly to some lockers, *Star Trek* circa 1970. She opened a few cabinets, not hiding a baffled expression. Maybe no one ever needed blankets at this stage of things?

Never mind, Ivy said. Just if it was available.

They should be here somewhere, she said and wandered off into dimmer recesses out of sight.

The door opened. This time the bed did have Nicky in it, small in the large expanse, looking as if the air had been flattened out of him. He did not look peaceful, but shattered. Two orderlies parked the bed in a near corner and the nurse with the ponytail appeared. In a bell-like voice, she asked Ivy to step aside while they checked his vitals. His eyes were puffed up, as if pummeled in a fight.

Vitals. Another word one didn't like hearing.

The other nurse appeared while the first slid Nicky's finger into a temperature sleeve, and cranked up his bed slightly, comparing notes about an apparently inept colleague. Did you see when Dr. Howard did the tracheotomy . . . ?

Ivy saw Nicky's swollen lips chattering. Aware she was a pest, but holding to the common wisdom that every hospital patient needs an advocate to speak on his behalf, she pointed out his shivering.

We'll get him some blankets, said the nurse with the ponytail, and she turned her finely drawn and made-up features toward Ivy. The direct gaze was almost shocking, like a shower of light. Ivy realized no one had looked directly at her for hours and she had needed it. She now loved this girl.

The nurse said, It's a normal reaction postsurgery.

The other nurse brought two warmed blankets and they laid them on Nicky. He was shaking all over. The skin of his face looked plastic.

He'll wake up soon, the nurse said, so chipper Ivy now wondered if they were both high. Nicky continued to tremble under the blankets.

Is this okay? Ivy said to their backs as they returned to their station, for the millionth time asking a stranger if something was okay.

Oh, yeah. His temp will be low, but they've given him medication to bring it back up. She tilted her head in the direction of the clipboard left by the orderlies on the counter.

Ivy leaned down close to Nicky's face. His eyes fluttered open, then closed. Hello, she murmured. You're all done. You're out.

His eyes opened wider, black, not seeing her. His teeth chattered and his body rattled under the blankets. You'll get warm, she told him, not believing it. You're fine.

After a few long minutes he stopped shaking and seemed to sleep. Ivy glanced up. Where had the old couple gone? She worried there was no one advocating for them. Her eye fell on the clipboard. She moved stealthily toward it. *Nicholas Cooper Scott* was typed at the top above a long list in small print of medication. Some she recognized. Lorazepam. Fentanyl. Jesus, she thought. All of these drugs had been pumped into him; no one had asked her permission. The drugging was nearly as punishing as the operation. How had she let this get so out of hand? She lifted the paper to a second page of medications. Suddenly her lax maternal attitude—allowing him to walk alone to the corner store, letting him do his homework on his own—felt reckless, if not downright neglectful. She had to take more care! She looked at his swollen waxy face and thought of all he'd been through—his tender throat sliced up, twice knocked out by drugs, three different hospitals, blood spattering into his hand. Fatigue socked her in the back ribs.

The clock above the door said 1:25.

What now? No one had told her. Then she remembered Dr. Estin saying he'd have a bed for the night, to keep an eye on him. *Keep an eye on him,* another chilling phrase. Ivy pictured herself slumping in one of the dim hallways, sleeping with her bag as a pillow in some alcove. Well, she'd do whatever she had to.

The nurse came bouncing over—definitely high, Ivy decided—and looked with satisfaction at Nicky, whose crushed eyes were opening.

Hello there! the nurse said and looked again at Ivy as if this collapsed mask of her son was proof. See? All good. Another fifteen minutes and you can go, the nurse told her. Someone from pediatrics will take you up.

The groomed woman in her sixties who appeared a half hour later looked like an older Eva Marie Saint in *North by Northwest,* in a grey cashmere sweater, gold necklace and pearls, her blonde hair one unruffled shape. Hello, I'm Gwen, she said in a low purr. She also sounded like Eva Marie Saint. I'll be taking you up.

They entered a wide silent elevator. Looks like you've had a long day, Gwen said.

Ivy mumbled something about how one never hopes for emergency surgery.

Well, he'll get a nice rest now, Gwen said.

Ivy noticed Gwen wore an elegant Cartier watch. Together they hummed upward.

The doors opened to a dark hushed hallway, lit waist high

with a coral band of light beneath a hovering blond railing. Facing were reflecting glass doors in a clean glass wall with a mysterious amber light behind.

Wow, Ivy said. This is us?

Yes, the woman said.

It's incredible.

We're very proud of our new pediatrics floor, the woman said, and rolled the bed forward. The lights are low like this because of the hour, she whispered.

They wheeled down a wide hall, passing an octagonal nurses' station with a profile at a distant desk, and glided through an open doorway into a high-ceilinged room with a wall of windows showing the starry buildings of Brooklyn in the distance and the satiny pleats of the East River below. A boat, flat and dark as a coffin, moved on the shimmering water.

Ivy gasped. This is amazing, she said.

Would you like a cot? Gwen said. People often just sleep on the window seat.

Ivy looked at the wide cushion in front of the windows with enough room for a family. Oh, she said, the window seat is fine. I mean, it's great. I feel like we're at the Four Seasons.

She was too wrung out to feel giddy, but there was giddiness deep within. River view!

Gwen said good night. As she left, in perfect choreography a nurse entered wearing white pants and a white button up shirt. She introduced herself as Angelica and said she would be there if they needed anything. Did he want something to help him sleep? Angelica asked. Ivy looked at Nicky who was starting to groan a little; she thought that might be a good idea.

Waiting for Angelica to return, Ivy put her palm on Nicky's chest and felt his small heartbeat. You're all fixed up now, she said.

His eyes were black blobs in the amber light. His puffed-up mouth barely moved when he spoke. I thought I was going to die, he said.

. . .

An hour later Ivy lay with a cheek on the hard pillow, staring at the silhouette of her son sleeping in this new bed. The shadows in the dim light looked almost sea blue. The hush was comforting, though her heart was loud and pounding. She basked in the stillness. Peace, she thought, that was really all a person wanted.

She turned to look out the majestic window. A small boat appeared occasionally passing by her knees on the hammered steel below. She felt as if they were on a great ocean liner, on a high deck, arriving at a port having dodged disaster.

Why did you have to have the wits scared out of you to feel sharp, to be content with being alive?

She closed her eyes, not ready for sleep but knowing she needed it, and skittering before her vision appeared the places she and Nicky had been in these last two days, the hallways, the rooms where they'd waited, the cabs bouncing, the beds where Nicky had been parked, lining up one after another, then jamming like logs at a turn in the river. She saw the faces which had regarded them blankly, or not looked up, the ones offering help, the doctor shining his flashlight. A filament ran through it all, beginning with the calmness of the first operation to the hectic flurry of the last. There was a boy carrying towels, peacock nails clicking keyboards, the counters against Ivy's ribs, sloping shoulders walking away, hands testing the IV tubes as if for warmth, the empty wheelchair. People, she saw, were brave and good and kind. She saw life was more astonishing and radiant than she'd imagined it, and she'd spent a lot of time imagining.

Out in the hall she heard a bed rolling by.

She was not aware of when she fell asleep; we never are.

9

Ivy

A strange passion is moving in my head.
My heart has become a bird which searches in the sky.
Every part of me goes in different directions.
Is it really so that the one I love is everywhere?

—RUMI

She felt she ought to be at the end of this by now. She looked back and saw that what she had thought was close to the end was more like only halfway through the middle.

It was hard to remember the loose abandon. She had felt it, but for it to be gone she had to stay out of reach. She would think of Ansel Fleming in two opposite ways . . . as a mirage which existed mostly in her brain, or as the radiance of magnificent sensation and feeling. Could the addict still respect her high?

She was looking for a hinge to connect one moment to the next, but couldn't do it in the old way. Those connecting faculties had been blitzed. How could she have taken on the job of being a mother when this could happen, this lack of ability?

To whom could she turn now? There was only one person, the one there all along. As Samuel Beckett would have it, I am I still here.

. . .

One morning walking to the Pink Room Ivy saw the figure of her neighbor the film director coming toward her slowly, talking on her phone. Ivy had never seen her walking slowly, her long legs were usually flapping in wide-legged trousers like Marlene Dietrich. As she drew closer the film director's handsome face looked as wracked as a medieval Madonna. Was it about a child? A parent? Was her husband making her suffer? The barrier of perfection which had surrounded the film director cracked apart and Ivy's heart went out to her. Such is the effect of sincere expressions of anguish on human connection. As she walked by, Ivy then wondered why another person's anguish had to be the reason she stopped judging her. A person expressing self-satisfaction did not inspire the same comradery.

She had put him away, mostly, then watching the news saw snow, a blizzard somewhere out West. It had nothing to do with him, so why did he appear? In white flakes slicing through streetlamps in the dark.

Ivy went to a memorial service on a farm. The woman, Diane, ten years older than Ivy, had died after years of on-and-off cancer. She was an exuberant person with three children from a first husband, and a boyfriend of twenty years named Larry who married her the week before she died. Ivy had met Diane and Larry years before when she was seeing a photographer from Montana and had kept up with them and used to visit their dairy farm in Connecticut which had belonged to Diane's family. Nicky got to milk the cows. There were always people there visiting the farm, the children, children's friends, and Diane made huge meals which got served late in the night and much alcohol was consumed. Ivy knew a few of the friends at the Saturday memorial. She did not bring Nicky.

At lunch Ivy sat with Diane's sister Iris and a small group on hay bales near the greenhouse where beautiful plates of food and flowers were laid out on the potting tables. Iris, slender with short red hair, had a few years ago at sixty-two married for the first time, a man she met on the internet. Andrew lived one town away from her upstate and was a retired professor. I couldn't believe he was interested in me, Iris said. On a nearby hay bale smiled a trim white-haired man with bushy white eyebrows. Then he seemed to turn off his hearing and concentrate on eating his pulled pork and beans because his face remained expressionless as Iris continued speaking. So now she had four stepchildren, Iris went on. One of them, Kimmy, had just fallen in love with a musician, so they were a little concerned about that. She was a singer, too, sort of, though young, hadn't made it and this guy was much older. Actually successful and seems perfectly nice, but he'd been in jail for a while, so who knew. I mean, only drugs, she said. But still. Anyway a month after they met they've moved in with each other up at our guesthouse and seem pretty crazy in love.

Ivy asked Iris what was his name, knowing the answer.

Later she went to the bathroom in the stable and felt her heart banging on the whitewashed ceiling. How long, she thought, how long.

Then there was a morning when she woke with no cobweb of dread. She practically levitated from her sheets. Birdsong entered in the windowsill space, the cheeps, the coo of the dove. Was there sadness in the sounds? Some. But the rest was a kind of miracle cloth. It was decidedly blissful to be alive. She heard Nicky in his room, humming. Another warbler! She sat up. Wait, her dream . . . it seemed to have rearranged her, only half remembered, a green suit, a white cliff, a red Chinese junk. Her brain felt as if the roof had been torn off and was wide as the sky.

She moved down the hall, feeling the soft weave of a throw rug under her feet. At his door she listened to Nicky moving his people around. You stay there, his voice said with a tender reassurance. I'll be right back.

. . .

She did have the dream—of flying. She would feel herself lifting up in a room and by flapping her arms would keep rising. Once up she might swoop through doorways or hover near the ceiling looking down on people. No one ever remarked on the strangeness of her being able to fly, but she felt the amazement of it, and its thrill and power. Outside she could fly high over fields, as high as a hot air balloon. She had no idea how she stayed up, how she was doing it. That was life: *not knowing how she was doing it.*

She was looking at a view, or out the oval window of a plane and the wisp of thought might come—him—like smoke, then vanish. And she had the thought that the Thing was only him. But now the Thing was her, too.

Life would not be different from now and the realization rather than being dull and oppressive seemed to release a rush in her, an opening of energy or light, as if the focus of every line had just been sharpened and the shapes of shadows in front of her were there to demonstrate simply This is how it is. Which was in itself astonishing.

This is how it is, she thought. Not how it was *going to be*. It was this, here, now.

It's hard to tell the exact moment a drop of water dries, or the instant that daylight turns to night. So Ivy could not have said when the preoccupation left her, but a time did come when he no longer occupied her brain.

Where was it, the vibration of him? It seemed to be gone.

Nothing passes away, Chekhov said. Perhaps he was still there, sitting quiet and invisible, but she mustn't look. She'd worked hard for its vanishing. The new space in her thoughts made room for appreciation. Her friends seemed to spill out of a dark forest into a field flooded with sunshine. She thought of each of their faces, so many she loved! How did it show? That remained to be seen. She felt it, though; that was the main thing.

She recognized the kindness of Everett answering her texts immediately.

Now she was paying her bills, if not exactly on time, at least closer to the due date.

At the cottage one winter night she stood on the porch looking at the sky and in the cold felt pulled in a new direction, seeing the stars flung frozen. She thought, I'm coming back a little. There I am. She felt more like the stars than herself standing there in a sweater, in this room with no ceiling. Getting into bed afterward she thought, One day I will die and he will never know how much love I had.

At John and John's dinner in their yellow rooms, Ivy felt, as always, wrapped in loveliness. What pretty glasses, she said, holding the green-and-white swirls. Aren't they? said John. We got them last trip to Venice. And the cheese, she said. We have a special cheesemonger, said John Two. We don't see you enough, John said, patting another new small dog, looking very much like Kitty, with long white hair. At all. Ivy appreciated it, then immediately thought, How can I keep up with their buoyancy?

At coffee Ivy told Irene and Daphne about the famous playwright at dinner the night before, now in his eighties, much celebrated, who told her, It's taken me this long to do the hardest thing in my life—like myself.

Don't believe him, Irene said, having worked with the man. He's one of those manipulators who knows what to say.

Ivy said it had worked with her and laughed.

You just have a bad asshole detector, Irene said.

Just standing myself is hard enough, said Daphne, ordering another decaf half latte, half chai, with almond milk. Then she had to hurry to an appointment.

Ivy stayed with Irene and they talked about Amy who after leaving her husband with the porn addiction had already found love—on the internet.

That's ironic, Ivy said.

They seem perfect for each other, Irene said. Ivy, you should try it.

Perfect for each other is, Ivy said, one of my red flags.

They laughed.

The way someone looks in a picture and how that person describes himself is the least alluring thing I can imagine, Ivy said. Don't you need to see the guy in action?

Well, you're never going to see if you don't make the effort, Irene said. I'll help you. I can live vicariously.

I never thought I'd say this, Ivy said, but I think I might prefer at the moment staying alone.

In the portal she watched Gloria Steinem being interviewed. She said, It is not so much about equality as about self-realization.

Everett came to see Nicky in the spring talent show—he and Oscar drew on mustaches and performed a "Who's on First?" comedy routine—and Ivy left for the weekend so father and son could have time together in the apartment. She went up the Hudson to Maira's. A year after his diagnosis, Tony's health was holding steady, but there was now another crisis: he'd fallen in love with a nurse. He'd told Maira the week before and had moved in with the nurse one town away. Maira was stunned. She and Ivy took long walks through the branch shadows on the roads and Maira related the up-and-down details of what had happened, weeping randomly. Tony had been lying for months and felt he should come clean. So big of him! Maira said. The nurse—her name was Alina—had a kid, and Tony had barely moved any of his stuff out and Maira wasn't sure if she wanted him to or if she hoped he'd change his mind. Ivy listened, truly as shocked as Maira. Maira had appeared so confident and sure of Tony. Turns out he felt neglected, Maira said. So, she said, why didn't he tell me?

On Saturday night they ate bowls of butternut squash soup by the giant fireplace and Maira poured more wine for both of them, watching the stream with puffy red eyes.

On Sunday Ivy and Nicky said goodbye to Everett on the stoop and watched him get in the cab with his backpack. Nicky ran up the marble steps before her. Let's wrestle, he said.

Are any marriages good? Harriet said, opening the oven, and flipping the—as she called them—aubergines.

Yours is, Ivy said.

That's what everyone says! Harriet laughed.

It certainly looks good.

Harriet closed the oven, and kept moving around the small kitchen area, shaking wet lettuce leaves, cutting a lemon, filling a ceramic bowl with wrinkled black olives. There are, she said, a few times in the day, a few times every day even, when I feel so completely utterly irrevocably lonely.

Ivy looked at her friend, mother of three, who worked as a film producer doing jobs she loved, who took Italian lessons on the side and swam two miles every day in the summer, who told her husband when he was looking handsome, and thought, I ought to pay more attention to my friends.

She called Bruno. They sat on stools at a bar. He and the architect were going to rent a house in Greece with friends. I don't know how it happened, Bruno said. I think I'm happy. Ivy asked him to tell her more. It seems as if he's not going to run away from me, Bruno said, mystified. And what about Ivy's razor blade? Ivy told Bruno that Ansel was married with a baby now. I thought that didn't happen, Bruno said. It didn't, then it did, she said, making him laugh. She told him she now spent more time worried about her maintenance or her insurance, something she probably ought to have been doing all along. When she came back from the bathroom, Bruno pushed a folded piece of paper toward her on the bar. For you to look at later, he said. After kissing him goodbye on the sidewalk she waited a few blocks before she opened the check with the illegible signature of Bruno Best.

Why is the book taking so long? Daphne said. She meant it to be helpful.

Ivy at the stove, stirring spaghetti in hot water, halving cherry tomatoes, grating Parmesan, listened to Oscar and Nicky side by side on the living room couch looking at the screen.

How'd I get on fire? Nicky said. How'd I get on fire?

Oscar said, It's going to look like I cheated. But I didn't.

I don't think you're in the sky.

Oh, snap, I'm a panda.

I'm a happy rainbow!

Let me see.

See my arm?

Ivy listened in a small rapture. It seemed they were speaking a poem. It was about absurdity and desire and life.

I'm all choppy.

What's this stuff?

It's grass.

Why is there a hole in the ground?

Wait, are we in the same world?

No.

Uh-oh, I fell into a hole in the ground.

Are you going to come into my world?

By the waterfall? Where is the waterfall?

Half of the waterfall's not there, Nicky said, weird.

Where'd you go? Where'd you go?

Um . . . I don't know.

You're all the way over there!

Where?

You're digging a hole!

I am?

Yes, you're digging a hole! Come into my world.

I'm trying.

How are you in a room? Oscar said.

How're you not?

It was the other John's birthday. They were making pasta from scratch and cooking the mail-order devil's beard mushroom they'd grown on a log under a glass, spraying it three times a day for a month. Pink champagne was poured. Ivy saw not a grain of resentment for her occasional neglect of their anniversaries, of their losses, and thought how their forgetting was a kind of grace. How could one return it? She brought three roasted marrow bones for the dogs and wore the Pucci slip that had belonged to her mother, knowing the Johns appreciated old school and, even more, appreciated effort.

There was a red geranium on the sill. Other plants came and went—the maidenhair fern, the orchids collared with taffeta in a box, even the cyclamen with its alert white ears in the winter did not last—but the geranium endured, with its soldered pipe stem and floating saucer leaves, not needing much water, or dirt, or even care. Its leaves had the same smell as the blossoms. Some things were orchid, some geranium.

The days of the future were set in a line before her, buckets waiting to be filled so they could then be dumped into the past.

For a long time it could still find her, the old feeling. She would stay motionless when it brushed by, dangerous, not wanting to give it any attention in case it circled back and rose up and she'd be ready again to give up her life.

. . .

Years later she was asleep in a small house with a wild garden tumbling into a forest and had the vivid dream that takes place where you actually are. In it, Ansel was there in the bed with her and they watched together, as Ivy often watched on her own, as dawn came up in the green or grey window. Later she woke again to the window, filling with the yellow splash of sun, and felt him still there.

All night the snow fell. Nicky was in his bed, quiet. Large flakes had started swooping down as they returned from his soccer game on the river, with the spotlights on the dark fields and the young figures breathless, running. As she watched shivering in the cold, Ivy felt vicariously the exuberance of the young people running on sturdy legs, the animal joy of movement. They high-fived each other like grown-ups. After a bath her cheeks felt an extra radiating warmth after the earlier cold as she painted with watercolors the curled form of Air on a yellow-and-red kikoi which Everett had given her. When she got into bed that night she felt clear. In the morning everything was covered in white.

A NOTE ABOUT THE AUTHOR

Susan Minot is an award-winning writer of novels, short stories, poetry, plays and movies. Her first novel, *Monkeys,* was published in a dozen countries and won the Prix Femina Étranger in France. Her novel *Evening* was a worldwide bestseller and became a major motion picture. She lives in New York City and North Haven, Maine.

A NOTE ON THE TYPE

This book was set in Scala, a typeface designed by the Dutch designer Martin Majoor (b. 1960) in 1988 and released by the FontFont foundry in 1990. While designed as a fully modern family of fonts containing both a serif and a sans serif alphabet, Scala retains many refinements normally associated with traditional fonts.

Composed by North Market Street Graphics,
Lancaster, Pennsylvania

Printed and bound by Berryville Graphics,
Berryville, Virginia

Designed by Soonyoung Kwon